Savage World

Savage World

Babel Series Book 1

Jennifer Slusher and Linda Thackeray

Contents

I

Sharks

"*Tommy please! Open the door!*"

Lisa's scream was muted by the seal of the airlock door and while he couldn't hear her, it was easy to tell what she was saying. Tom stared helplessly at her, feeling each dull thud of her fists against the small window as if they were stabs to his own heart.

An explosion thumped behind Lisa and belched a ball of plasma fire. Under any other circumstances, the electric blue columns of flame rushing towards her might have been considered beautiful, but at this moment, it gripped him with horror. Death reached the others behind her first, devouring their flesh with such ferocity, they barely had time to scream before disintegrating into the wall of fire.

At that moment, Tom saw the realization dawn on his lover's face. In the seconds before the plasma engulfed her, heat so intense any sweat was sucked dry, Lisa nodded. She understood. She knew. Jesus fucking Christ, she knew...

... and then she was gone, swallowed up in swirling tongues of sapphire heat. Tom thought he saw her start to scream but the sound never penetrated the roar of the fire or the thick safety hatch. Her gold hair, which he so relished between his fingertips during their lovemaking, ignited, giving her the halo, she used to swear she'd never earn. For a second, the mottled greenish blue hue of the fire gave his Lisa wings before enveloping her completely. From an angel to a living candle, fair skin now translucent and burning out too damn soon.

Later, he would curse himself for not acting faster and spare her the pain, but it didn't matter; he would pay for his sin every night in his dreams. Not for failing to save her, but because he let her burn.

And she'd known, she'd forgiven him in her last moment for his ultimate betrayal.

* * *

"*TOMMYYYYYYYYYY!!*"

Major Thomas Ian Merrick sat up in a cold sweat, shaking like a dog shitting razor blades, head pounding, trying to remember where the fuck he was. For a few seconds, he was still on that blazing ship, trying to save it as the plasma fire consumed the engineering deck. As the nightmare diminished, the scattered neurons in his brain regrouped to remind him where he was.

In a supply closet. Or, rather, *his* supply closet. In a whole other nightmare.

The closet had become 'his' because he'd commandeered the space to get a little privacy from the rest of the ship. The tiny room reeked of disinfectant and dust, with barely enough space to sit down or stretch one's legs. His back was pressed against a shelf, the edges digging into his shoulder, but it locked from the inside and, as far as Tom was concerned, it was fucking heaven. Beyond that door was hell.

He needed solitude and, on this ship, packed to the rafters with the remains of human civilisation, privacy was a luxury no one had in abundance. When he stepped past the door, he would return to the overcrowded, transformed cargo space he shared with the rest of his company. Once upon a time, a company commander could be assured of his own private quarters, but those days were over. Space on any ship in the fleet was at a premium and his comfort was not a priority.

In here, surrounded by the shelves of cleaning fluid, rags, and other janitorial necessities, Tom could hear the ever-constant hum of the ship's engines through the walls. Until this voyage, he never realised how much he loathed that bloody sound, now it added to the unquiet chaos on the decks of the ship.

At least in here, he was given a temporary reprieve from the noise, where he could drink himself into a stupor and not think about Lisa, the woman he was forced to sacrifice to save the ship.

* * *

A short time later, he got to his feet, legs tingling uncomfortably until the circulation resumed normal programming. Clusters of pain pulsed in his temples and the rotgut he'd been drinking had left a dead cat in his mouth. Steadying himself against the steel bulkhead, he searched the floor and found his grey, sweat stained t-shirt and pulled it on. Running his fingers over his close-cropped dark hair, he tried to fake some semblance of grooming, even if there wasn't much there to put right in the first place. After a similar inspection of his face made him realized he was in desperate need of a shave, he frowned. Water, like everything else on board was rationed to the point where two-minute showers were considered a luxury and no one would dare suggest using any of it for a shave.

Probably why all the women on board were wearing long pants and granny knickers.

The thought made him snigger until he stepped into the chaos outside.

* * *

In its day, the *HMS Rutherford* was a strictly military transport ship. She spent her time ferrying soldiers from one end of the system to the other, chasing down those mad Earth First bastards who were determined to halt mankind's colonisation of Sol by any means necessary. This usually meant disrupting mining operations on Calisto or the Ananke Cluster by using bombs and other acts of terror.

The *Rutherford,* or *Ruthie,* as she was more commonly known, was four hundred meters across and comprised of ten decks with a state of the art EM-Drive, capable of travelling at half the speed of light. Aside from transporting soldiers, she took passengers and equipment from Earth to the colonies and had a crew capacity of one hundred and fifty.

At present, she was carrying seven hundred.

When Tom stepped out of his supply closet, he walked straight into those seven hundred people who were mostly civilian refugees from Europa Colony. While seven hundred might seem high in the confines of the *Ruthie*, it was eclipsed by the number of how many were left behind. Being on the front line of the boarding process ensured the faces of everyone left behind were burnt into his memory.

Like they had when the sun went nova.

The noise level rose the instant he stepped into the hallway, into an assault on his senses. A group of children running past him, somehow managing to play in all this shit, made him pause and he watched them disappear down the corridor. The noise dulled into a roar just as the smell assaulted him. Even with the ventilation system working at capacity to keep things fresh, nothing could prevent the stink of so many bodies. Throw in water rationing and well...

It smells like a bloody barn, he thought, not for the first time.

Walking along the passageway, Tom no longer noticed the objects tacked against the walls and along the deck, turning the bulkheads into memorials for those left behind. There were photographs, toys, keepsakes, scrawled names against the grey steel and notes, left by mourners still shell shocked by the new world order. Tom no longer saw their faces, only their shapes disappearing into the walls, like living wraiths.

They in turn gave him a wide berth as he walked by, because everything about Tom Merrick said, 'go away'.

He was six feet of compact muscle, maintained by years of hard military discipline. Forever wearing a day's growth on his face (even when there was water), he wore a scowl made worse by his intense hazel eyes. If that wasn't enough of a deterrent, the uniform he wore certainly was. Tom was a lifer and lifers were hard bastards.

While it was easy to pigeonhole him because of his appearance, his sympathy for their situation would have surprised them if they'd known about it. Tom found it obscene he considered himself lucky to have lost his parents before Earth was destroyed. His mother passed years before his enlistment and his father followed her a decade later. Throughout this fucked up situation, he counted himself fortunate he was spared losing them the way most of the population had lost family, by the lack of space.

Although, truth be told, if Johnno Merrick had met his end in the nova, Tom would have lost no sleep over it. That bastard *deserved* to burn.

* * *

At six feet four, Gunnery Sergeant (aka Gunny) Derick Rickman looked like folded origami as he sat in a quiet corner of the cargo hold retrofitted for his unit, reading one of Tom Merrick's books. Trying to get lost in its pages, he raised his blue eyes at the rumble of voices intruding on his concentration. With no such thing as privacy anymore, Derick made do with the knowledge at present, this was as good as it was going to get.

Luckier than most because he came out of Earth's destruction with a brother who still lived, Derick knew most people had lost everyone they ever knew. Luke, who was currently on the *Olympus*, had made it onto one of the ships, unlike their parents and baby sister Lily. Thinking about them made his heart ache and he consoled himself with the thought they were with his older brother Chris now, and eventually he'd see Luke again.

BANG!

Derick jumped, startled by the noise. It had come from the centre of the room where one of the occupied chairs around the square table normally used for poker was lying flat on its back. He looked up just in time to see Corporal 'soon to be Private' Ozymandias Washington, flip the table out of his way and lunge for Private Linus Voight.

Cards, glasses, and poker chips cascaded to the deck as Ozzy landed on Linus, forcing the others to back away to get clear of the fighting. Only Private Alain Dupree made any effort to intervene, trying to drag Ozzy off the former *Heir* infantryman before the fists started flying. The other players opted to watch the show and those who were disinterested in the game earlier were now coming to egg on the two combatants.

Cursing under his breath, Derick jumped to his feet and stomped over to the impromptu arena. Under any other circumstances, Sergeant Joshua Jackson, whom everyone called Jazz, would have dealt with this situation, but Derick had spied Jazz leaving the room to go for a jog around the ship, so this was now his lot to deal with.

"WHAT THE HELL IS GOING ON!!"

Derick's bellow was so loud and uncharacteristic, the two men froze, fists cocked as if they were about to duke it out to Queensbury rules. The rest of the platoon was equally shocked, accustomed to this from their sergeant and the Major, but not from their even-tempered gunny. They gaped at him like fish panting for air. If he wasn't so damn pissed, Derick might have found the scene funny.

He was the antithesis of a typical lifer Marine and definitely not the average Gunnery Sergeant. He didn't bark for no good reason. In fact, in Tiger Platoon, Derick was the reasonable one. The Major could strip paint with a glare, or flash you a T-Rex's sneer right before he ripped you a new one. Nope, Gunny Derick Rickman was who you came to with your troubles, who'd talk you down when you wanted to blow yourself out of an airlock.

An outburst from him was nothing to take lightly. Even if he wasn't standing almost six feet four, with a solid build, a chiselled jaw, intense hazel eyes and a flop of hair that defied Marine regulations no matter how many times he cut it, Derick towered over most of the Sharks. While he looked just as hot, sweaty and smelly in his fatigues and canoe-sized boots, the authority he commanded was something they were all conditioned to obey.

Of course, it would be these two, Derick thought as he grabbed both Ozzy and Linus by the shoulders and yanked, as if he were pulling apart two brawling kids in the playground.

"Are you fucking kidding me?" He shoved them apart in opposite directions.

Linus stumbled backwards before he was halted by the body of Private Ren Richards, a stunning redhead with wild, wild hair. She shoved Linus back towards Derick, her face twisted in annoyance as if she couldn't believe this shit either. Derick met her gaze fleetingly and saw her shaking her head. Meanwhile, Ozzy did a little better. He didn't lose his footing and straightened up, almost matching Derick in height.

"Humanity is on the brink of extinction. We've got food riots and kids sleeping in the trash collection chutes because we don't have the room for them. At any moment, a dozen things could fuck us sideways and with all that, you're going to add acting like assholes to the list? I don't give a flying fuck about what started this! It ends *now.*"

Derick glared at them, silencing both men before his gaze shifted to the crowd. The onlookers fell silent, found their boots interesting to look at, stunned at their normally quiet Gunny going full hulk on them.

"In one hour, we've got to get our asses out there and maintain some kind of order during food distribution in the middle of a fucking famine. There will be enough people pissed at us, blaming us for enforcing the rules and here you two are, fighting like kids instead of watching each other's back!"

That sunk in. Whatever grievance had led to the fight melted in the face of that stark reality. They were Sharks and Sharks watched each other's back. Especially now.

"Sorry Gunny."

Ozzy's use of the nickname meant the message was received loud and clear and by the man's expression, it was one received with a side of shame.

"Pardon," Linus stepped forward and extended a hand towards Ozzy who met it with a fist bump instead.

"Peace, Kraut." Ozzy smirked, and Dupree smacked him on the back in approval at the gesture.

"Fuck you, American," Linus returned, but he was smiling.

"What's this, a fucking wedding?"

"Major ON DECK!" Someone belted out belatedly. Derick reacted immediately, recognising that voice anywhere.

* * *

Tom stepped into the billets his Sharks affectionately called the Cave, on the tail of a fight. He couldn't blame them. Not really. Their present situation and the close quarters didn't do much to help tempers. Being jammed into makeshift bunks in the cargo hold made them look and feel like penned sheep. Back in the day, soldiers serving on the *Rutherford* would have proper quarters but since the Exodus every space short of hazardous voids had become living quarters.

Now the *Rutherford* was one more lifeboat in a patchwork fleet comprised of military, cargo and cruise liners under the banner of what was being called the Earth Alliance.

Once in competition with each other, the various military organisations of Sol were forced to amalgamate to protect the remains of the human race. While the transition was easy enough with the flight corps becoming the Space Corps, the consolidation of Earth's infantry forces was far more complicated.

The American forces joined ranks with the remnants of other units, such as the British SAS, the Chinese Marines, French Colonial Troops, Israeli Givatis and other nationalities. Now consolidated, the reorganized force became the Security Heavy Artillery & Recon Corps. Its acronym, SHARC, gave rise to the nickname that quickly went viral.

Sharks.

Tom was given command of Tiger Platoon, composed of forty warm bodies, with ten to a squad and he had to admit it fit well. He liked the term Sharks better and it was a hell of a lot better than Marines, which he knew would rankle the non-American troops, himself included.

"At ease," Tom ordered with a dismissive wave of his hand when he saw everyone stepping to at his arrival. His head was split open now, thanks to the enthusiastic announcer but he kept his cool. Morale was already in the shitter without Tom tearing about like some drunken bastard.

He saw the dissipating hostility between Linus and Ozzy and guessed the earlier friction was forgotten once Derick reminded them Sharks watched each other's back. The big bloke knew how to handle short tempers. Christ knows they'd been friends long enough for Derick to handle his.

The kid was good value and their friendship went all the way back to a bar in Miramar when he was still a non-com. Tom was supremely grateful to learn Derick survived the exodus from Earth and wasted no time asking for the gunnery sergeant to be assigned to his new platoon.

Serving together was one of the few positives coming out of human civilization going to shit. Besides, Derick Rickman was the only Yank he'd ever met he didn't feel the urge to throttle.

"Good morning ladies," he greeted them with a nod and then met Derick's hazel eyes. "What's all this then?"

"Just a few assholes letting off steam," Derick saw no reason to go into details. Besides, chances were Tom already knew what's what. "It's handled."

Ozzy shot the Gunny a look of surprise but held back the confession on the tip of his tongue. If Gunny thought it was best to keep his mouth shut, then Ozzy wasn't going to argue with him. Besides, he had no desire to get his ass chewed out by the Major, who could yell even louder than Gunny. Meeting Linus's gaze, the two men agreed in silent solidarity for their benefit.

With Tom's arrival and the situation now under control, Derick's attention turned to his best friend and commanding officer. Tom was doing his best to hide it, but Derick saw the signs of yet another drink-til-he-passed-out respite.

He wouldn't say anything in front of the others. In private, maybe. Tom's trip down the bottle seemed to be getting worse. He was clearly nursing a hangover, judging by the bloodshot eyes, clammy skin, and the slight reek of stale liquor. Six months ago, Derick wouldn't have given a shit about how much Tom drank because he was right there next to the man, getting plastered.

Back then, Tom was a casual drinker who knew how to put the bottle away. Something changed after the Ruthie left Sol but for the moment, Derick was more concerned about the quality of the booze Tom managed to find. Derick swore if he found out who was making the rotgut Tom was poisoning himself with, he'd flush the son of a bitch out of an airlock himself.

"Good," Tom nodded, deciding to leave it if Derick considered the matter closed. Besides, he caught the critical way Derick was looking at him. It didn't require any clairvoyance on Tom's part to know why. The look was all too familiar. Derick was worried about him and as much as Tom might hate admitting it, the kid had cause. A conversation for another day, he decided.

"Right then, listen up!" Tom addressed everyone once they were a bit more relaxed, knowing there would be no repercussions for the earlier fight. "I just got word the *Obelisk* will be carrying half the rations it was going to. Seems the spoilage and the spread of supplies across the fleet is even worse than we thought."

An audible groan moved through the group. There would be hungry people on the *Ruthie* tonight. They would be angry, and the Sharks would be standing between them and what little food they were getting.

Derick cursed inwardly, a slight exchange of eye contact told him the Major was just as angered by this as he.

Glancing at his watch, Derick decided to shift their focus before they got too twisted up by a situation they could not change.

"Alright! We're on deck in…. fifty-two minutes. Alpha squad, you're up! I want equipment check in thirty. Ozzy!" he yelled at the man he'd just reprimanded. "Act like a soldier and go find Jazz…"

"No need Gunny, I'm here," Jazz announced himself as he stepped into the room. He'd been returning anyway from his run and caught Derick's orders. "You heard Gunny! Get ready!"

With Jazz barking orders at them, the crowd dispersed, scattering in various directions towards their billets. Derick spied the lithe body of Ren Richards following the crowd and spent a fraction of a second watching her crazy hair bounce off her shoulders. Glancing away quickly before he was caught, Derick frowned. He was her superior. He had to get over her. Dragging a hand through his hair, he turned back to Tom.

"Any orders, Major?"

His tone was formal but, in truth, they'd known each other for years and were best friends.

"Yeah," Tom nodded, taking a step closer to Derick and speaking in a lower tone. "Take Beta squad with you too. I think we both know how nasty this is going to get."

"That's a fucking understatement."

* * *

Derick Rickman never intended to be a soldier.

For as long as he could remember, he wanted to be a photojournalist. His dreams involved traveling Sol, taking pictures of important events and places, immortalising his experiences, frame by frame. An avid photographer in his youth, his collection ranged from modern holo-recorders to old fashioned film cameras and even video recorders. By the time he was ten, Derick mastered the use of all of them. Hell, he even had a vintage Browning he bought at an old junk store.

Daniel Rickman, his father, was career military and so Derick could hone his craft with each new posting on a different moon or planet. It was a hobby his dad encouraged because, Derick suspected, Dad believed his middle son might be just a little too smart and sensitive for the military life.

Derick's older brother, Chris, was the one who would follow in their father's footsteps. Born a year after Dan and Susannah's wedding, the couple decided to wait a few years before having more children. As a result, Derick was born four years later, Luke came three years after, and it was five years before Susannah got the girl she wanted in Lily.

By the time Derick was two, Chris had hung the moon.

Despite Chris indulging in his God-given right as an older brother to torment his younger siblings, he was never excessive or cruel. Charged to be the man of the house in their father's absence, Chris took the responsibility seriously. He looked after the younger children and helped their mother with chores.

For Derick, Chris had been his best friend and his confidante. Even when Chris had friends of his own, he never failed to make room for Derick. If Chris's friends didn't like a kid trailing behind them, then Chris didn't have time for them.

Unsurprisingly, Chris followed their father into the military, joining the Planetary Marines when he was old enough to enlist. Derick found it fitting. Chris was most like their father and it made sense that he would continue the family tradition. Derick was still in grade school, on an advanced track for college prep with an eye on every journalism scholarship he could find, when Chris left for boot camp.

Six years later, a month after Derick's high school graduation, Chris was killed in an Earth First terrorist attack on Ganymede.

While the others mourned Chris, Derick felt as if someone had dropped a nuke on his life, obliterating everything in its path. The enormity of it was more than he could bear and deconstructed everything Derick considered important to him. He gave up plans for college for a year with a half-hearted promise to go back later but never did. Instead, he lingered at home, consoling his father, who aged a decade after hearing the news, while trying to be there for his mother and siblings just like Chris would have done.

Even after Dan decided to take a permanent post on Earth, Derick found it difficult to get his life back on track. Chris's loss was profound, and the void left behind seemed vast and permanent. As Derick approached his twentieth birthday, his cameras and photography equipment lay forgotten as he cut a swatch through the local girls and spent too much time in one bar or another. His goals were gone, and he had no idea what he intended to do with the rest of his life.

His relationship with his father grew steadily tenser. Dan Rickman was always a hard man, one who saw no difference between soldiering and parenting. It was up to their mom and Chris to provide the emotional bedrock of their family. Dan's natural reaction to Derick's spiral was to take a hard-line approach, resulting in numerous screaming matches and even physical fights that ended up with Derick moving out of the house for a time.

One night, while drinking at a bar somewhere on Claremont Boulevard outside Miramar, where Dad was posted, on his way to another post-Dan-Rickman-argument bender, he started talking to a stranger. The guy looked like a junkyard dog, tough and mean with an accent that was part Michael Caine and part Crocodile Dundee. A guy, who could hold his liquor a hell of a lot better than a twenty-year-old college dropout could.

The drunker Derick got, the more he poured out his troubles to the stranger, who listened without comment. When Derick got through telling him about Chris and how his life had been upended by the loss, the man finally spoke.

"So, you're going to piss your life away because your big brother died in the service? Fucking rotten way to remember him, isn't it?"

Derick stared at him.

"Well, no…" Derick stammered a response. He hadn't heard it put that bluntly before. The crux of every argument he had with Dan Rickman was not that he was throwing his life away but of how Derick wasn't Chris and would never measure up to him.

"Look. You can spend your whole life crying about how he's gone but you got to remember one thing: he kicked it doing exactly what he wanted to do. Dying the way he did, with your men about you, in a fight, that's the way soldiers want to go. Fuck, that's how I want to go. I didn't sign up to die in a comfy bed, mate. I signed up to kick arse for something greater than myself, and I'm betting your brother did the same."

He was right.

Chris spent his whole life taking care of him, Luke and Lily. Joining the military was simply extending his protective nature to the planet. Yeah, he probably didn't count on dying so early, but Derick could believe it was exactly how Chris would want to go. Dying for something that mattered, protecting the people he cared about. It was a watershed moment, the jolt of clarity he so desperately needed, and he started weeping as it washed over him.

Instead of snorting in disgust at the appalling display, which was also a Dan Rickman special, the stranger patted him on the back and said quietly, "Get it out, mate. Get it out and let him go."

Sage advice from the man who would someday become his commanding officer and best friend.

* * *

"T- Minus thirty seconds and counting..."

The large passageway just outside a smaller cargo bay was literally crammed full of people. Every square foot was taken up, with barely any shoulder room. Bodies, nerves, and sweat in a stuffy heat the air scrubbers weren't designed to handle. The effect would make anyone claustrophobic. On the other side of the thick doors, crew members were preparing to receive the rations via shuttle and prep them for distribution.

Derick found a small crate in some supply closet and stood on it now, to give himself an elevated view of the crush of people lined up for their rations. With distribution run on a lottery system, chaos was barely threaded out by the presence of the Sharks. People picked up their rations in shifts, by the head of each household and their ID number. Zero's first, then ones, twos, so on and so forth. Each family would get enough rations for a week.

They were lucky one of the agri-haulers survived the jump.

Mostly, folks stayed orderly after a fashion. Derick made sure of it, even it meant being called things like 'Gestapo' and 'Pig'.

"T-minus fifteen seconds.... ten...."

The automated female voice sounded throughout the passageway, briefly silencing the low roar of the crowd. At least, until a voice carried over them, catching Derick's attention. From his viewpoint, he found the source easily. A large man with a slight gut and the sour look of one under duress. "Chu," Derick said quietly into the throat mike. "On your ri…"

"You're hurting me! Let go!!" Silence spread outward from the man as the crowd shifted and revealed a pretty, dark-haired, and exotic looking woman. The big man's hand was wrapped around her upper arm, nearly engulfing it. "You get your spic ass to the back of the line. You gotta wait your turn!" The man shoved the woman hard, making her stumble.

"HEY!" Derick shouted, jumping off his crate. He started through the crowd as a path appeared with everyone suddenly finding the space to get out of the big and pissed off Shark's way. "Let her go!"

"And what if I don't!?" Bubba or whatever his name was glowered at Derick sullenly. Easily Derick's height, no easy feat, and thirty pounds heavier, he seemed to be considering taking him on. "You gonna shoot me, you ass-RINE!?"

A red bead of light appeared on the man's chest and Derick looked up from it with a smirk. He jerked a thumb over his shoulder, towards Ren and her sniper perch. "No. But she will."

Bubba's chin hit his chest, eyes bulging at the bright red dot on his sternum.

"Fucking pork rind haolie!!" The woman jerked her arm free from the man's grasp. "I'm Hawaiian, not Hispanic!"

"You all look the same!"

Someone behind them shouted. The woman cursed and swung a fist, but Chu grabbed her in time, twisting her away as she protested. Derick grabbed Bubba, preventing him from retaliating and that was all the crowd needed to ignite. They pressed in on Derick and Chu, shouting and yelling, flash boiling to a riot.

"Stand down!!" Jazz yelled, freeing his nightstick when he lost sight of Gunny. "Beta! Crowd control right now!!" he ordered, yanking at the first body in his way to get to their gunnery sergeant.

"QUIIIIIET!!!!!!!!!!!!!"

The command rolled over the crowd, echoing off the bulkheads and stunning all of them into silence, even the Sharks.

The quiet left behind was like a vacuum, sucking every bit of fight out of the gathered refugees. Derick lunged to his feet, Bubba in hand as he sought the source of the noise. That had sounded like… yep. Derick grinned when he spotted Ren hanging up the intercom receiver near her position, looking at him smugly.

Now *that* was fucking effective. 'NICE' he mouthed with a wink before turning back to his charge.

"ID, name and billet," he ordered as he yanked a chip reader from his harness.

"Name's Jim Dale." The big guy glowered as he produced his bright green wrist band. "Billet 261."

Derick scanned it and when the device chirped in positive affirmation, he glanced at the screen to verify the picture. "Mr Dale, once I authorize the delivery to continue, you will be given your rations and escorted off the deck." Leaning in close, he grabbed the man's shoulder and dug his fingers into the flesh. "You have a problem with someone, you come to me. I catch you starting trouble again and your rations will be cut. Do you understand?" He growled.

Jim's eyes widened. The threat was an effective one. He glanced around, taking in the hostile stares directed at him. He swore under his breath, as if realizing he would have been responsible for things going sideways. Taking a deep breath and letting it out, Jim nodded.

"Good." The shame on the man's face was enough for Derick to decide that further action wasn't needed. "Anderson!" When the private appeared beside Chu, Derick let go of Dale. "Private Anderson here will make sure you get your fair share and will be your escort."

Leaving Anderson to handle him, Derick turned to the woman and motioned for her hand. "ID."

Shoving back lank, dark hair, she held up the bright green band on her wrist. "My name is Lani Kahananui. I'm a teacher…"

Fucking pork rind haolie was a teacher?? Where, a prison? Derick raised an eyebrow as he scanned her ID band.

The noise no one was supposed to be making oozed up again as she continued, raising her voice to be heard. "I'm in charge of the unclaimed kids." The crowd went silent again, staring at her when they realized exactly who she was. The unclaimed children were the poor kids separated from their families during the chaos of the mass evacuation. Lani had taken charge of them, sorting them out and organizing searches for family members.

Derick scanned her ID band and was rewarded with another satisfactory chirp. "Richards!!" he called out and received a sharp 'Yes, Gunny!' by the red-headed sniper. "You and Mayday are Miss Kahananui's escorts today. Once she gets the rations, please escort her back to her assigned billet."

Still humming with satisfaction from the smile she received from him earlier, Ren made her way through the sea of human bodies, gesturing at Junior Corporal Maya 'Mayday' Sanjay, a former medic with the British Army, to join her at his call.

"We're on it, Sir," she quipped, always wearing the slightest hint of a smile for him.

"Right behind you, mate," Maya echoed.

With the two civilians under trustworthy watch and the crowd under some semblance of control, Derick hopped back onto the crate and hailed Control to continue with the docking just as there was another shout.

Seeking the source out, Derick sighed. It was going to be a *long* day.

II

Survey

It was never wise to make hasty calculations even in the face of impending disaster.

Just being off by a fraction may seem insignificant, but in astrophysics, it was the difference between life and death. Instead of emerging from the Ribbon a little over a light year away from their destination, they'd overshot their exit point by *seven* light years. A journey intended to take four weeks now stretched into its sixth month. Never in the history of the world, were there such grave consequences for not carrying a zero.

Dr. Albert Nakamura stared at the faces before him, wishing it was anyone else but he who made it.

No one blamed him, of course, not the inventor of the Ribbon Drive responsible for saving humanity. His original prototype was being installed in a test flight ship given to him by his project funders, The Tiger Alliance (the federation of Asian nations). Albert had just been about to sign off on the installation when astronomers all over Sol flew into a panic.

Something very large had hit the sun, something with enough reactive material to destabilise its solar fission. Every instrument they possessed showed the core of the sun collapsing on itself and when critical mass was reached, it would go nova taking the *entire solar sys-*

tem with it. It would happen fast and no science they possessed could stop it.

Extinction would happen, not in seven billion years, but in a matter of *weeks.*

Suddenly Nakamura's drive went from being a prototype to humanity's last hope for survival. Frantically re-designing the device and increasing its output by a thousand, he worked around the clock to develop a working model while across the solar system, the evacuation lottery to choose several thousand people out of ten billion began.

As luck would have it, critical mass arrived a week early. One final act of Murphy's Law.

By that time, most of the people were already on board the ships and the military were on route to pick up final passengers. Nakamura made his calculations and rolled the dice, praying the Ribbon Drive would work as the solar system started to disintegrate and wipe out nearly ten billion people with it.

It did and humanity achieved the ability to fold space.

Twenty-five ships went through. For weeks before, smaller vessels not outfitted with a Ribbon drive had been leeched onto the larger ones with dry dock clamps and cables, like infant sharks pressed against their mother's belly. Of those twenty-five capital ships, twenty survived the gravimetric turbulence. Some of the older models, simply not made for such travel, broke up in transit. Nakamura tried not to think about the people on board who were lost. The drive's success was pyrrhic but at least they reached their destination on the far side of the spiral arm.

Ten years earlier, deep range probes transmitted data regarding the existence of a world with similar properties to Earth lying in a distant star system. The planet was sixty percent water and possessed a rich nitrogen-oxygen atmosphere capable of supporting life.

They called it Gaia.

It was a place to be visited someday, when they finally developed a real FTL drive capable of crossing the distance instead of the standard EM drives which allowed them to colonise Sol but nothing beyond.

The destruction of Sol changed everything. Gaia became the only viable destination for the surviving human race. Once again, Nakamura had to make calculations based on theoretical science not yet conclusively proven or field tested.

Fortunately, the Ribbon Drive did exactly what they needed, with the exception of the tiny, tiny mistake in his calculations. They arrived seven light years short of the planet.

From where the Ribbon deposited them, the journey to Gaia would take months. They simply didn't have the ability to make another attempt to fold space. With no other alternative, the fleet was forced to make the crossing using the EM Drive, travelling half the speed of light.

The months since pushed them to the very limits of their resources. All supplies were reaching dangerously low levels despite hard-line rations of water, food, and energy. Bodies were crammed into ships, running air and waste recycling systems beyond maximum operating capacity. Medical personnel were already dealing with the inevitable outbreaks of disease due to poor hygiene and bad air.

The bulk of the planet's diplomatic contingent never made it off Earth. Under any other circumstances, it was a situation ripe for a joke, but no one dare make it. What was left was an uneasy alliance of soldiers and scientists forced to work together to give birth to a new human civilisation. It didn't take long before they realised they needed a third component to function, a civilian faction to complete the triumvirate.

It was a shotgun wedding if there was ever one.

Now they were in sight of Gaia and it was none too soon; the entire fleet was sitting on a powder keg and they needed to get off before it exploded.

* * *

On board the Alliance Ship *AS Missouri*, President Philana Zubuqu stared across the conference table at the three people who made up the newly formed Earth Assembly. The Assembly, representing three distinct groups, the armed forces, the scientific community and the civilian population, formed to replace the now extinct Earth Alliance governing body.

"How soon can we land?" Philana directed her question at Nakamura, the Head of the Science Council.

A man in his forties, Nakamura never struck Philana as a scientist, certainly not the giant of propulsion and astrophysics he now was. He wore his hair long but swept back over his forehead. His severe expression and dark, sharp eyes belied the warmer personality Philana had become acquainted with over the years. She liked and admired him even before his Ribbon Drive saved them all.

Yet, he changed over the last few months. Instead of warmth and sharp intellect, she saw a man blunted by grief for not saving *enough* lives.

Running his fingers along the slate device in front of him, Nakamura brought the display alive and projected a holographic image above the centre of the table for all to see.

An iridescent world appeared before them, not Earth but not entirely dissimilar either. It was a place of blue oceans, greenish tinged clouds, and large greenish brown land masses. There were two moons in orbit. The moons weren't lifeless husks like Lunar but just as teeming with life as the world below them. Even as a hologram, their first glimpse of Gaia was breathtaking.

Nakamura refused to forgo the details even though the urgency of the situation was not lost on him. He knew about the escalating tensions throughout the fleet, the strain on all their resources and the civilians on the verge of rioting. Their fabricators could produce important things like medicines and machine parts, but food and water for ten thousand people was beyond even the most inventive engineer's capability.

"We can land any time," Nakamura answered, "but whether it is safe to do so is another matter entirely," he said, meeting Philana's brown eyes. "Since arriving in orbit, we have been conducting scans of the surface and what is clear to us, that wasn't before, is that there is an abundance of life on Gaia."

The announcement did nothing to allay anyone's concerns.

"Intelligent life?" Field Marshal Grigori Anisimov asked suspiciously. He was very much a Russian bear, towering, with a deep, booming voice and large hands that could break you apart if he felt like it. Grey eyes stared at the scientist, showing his concern at how the natives might react to ten thousand humans landing on their doorstep. As well as humans would, he suspected, if the shoe were on the other foot.

"No," Nakamura quickly dismissed the notion, seeing the fear it generated.

"There is an abundance of animal life, but we've detected no signs of intelligence. Of course, it is a big planet and we can't assume anything for certain. Until we are sure of what we are dealing with, I do not recommend landing. I propose we send a survey party first."

"And how long will this take?" Jyoti Sengputa asked impatiently. She was a petite thing who wore her dark hair in a tight bun, accentuating a strong jaw and eyes that looked older than her thirty-five years. "Life support is barely holding on as it is, not to mention people are becoming violent and desperate. They *need* to get off the ships. They need to feel the sun on their faces and breathe fresh air. They need to know there is an end in sight to all this."

Until a few months ago, Jyoti was the deputy secretary of the Solar Health Organisation. She had been off world investigating an outbreak of Miner's Disease on Ganymede when news of the disaster was made public. In transit when Earth was destroyed, Jyoti now found herself as the voice of the civilian population.

"It's difficult to determine. We are entering an entirely unknown ecosystem. We simply cannot assume the place is safe…." Nakamura tried to reason with her. He understood her concerns, they all did, but this could not be rushed.

"I agree with Albert," Grigori spoke and made Nakamura smile a little because the big Russian was the first one of the Assembly to address him as if they were more than colleagues, but rather soldiers in the same foxhole. "We cannot simply descend onto this planet. For all we know the dominant animal life down there could be dinosaurs."

Although that would simply be *magnificent*, Grigori thought silently.

"People are at breaking point," Jyoti insisted, her small fist thumping the table to emphasize each word. "We need to do something…"

"We *will*," Philana said firmly and with enough force in her voice to remind everyone they were in this together. Like the Zulu people from which she was descended, Philana's high cheekbones, full lips, and almost feline eyes exuded regal authority and confidence.

"Albert, put a survey team together. The sooner we send them down there the better. Have you selected a possible landing site yet?"

"Yes," Nakamura nodded and swiped the slate's screen to show another image. This one displayed a map, specifically a large continent shaped a little like Greenland but was the size of Africa. "This is the continent we have decided to call Laurasia. The name is an amalgam of Laurentia and Asia."

He widened the image further and showed a stretch of land on the south-east side of the continent. "We thought this might be a good landing site. There's a waterway of significant size travelling at least a thousand kilometres inland and gives us access to the sea. The land between the waterway and the mountain range is comprised of fertile plains and there are flatlands suitable for cultivation. The mountains will also give us protection from any harsh weather. The science team is calling it Babel."

"Babel," Philana smiled faintly. "I like it."

"I think the survey team should be accompanied by some ground troops," Grigori added. "With all due respect, Albert, we don't know what your team will be walking into."

"Fair enough, but I request that, in all scientific matters, my team leader has authority."

"And in all military matters, my officer should have the same," the Russian countered.

"Well then, gentlemen," Philana swept her gaze across the two men, "let's make this happen."

* * *

After Derick took out Alpha and Beta squad to manage crowd control during food distribution, Tom returned to the quarters he shared with a dozen other officers on board the *Ruthie*. Not only was he the only Shark officer present, he was also the only one with the rank of Major. The SHARC ranking structure, like most of the armed forces, was still a work in progress. Only the bird in charge of the *Ruthie* outranked him and she was a Yank promoted for being in the right place at the right time.

Before the Exodus, the room was a storage area of some kind and Tom swore he could detect a whiff of brain cell-killing chemicals through the wafting odour of sweat and stale air. Frankly, he didn't know which was worse.

The beds provided were no more than makeshift bunks and cots, while the grey, windowless walls and metal deck plates added to the ambience. At the foot of each 'bed' was a foot locker to store a lifetime of belongings. Most military men lived out of a duffel bag anyway, but Tom missed his books; not the sizeable library he stored on his personal slate, but the soft paper books he'd collected over the years. He'd taken what he could; the *Count of Monte Cristo*, the *Puppet Masters*, *Dune* and a few others, but the rest were sacrificed because the space was needed for the essentials.

This time of day, the room was empty and fortunately accessible by security code to keep civilians from coming in here and stealing. Desperation drove people to extremes and theft was just one of the things people were forced to take up to survive. With barter the only form of currency at present, thieves were always on the lookout for something they could steal to trade for something better.

Tossing in the bottle of rotgut he'd traded for a copy of *Moby Dick*, Tom grabbed a change of clothing from the chest and locked it shut. Leaving the room, he crossed the corridor to enter the communal shower used by most of the military personnel stationed on this deck. There were a few people in there already, some he recognised, and others he didn't.

Adhering to the etiquette of co-ed showers, Tom kept his eyes fixed on the porcelain tiles. It was extremely bad manners to steal stray glances at anyone's junk, male, or female. Self-consciousness at being naked in front of other people simply didn't come into it anymore, even with the nude bodies of the opposite sex beside you.

Still, it was harder (no pun intended) said than done when one came across the tantalising slick of glistening skin or the curve of a breast. At least, in those situations, everyone had the good manners to say nothing, even if it was affecting.

Tom stepped under the shower head and turned the knob. The spray rushing over him was lukewarm. Wasting no time, he pressed a dollop of gel onto his palm from the dispenser and began soaping up. He had two minutes to wash before the water switched off automatically. Biometric sensors on the tap knob identified him and ensured he was allocated his two minutes. After that, he'd have to wait for the next twenty-four-hour cycle to come along.

Once he was done, Tom got dressed and headed back to the Cave, still longing for a shave when he ran his hand across his chin and felt the stubble. At least, now, he looked somewhat respectable and not like a pile of dirty washing.

"Message for Major Tom Merrick at Com Station 14." Tom heard his name over the speakers as he was in the middle of the hallway. "Repeat, message for Major Tom Merrick..."

Tom hurried to the far end of the corridor, where a small secured room awaited. Punching in his identification code, the door slid open and he stepped into the cubicle sized space formerly used to let ship personnel make private calls home. Now it was used for ship to ship communication across their ragtag fleet. Shutting the door behind him, he sat at the station and took his call.

On the screen in front of him, the face of General Rhys Connor, the commander of the Sharks appeared, waiting to talk to him.

When the Sharks were first formed six months ago, Rhys, a Brigadier General of the British Army, introduced himself to his senior officers. Ironically, despite being a Major, Tom was one of the longest serving combat soldiers in the fleet. He'd started out as a non-com and come into his officer's bars late. Despite Rhys being a good fifteen years older, he was a career infantry officer who'd been in the trenches. Their shared combat experiences gave both men common ground as battle-scarred veterans of a changing armed forces.

He was a decent bloke. For a Pom.

"General," Tom greeted respectfully, feeling like he knew the man enough to recognize this wasn't a personal call. "It's good to see you."

"Likewise, Tom," the General replied from his office on the *Nelson*, green eyes resting on Tom with a similar affection. "I have some news for you and I wanted to talk to you face to face."

That didn't sound good. Tom wondered what fresh calamity was going to be visited on them now. "What is it?" He was almost afraid of the answer.

"Relax, Digger," Rhys grinned, seeing the man stiffen through the screen. "It's nothing bad."

"Digger," Tom grumbled, bloody Pom. Nowadays, it was a term of endearment and evidence of their growing friendship. "What can I do for you, Sir?"

"I need you to get two squads together. You'll be accompanying the science team planet side."

Tom did a double take, thinking Rhys was fucking with him but the man's expression revealed otherwise. "Planet side? As in 'off the ship'?"

"That's right," Rhys smiled smugly.

"Are we there? Did we get to the planet? When?" He fired questions like artillery shells, trying not to show just how excited he was at the prospect of escaping the *Ruthie*. After six months, it felt as if they would never reach Gaia, the Promise Land at the end of this nightmare journey through space.

Rhys didn't go into details, giving Tom just enough to proceed. "We slipped into orbit last night. They've done the initial scans and selected a landing site, but we need to go down there to confirm the data. So, you and your team will provide support to the squint team surveying the area to make sure that it's safe for the rest of the population to come down."

Tom didn't care if this was a babysitting detail. Not one bloody bit. The chance to see sky again, even if it was on an alien world, was the shot in the arm he needed after months of hell. Not just for him, but for his squad, who needed this excursion almost as much.

"We'll get it done, Sir."

"Good to hear. Just be aware that in all matters scientific, the head squint is in charge, but…"

Tom bristled at that but before he could voice his protest, Rhys raised his hand to stop him. "Unless of course, the situation becomes dangerous in any way and then you can assume command. Let them do what they need to do and take over if anything nasty jumps out of the bushes."

"Right." Tom could live with those terms. Besides, while they were scanning, he and his team would be out in the fresh air with the sky above their heads. He could tolerate a bunch of squints with that kind of perk. "I'll get the team together as soon as possible. When are we leaving?"

"At 1100 hours. Report to Captain Curran. She'll give you further details."

"Will do, Sir, and thanks for giving us the chance to get off this tin can." He was almost beaming.

"Yeah, I do recall how much you said you love space travel," Rhys replied dryly. "Good luck to you, Major. Connor out."

The screen went dark and Tom eased into his chair, letting out a sigh of relief. Finally, some good news.

It was about fucking time.

III

Jules

For a few seconds, she could do nothing but stare.

The ship was ablaze, from bow to stern, wearing the fire like a second skin. Dark space lit up like a newborn sun. The vacuum would extinguish the radiance soon enough, but for the few seconds while exploding bulkheads and ruptured hull plating allowed oxygen to escape, the flames lived. There wasn't an inch of the hull across the capital ship not on fire.

Elemental demons danced across the cracking plexiglass windows, invaded the vast turbines of the main engines and battered down airlock doors. They ran like wayward children through the hallways and slipped into the air vents, igniting fluids, greedily consumed furnishings, and sucked away flesh before the final damning explosion.

To those screaming, the fire's cackle sounded like laughter.

* * *

"We've got to find another ship!"

The hopper she was piloting carried fifty people, crammed in so tightly they could barely breathe. She promised them she wasn't leaving them behind and would get them to safety. The Asquith was an American battlecruiser, one of the largest ever built. It would be more than capable of handling a rough docking and providing refuge to her passengers for the trip through the Ribbon.

Except within sight of it, a solar flare lashed out with the fury of an angry god and smote the great ship like it was nothing. One brilliant eruption and the ship, with its crew of 400 was gone, incinerated. It was so quick, it staggered belief. She gaped through the cockpit windows, stunned for a moment until she remembered the people in her charge.

"Hold onto something!! We've got to get out of range before the engines blow!"

Pulling on the throttle, she banked hard, the hopper's systems groaning in protest at the sharp change in trajectory. Under normal circumstances, it was a bus, ferrying passengers from cruisers and transport liners to their planet side destinations. It wasn't made for speed or designed with the manoeuvrability of a fighter, which was what she was accustomed to.

Her Lidar Intercept Officer, or LIO, Chuck, grabbed an overhead bar and braced himself. Muttering under his breath, cursing whoever put the navcomp in the back of the cockpit on these barges, his free hand flew over the navcomp. Like Jules, he ignored the utter ruin of the Asquith even as they were bathed in the hellish radiance of the fire beyond the cockpit window.

"The Rutherford!" he called out finally. "Head for the Rutherford! She's taken damage but she's still flying. I'm feeding the coordinates into the nav!"

Jules wasn't listening, she was concentrating on avoiding the debris of other ships destroyed by the unexpected flares of their dying sun. Pieces of hull, whole sections, and pylons tumbled through space, hurtling at speeds that would destroy the hopper completely if struck. For the average onlooker, the craft navigated the debris field with drunken bobs, weaves and rolls but any pilot would recognise the precision flying necessary to achieve this.

When the Asquith exploded, it didn't need to be seen. It was felt.

The shockwave hit the tiny hopper from behind. Jules was thrown forward hard in her harness, as something hit the back of her flight helmet. She wasn't sure how, but she managed to keep both hands on the controls even as Chuck's body slammed into the cockpit window with an audible crunch before rolling off the console to crumple on the floor.

Jules glanced long enough to see his head bent at an unnatural angle and his bloody skull visible under a flap of destroyed skin hanging off his forehead. In horror, she looked at the window, barely comprehending the red smear where he'd made contact.
"CHUCK!"

* * *

Chuck Ferris had been her co-pilot from the moment she crawled into her first Zephyr. He was her best friend. She stood up with him at his wedding and would later break the news to his husband, Michael. She remembered having to wipe her tears and keep flying through the shockwave of debris and fire to reach the *Rutherford* because, even as Chuck lay dead on the deck of the cockpit, she had a job to do.

She landed on the *Rutherford* with the hopper and its passengers surviving the journey only to learn the ship was without a captain. The explosion that took the *Asquith* had also obliterated the command deck of the *Rutherford*. Upon managing to dock on the *Ruthie*, she was informed that most of the senior staff had been on the bridge. Before she could consider her actions, Jules was running towards Engineering, shouting orders to reroute command functions so she could get the ship under control and stay with the fleet to make the jump.

Somehow, with the help of a few terrified ensigns and one lieutenant, Jules had managed to set the *Rutherford* back on course to join the rest of the fleet heading towards the Ribbon.

When it was all said and done, Lt. Commander Juliana Curran, formerly of the US Zephyr flight wing was made Captain of the *AS Rutherford*.

She didn't know whether to laugh or cry.

* * *

She opened her eyes and found herself staring at the ceiling. The heat she could almost feel a second ago was replaced by cool, if somewhat stale air. Blinking once or twice to chase away the images of that terrible day, she sat up in her bed and scanned the room surrounding her like Alice waking up in Wonderland.

"Captain Curran?"

Already awake, the lit intercom over the bed prompted her to sit up in her bunk and reach for the light switch. The glare of light made her squint as her hand moved away from the switch to find the one allowing her to respond to the com.

"Here."

"Captain, General Shang is calling a vidcon in thirty minutes. You asked me to wake you?"

"Yep. Thanks. I'll be on deck in fifteen." That wouldn't be enough time to shower but Jules, like the rest of the fleet, was not wasting water. As Captain, she supposed she was 'entitled' to a shower when she wanted without the constraints of a schedule, but as a person? No, she wouldn't use water like that when the *Rutherford's* seven hundred survivors had to ration theirs.

Sitting up, she winced when something sharp scraped her hand. Lifting the sheet, Jules looked down when something thumped onto the carpeted deck. It took her a second to remember what it was. A clear framed photograph. She'd fallen asleep looking at it the night before. Bending over, Jules scooped it up and gazed at it for a moment. Emotion filled her as she took in her father's face next to her own. She was in her dress uniform and he looked like the rumpled, absent-minded English professor he was, even in his best suit. God, she missed him!

"Captain Curran?"

Nearly jumping at the sound, Jules shot a glare at the speaker over her bed. "I *said* I'm on my way."

"Captain, the vidcon has been moved up fifteen minutes. It just came over the links. There's a lag in the signal."

Of course, there was. During the journey through the Ribbon, the *Rutherford's* dish boosters were sheared off by the gravimetric turbulence. Replacing them was out of the question until their industrial fabricators were up and running.

"All right. I'm coming…" Jules returned the frame to the small crate serving as her bedside table before hastily getting dressed. Grabbing a brush, she swept the stringy mess into a ponytail.

It would have to do until she got her allotted shower.

* * *

"Is there coffee?" Jules asked when she entered the bridge. Her aide, a Chinese Navy junior officer named Wei Xin, presented a cup almost immediately. "I'll be in the office." She held up the warm mug to him as thanks and headed to the tiny room off the Command Deck.

Once inside the room, (more like a closet), Jules dropped into the old leather seat kept by the previous captain. Through some trick of engineering, this little room had survived the emergency decompression months earlier and still held memoirs of the previous captain. She hadn't the heart to get rid of anything. Just like she hadn't really packed up his things in her bunk. Initially, she bunked with some of the other officers until one of the other ship captains convinced her she would need the privacy offered by the Captain's quarters. She hoped the crew didn't resent her for that.

Bringing up the vidcon system, Jules punched in her passcode. After a moment and three chirps, the words 'YOU ARE NOW JOINING THE VIDEO CONFERENCE' flashed on the screen.

"Curran," she greeted simply.

"Good morning, Jules," Admiral Lian Shang, commander of the Space Corps stared back at her.

Lian, like Juliana Curran, arrived at her position a full decade earlier than expected. A career officer in the People's Republic Air Division, Lian was the highest-ranking officer left after their flight from Earth. Like General Connor who ruled the Sharks, Lian performed the same duty as commander of the Space Corps, with both branches commanded by Field Marshal Anisimov.

A classic beauty, with pronounced cheekbones and full lips, she was often mistaken for being soft when in truth, she had more in common with granite than flesh.

"Good morning, Admiral," Jules smiled at the other woman tightly. One of these days, maybe she'd want to take the liberty of using first names, but not right now. Besides, Shang looked like Jules felt: tired, in need of a hot shower, ready to scream, kill something, or all the above. "Are we waiting for anyone else?"

"No, it's just us," Lian replied with a relieved sigh. She did not wish to deal with that *báichī* SHARC General right now. *The English - we did not kill enough of them in the Boxer Rebellion.*

"General Connor is already in communication with your Shark counterpart on board the *Rutherford*. As you know, the *Olympus* has just entered Gaia's orbit. The planet is everything we hoped it would be and appears to be more than capable of supporting human life. Naturally the Assembly would like a survey team on the planet as soon as possible, supported by a Shark team from the *Rutherford*."

"Major Merrick, yes," Jules nodded. They'd met briefly in the early days of her captaincy when she was forced to run the *Ruthie* from Engineering. Amid the chaos of engineers, crewmen and command staff tripping over each other, he'd introduced himself and the only thing Jules could remember of the man was the accent.

"That's good news about Gaia. Let's hope that it doesn't turn into another *Andromeda*," she muttered under her breath.

Fifty years ago, before she was even born, humans tried to leave the solar system to colonise a moon in Alpha Centauri. On board the colony ship Andromeda, the journey took almost two years, with the crew being in regular communication with Earth during that time. A month after its arrival, in what would be the last communication, a Code Black was transmitted.

Do Not Rescue. Do Not Attempt Recovery.

Because of that transmission, no one knew what happened. When a probe was finally in range to scan the planet, there was no trace of the colony. Now, 'Andromeda' was used for the unknown, for things that went missing. People tended to forget, even now, space wasn't safe.

"Yes," Lian frowned. Their first and only attempt at interstellar colonisation. She hoped this effort turned out a good deal better than that. "In any case, you will provide them with a pilot and a hopper to rendezvous with the *Olympus* to pick up the Science Team for the survey mission."

Then, as an afterthought, she added. "If you feel like a field trip, you could go yourself. I wouldn't mind having another set of eyes on the ground. Besides, command of the operation has been given to the survey team, which means the Sharks are going to be at their charming best. You could provide a buffer between the two to make this expedition go smoother."

Jules chuckled, fed by a flare of excitement deep in her gut, and knew an opportunity when she saw it. A trip planet side? Hell yeah!

"You have a talent for understatement, Admiral." Her smile cracked a little wider. "I can be your eyes and ears as well as keep the peace. When do we leave?"

"1100 hours," Lian was glad to see Jules was pleased by this. There was so little reason for anyone to be happy about anything these days. "The Shark Major should be reporting to you soon." She paused a moment and collected her thoughts. "Have you had much dealing with the Sharks, Jules?"

"Just their American predecessors and only briefly." Jules's brow knitted. "Fighter pilots are a lot of bluster and bravado, Admiral. Marines can't be any worse."

Lian's silence spoke volumes.

* * *

Tom had yet to visit the new bridge.

In truth, he wasn't really that interested in seeing it. One bridge looked no different from any other and, frankly, it was Fleet territory, not his. Furthermore, reaching it would mean having to get through several decks of crowded people and that was more than he could stomach right now. Besides, any message relayed to him from the Captain of this boat could be done by an underling.

He'd met the bird once, paid his respects to her after she'd been promoted. Not that it was much of a meeting. The bridge was still buggered after the hull breach, so command functions continued to be rerouted through Engineering while repairs were being made. He'd showed up after a burst conduit had sprayed coolant everywhere. What conversation they shared was brief. She was covered in the stuff, swearing a blue streak and thoroughly unimpressed.

Since the last thing Tom wanted to deal with was 'pissed off woman', he got out of there quick smart.

As expected, the overcrowding on route to the bridge was just as bad as it was on the deck occupied by the Sharks. He also realised there were memorial walls on every deck, a painful reminder of the billions they were unable to save. Tom couldn't bring himself to think of the exact number. The sheer size of the loss would overwhelm him, and he was already drowning in guilt at the loss of one person. There was not enough alcohol in the fleet to mute the scream of billions in his dreams.

Since his security clearance gave him access to all the restricted parts of the ship, he could enter the bridge without difficulty. Stepping onto the central hub of the *Rutherford*, it took only a cursory glance across the work stations and command chair to see the Fleeters were just as mentally exhausted as his Sharks down in the Cave.

At the sound of the door, Jules glanced up from her aide. She had one finger against another, as if she was ticking off a mental checklist. She nodded curtly to the Shark Major and turned back to Wei. "I want Lieutenants McRae and Xu on standby. Did you notify the CMO?"

"Yes, Captain," Wei bobbed his head, fingers tapping away on his slate.

Tom did not immediately speak when she'd nodded at him because he was too busy blinking furiously, clearing the apathy from his eyes. Staring at the woman in the command chair, he was trying to process the realisation this was the same harridan he saw in engineering months ago. When he'd encountered her then, it was in the worst possible light but now it was as if he was seeing her for the first time.

Christ, she was bloody beautiful!

For months after their first meeting, they communicated through the ship's links, never with a visual, due to power restrictions. Their conversations were all very professional, occasionally tense, but they led to him forming an image of some no-nonsense career woman with a stick up her arse. What he did not expect to find was a dark-haired beauty with warm sultry features, flawless bronzed skin and Audrey Hepburn eyebrows arched over stunning brown eyes.

How the fuck was he supposed to manage any intelligent discourse when his first instinct was to ask her out for a drink? Who was he kidding? His first impulse would be to ask if she fancied a quick tumble in his supply closet. Guessing rightly that classy sheilas like this didn't take too kindly to such requests, Tom also reminded himself pointedly she was a captain and his superior officer.

That was hot too.

"Captain Curran," Tom slipped on his game face, avoiding the urge to look her over, to see if there was a body as equally stunning as the rest of her. "I'm assuming you got the orders assigning my Sharks to the squints going to Gaia? We'll be needing a hopper to get to the rendezvous point."

"I did." Jules dismissed Wei with a nod and finally turned her attention to him. This was the same man she met in engineering? How did she only remember his accent and not the lean, hardened body of a career soldier or the intense, hazel eyes? He was all bad-boy grit and swagger, the kind that made your Latina mother curse and your English Lit professor father think about dusting off the old 12-gauge.

And the way he was staring at her? Was Space Corps that different of a species? Maybe it was old prejudices, Navy/Marines, American/British? Whichever it was, she felt pinned by his stare. In an effort to take back control, she indicated the bread box off the command deck. "Would you join me in my office?"

"You have an office?" Tom blurted before he could stop himself. He cursed inwardly not wanting her to know how envious he was she had an office. The only reason he had any private space was because he threatened a janitor with bodily harm.

Of all the questions he could have asked, that one actually embarrassed Jules. Probably because she was hypersensitive about the privileges the rank of Captain got her. "It's more of a closet, but yes."

She was pretty sure it's original purpose had been a closet until someone realised a CO would need someplace private to conduct confidential matters. Stepping into the room after activating the panel that slid the doors apart with a hydraulic hiss, Jules slipped behind her desk as the Shark followed her in.

In here, she could smell freshly showered man (her favourite smell) and was reminded just how long it had been since she'd been intimate with anyone. Kicking herself, Jules shut those thoughts down. How could she think about something so selfish in this situation? Clearing her throat and her head, she decided to start off with the news that would rankle him the most.

"I will be flying the hopper to the planet." Anticipating an argument, Jules continued quickly. "Admiral Lian briefed me on the mission. I want you to know I am just the pilot. It's still your mission."

Under normal circumstances, Tom might have been annoyed by it, but his brain was still recalibrating after being confronted by the sight of her. In the small confines of this office, (he still couldn't believe she had a *fucking* office), the very female scent of her was overpowering. As much as he would normally hate having the ship's captain present, whether or not he was the one in charge, Tom couldn't deny going planet side with her wasn't the worst idea.

Clearing his throat, he resumed normal programming and ordered himself to stop behaving like a fucking teenager. Besides, she was Fleet.

"That's good to know, Captain. Squints, they like their poking fingers into every bloody nook and cranny. If I think something is going to bite it off, I will put a stop to it, and I'm not going to be airy fairy about it."

Jules hid a smirk. Nope, no difference at all from the Marines she'd known or her fellow fighter pilots. In a way, his manner was familiar and put her at ease. "Good. Do you have any questions for me?" she asked.

Fancy a shag over a half bottle of scotch in my supply closet?

Somehow, Tom managed to maintain a perfectly straight face as the question crossed his mind, leaving behind sinful trails of animalistic fucking and booze.

"We are buggering off 1100 hours, yeah?" He asked instead.

"Yes, 1100 hours. I don't know about you, but I do not want the scientists going off alone. I don't want the science teams...or anyone," she added belatedly. "Eaten by Godzilla. Or worse." Just as she wondered if she'd said that out loud, she realized by the look on Major Merrick's face that she had. Damn.

Tom smiled, feeling like he'd hit the fucking lottery. A sheila who knew Godzilla? What were the odds? Pop culture of the last century was his thing, especially bad Nip films. Oh, the Yanks tried a few remakes, but it just couldn't compare to the bloke in the rubber suit walking into power poles, stomping on papier mâché houses. Those were bloody magic.

"You like Godzilla?"

Staring at him for a minute, Jules finally smirked and nodded. "Who doesn't?" she grinned, glad to find some common ground with the bad-ass Shark.

"A bird with good taste," Tom grinned, feeling energised as he got to his feet. "Right then, see you at 1030 hours, Captain. Don't forget the sunblock."

She watched him leave and shook her head.

Jarheads.

IV

Departure

When the Sharks heard they were going planet side, Tom swore they whooped it up like they had won the fucking lottery.

He didn't know what made them happier, the fact they were leaving the ship or the possibility this exodus from Earth was finally coming to an end. Whatever the reason, he didn't care. They earned the respite after everything they went through since they'd boarded the *Rutherford.*

Being the buffer between an angry civilian population and the descent into chaos made the Sharks the focus of everyone's resentment. Sharks decided where people lined up, how they behaved, when they stood in line for rations, and shoved them back when they got pissy about how much they weren't getting. People needed someone to blame and the Sharks were the convenient scapegoat for everything wrong in their lives.

And they weren't afraid to show it.

Tom wondered if it was the same on other ships, if the Sharks there were going through the same shit as his own platoon. Sharks couldn't show fear since they had to be the ones who kept it together when everything else went to complete and utter shit. While they were tough combat troops capable of facing all kinds of danger, people tended to forget they had lost families and loved ones too.

They survived by relying on each other as family and Tom had to admit, the only thing keeping him sane, after what he was forced to do, was caring for his troops. Fuck knows, for many, the squad was all any of them had now.

Of course, the news only Alpha and Beta squad were getting the duty instead of the entire platoon was less well received and there were more than a few complaints lobbed at him. A well-placed bellow reminding them they were soldiers was all that was needed to silence the dissenting voices. Still, those forced to remain behind took solace in the knowledge their trek through space was almost over. For better or worse, the human race had arrived at their new home.

After a quick mission brief with Derick, he and Tom re-joined the rest of the squad in the Armory, where Tom unsurprised to hear energised chatter and genuine enthusiasm, beyond the usual Shark bluster. The feeling was infectious, and it was not lost on him. For the first time in weeks, he hadn't found it hard to leave behind the bottle of scotch in his footlocker. Maybe that's what he needed, the sun over his head and a job to do, so that he wouldn't dwell on the past. Maybe it what they all needed, to see a sky again and feel dirt under their boots again.

Maybe Gaia would chase the nightmares away.

"Well, well," Tom said, grinning with approval as he approached Sergeant Jackson. "Look at you lot. All smart and dressed up like you're going for a Sunday drive."

"Just waiting on you, Pa," Jazz retorted, handing the Gunny's rifle over to Derick.

Tom glanced at his friend as the man checked the blast rifle. Not since discovering his younger brother Luke was alive on one of the other ships had Tom seen Derick grinning so broadly. "Right then," Tom nodded at Derick, "let's not keep Captain Curran waiting?"

"Captain Curran?" Derick looked up from his rifle. "What, is she giving us a send-off something?"

Tom didn't meet his gaze. "She's piloting."

Derick stared at him, brow knotting with suspicion. "Why?"

"Probably to make sure I play nice with the squints." Tom's answer was evasive, and he was certain Derick would question why he wasn't more upset than he was. Under normal circumstances, Tom would be on a tear at being chaperoned by some Fleeter.

"And you're okay with this?" Derick eyed Tom like the man had undergone an exorcism or something.

"Got not much of a choice in the matter and I'm not going to bitch when it's a chance to get off this fucking can."

You lying, lying bastard, a Cockney Jimmy Cricket chided him in his head.

What the hell was he doing? The instant they showed up at the hangar, Derick would know exactly why he was so at ease with Captain Curran piloting the hopper. After all, it wouldn't be the first time the big bloke saw him on the pull. How many furloughs had they spent together where they went drinking and partying like a bunch of kids at spring break? Tom couldn't even count the number of strange places they'd woken up in (cough…cough…yoga studio and insurance office), with women they bedded tangled around them.

True, his present infatuation with the Captain of the *Rutherford* was a little different, but the reason for that was plain. She was quite possibly the most beautiful woman Tom Merrick had ever seen. With those brown eyes and amazingly full lips, his heart had been ready to pound out of his chest, like some cartoon character, at first sight.

And she liked Godzilla.

It was like winning the lottery. Beautiful, brainy and Godzilla. She could not be more perfect if she tried.

"Okay." Derick shot him a last cocked eyebrow before turning around to push his way to the front of the room. "Alright!" Derick shouted at the squads, glancing at his watch. "On the line! Time to earn that pay check! Sergeant are we ready?"

"Locked and loaded, Gunny!" Jazz called, weaving through the group to join the Gunny.

"Right, ladies; let's get our arses into gear," Tom added. "We've got a hopper with our names on it. The sooner we get there, the sooner we get off this boat for a bit."

With that, he turned on his heels and headed out the door, confident Derick and his squad would be right behind him.

* * *

As her squad prepared to move out, Private Renee 'Ren' Richards took the opportunity to tuck a wild red curl beneath her helmet. She had tied it up, but the tight curls never seemed to stay put and always found some way to cause mischief. As her green eyes glanced briefly at Major Merrick leading them out of the Cave, Ren couldn't help but let her gaze linger on Gunny falling into stride with him. Their eyes met for an instant before Derick flashed her a grin and turned his attention elsewhere. The contact was brief but satisfying and, not for the first time since she laid eyes on him, Ren told herself she was playing with fire. She couldn't help it, he was simply too pretty.

The same curl popped free again and she sighed and ignored it. Speaking of hair, she packed two objects in her kit that weren't regulation. A bar of scented soap and a razor because, goddamn it, she was shaving her legs the first chance she got. Just because she was a Shark, didn't mean she ignored all forms of feminine grooming. There wasn't much she could do about getting a bikini wax, but she could at least stop causing herself third degree lacerations whenever she scratched her calf with her toes.

"I'm bringing my razor, what about you, Mayday?" She glanced over her shoulder at Maya. "You going to take advantage of the natural environment to get in some much-needed grooming?"

"Same," Maya whispered, dark eyes flashing wickedly. Her thick dark hair was braided and neatly tucked under her helmet as well. "It's all peace and free love down there." She glanced at her friend as they filed out into the passageway. "Eddie says it's like shagging a bloody Sasquatch!" Even though the words were crass, Maya's posh British accent made even the foulest language sound classy.

"*Ben-zona!*" Private Isaac Jager, better known to his comrades as Jag hissed in his native Hebrew as he overheard more of this conversation than he needed to. "As fascinating as it is to hear what you two are planning for your nether regions, please stop. Really."

"Suffer, Jag," Ren gave him an unrepentant look before winking at Maya, "suffer."

* * *

Even though the ship was a small, kind of chubby and blockish troop transport and not her beloved Zephyr, Jules was not complaining. She dubbed the ship *Firefly*, after a bit of pop culture from the last century she knew Tom Merrick would get. It seemed to fit the economically-sized, bullet-shaped craft. Being back in a cockpit, being a pilot once again, felt good. While commanding the *Rutherford* was an awesome responsibility and one she would not surrender now she was in the big chair, she missed the freedom of being in a fighter.

And it wasn't the same without Chuck.

Jules swallowed, forcing away her grief about Chuck, whose absence felt like an abyss. She missed him even more now she was captain because the rank would make no difference to him. He'd call her out on her shit or tell her to take the stick out of her ass when she was being especially testy.

With a slight grin, she ran a gloved hand over the console. She'd learned to fly in these things, all the pilots did. Her TO had made sure she knew everything the hopper could do and what it wasn't supposed to be able to do. They disproved those a couple of times, hadn't they?

Behind the cockpit, the walls were lined with jump seats with five-point harnesses. Divots marked the floor, sporting lay-flat hooks to secure equipment, pallets or whatever. The ship had seats for 40, including the co-pilot spot beside her. At least this would be a smoother flight than the last time she was in such a craft.

The sound of the Sharks entering the bay caught her attention and she sat up, leaving off bad memories that were no good to anyone.

Pulling on the headset, she brought up the communications console to start the pre-flight procedures.

* * *

Tom led the way into the hangar and as expected, the hopper was there, opened up and waiting. There was no sign of the Captain, but Tom was taking no chances. Glancing slyly at his best friend behind him, he spoke almost nonchalantly, "I call dibs, mate."

No doubt, Derick would be wondering what the fuck he was talking about, but Tom wanted to stake his claim before Juliana Curran showed up.

"On?" Derick eyed the hangar bay, not seeing anything worth that kind of claim. No Victoria's Angels, no pole dancers. Newp. All he saw was green. Crates, the hopper and green-clad Sharks. He was about to say more when a woman appeared at the ramp extending outward from the rear hatch.

Gorgeous tanned skin indicating Spanish ethnicity, her hazel eyes were browner than green but still appeared luminous. Her dark hair was pulled back in a French braid. She was clad in a flight suit that did nothing to hide her curves and goddamn, she was flawless.

"Dude, who is that?" Derick asked in surprise, too stunned to put two and two together.

At the ramp, Jules surveyed the Sharks, impressed that even after the last few months, they still looked sharp and energetic, ready for anything. Once upon a time, she'd served under a captain who took it upon himself to greet every single crew member in person. He was the best she served under and morale was always terrific. Granted, she hadn't done much like that since leaving Earth, but it was never too late to start, and she had time while the pre-flight did its thing.

Stepping off the ramp, she nodded to the tall Marine officer and his moose-height gunnery sergeant. "Major Merrick. Gunnery Sergeant," she said, extending a hand to the latter. "Captain Jules Curran."

"Cap... Captain." Derick raised an eyebrow at Tom but shook the woman's hand. He should have called the team to attention, but it was too late, she'd introduced herself.

"Captain Curran," Tom greeted her as professionally as he could, hoping she couldn't detect all the unpardonable thoughts running through his head upon laying eyes on her again. Derick's reaction told Tom it wasn't just him and they had somehow landed the prettiest captain in the fleet.

"This is Gunnery Sergeant Derick Rickman," he introduced, the barest hint of a smile tugging at the corner of his lips. *Dibs mate*, his eyes said silently, even though the distance between ranks made any kind of fraternization impossible. Still, it was a necessary part of the *bro code*.

Derick shot Tom a good-natured dirty look before turning back to her. "Nice to meet you ma'am."

"And you." Jules smiled at them both and glanced over the other Sharks. "So, Major? Are we ready to go?" She couldn't hide the real excitement in her voice because they were about to get off this heap and hit the turf.

"We are," Tom avoided Derick's gaze as he spoke, quite sure he was on the receiving end of what the Yanks like to call the *stink eye*. "My people are itching for the sun and, with any luck, a look at Godzilla." He threw in that last bit for her benefit.

Jules rolled her eyes, lips pressed together in a somewhat failed attempt to hide a smile. She was never going to live that down.

Jesus, Tom was showing his nerd, Derick groaned inwardly. Time to intervene, as any good wingman would do. Hitching his pack over a shoulder, Derick made sure that it 'accidentally' hit Tom's arm.

"Oh, sorry sir." Wiggling his eyebrows, he headed towards the hopper. "Jazz, load 'em up!"

Watching the Marines line up, Jules watched them approvingly. "If I were them, Major, I'd be more worried about stepping in Godzilla crap." Jules couldn't hide the grin this time as she went past Tom and returned to the *Firefly*.

"All a part of the job, Captain," Tom replied, reminding himself he had to stop wanting to call her 'luv'. "After you," he said, motioning for her to go first. Not because she was the pilot or the captain of this boat, not even for any sense of out-dated chivalry.

He let her go first because he wanted to check out the view.

* * *

"Nice."

Ren heard Jag say and made a face at the man. "Great, I'll bet *she* has water to shave her legs," she threw sourly at Maya as they started to move out.

"Hot water at that," Maya grumbled. "You know if men had to deal with shaving their bloody legs, we'd have hot water all day long."

"My brother was a competitive swimmer. He had to shave his legs and chest and he didn't whine as much as y'all are," Ozzy teased as he came up behind them. "I thought ladies liked stubble..."

Maya frowned at him and flicked his chest. "I curse you with razor burn..."

"Enough chit chat, ladies!" From the loading ramp, Jazz pointed at Maya with an expectant look.

Maya feigned innocence as she filed in behind Ren and the others.

* * *

Leaving the *Rutherford* put everything in perspective.

For weeks, they could only see their predicament in the microcosm of the *Ruthie*. Their understanding of their situation was limited to personal loss, to the mourning of the lives lost and the ones they could not save. It was easy to let their suffering be defined by the lack of creature comforts, the absence of personal space and the threat of dwindling resources hanging over their heads like the Sword of Damocles poised to fall.

Those complaints were silenced once the hopper left the ship and they could see the vastness of space surrounding the ragtag collection of ships containing the entirety of the human race. A civilisation of twenty billion now numbered a paltry ten thousand, trapped in dozens of ships carrying food, equipment, livestock, and every piece of cultural heritage they could salvage.

Looking at those ships made Tom realised just how fragile and alone they were.

In a part of the galaxy known to them only by maps and long-range probes, there was no guarantee they would survive. For so long, humans confined themselves to countries, building walls around each other as they jockeyed for power and resources on foreign patches of dirt. What had it all been for?

Seeing the fleet limping along in space, Tom realised it wasn't just about them starving to death or going crazy in these ships. It was about *extinction*. Mankind was now as scarce as the buffalo or rhino, a species on the brink of oblivion. If humanity didn't start seeing themselves as one organism, they would never survive, even if they landed on the new world.

Looking at the stars, Lisa entered his mind. Usually, he buried thoughts about her in drink or deflection but, gazing out the hopper window, he thought about what would have happened if he hadn't purged the airlock. The entire ship would have been compromised and ten thousand would be less seven hundred. Blinking slowly as he digested that, he knew he had to get past it.

The kids under his command needed him to. It struck him just how young the members of Alpha and Beta squads were as he observed them on the deck. He and Derick were veterans, but the rest— they were all so young! Most had seen some action in the last five years, but they weren't lifers yet, not the way he and the big bloke were. Half of them looked like they should still be in school and the other half just looked out of place.

A familiar laugh caught Tom's attention and he looked down to where Corporal Ren Richards, was speaking in whispers to Private Maya 'Mayday' Sanjay. Those two, shared more in common with schoolgirls up to mischief than a sharpshooter and a top-notch medic.

* * *

"Look at him," Maya rolled her eyes and gestured at Private Colin Macon, her boyfriend who sat four seats down. Like he usually did, he'd dozed off in his seat within minutes of planting himself in it. "He can sleep through anything!"

"Not everything I hope," Ren nudged her and the two erupted into peals of laughter.

Tom hid a grin, pretending he hadn't heard the conversation. Next to them, Jag was listening with a grin, despite his numerous complaints about their ribald chatter.

Across from them, Ozzy and Linus sat next to each other, arguing about everything from who took what seat to how much they were invading each other's space. Even though they were fully kitted, both were nudging and fidgeting like two lads spoiling for a fight in the schoolyard. Tom gave it another two minutes or so before Derick lost his head and threatened them both with death.

Dupree, whom Tom called French because he didn't give a shit about cultural sensitivity, was sitting beside Private Lorio and Anderson. The two came out of boot a few weeks before everything went tits up and still wore 'what the fuck just happened' looks on their faces. French, who came from a large family in Provence, took them under his wing, for which Tom was grateful. He couldn't imagine a worse baptism by fire than what these two kids had endured these last few weeks.

Meanwhile Ozzy and Linus continued to bicker, their voices getting louder as they once again launched into an argument the others had become familiar with over the last six months. Jnr. Corporal Shaini 'Shiny' Ndlovu, the squad's comtech, sat two seats from Ozzy, wearing a grimace as her exasperation grew the more intense the debate became.

"Oh, for the love of GOD!" Shiny finally snapped, dropping her head back in exasperation, her helmet smacking the wall lightly. "Will you two shut up about cavemen and astronauts? I can't believe you keep arguing about this same shit!"

"Well, who do you think would win?" Ozzy asked, just to get her goat.

"Ren toss me my gun!" Shiny called out. "You're nearest to the weapons locker."

Ren laughed and then spoke up. "Don't worry Shiny, you won't need it. I already know who's going to win."

"Who?" Everyone looked at her.

"Shark chicks armed with blast rifles."

Tom laughed as Ren received a chorus of cheers from the handful of Shark females before tilting his head at Derick and whispering, "We'd be fucked for sure."

"Yeah, we are," Derick snorted, gaze lingering on Ren for a moment before he went back to the book he'd stuffed into his pack.

"Hey Major," Jazz asked, slapping Linus' helmet "Any chance we'll see people down there?"

"Negative, mate," Tom replied, having read the mission briefing Connor sent him beforehand. "Lots of beasties, but no people."

"Sorry, Pookie," PFC Tonie Edwards, a perpetually cheery blond, sang out to the tall Pacific Islander fastening the strap on his battle harness. "No alien princesses for you today!"

"Blondie, I swear, you call me that again I'm going to shoot you!" Private Kenan Pookalani warned, miserably aware he was stuck with the unfortunate nickname for all time. "Besides, you don't know where an alien princess has been. That's why it's best to eat local," he winked at her with a shit eating grin.

"If there's any shooting of my Sharks, it's going to be me shooting you all for threatening to shoot people," Derick retorted good-naturedly, glancing up from the pages of his book.

"Yeah!" Tonie stuck out her tongue at Kenan and then added, "I'm saving myself for marriage!"

"So that Fleeter you were doing in maintenance doesn't count?" Private Evan Chu, one of the Betas, rose immediately to the defence of his buddy, Pook...uh Kenan.

"Of course not," Tonie said with a smirk, "Fleet never counts."

Even though he maintained his typical scowl, Tom was glad to see them laughing and mucking about as they waited for the flight to begin. It felt like things were starting to normalise again after the last few months on the *Rutherford*. Carrying out a mission suited to their expertise instead of playing policeman to a ship full of dissatisfied and angry people would do a world of good for their morale.

With any luck, this operation would be the beginning of a new chapter for all of them.

V

Olympus

On the hangar deck of the *AS Olympus*, the largest battleship in the Alliance, the scientific team chosen by Dr. Nakamura made the final preparations for their survey mission to Gaia. With anticipation running high, the expedition was the tonic they needed after months of confinement and grief. Like the Sharks escorting them, they were eager to get underway. Discoveries awaited on the planet below and every second they spent waiting to leave felt like time squandered.

Most of them were experts in their fields of study, mined from the numerous refugee ships trailing the *Olympus,* after it finally sighted the planet Gaia. Nakamura assembled the team with the aid of an experienced expedition leader, Dr. Olivia Hall. A foremost expert in the field of planetary surveying, her place in the fleet was secured long before they left Earth. Dr. Hall was essential for the colonisation of Gaia, and the Alliance was not about to let her take her chances with a lottery, no matter how poorly that sat with her.

Their survival depended on it.

For almost twenty years, Olivia was present for nearly every colonisation project in Sol. From Miranda to Neptune, whether it was a gaseous rock or an icy wasteland, Olivia and her team were there first, laying the groundwork to ensure the successful colonisation of the new frontier. Thanks to her contributions, humanity spread across Sol, beyond Earth and Lunar.

In Nakamura's opinion, there could be no one better to determine if Babel was safe for humans.

Sadly, due to Sol's premature destruction, not all of Olivia's survey team reached the fleet in time to escape. As a result, there were visible gaps in her team's roster and working together, they had cherry picked the best candidates from what remained of humanity's academic pool. Some had the skills necessary to be of value in the expeditions. Others were chosen because there was no one else left.

It was a painful reminder of just how many brilliant minds were lost.

* * *

"So, your brother doesn't know you're on this mission?" Dr. Tamara Adelaide, specialist exobiologist, asked Engineer Luke Rickman as he secured their scanning equipment in the appropriate cases.

"Nope, "Luke snapped the metal lock into place and ran his hands along the seam of the case to make sure he got the others as well. "We spoke to each other a few weeks ago but not since. You know what com traffic is like."

She did. Once the list of survivors was released across the fleet, there was an unholy swell of people demanding to talk to loved ones after discovering them on other ships. All were desperate to regain the sense of family the nova had so effectively destroyed. Unfortunately, this meant the com systems were running around the clock and people were stuck on waiting lists that were days long for the chance of any link time.

Luke knew he was lucky.

When news of the nova first became public, Luke was working on Haumea, one of the planetesimals in the Kuiper Belt, as an engineer. Like the rest of the station's contractors, he'd headed home immediately because family was where you wanted to be when the end came. He made it as far as Ganymede when the sun went nova prematurely without ever seeing his parents or siblings again. In the last days of Sol, communication traffic was so frenzied, with everyone trying to contact their loved ones, Luke was barely able to call home before it was too late.

When he did speak to them, he was allotted a savagely short five-minute transmission to say goodbye to his parents and sister Lily. At that point, he had no idea what happened to Derick.

A month after they passed through the Ribbon, when Luke was still devastated from the loss of his family, he learned his older brother survived the destruction of Sol. It was a miracle he was not about to question because, until he saw Derick's name appear on the survivors list, he truly believed he was all that was left of his family.

When he spoke to Derick for the first time a few weeks later, the sheer rush of emotion at hearing Derick's voice almost moved him to tears. Even Derick's typical Marine bravado had crumbled. For one moment, they were two siblings taking comfort in each other because everyone else they loved was dead. Now, all they had was each other and those bonds never felt more desperately urgent than now, when they were on the edge of everything.

"I'm glad," Tamara's soft voice hid the sadness of her own loss, even if she was happy for him. Her mother and brother died together in their family home at Okinawa. If not for the appointment to Dr. Hall's team, she would have died with them. She was fully prepared to. However, Matsuko Adelaide, ever the pragmatist, insisted she accept the lottery ticket. A chance at life should never be squandered, she said.

Tamara liked to think Matsuko and Aaron spent their last days together as if they were celebrating the holidays, by sharing memories and giving thanks to God for all the good times.

The flutter in her voice made Luke pause immediately and glance over his shoulder. "You okay?" He eyed her with concern.

"Yes," she nodded, wondering how odd it was they'd forged this friendship when in the beginning she could barely stand him.

They met on Ganymede. Luke was trading his expertise on ships for passage back to Earth and his family while Tamara was leaving hers to join Dr. Hall's team. To her, he was nothing more than a skirt chaser who bedded every woman in sight. Tall, handsome, and broad shouldered, Luke's blue eyes and charming smile could have been labelled a weapon of mass attraction. Tamara remained uninterested, finding his cocky, arrogant swagger obnoxious instead of charming.

Everything changed with Earth's destruction and they found themselves on the same ship, sharing the same grief. Pain had made them friends. Throughout the next five months, their sorrow forged the friendship she now came to cherish. He was her best friend and filled the void left behind by Aaron and her mother.

"We're going to get through this, right?" He stood up and rested his hand on her shoulders, making sure she looked up when he spoke.

She was such a little thing, he thought, standing over her. Just an inch over five-foot, she was a porcelain beauty with Asian and Caucasian parentage. Hidden behind the nerd-girl-chic glasses was a beautiful woman who reminded him of Lilly. As any big brother would, he'd slotted Tamara into the role of little sister and saw it as his duty to protect her from the meaner things in life. Taking care of Tamara during the voyage through the emptiness of space saved him from going crazy.

He didn't want her to think she was any less important to him just because Derick was still alive.

"Yes," she rewarded him with a grateful smile. "We will."

"Good," he lowered down and planted a soft kiss on her forehead, "You'll meet Derick, and then it will be three of us, just like the Three Musketeers. All for one and one for all."

Tamara laughed, finding his enthusiasm infectious. "Right," she beamed. "One for all and all for one."

* * *

Something about guiding a smaller ship onto a larger one, while going approximately a billion miles an hour NEVER got old. It didn't matter if the smaller ship wasn't a Zephyr or a fully decked out troop carrier. To Jules, flying was familiar and welcome. After months of pulling decisions out of her ass (or so it felt), it felt satisfying to do something she knew she was good at.

It was certainly a far smoother ride than the last time she put a hopper on a ship.

"*Firefly*, this is *Olympus* Flight Deck, Chief Edmund at your service."

Jules smiled as she tapped her headset to activate the link and leaned forward. A busy landing bay loomed overhead and there was a single figure standing on the edge. The man's arms were in the air, a glow light in each hand above his head. "I see you, Chief."

"Roger that, Captain Curran. Once you breach the barrier, proceed to slot eleven."

"Slot eleven, aye, Chief." Yep. Familiar felt good.

* * *

Despite the *Olympus* being larger than the *Rutherford*, Jules could see they suffered the same lack of space. Crates, crates, and even more crates lined the walls of the flight deck, secured into place all the way to the overhead ceiling. On her ship, most storage lockers were converted to habitable space and the cargo was stuffed anywhere they would stay put. She suspected it was the same here.

Catching sight of cots lining the back of the flight deck, Jules realized they must be for the deck crew. The *Rutherford's* crew did the same, giving up their berth for the passengers. Hell, they even had people living in some of the hoppers. She made sure every single one of them was acknowledged for their sacrifice with letters of recommendation. For whatever it was worth.

Following the crew member's hand signals, again so familiar, Jules waited until his gloved hands fisted before she started the landing sequence. The *Firefly* bumped softly against the deck and, 3.2 seconds later, a light blinked green on her console. The maglocks were in place and they were secure. She popped her harness and reached for the intercom.

"Major Merrick, we are on deck. You're clear."

Popping his harness, Tom keyed his headset to respond. "Thanks, lu... uh Captain," Once again Tom kept himself from finishing the word and cleared his throat, ignoring Derick's pointed smirk. "I don't imagine this will take long. We'll give the squints some help loading up and then we'll be off. General Connor wanted us to get down there quick smart. Keep the engine running," he said into his headset as he moved towards the hatch.

"I'll keep her hot," Jules grinned as she got to her feet to stretch.

* * *

On Earth, Olivia Hall hadn't had much of a family. No husband, no kids... not even a goldfish. Well, she did try to make a husband work once but Sayed felt he had to compete with her job... and how could he, when the thrall of visiting unknown worlds had such a hold on her?

They hadn't lasted long, and she'd gone back to the people she was more comfortable with. Her team was hand-picked and while some of them were young, they were ambitious and knowledgeable in their fields. Some, like Luke Rickman and Tamara Adelaide, she considered her 'kids'. Others were sisters and brothers, their loyalty earned by the shared dangers of their adventures.

Standing in the prep area they'd been given on the flight deck, Olivia watched her team check and recheck their equipment. Clad in a version of the Sharks field fatigues, they were energetically conversing, stuffing things in pockets, and running last minute calibrations.

Finally, her dark gaze fell on Luke and warmed. At first, she had debated on bringing him on this trip. What if any of the 'projects' his genius level IQ started was a cure for cancer or a way to feed everyone and she was keeping him from that? The scientist in her wanted to make him stay put.

The 'auntie' she was to him had cashed in a favour to learn his brother would be one of their Shark escorts. Despite being brothers, they were adults and had not been reunited. A fuel conservation mandate limited travel to only emergencies and reuniting minor children with their family members. Anyone else, like Luke and his brother, would have to wait until they made Gaia.

Olivia wasn't about to consider 'if' they made Gaia.

"Dr. Hall?"

"Yes?" She looked up to find a young crewman standing before her.

"Your ride's here, ma'am. Bay eleven," he indicated a just-landed shuttle on the other side of the loading bay.

"Wonderful. Thank you," Olivia smiled, a soft hint of Georgia peach in her voice and turned to address her team. "Ladies and gentlemen, our limo has arrived," she announced, glad to see the team perking up even more at the news. She couldn't blame them. They weren't the only ones counting the hours until they could put boots on the ground and breathe fresh air. "Dr. Akiyama?"

The Japanese oceanographer looked up from the case she was securing. "Yes, Dr. Hall. Ready!" Hanae shot her a grin that belied the natural serious countenance of the young woman's face.

"Good. Dr. Adelaide?" Olivia smiled warmly at the other younger woman. "Ready?"

"Uh, yes ma'am. I mean, Dr. Hall," Tamara piped up, pushing her glasses further up the bridge of her nose. "We're all packed here, now, thank you."

Luke winced and shook his head. She was quite painful to watch sometimes. "It's secured, Liv!" He grinned with a wave, winking at the woman and telling her he was still not above chasing cougars.

Olivia shot him a wry look. "Put your crazy back in, boy," she told him affectionately. He and Tamara Adelaide made an odd pair of friends and she wondered how the two came to such a relationship. Dr. Adelaide was like a younger version of Olivia and Luke... well. She'd known tomcats with more shame. She just hoped his brother wasn't such a flirt. "Let's go, we don't want to keep them waiting." Speaking of the other Rickman, Olivia turned back to her own gear so she wouldn't give away her surprise.

Tamara waited until Olivia's head was turned before she reached out and swatted Luke on the back of his head.

"Ow! What the fuck...?"

"She's old enough to be your mother." Tamara shook her head and picked up the case at her feet.

"She's not my mother and I'm not ageist."

"Oh, my god," Tamara's jaw dropped open, staring at him aghast. "You're a total man whore, aren't you?"

Luke snorted. "What, you just figured this out…?"

* * *

When the ramp extended outwards, Tom and Derick stepped out of the hatch first and scanned the bay, seeing the same desperate situation playing across the ships left in the fleet. From the files he'd read before the mission, he knew exactly which one Dr. Hall was and, while he wasn't a regular subscriber of *Scientific Sol*, he knew her by reputation. If they were going to survey the planet destined to be the new home of mankind, at least they had the best person for the job.

"That's Dr. Hall," Tom pointed her out. "She's surveyed more new sites than I've been on missions. Logged a fair bit of space time, which means she won't be a complete pain in the arse."

"Cool." Derick's gaze homed in on the dark-skinned woman. She was wearing fatigues, more generic than the Sharks. As appearances went, he wasn't sure what he was expecting. Shouldn't someone in her line of work have a fedora and a bullwhip, like some kind of Indiana Jones? His gaze didn't stay long on her, shamelessly half-listening to Tom as he surveyed the deck.

Derick couldn't help it. He was on the *Olympus*, so close to…

"Luke!!!" Giving up all pretext, Derick jumped off the shuttle ramp and broke into a run, shoving his way past the flight deck crew and other people.

Luke forgot what he was doing the instant he saw his brother and dropped the case he was carrying onto the deck with a clang. Breaking into a wide grin, he didn't realise he was running forward until he saw Derick inches away from him.

"Holy fuck! Brainiac!" Derick swept Luke into a bear hug and nearly lifted off his feet as he hugged him tightly.

"Bigfoot!" Luke bit back, laughing at the nicknames their big brother Chris had bestowed on them as kids. Even though he was grinning from ear to ear, his eyes were moist, unprepared for the swell of emotion gripping him at seeing Derick face to face. There was so much to say, so much to mourn, but it could wait for now. Later, they'd get drunk and talk about the losses. For now, they were together, and it was all that mattered.

* * *

Tom was smiling as he watched the meeting between Derick and his brother. He was happy for the big bloke. Derick had been close to his siblings, and the death of almost all of them affected him more than he let on. To Tom, Luke was as much family as Derick, but he chose not to intrude on the reunion. Instead, he headed towards the head squint, a woman who demanded respect, even from the likes of him.

"Sergeant!" He motioned Jazz to follow him.

"Dr. Hall?" Tom called out on approach. "I'm Major Merrick and this here's Sgt Jackson. Are you ready to go? My lot can help with any equipment you needed loaded up."

"Major," Olivia smiled warmly at the man. He looked every bit a Shark. Hard, no nonsense and highly capable. "It's nice to meet you both and yes, we're ready," she indicated her crew behind her. Most of them had cases in hand and backpacks on, save for Luke. As her gaze went to the Rickman boys, she had to clear her throat before continuing. "If your Rickman is anything like mine, the faster those two get off the ship, the safer the female population of the *Olympus* will be."

"Boys will be boys," Tom smirked, making no apologies for either as he spied the gunny gesturing his brother and a cute librarian, towards the hopper.

The other squints were following suit, picking up their gear, preparing to board the craft. Some of the cases appeared large and unwieldy, too much for squints to manage on their own even if they were making a valiant effort to try.

"Your people look like they've got things under control, but my lot will help, just to move things along," Tom offered, telegraphing his eagerness to get down to the planet.

"I've a long-standing rule on my team," Olivia gestured to the group. "If you can't carry it, it doesn't go and if it can't be abandoned, it doesn't go." To date, all her survey expeditions had returned alive. It was a record she planned on maintaining.

"Good on 'em," Tom complimented her sensible approach. He'd met more than one egghead who'd go into palpitations at the idea of leaving anything behind. "Still, might as well be useful, right?"

Jazz nodded and reached out to take the case from the doctor. "May I, Doc?" he smiled. "I will be careful."

"Sure," Olivia replied, giving Jazz a look that said his ass would be so much Gaian mulch if something happened to the spectrometer case she was handing over.

Tom caught the look and smirked inwardly, his respect for the woman hiking up another notch. Anyone who could, with just a look, intimidate a Shark sergeant armed with an arsenal was a woman worthy of his admiration.

VI

Babel

When the *Firefly* descended through fluffy, pale green clouds, she trembled, excited to finally be in the sky, searching out unexplored territory.

Jules tore her eyes from the skyscape to the console as the yoke shuddered in her hands. Instinct and training told her the cause, but she checked the instruments anyway and found she was right. Atmospheric ionization. With a frown, she relayed the information back to the *Rutherford*, along with an order to complete a full scan, to ensure a larger storm wasn't on its way.

Once the little ship dropped into the atmosphere, Jules headed towards the appointed landing site. Soaring over tall, tall trees and endless green plains, Jules noted that from up here, Gaia didn't look that different from Earth. Except for the clouds. They were a greenish tinge, reminding her of fluffy cotton candy from her childhood. A thought occurred, and Jules switched off the HUD. Yep, she grinned. Still a pale, light green. Flipping the HUD back on, the realization she was the first person to see their new home hit Jules like an avalanche.

A near sob sucked her breath away and Jules inhaled to regain control. The elation was bittersweet and heavy. Chuck should be here, beside her. A deep ache squeezed Jules's chest at her friend's loss, hurting more in this moment than his absence had done throughout the last few months.

He would be the first to tell her to get back on her feet. There was too much to be done, too many people depending on her.

Someone in the back laughed, drawing Jules out of the darkness of regret and loss. When they laughed again, not even the hum of the engines could hide the contagious nature of it and before she knew it, she was smiling too.

* * *

Twenty minutes later, Jules set the landing sequence and called back to tell the Major they were setting down. There was more commentary from the back, until a slight thud reverberated through the soles of Jules's boots. The others would have felt it and when she switched off the HUD, Jules had to take another minute to look outside on their new home.

In the distance, white caps dotted an ocean stretching past the horizon to her right. In front of her, the sea marched right up to impossibly high cliffs and crashed against a series of huge, jagged rocks. Spanning out from her left was a huge, flat expanse of plains, covered with scrub and steppe plants. A river sparkled and emptied out into the bay in front of her.

There was so much colour it seemed everything was in brilliant bloom. And she was the first to see it. Was this what Earth was like thousands of years ago? So beautifully raw she felt incomplete and primitive compared to the forces capable of breathing life into such an amazing place?

* * *

"We good to get off this... oh." Tom poked his head into the cockpit to ask but was awestruck into silence by the amazing sight beyond the window.

After waiting patiently for her announcement once they'd touched down and then hearing nothing but silence, Tom decided to investigate. Everyone was jabbering with excitement as he passed them by and Tom gave no cause for concern when he made his discreet exit out of the cabin.

Once he stepped through however, he understood immediately the reason for her silence.

The planet beyond them was breathtaking. It wasn't Earth and oh, how it wasn't. There were enough subtle differences here and there, but it was the not so subtle ones reminding him they were light years away from home. The beautiful vista before them could have been lifted from the pages of a fantasy book, depicting an idyllic non-existent world of sunshine, stunning forests and spectacular mountains. After weeks of looking at nothing but grey walls and even greyer faces, the explosion of colour was almost overwhelming.

"Bloody hell!" He sank into the empty co-pilot's seat beside her, "Now that's something."

Jules simply nodded and glanced at him. And did a double take. "Oh shit." She winced and shook her head, not believing she'd been so out of it. "I'm sorry, I forgot about everyone…"

"Don't worry about it, luv." This time he didn't bother to correct himself. "Seeing this for the first time would make me forget about my lot too. I never thought I'd see an ocean again. Didn't have them where I grew up, but I never forgot what it was like to see the Pacific for the first time."

"I loved the ocean." Jules couldn't take her gaze from the window, but she was glad he was there. They didn't know each other very well but sharing the moment with him felt right. "My dad used to take me every year."

"I grew up on Ganymede and only saw glaciers." Tom couldn't imagine what it must be like to have a father who was arsed enough to take you anywhere. "I only saw the Pacific when I was sent to Boot on Earth."

Tom glanced her way and was struck by the expression on her face. Her almost hazel eyes sparkled and the smile tugging at her lips was both sad and haunting at the same time. It plucked at the strings of his heart and made him want to wrap her up in his arms, so they could lean back and just take it all in, like a pair of kids admiring a starry night.

Oi Fuck Knuckle! Get your head back in the game!

The reproachful voice of Drill Sergeant Wayne 'Pod' Barnes barked in his head, reminding Tom with jackbooted precision, he was on mission. Pod, as he was known to the recruits of Kapooka Army Base, was the hardest bastard Tom ever met. Called Pod, short for Prince of Darkness, the man made Tom appear positively cuddly.

Dispelling his love-struck mooning about the Captain, Tom cleared his throat and reminded himself they were on an alien planet on an extremely high-risk mission and he needed his faculties intact. There would be time to offer her a beer and a shag after this was all said and done.

"Right then luv. Want to open hailing frequencies and tell the *Olympus* we landed here safe? I'll go get the Sharks and squints ready for deployment."

"Now, that's an idea," she chuckled, glancing at him. So far, he was proving to be different than what she expected. Sure, he wore the tough Shark persona like a second skin but there was a shadow of something more beneath it. She smiled slightly and turned back to the console with the moment dissipating. "All right, so atmo is breathable, which we knew." Always good to have a second opinion when it came to breathing. "No one's wearing a red shirt under their uniform, right?"

"No red shirts in my team," Tom replied, still admiring the view outside. In retrospect, it was almost as mesmerising as the view *inside* the cockpit. Once again, the comment about red shirts reminded him this was an alien world capable of killing them a dozen ways before sundown.

"*Olympus*, this is the *Firefly*," Jules hailed the flagship as he left her to it and made his way out of the cockpit. "We are on the ground at latitude 170 west, longitude 160 north. 1002 hours, sierra tango." An answer would take a minute or two to come, so she initiated the shuttle's sleeper mode to conserve energy. When it was done, she checked the clock, noting the time. Nearly five minutes. Was the *Olympus* crew asleep? She reached for the link again when it went live, making her jump with a start.

"Copy *Firefly*. 1005 Sierra Tango."

Finally. "Be advised we are exiting the hopper under protocol. Sending reports every thirty mikes. Sierra Tango 1006 hours. *Firefly* out."

When the response didn't come back right away, Jules frowned before chalking it up to some signal lag.

"Copy that, keep your eyes open."

Oh, that wouldn't be a problem, Jules snorted. She hopped to her feet, grabbed her pack, and headed down the corridor to the others. Really, she wanted to sit and stare at the scenery some more but that would bring Major Hotness back here and then they'd both be ensnared by the planet's beauty. That would definitely inspire confidence. Not.

* * *

When she entered the carrier compartment, the Sharks were in full roll-out mode, so Jules turned her attention to her pack. While not as heavy as a Shark's, Jules carried a survival kit, protein bars for food, (chicken a la king her ass), and a water zapper among other things. Removing her sidearm and its holster from the pack, she quickly strapped it into place around her thigh.

Reminded of what was agreed between them regarding who was in charge down here, Tom made his way to the leader of the expedition.

"Dr. Hall, you ought to be the first one out. We'll still be escorting you, but it will look better in the history books. Once we've had a look about and established a campsite, your team can get set up to do their bit."

"Thank you, Major," Olivia grinned at him, teeth brilliantly white against her dark skin. "I could care less what the history books say, but I don't mind sharing," she teased before turning to her team. "Do you hear that, ladies and gents?" Olivia raised her voice to make sure they all heard her. "There will be no movement until the Sharks give us the go. If you do not listen…" She nailed Luke with a raised eyebrow. "And you survive, I will make you suffer."

Luke opened his mouth to speak but Tammy slapped a palm across his lips and pinned him with 'the look', something only girls with brains (or moms) could do with surprising effectiveness. "Behave." She said simply, and Luke exhaled sharply in surrender before she really got surly. Doctor Hall's 'punishments' for not listening or letting eagerness override safety were notorious.

Noting the movement, Derick cocked an eyebrow at his brother over Tamara's head. 'Whipped', he mouthed at Luke before continuing. "Alpha Squad, you're on guard duty. Beta Squad, I want a 25-yard perimeter set up!" He swept his gaze over his teams, resolutely not lingering on Ren Richards or yet another errant curl escaping her efforts.

As the squad leaders called out their responses, Maya took the opportunity to poke Jag in the shoulder. "Oi! You heard the woman. No stepping in sinkholes, yeah?"

Ozzy snickered, and Linus was right behind him with a snort.

Maya fixed them both with a glare. "Oi, you two, Tweedle Dum and Tweedle Dunce, no touching yourself after you fondled unidentified plants this time!"

Ozzy and Linus were the terrible twins, feeding off each other, and she didn't like anyone picking on Jag but her. Well, Ren was allowed of course.

"Hey!" Ozzy glowered at her and tossed his friend an odd look. "What happened to patient/medic privilege?"

"Oh, I say it ended when we all saw you scratching your nuts like a cocker spaniel with fleas," Corporal Cori Harwood of Beta squad smirked.

"No shit," Ren fist bumped Cori at that. Like everyone else, Ren was eager to get out and see the world to be their new home, not to mention some alone time with her razor. "Come on, let's get going, there's grooming to be done."

"You got a hot date with your rifle Richards?" Ozzy cracked, winking at her. Beside him, Linus stifled a snort until both of their heads jerked forward under a solid 'thwack'. Ozzy swore, rounding on whoever hit him but froze when he met with a glowering Gunny. "Oh…uh…"

"Uh is right," Derick retorted, shoving past Ozzy into the middle of the group. While his unit teased and roasted each other all the time, Ozzy tended to get too personal (and take things too personal) and Maya had been out of line. He'd talk to her later. While Ren could handle herself, he intervened before someone got shot. He wasn't even going to give any thought to how much Ozzy's digs at Ren rankled him. Not right now, anyway. "If Annie shoots you, I have to fill out the paperwork and then I'm down two good soldiers."

"Two?" Ren didn't give Ozzy *that* much credit. "Sure, whatever you say."

Nevertheless, she did flash Derick a brief smile of gratitude before she went off to help Maya who was trying to deal with a dangling strap on a hard to reach place on her pack. She could see Colin itching to help the medic and wanted to spare them the crap they'd get from the rest of the Sharks if he was seen doing it. Everyone knew the two were an item but for the sake of Gunny and Sarge's sanity, it was best if they kept it discreet.

"Bloody… mother… of a goat…" Maya swore under her breath, one hand scrabbling for the strap in question. When she felt the weight of her pack lift, she grabbed it and turned to Ren. "Thanks, mate."

"No trouble," she replied and then regarded the Major who'd just returned from the cockpit and the Captain with the undoubtedly shaved legs. "Sir, we're heading out? Me and Mayday got our dancing shoes on!"

Tom kept his game face on, but his tone was light. "Keep your knickers on, Orphan Annie. Gunny, you and me are going to escort Dr. Hall outside for a look about. Captain," he turned to Jules, "you mind watching the squints, so they don't wander off?"

"I think I can handle it," Jules exchanged an amused glance with Dr. Hall. "Don't be long or I'll send them out to search for you and I'll make sure to tell the other Shark units." Said squints would probably use all their gear and locate the Sharks within minutes anyway. Maybe she wouldn't tell the other Sharks but she sure as hell wouldn't let Tom live it down, either.

Tom cracked a grin.

Ren rolled her eyes. *Typical.*

"Right then, Doctor Hall," he turned his attention to the woman who was going to make history if this world was everything they hoped it to be. "Ladies first."

"I see chivalry isn't dead," Olivia smirked at the Marine. She'd meant what she'd said earlier. She really didn't care who put boots on the ground first, but she was grateful for Major Merrick's consideration. For someone that looked like the human version of a junk yard dog, there was more to the man than he let on. "All right, let's get this show started."

* * *

The change in air pressure made Olivia's ears pop as the outer door of the main hatch unsealed. Sunlight stabbed her in the eyes as a soft, fragrant breeze rushed into the shuttle, as if welcoming them. Inhaling deeply, Olivia let it out slowly, savouring every bit of virgin, crisp air. Like the rest of the fleet, she was starved for fresh air and the slightly cool wind that washed over her exposed skin felt delicious.

We'll never be able to say the sky is blue again, Olivia thought, squinting at the pale green sky and the languid, lime-coloured clouds before she moved onto the lowered ramp. All her training babbled on about how the colour was due to atmospheric conditions, water vapour, and light spectrums but the little girl hidden deep inside was thinking how much it looked like her grandmother's sea foam divinity.

Captain Curran had put them down on the edge of the plains, several hundred yards from a river gorge. In the distance, where the gorge snaked off to the horizon, it was lined with massive copses of trees as big as Redwoods but bore some resemblance to eucalyptus.

"Gentlemen," she didn't look at the Shark major or his gunnery sergeant, too entranced by the view. "Shall we?"

"After you, Doc."

Tom, like Derick next to him, was basking in the view. This was going to be home and it was beautiful. Earlier in the cockpit, he was distracted with Jules but now, seeing it up close, he marvelled at what lay before him. After the last six months in space, Tom would be content to spend the rest of his life on this world without ever logging another second of space time again.

The doctor descended the ramp, and for posterity's sake, the two Sharks remained one step behind her for the occasion, but no farther than that. For all its beauty, this was an alien world and her safety were Tom's primary concern.

Despite the fact, she had several exploratory missions under her belt, the thrill of stepping foot onto a new planet never got old. For a split second, Olivia was Buck Rogers or John Creighton or even Diana Prince, stepping forth to the unknown. Silly, but once upon a time this had only been a dream. Smiling to herself, Olivia unclipped her slate and stepped off the ramp. Her boot sank slightly into the loamy, moist soil as a faraway *ca-caw* echoed faintly.

Fanning out to stand beside the hatch, Derick breathed in deeply. No body odour or sweat, no fear, no overtasked sanitation facilities. Just fresh, fresh air. He took another deep breath, and another, feeling healthy for the first time in months. Around them, fragrant flowers bloomed from various plants and the scent reminded him of his and Luke's mother, Susannah. A master botanist, she would have been ecstatic by this. Loss squeezed his chest, making Derick shut his eyes for a brief second before giving himself a shake and checking the bioscanner strapped to his wrist.

"Bio-trackers show only little critters about," Derick announced as the screen homed in on and tracked various tiny heat signatures.

For a moment, Tom didn't respond. He was surveying the landscape and though it was all very beautiful, especially to eyes confined for months to a grey, steel box in space, the allure was wearing off. More in charge of his faculties than he had been in a long time, he was mindful of the alien world they were venturing into and presuming to tame.

The slate might show all was safe, but Tom knew technology was fallible and they couldn't arm themselves against what they didn't know.

That's what the squints are for, Pod's voice reminded. Keep them safe as best you can but never assume there's not something ready to fuck you over around the corner. There usually was, Tom admitted grudgingly to himself and turned to Olivia. In the end, it was her expedition, he was just her minder.

"You good to go, Doc?"

"Yes," Olivia nodded once, moving away from the hatch. Overhead, a flock of indigo coloured birds with crane necks soared overhead. She looked up, smiling when the birds chittered at one another. Checking her slate once more to confirm the readings, she grinned at the Major. "Bring out the troops."

Tom threw a side glance at Derick. "You heard the lady, Gunny."

"Yes Sir," Derick stepped back up onto the hatch from the side. "Alpha, Beta squads, you have your orders. Move out!"

"Roger that, Gunny."

Thank God, Jazz thought silently. He didn't think the rest of the expedition could remain patient any longer, not with all the rustling of boots and uniforms he could hear. The squints wanted just as much off the ship as Alpha and Beta squads. The anticipation in the air felt tangible, like something to be seen and touched. Hell, he almost wanted to rub his fingertips together to feel its texture. Severing the link to Gunny, he turned to his team.

"We're up, chicks and dicks!" he called out, momentarily forgetting about the squints and the *Ruthie's* Captain in their company. Checking his rifle one last time, Jazz delegated his people. "Twenty-five-yard perimeter, I want a body at each transponder. Ozzy, you're on point. Richards, you're in charge of the transponders. Everyone else, hold position until we give you the word to move out."

This produced a groan among the scientists, but Jazz ignored it. This order was not to be disobeyed and they wouldn't be held up for long. The squints needed to give this world their okay, so the rest of the fleet could come down. The brass wanted it done as quickly as possible.

Eager to head out, Ren picked up the transponder units, stored in their protective cases, against the wall with all the other equipment. Once activated, the transponders would give the fleet a signal lock on their position.

"You coming, Mayday?" she asked as she headed towards the door, following the other Sharks making their way out.

"Yup." Maya quickly fell into step behind her friend, shrugging her pack into a more comfortable position. Tightening the strap on her helmet, she strained to see around Ren, to get a glimpse of what the fresh air was teasing her with. "This is better than sex."

Ren threw her friend a wink, aware Jag was in earshot before adding, "Then you haven't been doing it right, Mayday." As a rule, they didn't behave like Catholic schoolgirls all the time, but it was fun seeing Jag blush. The co-ed situation was something the Israeli was still getting used to.

"Think I bloody have if I'm getting it," Maya retorted, smirking at Ren.

Shaking his head, Jag grumbled. "It's all sex with you women."

"Anyway, I can't smell Jag's socks anymore," Maya continued.

"Thanks a lot," the beleaguered Shark gave up and followed his comrades out of the hopper behind Jazz who was leading the way.

* * *

"Mac, you and Tonie head north west of the perimeter," Jazz ordered once they were outside the *Firefly*. "Open links and make sure your camera is recording."

"No problem," Colin replied in his laconic voice and glimpsed Maya heading off with Ren to install the transponders. Their eyes made contact briefly and, though nothing was said, Maya flashed him a little smile, a promissory for some alone time later.

Smiling to himself as the warmth she engendered in his heart flared briefly, Colin returned his attention to Jazz who was still barking orders at the rest of Beta Squad.

"Harwood, Tehea, head east but do not cross the river!" Jazz remarked, studying his slate and the topographical map of the area. "Stay within perimeter and for fuck sake, check in at regular intervals, all of you! We've got no idea what's running loose around here."

As if to emphasize his warning, another distant *ca-cawwww* reached them.

"Oh, don't worry Sarge," Tehea, sometimes called Teacup, quipped. "What's the worst that could happen?"

"Don't say that!" Kenan groaned, slapping his forehead as she spoke. "Don't you know the most sure-fire way to get us all killed is to say that?"

"Grow up!" Linus smacked him on the back of the helmet. "Next thing you know, you'll be tossing salt everywhere like a demented chef."

"I'm just saying," he pointed out, heading out with Linus following, "better safe than sorry."

* * *

"This sucks. We should be going with them." Luke shot Tammy a look of disappointment as he watched the Sharks, including his brother, empty out of the *Firefly* into the new frontier beyond. The fresh air was wafting through the open hatch like a siren song and he was itching to get out there and see for himself.

"How do they know they're not going to run into a face-hugging alien or green-tentacled monster?"

Tammy rolled her eyes.

"If Dr. Hall sees anything like that, she'll know what to do." Hanae smirked, glancing over at the opening that was oh so close and yet so, so far. "I hope we find krakens."

* * *

It was time for her people to do their jobs, Olivia decided after the Sharks spread out over the area.

Ten minutes after their deployment, there was no indication of trouble although Olivia was painfully aware of how little time that was to gauge anything. It was beautiful — like Earth, but not like Earth. It didn't matter if it wasn't, Olivia decided. Humanity could not take another few months cooped up in the ships above. They'd tear each other apart and the question of finding a new home world would become moot.

"Major?" She met his gaze and said no more, the look in her eyes speaking volumes.

Tom nodded and tossed a sideways glance at Derick. "Cut them loose. I think we've all earned some time out in the open, even if it does turn out this is an alien hunting ground and we're all about to die horrible, horrible deaths."

As Derick went back to the *Firefly* to usher out the scientific members of their party, Olivia chuckled. "Major, your idea of a pep talk leaves *a lot* to be desired."

VII

Skewers and Storms

Once the squints were allowed out of the *Firefly* to begin the survey, Jules had little to do but monitor the sensors and keep a vigil for any changes in the environment. Even if the visual provided them with an idyllic view of their landing site, the planet was teeming with life and the probabilities of danger were high. Their sensors were sophisticated enough to register life, but they had little to no idea of how that life would manifest. For all they knew, everything here could be toxic to them or the indigenous fauna too hostile for a colony to be established.

It didn't matter, she told herself upon leaving the hopper in search of the Major. Humanity didn't have the luxury of being picky. This was the only planet capable of sustaining them and they simply did not have the resources to search for another. As she stepped out into the open and glanced at the sky, the odd green-tinged colours still struck her.

It was beautiful but so very alien.

Using her slate, she traced Tom's location using his personal data implant. In the past, such devices fell squarely within the crosshairs of civil liberties groups screaming privacy violations. The idea of tracing the movement of billions was invasive, to say the least, but it was standard issue for all military personnel now they were a spacefaring species.

It made it easier to recover bodies.

Making sure she did not venture into the tree line, Jules skirted the great forest that awaited exploration once their preliminary surveys were complete.

The heat was delicious even if she felt beads of sweat beneath her flight suit. After breathing nothing but circulated air at a maddeningly constant temperature for the last six months, she was happy to put up with the unpredictability of a natural climate. The air bore the fragrance of pollen and sap, with small insects buzzing about, oblivious to the new arrivals in their ecosystem. Chirps and trills peppered the air and Jules swivelled her neck each time to catch a glimpse of the animal or bird it came from.

Along the way, she spied the squints hard at work. They were conducting a battery of tests on the environment, taking air, water, and mineral samples, collecting specimens of plant and insect life. Whatever their duty, she saw the delight at being in the open air on all their faces. The Sharks, despite being more jaded and cautious, were similarly enamoured and a strange sort of camaraderie had formed between the two very different camps.

She found the Major on the banks of the unnamed river, playing escort to another group of squints. Carrying a gun, more like a miniature cannon she thought, it appeared he wasn't above guard duty like the rest of his squad. She watched him admiring the scenery, taking in the beauty of it all. Beneath the clear water, there were bushes of aquatic plants of deep red, yellow, and amber. The result was a river painted in colours that took the breath away.

"Oh wow!"

At that, Tom glanced over his shoulder to see Jules's awed expression as she gaped at the river. Her expression made him smile inwardly. "Bloody amazing, isn't it?"

"It is," she nodded in agreement, her eyes drinking in the visual feast of alien colours.

"The squints are taking water samples," he gestured further up the bank where Hanae was ankle deep in water collecting samples in little test tubes with her assistant, Mahmud, a kid who was twenty-five but looked seventeen. Worse yet, to avoid being mistaken for a teenager, Mahmud wore a beard that covered half his face and a man bun that made Tom Merrick want to belt him on sheer principle.

"I've given up telling them to be careful. I'll JUST SHOOT THE THING THAT BITES OFF THEIR LEGS!" Tom hollered loud enough for them to hear.

Hanae's response was a tongue stuck out in his direction.

Jules stifled a smirk, admiring the balls on the Japanese scientist who knew perfectly well she could take such liberties with the Shark Major due to her civilian status. Still, judging by the faint smile on his face, it was clear he wasn't taking any offense either. Like the rest of the expedition, Tom Merrick's spirits were buoyant just by being out in the open.

"Think of it this way," Jules shrugged. "There's no sight of Godzilla yet."

He uttered a short laugh and Jules found herself studying him closely for a moment. He could never be considered beautiful, but he was ruggedly handsome and personified alpha male. Aside from the accent and the ripped physique, the man oozed bad boy in every conceivable way. As her *Mami* would say, '*That kind of boy is no good for anything but trouble.*'

Realising she was staring at him thoughtfully, Jules averted her gaze and remembered why she'd sought him out in the first place. "There's a storm on its way. Judging by the sensors, it's about an hour out. It's a Category 1, so I suggest we get everyone inside before it hits."

His gaze shifted up instinctively, trying to see its approach in the painted sky; but for the moment, the winds were pushing the greenish clouds through the air at a lethargic pace. It was approaching noon and Tom felt a pang of disappointment at having to leave this place so soon after arriving.

"They're not going to be happy," Tom frowned studying Hanae and Mahmud who were now wading knee deep in the water, much to his chagrin.

"I don't think anyone is going to be after being cooped up on the ships, but we have no idea what storms on this planet are like. We need to be smart about it."

"Agreed. Just pointing out the obvious. The hopper going to be steady enough for us to stay put, or are we going to have to take off to another spot on the planet?" Tom didn't want to suggest the idea of going back to the fleet because no one would be happy about *that* alternative, himself included.

"No, we're good to stay put," Jules was confident about that. She'd flown a shuttle through a solar flare, riding a wave of heat that should have melted the hull right off its frame without too much trouble, she could handle this. "The storm doesn't appear to be very large and readings indicate it's moving fast. It should be over us and past in about twenty minutes."

Twenty minutes, he could live with that. "Right then," he nodded and tapped his headset. "Gunn…"

He never finished the word.

Tremors like an earthquake suddenly rumbled to life around them. The ground shook with enough ferocity to send shudders through their bones. Leaves shook on their branches and birds took flight hastily, the large flocks becoming dark clouds against the green. Jules's slate started squealing in response as she snatched it from her belt, raising its display to her face.

"OUT OF THE WATER!" Tom waved Hanae and Mahmud out of the river, not waiting for Jules to tell him what was going on. The two scientists were standing in place, their faces frozen in shock until his military bark got them moving. They waded out of the river, splashing noisily to reach land.

"What is it?"

"Major, what's going on?" Tom heard Derick's voice in his headset. "My slate just picked up a pretty big bio reading coming from your area!"

"It's coming from the woods," Jules declared, her eyes studying the blips on the small screen too numerous to count. Thirty… maybe forty, she thought, emerging from the tree line on the other side of the river. As she spoke, a small cloud of dust appeared like a fog rolling in through the thick tree trunks.

"Look!" Hanae pointed.

"Oh, my God!"

Jules stared at the herd stomping through the wall of dust towards the river. The size of rhinos, they were just as sturdy, with impressive horns that extended almost three feet beyond their bovine faces. Covered in long grey fur, their eyes were almost hidden by an equally shaggy fringe. They looked like yaks except that the tip of each horn, separated by inches, was spiked with bluish energy. Led by an alpha, the herd paused within reach of the river, sniffing the air as it picked up the unfamiliar scent of the newcomers.

"Nobody move," Tom warned. "I don't know how deep the river is, but I don't want to find out the hard way whether those buggers can swim. If they decide to stampede, we're going to be in a lot of bloody trouble. Derick, tell everyone to hold position."

"But..."

"You heard me Gunny," Tom repeated himself, his hand on his weapon. To him, they looked like cows, but Tom was no xenobiologist to say for certain.

All four of them froze on their side of the river, watching the alpha come to the edge of the water. The creature stared at them for a long moment, trying to decide if they were dangerous or not. Tom marvelled at the electrical charge running between the creature's horns. It cast a bluish aura around the animal, making it look even more unreal than ever.

After what felt like ages, it seemed to make up its mind they were harmless and reared up its large head. Opening its mouth, it released a loud trumpet-like bray that beckoned the others forward.

The herd rumbled towards to the water's edge before lowering their heads to drink. It appeared not all the creatures bore the impressive horns as others sported extended cheek flaps like those found on orangutans. Tom wouldn't be surprised if those were a different gender. The younger calves bore neither flaps nor horns and these did resemble the yaks of Earth.

"They're beautiful," Jules found herself whispering.

"Well, they're different," Tom admitted, not willing to go so far as 'beautiful'. Next to them, Mahmud was recording the creatures' morning drink with a hand-held holo recorder while Hanae was scanning the herd from across the river.

"We should name them," Hanae suggested.

The creatures raised their heads at the unfamiliar sound of human voices, stared for a second and then returned to their drink, indifferent.

"Skewers."

"Skewers??" Jules turned to Tom.

"Would you want to get in front of those things?" He indicated the long, impressive and electrified horns.

"Good point," Jules smiled in agreement, turning her attention back to the Skewers, watching the herd go about its business in wonder. Clearly, the creatures, who never encountered humans before, did not view their observers with concern and Jules wondered what other life forms would make themselves known before this mission was over.

* * *

Once he was assured there was no danger, Derick and a few of the Sharks wandered over to the river bank to look at the herd of animals Tom was calling 'Skewers' for now. He suspected the name was going to be temporary. No doubt, Dr. Hall and the other eggheads would want to give it some biology class name like *Genus Whatsit* or *Bovidae Skewer Merrickus*.

Captain Curran joined Hanae and Mahmud on the river bank. To Derick's horror, the two scientists were back wading in the water. If they knew what he did about rivers, Derick thought. In his experience with the Corps, bad shit always lurked in rivers. From glow in the dark leeches to carnivorous, ten-foot-long fish…Derick did not trust the water. He rolled his broad shoulders slightly, to loosen them up and readjust the assault rifle clipped to his battle harness as he approached his friend.

"You never said she was hot," he nudged Tom as he glanced at the woman in the nearby distance. She was gorgeous. He didn't blame Tom for the lie but he sure as hell wasn't going to let his friend live it down. It was too much fun.

"I might have left a few things out," Tom was not at all repentant.

"You mean flat out lied, you Aussie bastard," Derick accused good-naturedly.

Laughter caught his attention, bringing Derick's gaze to where Orphan Annie and Mayday had their heads together. They were staring at the herd, taking pictures like frigging tourists, and who could blame them? It was the first extra-terrestrial species they'd ever seen on this world. Not little grey men but alien cows. It was worth commemorating.

"Just make sure your brother keeps his hands off Orphan Annie," Tom served back, aware of the younger Rickman's reputation with women. Of course, it was just possible this particular Rickman didn't know the girl preferred him.

Derick's eyes narrowed, and a muscle ticked in his jaw and he looked away from Ren and Maya.

"She's not his type," he shrugged, going for nonchalant and hoping he passed muster. Why did everyone give him crap about Ren? He wished he could tell them to stop, that what they found oh so funny wasn't helping his predicament, but then that would mean discussing said situation.

He simply couldn't entertain such thoughts or the dreams that he fought hard not to have. She was his subordinate, a Corporal to his Gunnery Sergeant and anything outside of a familiar friendship was against the rules. Not for the first time, Derick cursed the urge to follow the rules and regs bred into him from the day he was born. His desires were completely unprofessional. Sometimes, they were downright disrespectful.

"So, the Captain says there's a storm coming?"

"Yeah," Tom nodded and glanced at his watch, an old-fashioned thing you had to wind up. It had been his father's and one of the few things from the old bastard he bothered to keep. "It should hit in about forty minutes. Give the squints another twenty and we'll start to round them up and get them inside the hopper. Jules reckons we can sit it out for an hour and then resume the surveying again."

"Good," Derick made no comment on Tom's familiarity with the Fleeter. He took another deep breath, as he had been doing since they landed and frowned, head coming up to scan the horizon. "I smell ozone..."

"Captain Curran?" Dr. Hall's voice interrupted him on the all-call channel. "We're detecting heavy ionisation in the atmosphere, higher than the norm."

Jules touched her headset and looked up from her conversation with Hanae. She turned to the darkening horizon, body language returning to all business.

"How heavy?" she asked, turning back to head towards Tom. Hiccups in communications and atmospheric changes were two very different readings.

"Heavy enough to suggest you calibrate the frequencies if you have difficulty reaching the fleet. It might become worse with this storm. I believe it is a naturally occurring element of the planetary ozone."

Jules reached Tom, both frowning at the same time.

"Bugger," Tom cursed. "We're going to have to get the engineers to reinforce all our communications equipment with some kind of shielding if we want clear transmissions."

"It's something we'll have to think about when we begin colonisation," Jules said with a sigh, glancing back towards the darkening sky. "Any idea if it's tied to those rain clouds heading our way?"

There was a pause before Olivia's response came through. "Possibly. We'll need a few minutes when it hits to get more specific scans. I'd like to interface the atmospheric readings from my slate with your sensor array for more accurate data."

"I don't know whether I like the idea of our communications being disrupted during the storm, Captain," Tom said to Jules, switching to a more formal tone now that others were around them.

"We may not have a choice." Jules could appreciate his concern, especially since it mirrored her own. A breeze gusted up off the river, stirring the grasses around their feet. "If worse comes to worst, we can take off, get out of the storm and into the atmo to send a signal that way.

That sat better with Tom because the storms like everything else on the planet were a mystery. While the squints might claim it was comparable with what was found in Sol, the truth was they just didn't know where those similarities ended.

Assuming nothing would go wrong was just tempting fate.

* * *

"Holy shit, those are some big flowers."

Tonie lifted her digital recorder to her eye and moved closer to the plant that stood almost waist high and six feet in diameter. The stamen was a bright maroon bud surrounded by clusters of florets in colours of yellow, amber and green. Standing above it, she felt like she was looking down on a dome of vibrant hues and she leaned forward to take a few shots, still awed she was the first person to ever see these flowers.

As ordered by the Sarge, she and Colin reached the outside edge of their prescribed 25-yard perimeter. The clearing had thinned out and the remaining space between the thickets of massive trees were taken up by the enormous plants. In the distance, they could see large leaves hanging off thick branches high overhead. They would provide excellent shade from the sun when they began surveying.

While Tonie's fascination was with the flowers she was currently taking pictures of, Colin was moving through the flower bed towards the trees, trying to get as close as possible without Sarge or Gunny tearing him a new one. The trees seemed even taller than his home state's massive Redwoods. Taller but not as thick, although he knew his fingers would not meet if he hugged the trunk. Not that he would do that, what with the thick, ugly, thorn-covered vines winding up the bark. They looked oily and nasty and instead of pointing outward, many of the hand-length thorns were buried in the wood.

Glancing over a shoulder to check on his partner, Colin frowned. "Hey, don't get too close," he warned, "let the squints scan it first."

"What's wrong, afraid of some flowers?" She reached down and ran a finger over one of those clustered petals. Warm and leathery, not like a plant at all. Tonie sniffed as she studied the plant. "Do you smell that?" she asked Colin, nose wrinkling as the odour thickened in the air. It didn't smell like a flower at all. Instead, it smelled like curdled milk or something rotting.

"Jesus that stinks," Colin grimaced as he backed away from the plant. "Smells like an old slaughterhouse."

About to ask him how he knew what a slaughterhouse smelled like, she froze when the bud in the centre of the thing fluttered open. Craning her head to look at it, Tonie jumped back when a thick, slimy appendage shot from the opening and paused in the air, wavering like a stalk of grass in a breeze. At the very end of it, small feelers rolled out of the opening, as if testing the air.

The surface of the flower shuddered and opened even more. Several seconds went by before Tonie realized she was staring at a gaping mouth, lined with rows of serrated, jagged teeth.

"Ohshi…." The appendage snapped forward, coiling around her body, arms and all. "COLIN!!!!!!!" she screamed, struggling against the tentacle lifting towards her. "Shoot it!" Fetid air wafted upwards from the opening, making Tonie gag even as she screamed again.

Without hesitating, Colin opened fire, aiming for the area where the tongue (it was a fucking tongue!) emerged from the main body. The bullets shredded the meat around the mouth, tearing huge, wet gashes into its flesh. A pained, outraged keen filled the air as Tonie was flung to the ground, landing on her side with a crack of bone that was surely her ribs.

Struggling to her feet, she spotted Colin hurrying towards her just as a second of the 'flowers' seemed to awaken. As its mouth opened, she tried to warn him but lightning quick, the tip of the tongue speared through his neck and out the other side in a burst of blood. For a moment, he looked like he was wearing one of those ridiculous novelty arrows you wore on your head.

Suddenly, Tonie realized Colin wasn't on his feet on his own. That thing was holding him upright. "Oh Jesus...Colin... shit...!" Snatching her link, she thumbed the line open. "Edwards to base! Macon's down!!"

VIII

Audreys

If things can get fucked up, they usually will.

Another Pod gem, Tom thought as he, Derick and Jules, not to mention the rest of the expedition, heard the terrified message through their headsets. Even as his well-trained ear zeroed in on the source of the gunfire, a massive flock of birds lifted noisily out of the trees to mark the spot. Bolting from the river in a dead run towards it, Tom felt like he'd dropped his guard.

This world was their salvation, but it could also destroy the remaining dregs of the human race. One minute they were talking about ionisation and link frequencies, oohing and aahing about the skewers like a bunch of fucking tourists and the next, they were racing to reach a Shark under attack by something native.

Easily clearing downed trees and zigzagging around others in his way, Tom realized Edwards had gone silent, save for the distortions against the mic on her headset and the dying bursts of gunfire. A shaky flashback of watching Lisa burn made Tom put on an extra burst of speed. Derick appeared at the corner of his eye, nearly even with him. Who he didn't see was Jules.

Slapping his link, dropping off the main channels where Derick was busy barking orders to various Sharks, he hailed the *Rutherford's* Captain. And damned if it wasn't Lisa again, screaming in eternal death. "Jules? Jules, luv, where are you?"

Three heartbeats went by before she answered. Her voice nearly made him stumble. "On my way, back to the *Firefly*!"

Good, he didn't want her anywhere near what they were heading into.

* * *

When Edward's screams ripped through the relatively quiet background, Ren, Maya and Jag were playing escort to a squint team.

They weren't too far away, Ren figured, since it was only twenty minutes or so since the duo passed her team and the small group of squints they were assigned to babysit. Maya and Colin had swapped some flirtatious barbs with Tonie making gagging sounds before the two headed off. Maybe it wasn't exactly professional but who was Ren to get on her friend's case just because her own crush was someone she couldn't have?

"Colin!?" Maya called into her headset before Ren could give orders.

"Mayday!" Ren called to her friend, grabbing the other woman's battle harness as they both glanced towards a renewed burst of gunfire. "Maya, get everyone back to the *Firefly*! Jager, with me!"

"What?!" Maya stared at her friend, trying to work the redhead's grip off the webbing of her harness. "Ren, Colin and…"

"Do it, Mayday!" Giving her a slight shove, Ren hoped her friend would forgive her later. Especially if something terrible had happened to Colin.

Even though Maya might claim she and Colin were 'just shag mates', Ren knew he meant a lot more to her than that. She wanted to spare her friend the nightmare of finding a loved one dead. Not to mention keeping their only medic and her best friend from losing her shit if the worst was revealed. "Take them back and come on when you're done, Lance Corporal!" Not giving her another chance to argue, Ren took off after Jag towards the fight.

Conditioned to follow orders, Maya still couldn't help the sting of her friend pulling rank. She watched them disappear into the trees before turning back to the science team. "Leave it!" she snapped at someone trying to throw things into a backpack. "We need to get back, NOW!"

* * *

Ren didn't stop running even when the gunfire stopped. If anything, the silence made her run faster. Within moments, she broke into a clearing with Jag right behind her and they both skidded to a halt in horror.

"Edwards! Macon!" Ren yelled, scanning the ringed clearing as she firmed her grip on her rifle. The entire clearing was filled with massive, leathery looking plants, one of which was shredded into a white, pulpy pile of chunks that looked like something her dog used to hork up. Movement to her right caught her attention. One of the plants was shuddering and twitching. Using hand signals, she motioned Jag to move around to the other side. "Toni! Talk to me!"

Ren circled to the left, her boot squelching in something smelly and viscous. She looked down and grimaced. "That's nasty..." she groaned, dragging her boot on the grass to clean it off.

Jag's blistering curses in Hebrew made her look up to find him staring at the ground.

"What is...?" Ren stared past Jag, where he had dropped to one knee. Behind her friend, one of the plants... who the fuck was she kidding. It was not like ANY plant or animal she'd ever seen. The body of the thing rising behind Jag was shaped like a bulbous onion, covered in glistening scales and set atop black rows of undulating, articulated legs.

A dark opening appeared in the middle of its leathery 'petals' and the sunlight glinted off something hard and sharp. Lots and lots of very, very sharp pointies. "DOWN!!!" Ren bellowed, giving Jag a split second to obey before she opened fire on the creature about to grab a very kosher snack.

As if a call to arms was sounded, the remaining 'plants' in the clearing awakened at once, each of them rising up on those ugly legs and opening their nightmarish mouths.

Watching them in horror, Ren's first thought was not for her safety or that of Jag's but how much these things looked like some mutant version of Audrey the alien plant in *Little Shop of Horrors*. *Audripede Renee Whattheholyfuckidaii.*

"Richards!" Jag threw a hand into the air and Ren followed him, to find Tonie Edward's limp body dangling in the air, impaled on a spear-like tongue extending from the mouth of the creature. There was no sign of Colin and Ren's stomach sank as she imagined what might have happened to him.

Oh God, Maya. I'm so sorry.

When the tongue began to retreat, drawing its meal into its open jaws, Ren snapped back into action. Tonie was NOT going to end up as this…this…Audripede's food! No Shark deserved to go that way.

Pulling the trigger on her blast rifle, she was remotely aware of Jag doing the same, except he was shooting behind *her*. Something splattered against her cheek and her neck, soaking the collar of her uniform shirt. As the creature behind her collapsed to the ground, Ren swiped the mess off her neck, glancing at it. Thick, milky white fluid covered her gloved hand. As Ren shook her fingers to get it off, the beast holding Tonie screeched in anger, whipping her body about with an ear-splitting screech.

In retaliation, the remaining Audripedes shuffled towards Ren and Jag with speed that belied their bulk. Out of nowhere, a speared tentacle thunked against the chest plate of her body armour, hard enough to throw Ren to the ground on her back. Another creature shuffled forward, it's 'tongue' rising high in the air over her. She rolled quickly, just in time to avoid impalement by the javelin-like tip. Instead, it buried itself in the dirt beside her.

Rolling again to her back, Ren swiped her pistol and fired at the beast. Its flesh erupted in more of the nasty white fluid, but it screeched a retreat that allowed her to get back on her feet.

She stood up with the intent of finding Tonie but suddenly she was overcome with a wave of dizziness. Shaking her head, Ren tried to clear her mind and failed.

Focus, Richards! Gunny's voice barked in her thoughts, but not even her conditioning to obey him cleared the fog in her head. There were two of everything, just like it was when they went through the Ribbon and the ship had been shaking so hard.

As soon as the first creature died, Jag found a second target and was firing at it when he realized there wasn't enough noise. "Corporal?!" Turning, he spotted Ren and instantly knew something was wrong. The redhead was wavering on her feet, her gun silent as she swayed and shook her head. "Ren!"

When she didn't answer, Jag started towards the woman as she staggered back a step. "Richards... CORPORAL!!!" he shouted, when he realized he wasn't going to make it to her side in time.

Her lack of a scream as a speared tongue pierced her thigh was something Jag was certain he would never forget. "She's hit!!" he yelled into the link, tracking the tentacle to find the monster it belonged to and firing at it. "Major!! Gunny!! Richards is hit!"

"We're here!" Tom yelled as he skidded into the clearing, Derick right behind him.

"REN!"

Tom barely managed to grab Derick's harness as his friend shot by. "Go that way!" he ordered, indicating for the big Gunny to skirt the clearing. "I'll distract it, you grab her. Jag keep the others busy!" He'd never be able to stop the big bloke from going to Richards' aid, so he might as well make it something he could use.

Waiting until his friend was in place, Tom took aim at what he determined to be the king beast and opened fire on the round, fat body.

As bullets ripped through it, Ren was whipped to the right and then into the branches of a tree before Tom saw Derick make a grab for her. Once he did, the limb holding her yanked hard, trying to free its prize from the nasty creatures hurting it.

Grabbing Ren about the waist with one arm, Derick yanked his machete free and slashed at the limb, severing it. As it snaked away, he scooped Ren into his arms and hurried out of the kill zone.

With the world swimming in a haze of pain and something else, Ren blinked as her eyes finally focused on the face above her.

"Hey, Der...ick." Her words were slurred and the smile she gave Derick was weak and tired.

She'd never used his first name. He'd always been 'Gunny' or 'Sergeant'. He'd never called her 'Ren' to her face, until today. No matter how much they teased, joked around, or took digs at each other, they'd never breached that one protocol. The only protocol Derick suspected they both kept in place to keep them from going to places that would only end in trouble.

Seeing her this close to death destroyed that last barrier. Derick pulled her against him and pressed his lips to her forehead. "Shh, baby, I'm here," he murmured, carefully lowering Ren to the ground to assess her injuries. Swiping gently at the blood swelling from a cut on her cheek, Derick was horrified when he spied the large, bloody hole in her thigh. Clamping a big hand over it, he reached for the link with his free hand. "Mayday, I need you on site!" he ordered sharply.

"Almost there, Gunny!"

* * *

A handful of Alpha Squad Sharks joined the fray and Tom had quickly commandeered a grenade launcher to get the upper hand. Some of the beasts were dead, collapsed across the clearing under plant chum and a milky white, pus-like substance that slimed the grass. An acrid, nauseating odour permeated the area, like burnt flesh and rotting bodies.

When Derick's all-clear came through, he raised the thick-barrelled weapon to his shoulder and aimed at what he'd named the king beast. Bigger than the others by a few feet, it was also twice as ugly. Dropping his cheek to the sight, Tom put the monster in the crosshairs and fired.

Firing two in quick succession, Tom dropped to one knee as the first grenade hit the ground just in front of the monster and the second plunged into its massive belly. They exploded within a second of each other, showering the entire vicinity in burning grass and dirt and the occasional wet *schlack* from a piece of meat hitting the ground.

With the 'king' dead, the remaining creatures shuffled into something resembling a retreat. "Hold your fire!" he ordered loudly. They could finish the beasties, but Tom wasn't so sure they had the right to. In the last century, hadn't humanity done enough damage? No longer was the rape of the natural world permissible for the sake of expediency and doing so felt just as dishonourable as shooting a fleeing creature in the back.

Turning his attention to the clearing, his mind began cataloguing the wet and burnt chunks of meat before Tom even realized it. As a result, he stared at one particular piece for a full moment before realizing he was staring at a human hand. He turned away in disgust, aware they would have to collect the remains eventually and afford the victims a decent burial. After they identified whether the remains belonged to Macon or Edwards.

Only when he turned away and found the ruined body of PFC Tonie Edwards did he realize identification would be fairly easy, after all. She had both hands so the grisly question of who the stray hand belonged to answered itself.

"I'm here!!"

Maya Sanjay burst through the underbrush, coming to a halt beside Tom. Aware of her relationship with Macon, he cast a hasty look at the disembodied hand and was relieved to see no obvious signs of Macon's body. "Mayday, see to Richards!" he ordered, pointing to where Derick knelt over the corporal.

When she didn't see Colin, Maya shut out the facts and hurried to her friend's side. Dropping to her knees, she yanked the quick release latch on her pack and dumped it beside her to dig into it. "We've got to stop the bleeding on that leg," she said quickly, no trace of the playful schoolgirl with the crass humour from earlier. Coming up with two large, triangular gauze pads, she slapped it over the Gunny's hand and nodded for him to pull back. When he did, Maya put the second pad on top of the first.

A few minutes later, after sorting out the Sharks and setting a watch in the clearing, Tom approached the group with Jag. Derick was cradling Ren's head in his lap, with one hand cupped under her chin and the other gently swiping blood from an oozing cut on her cheek. Whether his big friend wanted to admit it, the Gunny's crush on the Corporal was just as big as the one she had for him.

Before the Exodus, had he learned of the attraction between the two, he might have counselled Derick on the issues created by a relationship in the ranks. Now? If two people could find comfort in each other after the end of the world, who the fuck was he to bitch about it? Besides, he figured eventually folks would realize that with less than 10,000 humans left, the survival of the species would take precedence over traditional military protocols.

"Status, Mayday?" Tom asked as he tapped Jag's arm and pointed over to Ren's rifle on the ground several feet away. Ren's pants leg had been cut away and bandages had been secured around the slim, muscled thigh. Maya's medical tab was lying on Ren's stomach, blipping away.

"Don't know yet," Maya said abruptly, fastening an outer bandage around Ren's leg before pulling a hypo from her pack. "She's been dosed with some kind of toxin. The database is trying to pin it down. Gunny, we'll need the…thing…" she said, making a face at the leftover appendage laying in the dirt by her friend.

Grabbing a small, compressed air can out of her pack, Maya turned to the cut on Ren's cheek just as her med slate blinked.

"What is it?" Tom asked, having dropped a surreptitious hand on Derick's shoulder.

Frowning at the med slate, Maya yanked her pack closer. "It's some form of atracotoxin, like a spider would make," she said, digging out an anti-tox kit. Priming it, Maya dialled up the closest antidote she had for such a thing and applied it to Ren's arm. "This is a generic anti-toxin, but the shuttle's Med Station should be able to synthesize the exact recipe. We need to get her back to the *Firefly*."

"No problem," Derick answered immediately and moved to Ren's side to pick her up.

As he stood with Ren cradled against him, Maya rose to her feet as well and glanced around the clearing. Biting her lip, she bent over her pack. "What about Edwards and Col... I mean Macon?"

"They didn't make it." Tom squeezed her arm in sympathy, watching her. "I'm sorry, Mayday."

The news was taken as he expected. Months ago, he informed her none of her family were among the survivors evacuated from London. Now, like that day, a mask dropped into place and she looked down at the ground. There was no sobbing or curses, just a sharp intake of breath as if the news needed breathing in to be accepted. When she lifted her chin, Tom saw the Shark he knew in place.

"Thank you, Major," she nodded, her voice sedate. "Let's get Ren to the ship."

Atta girl, Tom thought silently, thinking it was weak praise for the strength she was showing.

IX

Retreat

Both Sharks and Squints were waiting for Jules when she returned to the *Firefly*.

The science teams were being herded onto the shuttle and being ordered to leave their equipment outside. Only a handful of them were arguing with the Sharks' urgent requests and she could see their nerves were quickly becoming frayed. Thanks to the roar of gunfire and anxious cries emanating from where Tom and Derick had headed, tempers were getting short as well.

"We're not lifting off yet!" Jules called out, climbing on top of a crate so they could see her. As she'd hoped, the group went quiet. "We're not lifting off. This is just a safety measure. I promise, if we have to leave the equipment, I will make every effort to come back for it."

Several of the team glanced to Dr. Hall, who nodded and indicated the shuttle. As the group started filing on board, Jules was pleased to see cooler heads prevailing. She had just stepped off the crate when she was addressed.

"Captain?"

Turning, Jules wasn't surprised to see Dr. Hall and Luke Rickman.

"Where's Derick? What's happening?" Luke demanded, glancing behind Jules where distant gunfire echoed from the trees.

With the noise on stereo in her headset, Jules winced. "All I know is two of the privates were attacked…" She paused, listening to the tense voices over her headset. It wasn't lost on Jules the scientists were growing more agitated by this latest turn of events. "Gunny was fine last I saw him," she told Luke, waving at Sergeant Jackson.

"Yes, ma'am?" the dark-skinned man asked as he jogged over.

"Can we do something about the comms? I don't think it's helping anyone's nerves to hear what's going on." She tipped her head in the direction of the scientists who were clearly affected by the violence beyond their view. Not that she blamed them.

Jazz glanced back at the others and nodded in understanding.

"On it," he replied, with a sharp nod. Despite having sent a team to help the Major, Jazz was fighting the urge to go his unit's side. "Shiny!"

As their comtech, Shiny had proved to be a wiz with electronics during previous missions. She joined him quickly, armour jiggling slightly on her slender frame. She'd been working on calibrating the transponders when the order to withdraw was given.

Grabbing her arm, Jazz tugged until she followed him a few feet away, so they wouldn't be overheard. "Cut the comms for the squints, except for Doctor Hall, yeah?"

"But..." Shiny glanced at him with her grey eyes and then at the others before nodding. "Yes, Sergeant. Are we going after them?"

"Not until he gives us the word," Jazz answered as they shared a look. She was feeling it, too. "I sent Tonkin and his team. They're not alone."

"All right," she nodded and headed back towards the shuttle to access its communications terminal.

An explosion made Jules and everyone else jump before every face turned towards the tree line.

"Keep moving!" she shouted above a second explosion, hoping no one panicked. While they seemed to maintain their senses, she could see real fear. In contrast, every single one of the Sharks started checking their equipment, all of them looking towards Sergeant Jackson. Jules couldn't blame them. It had to be difficult to sit here when it was clear their comrades had encountered something hostile.

Hell, Jules wanted to go investigate herself but her agreement, her word to Tom, had been that she would defer to him in matters like this. Her place was here, with the hopper. But damn it all, this wasn't her nature. Six months ago, she'd be the one being called out to join the fray, to lay down cover fire or dropping to put more troops down. This sitting back and letting the others do the fighting for her had her chomping at the bit. There was also this little issue of what her stomach did every time Tom Merrick smirked at her. Despite their brief encounters and short acquaintance, she quite liked the man.

"Sergeant?" Jules called finally, unable to keep quiet any longer. The younger man looked on edge, like a bow string being pulled back.

"Those were grenades, ma'am. Tonkin had a launcher with him," Jazz answered, studying the horizon.

That was the last straw. Jules tapped her comms. "Major?" When he didn't answer, she let loose several curses heard only in the bowels of aviator bars.

"I'm sure the Major is handling the situation," Olivia offered, hoping her words helped the younger woman. She hated this too, hated waiting, and really, really hated not knowing.

Jules glared into the distance, straining her ears to hear something. Anything. "Sergeant," she began just as her headset came to life.

"Jules, get the med station ready! We've got wounded!"

"Better not be you," Jules growled, tamping down the relief she felt at hearing Tom Merrick's accent. "Roger that!" she replied. "Sending some Sharks to help!"

The grin Jackson gave her before he called for a team to follow him would be worth whatever burr got under Tom's saddle over the order.

* * *

A short time later, Luke Rickman paced outside the *Firefly*, much to the annoyance of the petite young woman parked on a crate nearby. Tammy was given a description of the beasts along with the sample tentacle and parts of the corporal's shirt. Immediately, she'd set up a makeshift lab to run scans. Glancing up at Luke as he stomped by her for the hundredth time, she sighed but couldn't bring herself to chide him for being distracting.

"Your brother didn't look injured," Tammy patted the crate next to her. "Sit down, big brother." That would get Luke's attention for certain.

Pausing, Luke glanced back at her and dragged a hand through his hair. No, Derick hadn't been hurt, (at least, he didn't think so), but the emotions he'd seen on his brother's face during that brief glimpse made Luke want to be at his side.

Despite being the only Rickman in their family to avoid the service, Luke understood the realities of a military life. Their father was a career soldier and their oldest brother Chris was killed in action. When Derick enlisted after Chris's death, Luke hadn't been as accepting of the decision as he should have been. In fact, he hadn't come to terms with it until Derick was gone for a year.

Now, with Earth destroyed and all of his family but Derick gone, and faced with the actuality of his brother running into the fray, Luke nearly lost every term he'd thought he'd accepted. "I need to see him," he said, dropping onto the crate beside her.

"You can, you know," Tammy replied, holding up a small vial and tapping it with her fingers. She suspected Luke was out here because of her and the way he looked at her just now proved it. "I'm a big girl Luke. I'll be fine," she smiled. "Just don't get in their way, okay?"

Luke didn't respond - he was already back on his feet and heading for the shuttle.

Once inside, he headed through the passenger cabin to the Med Station, where he could see his brother taking up the entire doorway to the partitioned cubicle. He could hear the medic's crisp British accent and Liv's quiet but strong voice. Pausing behind his brother, Luke put a hand on Derick's shoulder and squeezed. When his brother scooted to the side, Luke could see the redheaded corporal on the medical bed. On one side, Lance Corporal Sanjay was working on her. On the other, Doctor Hall was holding the medical tab over Ren, using the light to illuminate Maya's workspace.

Tom was just inside the room, to Derick's right and a third Shark was at his left flank. All of them were covered in mud, blood and what looked like plant guts, watching Maya work on the corporal. Not for the first time, Luke felt a little ashamed at being grateful that none of the blood was Derick's. "What happened?" he asked quietly.

"Carnivorous plants the size of fucking rhinos," Tom answered for Derick, who was staring fixedly at Ren on the bed. "We lost two people to the bloody things."

A pair of forceps clattered to the deck and Tom winced in reaction. Fuck. Still, Mayday was a pro and didn't bat an eye as she grabbed another set.

Unnerved by his brother's silence, Luke glanced up at him and did a double take because, for once in his life, he couldn't read Derick. His brother wasn't known for keeping his emotions in check and yet, Derick was oddly restrained as he watched the girl on the examination table.

Luke wasn't sure what to think of that, other than the obvious. He looked at the Shark on the table, where the medic was extracting segments of alien pulp from her thigh with thin forceps. "Are we getting out of here?"

"I'm not sure yet," Tom answered honestly, glancing past his shoulder at the aisle leading back into the passenger cabin and the cockpit. "I'll be back in a bit. I need to check in with the Captain."

When Tom squeezed past him out the door, Luke took up the Major's spot on the wall. The other Shark opted to leave as well, perhaps sensing the two brothers might need some privacy. He nodded at Luke before leaving. Now alone, mostly, Luke looked up at Derick again. He didn't appear to notice Luke, his gaze locked on the unconscious girl on the table. A tic had started in Derick's jaw, finally exposing just how worried he was. That alone warranted another look at the woman.

Even bloody, unconscious and half covered in alien goop, she was a looker. Red, corkscrew curls escaping from her braid and pale, freckled skin made her look like she belonged on some hilltop in the Scottish Highlands instead of here, having alien crap picked out of her. With high cheekbones and full pouty lips, Luke imagined she had green eyes to match her fiery red hair. He looked up at Derick again and nudged his elbow. "You okay?"

Derick barely took his eyes off the redhead. "Yeah, not a scratch."

"I didn't mean that." Luke tilted his head subtly at Ren.

Derick stared at Luke for a full minute this time before turning back. "I'm fine," he answered, not at all prepared to talk about what he was feeling or thinking. Not until he knew Ren was going to be all right. Which she had to be, because she was too damn stubborn to survive the destruction of Earth only to be killed by an overgrown houseplant.

Luke raised an eyebrow but didn't press the issue. The Rickman family, even the two surviving members, didn't discuss women or feelings. Gabriel Rickman hadn't raised his boys that way. Instead, Luke remained at his brother's side in a silent show of solidarity and support. He'd also be there when and if Derick owned up to caring about the young woman on the examination table.

* * *

With the immediate danger gone, Jules had been in the middle of sorting out the Sharks and the scientists when her comms blipped at her. Realizing she'd completely forgotten about the approaching storm, Jules ordered the teams to stay within eyesight of the shuttle and returned to the cockpit to track the storm's progress. Despite the task at hand, Jules couldn't help but think about the lost Sharks. She hadn't known them, but they'd died on her watch. That was hard to swallow.

Even more hard to swallow was the idea that dying within twenty-four hours of reaching their goal just wasn't right. Edwards and Macon suffered with the rest of them and had the right to share the accomplishment of reaching their new home. Now, they would be footnotes in history as the first casualties in the colonisation of Gaia.

Sitting back, Jules rubbed her eyes and turned her gaze towards the horizon.

"*Mierda*," she breathed, eyes widening as bluish-purple lightning sparked brilliantly across the face of the largest anvil cloud she'd ever seen. She even had to lean forward to find the top of the construct.

Only when thunder rumbled from one end of the sky to the other did she break her gaze and look down at the console. Reaching for the stabilization controls, Jules glanced up when she heard someone behind her.

When Tom paused in the doorway of the cockpit, Jules indicated the co-pilot's chair.

"I figured you could use this." Tom held up a covered coffee mug. "There's no cream or sugar but you Yanks need to learn how to drink it properly anyway."

Jules snorted and took the cup. "Thank you," she murmured quietly, testing the temperature before deciding to drink it anyway. The first sip scalded her tongue and she tried not to wince. Not like she needed taste buds but the warmth felt oh so good. Glancing down at the cup, she frowned and looked at him.

"How do you get used to it? Losing people? Is it part of the job for you?"

"It is." Tom glanced at her and shrugged before looking out the window. "Ground troops. Bullet catchers, that's the way it is for my lot." An ugly memory invaded his head, making Tom frown. In that moment, it was hard to feel the nonchalance he needed for his answer. "It's the job but not one we ever get used to, no matter how many years we've got under our belts. It's when you stop caring, stop giving a shit about the bloke watching your back…"

He should have had Lisa's back but had chosen the ship instead.

Clearing his throat, Tom snagged Jules's cup of coffee and took a sip before handing it back. "When that happens it's time to quit."

So, it didn't get easier, Jules thought bitterly, not missing the dark shadows on the man's face. "Six months ago, I was just a pilot," she said quietly, wondering if a friendly squeeze of the arm would be accepted. "The only person I was responsible for was my ship and my LIO. Now, I have a whole ship full of people I'm responsible for. Sometimes, I think I got this. I can do this. Other times, like right now, I wonder what the hell I was thinking."

"Life's like that, Jules," Tom propped a boot on the flight console. "Sometimes, it doesn't give you a choice. Most of the time, life's a bitch that just sneaks up on you and screws you right and proper."

"Charming. Get your foot off the ship," Jules replied dryly, shoving his leg.

He was right of course. Not that she'd tell him that. Jules knew she had it easier than most. Yes, she'd lost the man she considered family but too many had lost so much more. She'd had no family alive when Sol was destroyed, having lost her mother when she was young and her father three years before. If the worst thing to happen to her life with this upheaval in human civilisation were her new responsibilities, she had no right to complain.

"That's me, luv," he winked, dropping his foot to the deck with a thump. "Prince fucking Charming."

Prince Charming? Hah. Jules studied his profile as he looked out the window, apparently noticing the clouds. In that moment, she decided she was glad he wasn't the fictitious man in question. Tom Merrick treated her like Jules, not Captain Curran. He had no filter, said exactly what was on his mind, whether it was appropriate or not. Before the Exodus, she might have wanted someone more refined, but the truth was he treated her like an equal. She hadn't expected that, not when some of her own, supposedly refined peers still had trouble doing so.

"Is that bloody normal?" Tom asked, indicating the clouds and stirring Jules out of her reverie.

Right. Storm. Alien planet. NOT the time to realise she might be attracted to this Shark.

"No, actually," she replied, sitting up to activate the HUD. Pointing to the graphs on the display, where are least two were pegged to the right, she continued. "There's a lot of electricity in those clouds. Atmospheric levels are at five hundred million kilowatts. I've never seen anything like it."

Fascinated by the indigo masses and the spidery webs of electricity, Tom only nodded. "I wonder if it's normal for Gaia," he ventured, looking back at her. "Are we talking hurricane scale? Can we take off if it gets too bad?"

The idea of riding that monster out didn't appeal to him, especially on the heels of Macon and Edward's deaths. Just then, a gale blew across the shuttle, making some of the people outside turn their backs to it. In the distance, the trees had started to bend and sway with gusts sweeping across the flat space like an invisible creature on the run.

"Possibly," Jules frowned, not looking forward to the possibility. "We could take off but with the ionization so high and all that lightning, we really shouldn't be in the air. As it is, we're going to have to shut everything down but the red systems. The shuttle has surge protection against high electrical discharges, but I don't want to test it against what's happening out there."

"I hope everyone took a bloody shower before they left," Tom grumbled even though he couldn't complain if he got stuck in closed spaces with Jules for a while. At least the cockpit was bigger than his closet on the *Ruthie*. Against his will, the idea about asking her if she'd like a shag and a bottle of scotch resurfaced in his mind.

Jules eyed him dubiously. She couldn't tell what he was thinking but decided it most likely wasn't anything professional. Men.

Oh, this was going to end well, Tom thought silently.

X

Sky Crabs

As Jules and Tom watched the approaching clouds, the wind whipped up again, scouring the windshield with grit and dirt. Overhead, Tom heard the sharp *drip, drip, drip* of water against the hull as fat raindrops splattered against the glass. Outside, a handful of Sharks and Squints were rushing to cover or gather equipment to get it under shelter. Down the corridor behind them, they could hear everyone gathering inside the shuttle. Overhead, thunder rolled again, loud enough to make both officers raise their eyes upward.

"I do not fancy riding out a hurricane again," Tom grumbled.

"Again?" Jules stared at him. "How many have you…"

"Four. Last one was the Deimos Colony evac two years ago. Everyone survived but my platoon got caught on the island during the storm, along with about a hundred colonists."

"I remember that," Jules nodded, the revelation hiking her opinion of the Major up another notch. The evac had been a mess, both politically and in real life. A mud dam had collapsed at a critical juncture, forcing the remaining colonists and military personnel to abandon the base camp and take refuge in caves in the surrounding mountainside. Was that him? The kind who never mentioned his actual heroics but was larger than life everywhere else?

"I'm going to check on the corporal," Tom announced. As well as his Gunny and his medic. Make sure they both hadn't gone nutter on him.

"I'm coming with you," Jules stated, tucking her now empty coffee mug against the windshield as she stood up. She rolled her neck, popping it in relief before following Tom.

* * *

"She's going to be all right," Maya spoke up, addressing the Gunny as she secured a blanket over the now sedated Ren. He barely moved, only nodded to acknowledge her. Was he going to stand there the whole time? Would Colin have... her stomach twisted, and Maya shook her head as she went to the small sink to scrub her hands once more. She had to stay busy. Maybe check her pack once more. A noise like a banshee's wail caught her attention, making her look up. "What was that?"

"A bloody big storm," Tom replied as he slid past Derick, one hand quickly gripping his friend's arm. "How is she?"

Free of her uniform and body armour, Ren seemed small and too pale for Tom's liking. Accustomed to her lively personality, seeing her like this, with tubes poking out from the blankets and the various machines pinging around her, made Tom feel she was setting up camp on death's door. Perhaps she had been. Tom dismissed the thought immediately.

He had to, for Derick's sake.

Maya nodded at Captain Curran when she appeared behind the Major, addressing all three of them. "She was lucky. The tentacle missed the femoral artery." Had been bloody fucking close, though. "There was some blood loss, but it wasn't significant. Our supplies could keep up. There was also minimal muscle damage, considering."

"What about the toxin she was dosed with?" Tom asked, hating the dullness in his medic's tone. Maya and Ren were a set, beams of light bouncing against each other, elevating the mood by always cracking jokes and being snarky.

"It's definitely some kind of paralytic. The anti-toxin we have on hand appears to be working and I handed everything over to Doctor

Adelaide for analysis. She mentioned making something specifically for that creature, so we'll have it on hand."

"Thank you, Lance Corporal," Jules said kindly. "Does she need to go back to the *Olympus*?"

"No ma'am," Maya answered, glancing at her friend. Despite knowing how important this mission was, she wouldn't have hesitated to say yes if she felt Ren was truly in trouble. "She's stable and will be back on her feet in twenty-four or forty-eight hours."

"That's good to hear," Jules relaxed at the news and saw Tom and Derick doing the same. "Now, this storm. We think there's a lot of electricity in it. We'll need all non-essential systems shut down."

"I can do that," Maya nodded, moving towards Ren's side. "I can check her vitals the old-fashioned way."

"Great. Make sure she's strapped in, just to be safe," Tom exchanged a brief look with Jules as she headed for the door. "Let us know if anything changes, Mayday."

Pausing for a moment, he debated trying to find some words of comfort to give his medic solace but dismissed the notion almost immediately. Tom was smart enough to know the only 'cure' was time. Turning away from her, he found Derick standing behind him instead. The big bloke was looking over his shoulder at Ren, a war of indecision on his face. Tom didn't need to be a mind reader to know why he was floundering. Derick wanted to stay with Ren, but duty was calling.

"You coming, mate?"

That did the trick. Derick snapped back to the here and now, getting the mental jolt he needed to reach a decision.

"Right then. Come along, we got shit to do," Tom told him, giving his thick bicep a hearty slap and headed out. Derick was right behind him.

* * *

In the main compartment, the noise of so many people gathered in one spot drowned out the whistling wind and whatever was being tossed against the hull. Someone had shut the hatch, so Tom hoped that meant everyone was indoors. The voices died down when he entered with the Gunny behind him.

"Carry on," Tom muttered, spotting Jules in the corner with Dr. Hall and another squint. Both scientists were wearing an expression of urgency that immediately put him on guard. "What is it?"

Dr. Hall nodded towards the face he didn't know. "This is Dr. Dmitri Andropolis, my meteorologist. Andy has been part of my team on almost every survey mission I've..."

"Right, he's an expert. What's the problem?" Tom cut in impatiently. Jules winced in the corner of his eye. Well, he'd warned her.

Before Olivia could answer, Dr. Andropolis, a thin bespectacled man with sallow features, answered just as quickly. "It's this storm. It's not exhibiting any of the characteristics of a naturally occurring weather front."

"And that means what?" Tom asked, looking from Dr. Andropolis to Dr. Hall. He knew better than to look at Jules.

The droll look the scientist gave him made Tom suspect this guy liked military as much as the military liked his lot. Which meant they wouldn't be chatting over a cuppa and cucumber sandwiches any time soon.

"I reviewed the external sensor readings in the cockpit," Andropolis explained, his expression showing genuine worry. "I wanted to record the atmospheric levels for review later. I noticed how the storm was formed. From what I observed, the storm is a thunderhead or a cumulonimbus, usually formed by upward currents. These usually become tornadoes and cyclones."

"Okay, with you so far," Tom returned, wishing the man would get to the point. "This one is a bit strange. We are on an alien planet after all. It wouldn't be just like the ones in Sol."

Andropolis let out an insulted huff and shoved his glasses up his nose with his middle finger. "Of course, I know that! We are in trouble Major! Storms, even alien ones, follow patterns. This one doesn't. It didn't form by upwards currents. It's like it just appeared out of thin air."

"Okay. That means what to us?" Jules intervened before one of the two men strangled the other. "It has been generated by *something*. Storms don't just appear out of nowhere." As a pilot, she was more cognisant of weather patterns than most, save Andropolis himself. Atmo training required entire units to read the weather, temperatures and wind currents. Storms took time to manifest. They simply did not spring out of nowhere like Athena, fully formed.

"OH MY GOD!!" The shout grabbed Jules's attention sharply. Just when she located the speaker, others started shouting.

"HOLY FUCK!!"

"Major!! Captain! LOOK OUTSIDE!"

* * *

Jules sprinted towards the observation window, Tom following close behind.

He found her, face pressed against the observational portal long enough to unleash curses potent enough to wake her mother from the dead before bolting for the rear hatch.

"Jules, wait!" Tom hurried after her, not bothering to peer through the observation portal at what sent her into such a state of panic. It was enough that it had. Tom reached her just as she activated the hatch, allowing the wind to rush into the airlock vestibule. Cursing, he shielded his eyes against the grit but caught sight of Jules hurrying out to the edge of the ramp, riding it down to the ground.

"Have you lost your mind?" Tom yelled over the wind, wishing she'd be just a little cautious for the sake of his sanity. "Jules!" he shouted again, following her out and grabbing her arm.

The wind whipped at them both, tearing her dark hair from its braid. Tom could see she wasn't even paying attention to him as the long strands lashed against her cheek while the pelting rain soaked her uniform. Above them, neon blue lightning crackled against the underbelly of the clouds, casting an eerie glow over everything.

"Jules, get inside!" Tom held fast on her arm, prepared to throw her over a shoulder if he had to when she grabbed his sleeve.

"Tom, look!" she yelled, thrusting her free hand towards the clouds.

He raised his eyes to the air and forgot all about the wind and the rain.

"Holy fuck."

Balmain Bugs, that's what they are.

It was his thought at seeing massive creatures moving in and out of the swirling purple clouds. Balmain Bugs, the nickname given to the butterfly fan lobsters native to his parent's homeland of Australia. Except these were flying, not scavenging about in the ocean.

Iridescent colours swirled along huge, flat carapaces and rippled towards fat tails that trailed blue and green tendrils of electricity. They moved in and out of the clouds with purpose, like a pod of dolphins chasing a ship. And they were easily the size of the *Firefly*.

"It's them! They're making the storm!"

"Come on!" Tom tugged her arm, making his words a command. "We need to get inside, now! I don't know if those bloody sky crabs are friendly or not, but I rather not find out while we're out here!"

This time she listened, ducking her head and allowing him to pull her into the airlock. The wind seemed to scream in anger at their retreat to safety and the gusts chased them into the airlock, forcing Jules to grab Tom by his battle harness.

Bloody oath! Tom slapped a hand on the controls and half-turned, throwing an arm over Jules's shoulders as stuff too big to be called grit scoured against them. He pulled her to his chest and squatted, burying his face in her shoulder as the wind became a howling demon. Christ on a friggin' crutch, how long did it take the fucking hatch to close? It had to be that damn wind!

He wasn't sure when the hatch closed but when there was much less noise and no wind tearing at them, he lifted his head. Rubbing the grit out his eyes, he tried to assess the situation. There was no blood and none of them were finding God so everything was Mickey Mouse. He'd take it. When Tom's eyes were finally clear, he patted Jules's back. "Look."

As if just now realizing the wind had stopped, Jules popped her head up and swept her hair from her eyes with one hand. "Oh wow."

The airlock deck was nearly covered in leaves and dirt and broken bits of vegetation. Wow was right, Tom thought as he rose to his feet, pulling Jules with him. About to ask if she was all right, he chuckled instead and pulled a twig from her hair.

"Stop laughing," Jules wrinkled her nose at him.

"Am I interrupting something? I mean, we got this big storm going on…"

Tom and Jules stepped back from each other so fast that Derick chuckled, making Tom glower at him over Jules's head. "Laugh it up, Big Foot," he grumbled.

Derick opened his mouth, but he was silenced by Jules.

"Both of you, come on. We need to get everyone strapped in," she ordered, pushing past the big Gunny.

* * *

"I think we should stay put," Olivia offered, joining the two officers in the cockpit. "They may pass right over us and not even see us."

Jules didn't like that idea, but she supposed Dr. Hall had a point. She could tell Tom was of the same mind. "Makes sense," she shrugged. "If we stay here, it's 50/50 they see us. If we take off, they will *definitely* see us. We need to avoid any action that could be taken as provocative."

"Seven hundred meters… Six hundred…" Derick's voice echoed down the passageway towards them. "Those things are moving fast!"

"Sky crabs," Tom called out helpfully.

"They look more like sky lobsters!" was Derick's reply.

"Sky crabs is easier to say!"

"Really?" Jules gave Tom's arm a shove and shot him a dry look.

"Sorry," Tom threw her an embarrassed smile. "You were say…"

Something hit the hull of the *Firefly* hard enough to make the ship shudder. Thunder clapped so loud and so close, it was like it was *inside* the shuttle. Tom was thrown against his harness as Dr. Hall tumbled out of view. Beside him, Jules was bracing a boot against the console as again, something crashed into the ship, less violently this time.

Screams and shouts came from the passenger area as the unmistakable scent of heated metal reached Tom. Taking cue from Jules, Tom planted a boot against the console.

"*What the fuck was that?*"

Tom didn't recognize the voice.

"Lightning hit the hull!" Derick announced.

"Doc, back to your seat," Tom ordered the scientists but found he was talking to the woman's back as she hurried down the corridor.

Lightning crackled again, rocking the *Firefly* once more. Jules realized one side was being lifted off the ground. Before she could call out a warning, the shuttle slammed back to the ground as cries for quiet were drowned out by another ear-popping crash of thunder. Something moved against the glass in front of her and Jules gasped. "TOM!"

There, against the glass was a slitted, iridescent blue *eye* the size of a basketball watching them. It disappeared, just as the ship was hit again. This time, Jules felt it more in her boots and she knew they were going to flip.

"BRACE!!" she yelled, Tom echoing the command as her stomach dropped and the world went ass over teakettle, to the right.

There was a different pitch in the scream that came out of the back, but Jules could only hold onto buckling metal. Crashing gear and breaking glass drowned everything else out. Suddenly, they were upright again. Someone screamed for Dr. Hall as the on-board lights flickered and died, leaving them all in the pitch dark. A moment later, lightning crackled over the outer hull, nearly blinding Jules.

"Fuck!" Tom cursed, just as the ship was struck again and this time, they rolled to the left. Anything that hadn't come loose the first time gave up the fight now in a cacophony of deafening noise. A hiss and a different kind of sound turned Tom's attention to the windshield, where a foot-long crack had appeared.

Something metallic hit the windshield, making both Jules and Tom jump.

"Hull plating!" she called over the noise. Suddenly, the hair on her arms stood on end and the air became acrid with the smell of burnt wiring and electronics. Something roundish and blue appeared in the air near the ceiling and pinged around the cockpit before dissipating against the glass. "Ball lightning!" she yelled as the air crackled again and another bluish light zoomed out of the cockpit and down the passageway.

The ship lifted again. As Jules recognized the direction, she grabbed Tom's sleeve as the shuttle was rolled on its end and then slammed onto its roof in a bone-jarring crunch of metal and rolled over its end once more. Something popped in the dark as the ship was lifted again, this time rolling to the right. The shuttle slammed to a stop before being yanked to the left.

This time, when the nose of the shuttle went into the air, there was a different feel to the lift. Jules's eyes went wide. The ravine with the river at the bottom. Frantically, she tried to recall. Was it a drop to a shelf and then a drop to the river or was there a slope? *Shitshitshit.*

As the shuttle was slammed onto its roof again, Jules's head hit the headrest hard enough to put stars in her eyes. She couldn't hear anything but the ship being torn apart. Was Tom alive or like Chuck, was he lying there, dead? A muttered curse blistered the dark, making Jules breathe a sigh of relief. The shuttle rolled onto its side where the abuse proved too much for the windshield. The crack raced across the glass and spidered out as their movement changed again.

"We're sliding!" Tom's voice was a beacon in the dark. They were, indeed, sliding downward on Jules's side. Metal screamed in the darkness, as if the ship was finally realizing the trouble they were in.

Suddenly, they crashed against something that halted their momentum so violently Jules wasn't even sure if they'd actually stopped or were falling. Minutes ticked by before she realized that they were upright; a soft light was coming through the windshield and that noise rushing in her ears was silence.

"T—" Her voice cracked. "Tom?"

"Fuck me." Yep, he was fine.

"Later." As sunlight filtered into the shuttle once more, Jules heard Tom hit the release on his harness. She followed suit and rose to unsteady legs.

As a kid, Tom Merrick had adored roller coasters. The loop-de-loops, the ones that spun like centrifuges and even that poofter tea-cup one. Now, swear on the Queen's knickers, if someone brought up building one, he was gonna shoot the bastard.

"SITREP!" he yelled before he was even out of the chair. Jules was getting to her feet, thank god, and looked to be still in one piece. No missing parts or new openings.

"DOCTOR HALL!!! Mayday, get over here!!"

Jules met Tom's gaze and they turned as one another before running towards the passenger compartment.

XI

Damage Control

"Oh my God, they're magnificent!"

Luke barely glanced at Tammy, who was facing the observation window instead of being parked in her seat beside him and strapped in. "That's not the word I'd use," he muttered. Twisting in his seat, he could stare at the creatures with the rest of the scientists and Sharks. He couldn't blame her for goggling like a schoolgirl. For someone in her field, the massive beasts had to be a dream come true.

"Look at them," Hanae, who was the same from her seat, added. "They're like the moray eels on Earth."

Luke wasn't so sure about that. While it did appear that they were generating the electricity driving the storm, they were much larger than any moray eel he'd ever seen. More like the size of blue whales.

"It's not so surprising," Tammy eyes were still glued to the window. "With an environment this ionised, it would make sense the life forms evolving here would generate a higher than normal electrical field. On Earth, it presents in marsupials and insects."

"Like the Skewers," Hanae remarked.

"Skewers?" Luke glanced back at the oceanographer.

"That's what Major Merrick called the bovine-like creatures we discovered at the river," she explained, making 'horns' at her forehead with both forefingers.

Of course, he would. Luke resisted rolling his eyes and went back to staring at the new lifeforms.

With the beasts mostly keeping to themselves and the Gunny calling out the closing distance, Tammy didn't think the *Firefly* and its occupants were in any immediate danger. Having observed lions and other animal groups in the wild, she was confident in her ability to read a situation, regardless of whether the animal was a lion or an overgrown lobster.

Suddenly, the ship vibrated and hummed in a flash of blue light. Luke sat up straight. "That was a lightning strike," he told his brother as Olivia entered the passenger compartment.

"Great." Fan-fucking-tastic. "I want everyone strapped in, NOW," he ordered, glancing towards the expedition leader who had moved to the window beside Tammy. "Including you, Dr. Hall," he said in a more respectful tone.

Grumbles of disappointment met his command, at least until the next energy surge hit. It was a good reminder and lit a fire under any stragglers. Around him, harnesses snapped into place audibly as Ozzy and Jazz walked up the rows to conduct a quick check. After a few moments, both men informed the Gunny everyone was packed in before heading back to their seats.

As Ozzy walked by the observation window, he glanced out of it and stopped. "Uhh… Gunny?" he called out, waving the man over. "We got two of the creatures on approach."

"What?" Tammy loosened the chest strap of her harness, so she could look behind her, ignoring the Gunny's demand she sits back down. Sure enough, two of the flying behemoths had broken off from the pod and were now approaching the shuttle. Light pulsed through their blue-green carapaces, turning them a deep purple as their long tails swished from side to side, not unlike agitated, or pissed off lions.

"Olivia! I think we might be in trouble."

Popping her harness, Olivia slipped out of the straps, ignoring the Sharks' protests and moved to the window. While Tammy was an exobiologist, Olivia had anthropology and zoology degrees.

"Oh hell," she muttered, within a second of reaching the window and realizing the younger woman's intuition was on target. "They might have interpreted our ability to take a hit as a threat," she began, turning for the cockpit. "We need to get out of here NOW."

"BRACE!" Someone yelled, a second before the ship was hit so hard, it was lifted off its landing struts and slammed back to the ground. The few people on their feet when the hit occurred were tossed across the deck.

"I got you!" Simply reacting, Luke grabbed Tammy first, a brotherly instinct making her his priority. Ozzy tumbled back into the boots of the row across from him with a yelp and Olivia disappeared out of his vision. Swearing, Luke dug his fingers into Tammy's arm to pull her back into the seat beside him.

The next hit came from the other side and all but tossed Tammy back into her seat. With Luke's help, she scrambled to get her harness secured. "Where's Olivia!"

Looking up, Luke felt panic stab at his chest. There was no sign of Olivia. Across from him, two Sharks had a dazed-looking Ozzy by his body armour and were strong arming him into a seat, but there was no sign of the expedition leader.

Another strike sent any thought out of Luke's head as the shuttle was flipped and tossed like a child's toy. With nearly neck-breaking movements, the 80-foot-long shuttle was thrown from end to end and rolled over like a cat's toy. Everything and anything that wasn't secured or bolted down became projectiles in the topsy-turvy tumble, raining down on their heads one moment and then pelting them from all directions as they were rolled again and again.

The fourth hit took out the lights, setting off several curses and a couple of screams. The stinging odour of burnt electronics hit his nose a second before hissing and popping sparks lit the air somewhere to his left. At some point in the last six months, a very bored Luke had memorized the entire manual to one of these ships. The panel that just went housed the main communications transceiver. Shit.

As the ship slammed into the ground once more, Luke realized the entire ship was being crushed. In the intermittent light, he could see places where the bulkheads were bowed in and parts of the roll-cage struts had buckled. Calculations regarding foot pounds of pressure needed to do such damage rolled through his head like a ticker stream, as did the numbers stating just how much more the ship could take. He *really* wished he hadn't read that damn manual.

There was another sizzling, crackling sound as a bluish light lit the compartment. Luke didn't need Andropolis's shout of 'Ball lightning!!' to know what it was. "EVERYONE BOTH FEET FLAT ON THE DECK!" he yelled as another roundish ball popped through a bulkhead and shot across to the other side.

The ship rolled once more, shaking their very bones as it was slammed into the ground. When they began moving again, Luke recognized a change in the pattern of movement just as he heard Tom's distant shout that they were sliding.

After what seemed like forever, the ship's slide came to a sudden, abrupt stop. Around him, people were swearing or crying. Or throwing up. Gross.

"Derick!" Luke called in the darkness.

"I'm here! You okay?"

"Yeah!" The only other time he came this close to fainting was when he first found out Bigfoot was alive and only a ship or two away. "Olivia!" Luke called out, over top of the Major's demand for a SITREP. He didn't answer, figuring Tom or his brother wouldn't be appreciative of him stating the obvious. Instead, he let Derick answer it.

"Can someone see Dr. Hall?!" he called out. They hadn't moved in a good two minutes and he could hear harnesses being released. Most likely, the Sharks, since Derick was ordering the squints to stay put. A light flared to life and was followed by a handful more beams piercing the dark amidst cries of protest.

"Dr. Hall! Mayday, get over here!"

"You found her!" Tammy undid her harness, but Luke held her back. He recognized the voice, it belonged to the comtech, Shiny, but her calling for the medic couldn't mean anything good, nor were the shouts for help to 'get this shit off her!'

"Tams, stay put," he warned as the Captain and the Major came in, looking just as tossed and addled as the rest of them. His brother called them over to Shiny's location. "I'll go see."

"But..." Tammy glared at him and huffed back against the bulkhead.

Silencing her with a look, Luke unfastened his harness and got to his feet. Picking and stepping his way over the equipment and various instrument cases littering the floor, he stopped when Derick's shoulders sagged, and Jules covered her mouth. In that moment, Luke knew. Olivia was gone.

He didn't have to see Olivia's head turned at an unnatural angle or Shiny respectfully closing the woman's eyes. He didn't need to smell the release of death from her body. The woman had taken a chance on him after the destruction of Sol, giving him purpose during those dark months when he thought everyone he loved was dead and gone. She'd scoured the survivor lists when he was crushed in the depths of despair and delivered the good news his brother was a confirmed survivor on board the *Rutherford.*

Jesus, she was gone! Luke stumbled back towards Tammy, who was shaking her head as tears leaked from her eyes.

"No. No!" The young woman's lower lip trembled, the facade of strength shattering when Hanae threw her arms around her to share her grief. Reclaiming his seat, he pulled both women to him as word spread through the expedition team.

* * *

"Jules, look at me."

A hand touched her chin gently, pulling Jules's gaze away from the body of Dr. Hall. She stared at Tom, shaking her head. "I-I should have taken off," she nodded. "I should have..."

Tom glanced around them and even though no one seemed to be paying attention to Jules, he didn't want them to see her like this. Not when she had an uphill battle anyway as the replacement Captain to the *Rutherford.*

"C'mon," he said, taking the liberty with the woman to slide his arm around her waist. "This way."

Tom led her through the aisle towards the cockpit, but it wasn't easy. Tangles of wire and conduits clawed at them from the ceiling and the walls like brambles. Once in private, he lifted her chin again to get those beautiful eyes to look at him.

"Jules, luv. Listen to me. I need the *Firefly's* status. I need to know if we can fly."

"I should have taken off," she whispered more to herself than to him. "I should have just gotten us out of here and circled back when the storm was over."

The profound regret in her voice was something Tom recognised all too well. Hadn't he been drinking himself into a stupor since they'd left Sol to avoid his own demons?

"Jules," he squeezed her shoulder. "You couldn't have known this was going to happen and it was a good call."

Jules looked up, hardness seeping into her normally warm brown eyes. His words were kind, but she couldn't absolve herself. Not yet. "Maybe, but when I saw those damn things, I should have left. It was too much of a gamble they wouldn't attack. I shouldn't have risked it."

"You made a decision..."

"And it was wrong!"

"You couldn't have known," Tom's voice was firm, now planting both hands on her shoulders. "Bugger it, neither of us saw it coming. Look, there'll be time enough for us to think about where we went wrong, but right now, we need to know if the hopper can fly. You're the only one who can do that and, however bloody bad it is, we'll manage. I trust you."

Closing her eyes, Jules inhaled deeply, letting it out and nodded. Later, she'd examine how much his trust in her at this crucial moment meant but he was right. Rubbing her face, Jules sniffed and considered his question.

"Right now, no. Even if the hull is intact and airtight and we can repair the windscreen and the windows, I need to inventory the systems that are offline and see if they can be repaired. I'll need someone who can do that…"

"Luke Rickman," Tom volunteered without hesitation. "Luke's your bloke. The kid's a genius, I swear on the Queen's knickers."

A snort escaped Jules before she realized it. "You have a fascination with a dead woman's underpants, you know that?"

"Safest place in the universe," Tom quipped back as if it were a no brainer.

Rolling her eyes, Jules gave him a gentle push. "Then send him up to me. I've got to get started. Tom?" When he turned back to face her, she gave him a sad smile. "Thanks."

"For what?" Tom winked before turning away to head back to the others. When it was all said and done, when everyone was safe, he'd make sure Dr. Hall was remembered like the top bird she was.

Right now, he had to make sure they didn't end up just as dead.

* * *

"Thank God, you crazy woman," Maya told the unconscious but relatively unaffected Ren Richards as she shoved a cabinet away from the side of the medical bed. She'd left Gunny to handle moving Dr. Hall's body, with a promise that she would let him know how Ren fared. The redhead was sporting a few new cuts and maybe a slightly scrambled brain (who the hell didn't after that ride), but she was breathing and still secured tightly to the bed.

Too bad Maya couldn't say the same for her Med Station. Almost all the cabinets had fallen open and the once neatly stowed supplies were now strewn all over the 12 foot by 12-foot space. Only the cabinet reinforced with a lock remained intact, save for the dent made by the office chair. Bloody hell, there were even loose Band-Aids tangled in Ren's hair.

Brushing those away quickly, Maya checked the IV in the crook of Ren's arm. Her tape job had held and there was no blood backing up the tube, even though the bag was dumped on the floor. Scooping it up, Maya carefully unkinked the line and draped it over a monitor mounted to the wall. That would have to do until she could get back and sort out the mess.

Her medical bag wasn't where she'd left it, but Maya found it easily enough. She threw the strap over her shoulder, glanced at Ren once more and headed for the door, stopping short when the Major himself appeared. He looked no worse than he usually did.

"Major."

Aware that Derick was busy sorting out the clusterfuck their mission had become in the last ten minutes, Tom took a moment to stop by the Med Station on his behalf. Not that Derick was the only one who would want to check on Richards and Mayday. The young medic was soldiering on in the best tradition of the British Army, even though the raw wound of her personal loss was given almost no time to scab over.

"You both all right?"

He was not surprised to find Ren mostly sorted; Mayday wouldn't have permitted otherwise. But right now, his question was more for the medic, even though he was trying to be subtle about it.

Despite surviving the destruction of Earth, swimming at the bottom of a bottle, Tom had sobered enough to realise being a squad commander required a whole different set of skills. He wasn't just their Major. For some, he was the unofficial patriarch of their fucked-up family. While his own dad was no prize, he'd served with many good officers who knew how to straddle the line between commander and mentor with success.

"The corporal is still good," Maya replied, checking her pack so she could claim ignorance of her CO's subtle question. Of course, he would know about her relationship with Colin. Anyone would be hard pressed not to, considering they'd lived in each other's faces for the last six months. She just wasn't ready to answer questions about whether she was fine. In Maya's eyes, she didn't have a choice. She had a body and injured needing her. Shouldering her pack, she turned to face him, the epitome of a British stiff upper lip. "If you'll excuse me, sir, Sergeant Jackson is triaging for me. I need to see the injured."

"Off with you then," he respected her choice to say nothing which meant the hurt was bone deep. "Oy Lance Jack?"

"Sir?" She stopped on her way past him, fingers tight on the strap of her pack.

"Good job."

In the face of her loss, he admired her ability to focus on the job and even if it was too awkward to say out loud, he hoped the simple compliment did the trick instead.

Two small words, but Maya had needed to hear them. The corner of her mouth flickered, a ghost of the mischievous, outgoing personality. "Thank you, sir." She nodded once before heading out of the Med Station to get on with things. There was no choice, no option for her or the other expedition members.

XII

Reconnaissance

From the inside, the *Firefly* seemed to have withstood the worst of the assault. From the outside, the three Sharks assessing the damage were having trouble believing they were all still alive.

Rain beat against them, soaking their uniforms as they braced each other against the wind, gawking at the battered ship in a mixture of fascination and horror. Occasionally, one would glance at the other two to make sure this wasn't a fucked-up dream. Considering the thrashed ship was their only source of solid shelter at this moment, their anxiety was understandable.

The *Firefly* had settled on its belly, up against a group of young trees now mostly devastated. Its gun-metal grey hull was covered from stern to bow with massive dents, some so severe the metal had creased or been ripped open altogether. A six-foot gash laid her port side open, exposing the interior insulation and shielding, while mud caked around the long tear and in the portals and vents all around the ship.

The Sharks stood in deep furrows of thick, dark mud created by the ship, in front and behind them, beginning from the top of the hill they descended. The hillside was shredded, with destroyed and crushed trees, plants crushed to pulp and exposed rocks that still tumbled down past them every so often.

"Fuck."

Jag threw a sidelong glance at Ozzy who was wiping water out of his eyes with his forearm. "No kidding," he agreed, trying to ignore the wind that howled like a banshee around the downed carrier. "How far are we from the landing site?"

Shiny unhooked her tab and studied the device. She swiped water off the screen before answering. "According to this, we're eight hundred meters away from the nearest transponder."

"I can believe it," Jag followed the hill's incline from their position to the top and estimated its length made that number entirely feasible.

Ozzy trudged around the end of the ship and froze, his curses at the mud sucking his boots going quiet. "Fuck me, we were lucky."

"What do you mean?" Jag exchanged a glance with Shiny before joining him.

"Oh my God!" Shiny gasped, her stomach bottoming out as she joined Ozzy where he stood on the muddy edge of a cliff and the massive gorge the drone sweeps had found. She aimed her slate at it and tapped the screen. "Dear God, that thing is over three thousand feet deep," she said, just above a whisper.

Beside her, Ozzy swallowed audibly, and Jag swore in Hebrew. A boulder-filled, white-water river was at the bottom, swirling high and fast in the rain. If the ship hadn't ground to a stop and had covered another six meters, they would have gone over and there would have been no survivors.

"Look." Jag touched Shiny's arm and then Ozzy's, pulling their attention from the Death River of Doom to the massive felled tree that spanned the gorge. As big around as the *Firefly*, it was an ancient sentinel that made Jag feel very small. Lichens and moss covered the dull, lifeless bark, while mud caked around the ragged base, solidifying its metamorphosis into a makeshift bridge.

Their eyes followed the tree trunk to the other side, where the jungle seemed wild and alive. Thick, ropey vines spiraled out of more massive trees, each of them bearing a thick canopy of leaves and branches. Waist-high underbrush covered the ground between the trees and, even in the rain, they could make out insects and small avians and even frog-like creatures jumping in the muddy puddles created by the rain.

"Report."

All three jumped slightly and Jag quickly answered the Gunny's demand as he led the way back from the edge. "We're stopped at the edge of a hill just before a three-thousand-foot drop. It looks stable for now but recommend we evac everyone to safer ground once we've conducted our sweep, Gunny. There's a big tree bridging the drop with more jungle. Permission to make a sweep."

"Negative," Derick's voice returned. "Hold position. We're joining you."

Jag's shoulders sagged, disappointed because he wanted to see what was on the other side of the bridge.

"Yes, Gunny." He shrugged at Ozzy and Shiny when a nearby rustle of underbrush made all three Sharks go for their guns. Watching the plants shimmy slightly, no one said a word as they readied their blast rifles. There was another shake, spraying raindrops off the leaves.

"Shiny?" Jag hissed, missing Ren and Mayday suddenly.

Studying her tab, Shiny shook her head, "It's a lifeform..."

"Well, yeah, but good or bad?" Ozzy wanted clarification, his eyes not leaving the shuddering underbrush. "Like the kind that just thrashed our ship?"

"I was get..."

"Look," Jag whispered, silencing them both.

A snout poked out of the dull green leaves, sniffing at the air before the rest of it came forward, trundling out of the bush. No more than two feet tall, the quadruped was covered in soft spines resembling hair. Jag was reminded of a wombat, except this thing had floppy ears like a rabbit and small, almond shape eyes. It shuffled towards them, still sniffing, head turning side to side to study them.

Ozzy stiffened in reaction, hands tightening on his rifle.

"Hold your fire, Oz!" Jag hissed at his fellow Shark, not wanting to spook the creature. "It doesn't know what we are."

"The small, cute things are always the deadliest!" Ozzy retorted under his breath, half-frozen as he tried to track the creature's progress.

"You watch too many movies!"

"You don't wa…"

"Oy! Frick and Frack, shut it!" Shiny ordered, her voice just as hissed and quiet as theirs. She didn't move much, just shot them both a hairy eye they'd best not ignore. Carefully turning back, Shiny watched as the creature shuffled towards her first, the blunt snout snuffling at her boot. Curious but cautious, the creature chuffed at her pants leg before looking up with grey eyes and barked.

Naf!

"Oh, that's a weird bark," Shiny grinned and glanced at her comrades. "It's kind of cute though."

"You can't keep it," Ozzy rolled his eyes. What was it with women and cute, fuzzy things? "It could be…"

Ignoring him, Shiny bent down slowly and stretched her hand out, offering her fingertips for the creature to smell. When it didn't move away, she gently rubbed her fingers across the top of its head. Its floppy ears stood up straight and the spines along its back changed colour from its dull green, to a bright amber.

"Oh wow, it's like a chameleon!" Shiny exclaimed, her voice sounding almost girlish.

Naf! Naf!

Jag looked up from the creature to see three more emerge from the undergrowth. One was almost the same size as the first while the other two were much smaller, with shorter ears. Cubs? Jag decided and was glad Ren and Mayday weren't here. No doubt, both women would have adopted the things by now. When Shiny cooed over the approaching babies, Jag smiled faintly to himself. It would seem their tough as nails comtech was no better.

"Whatever you do, Shiny, don't feed it," Ozzy told her with a frown.

"Too late." Shiny held up a ration bar she'd quietly removed from her pack. Tearing open the foil, she tore off a bit and offered it up. "Ignore him, he's a city boy," she teased gently as the creature sniffed at the food suspiciously. Cautiously, the small beast opened a mouth full of teeth and nibbled the bite out of her fingers. Shiny removed the wrapper from the bar entirely and laid it on the ground. "There you go." The creature promptly snatched the whole bar and trundled back to its family.

"They're hungry," Jag observed, watching the two small cubs fall ravenously on the ration bar first. He was digging a bar out of his own pack when pieces of an unwrapped bar landed on the ground near the first one. When he looked up, Ozzy was stuffing an empty wrapper into a pocket.

"What?"

"Nothing," Jag grinned, stowing the bar he'd been about to offer and turned his gaze back to the creatures and the occasional 'Naf!' At least some lifeforms on this planet were friendly, he thought with a sigh.

* * *

The discovery of apparently friendly creatures did nothing to lessen the blow of Olivia's death.

The scientists who worked with her daily, who knew her personally and shared friendships spanning years, were devastated. After all the wounds suffered since Earth's destruction, this one seemed the unkindest cut of all. While the Sharks did not share the same connection to her as the squints in their charge, they knew the doctor from reputation. She was a celebrated planetologist who embodied the pioneering spirit.

Derick saw to Olivia's body, sealing her away in a body bag until such time when she could be properly buried. He'd only known the woman a short time, but her death affected him because it affected his brother. Of the three of them, Luke always had a welcoming smile and a contagious, ready-to-fire laugh. That was one of his first memories of the happy baby Luke had been. Securing Olivia for now, Derick made a quick trip to the Med Station to check on Ren and then headed outside, to join Tom and Jules.

"You think she could still fly, Captain?"

Jules propped her hands on her hips, studying the ship. "I could lift off but we're talking atmo only and short trips. She's not space worthy," she said, shaking her head as one hand indicated the long gash in the *Firefly's* side. "And that's only if we're able to get the stabilizers and thrusters back online."

"We got a lot of smart squints here," Tom gestured to the group being led out of the damaged ship by Sarge and the rest of his Sharks. "We could seal the breaches, scavenge the inside of the ship for bits."

"We'd need a laser welder," Jules told him by way of answering. "And if we can't neg-press the inside..."

"Neg-press?" Derick ventured, glancing at Tom.

"Negatively pressurize the interior so we don't implode when we hit space." Jules looked up at Tom. "Don't get me wrong, the ship could possibly be repaired, but we'd need the equipment and the people. The Squ...scientists are mostly from the biological sciences. Aside from Luke, there's not one engineer among them. I told the Fleet we'd check in, in 24 hours because of the ionisation in the atmosphere. If we don't, they'll know something's up."

"Twenty-four hours when?" Derick prompted, glancing at the matte grey combat watch he wore on one wrist.

Jules frowned and pulled her tab out of a cargo pocket. "That was... Wow. That was six hours ago. That gives us another eighteen before they realize something's wrong. Assuming the *Olympia* Sharks are ready to go, and they can launch immediately, that's another hour and a half. Almost a day before we get support. We need to get comms up," she said.

Glancing at her, Tom was about to say something when an idea popped into his head. Looking towards the disembarking squints, he spied the man he was looking for, helping the librarian-cute squint off the ramp. "Oy Luke, get over here!"

When the younger Rickman joined them, Tom noticed he'd lost his usual cocky swagger. Olivia's death must have hit him hard as well, but the kid was made of strong stuff, just like his brother. He made a mental note to have a chat with Luke when he could, just as he had with Maya.

"Yeah what's up? Can I help? Although," Luke let out a low whistle as he surveyed the gash in the hull. "If you want me to fix this, I think you're overestimating my abilities."

"No, no," Tom shook his head and crossed his arms over his broad chest. "Those transponders we use to establish a perimeter, can you rig them up to boost a transmission to reach the fleet?"

Jules snapped her gaze to Tom. Colour her impressed. Even if execution wasn't possible, the idea had merit.

Tom caught the look and winked. "Not just a pretty face, Captain."

"Or a bald one," Jules retorted with a soft chuckle and smiled at Luke. "Can you do it, Mr Rickman?"

Luke exchanged a sarcastic glance with his brother at the two officers getting their flirt on before setting his mind to the question asked of him.

"Yeah, it's doable. We'd have to wait until the storm passes completely. All that electricity in the air might harm the signal more than anything else. If we can get enough of them, I say let's give it a try and just call me Luke."

"Or Baby Brother," Derick grinned, not flinching away from the punch Luke landed on his shoulder. "We're going to have to go back up there and get those transponders."

"You think you can take a squad and go get them?" Tom framed the order in a suggestion, a habit he'd formed since Derick and he started serving together.

"No problem," the Gunny said confidently. "Just give me ten minutes to unpack my party dress."

"He loves silk underwear too," Luke nodded at Jules, making her smile. "I can look at the communications array while he's doing that, make sure it didn't sustain any serious damage. You want me to make that my priority instead of the support systems?" It was the exact thing he needed to get his mind off Olivia.

"Yes, thank you." Jules was sincerely grateful for his help. They hadn't needed an engineer for this mission, so Luke's presence was an unexpected bonus. Considering their present circumstances, Jules suspected it could now mean the difference between life and death.

A massive cracking noise rent the air as something wooden gave way and the *Firefly* shuddered before settling with a heavy boom that reverberated through their boots. Squints and Sharks scrambled away from the ship as it shifted and finally came to rest with another ear-piercing crack.

"Jesus Christ!" Tom stared at the craft. "I thought that bloody thing was going to go! Sarge!" he bellowed at Jazz and indicated a clear spot about thirty feet away. Should something else give and they started to lose the *Firefly*, at least no one would be in its way. "Rally everyone over there!"

"Yessir!" Jazz hollered back. Not missing a beat, he started issuing orders for the Sharks and the squints to muster in the indicated spot.

"We can't stay here," Tom stated the obvious.

"No kidding," Derick ran a hand over his shortly cropped hair.

"Yeah, with the weight of the ship, all that rain we just got…" Luke dug his boot into the soft earth beneath him and drove the tip in, testing the soil compaction. He stared back up the hill, where small stones were tumbling loose. "If we get some heat, the earth might harden enough to hold the hopper in place…"

Jules glanced at the sky and then her slate. "Sun down is in four hours. I don't think we can count on that."

"And if it rains again, we'll be right and properly buggered," Tom finished off, following Luke's gaze up the destroyed hill.

"That's about the size of it," Luke shrugged.

If there was a landslide, not even that enormous tree bridge was going to keep the ship from tumbling into the chasm.

"We can't stay here," Tom said finally, noting Jules shaking her head in agreement. Good, one less argument. "Right, then. Gunny, get moving on those transponders."

"I'm already gone," Derick nodded to Luke before heading off towards Jazz and the others.

"Check out the communications array before he gets back," Tom told Luke. "You feel so much as a twinge from the ship, you're out of, there right?"

"Trust me, I'll be running out shit scared and that will be fast."

"Good. Anything happens to you; the big bloke will never let me forget it." And that was if Derick let Tom live.

"What do you have in mind?" Jules asked, narrowed eyes studying the Shark Major. He had a plan and she was pretty certain it involved going for a hike.

"I'm going to take a scouting party and see what's over that bridge," Tom gestured to the jungle on the other side of the chasm. "Our maps say there are mountains in that direction, we might find caves or someplace better to shelter for the night."

"In there?" Jules stared at the dense woods that reminded her of a Middle Earth setting. Or a Godzilla flick.

"We can't stay out here in the open, Jules. This planet is full of beasties and I'd rather be undercover when night comes."

Remembering it was his call while they were planet side, Jules was grateful he tried to include her on the decision-making process, unlike too many others she'd crossed paths with. "Fine. I'm coming with you."

Tom's eyebrows ratcheted skyward and he shook his head. "Negative. Not a good idea and the squints..."

"Have your sergeant to keep an eye on them," Jules met his gaze with her dark one, as if daring him to deny her.

Derick was missing this, Luke chuckled to himself as he took a step back, not wanting to be in the line of sight of either officer.

"No."

"Yes."

"It could be miles of hiking through dense—"

"I'm going." Jules's head swivelled back on her neck defiantly.

"Fine! Be ready to go in fifteen minutes!" Tom fired at her, wondering if she was going to win all their arguments. Oy, he couldn't think about that. She was the Captain right now, he reminded himself, and not for shagging. Not. For. Shagging. "Bloody bossy women," he grumbled at Luke as he stalked past. "Go on, show's over."

Nope, Jules snarked to herself. Definitely NOT Prince Charming.

XIII

Jungle Trek

When Tom insisted Jules wear a borrowed pair of combat boots from one of his Sharks before they began their trek through the jungle, she balked at the suggestion. After all, it wasn't as if she were wearing high heels but rather flight approved combat boots. The Space Corps pilot she was railed at the notion of surrendering any part of her uniform to the prejudices of ground pounders even if the advice seemed reasonable enough.

His expression at the suggestion she keep her own footwear was so infuriating, she almost decked him on principle.

"If you want to go trekking through that jungle, you're going to wear proper boots instead of those ballet slippers you Fleeters wear. We've got no bloody idea what's in there and a jungle that thick will be crawling with nasties that will have no trouble sneaking into those boots of yours."

The notion of anything crawling into her boot won his argument.

An hour later, she was secretly grateful she yielded the point because he was right, (she sure as hell wasn't going to tell him that). The jungle they were currently trudging through resembled the ones she'd seen in documentaries about the Amazon Basin or the thick rainforests of Australia. From the other side of *Firefly* Bridge, (what they'd end up calling the huge tree bridge), it seemed ominous and foreboding.

Now, in the thick of it, Jules felt smothered and downright spooked.

Around them, the forest was in various stages of growth. Small, young saplings grew in the spots of sunlight that speared through the overhead canopy, fighting for space among bushes, brambles and various vines and ivies. Some of the trees were massive, even larger than the behemoth across the gorge. From their splayed branches, thick, ropey vines dangled haphazardly, creating a web-like lattice-work overhead. Others were wrapped tightly around the wide trunks, clinging to the bark like desperate lovers. Some dug into the soft, moist earth, looking like moorings holding the giant titans to the ground.

Among the overload of green were bright, vibrant spots of colour. Here and there, creepers encased downed logs in velvet shades of lavender and red. Insects flitted about, sunlight reflecting off metallic wings. Small creatures skittered about, freezing in place as Jules snapped pictures on her slate. Big, round eyes tracked their progress as things hopped and slithered around them. There was still more to see; butterflies with gossamer wings, snake-like creatures with delicate, translucent limbs that looked like they were hovering. Were they venomous? Did they bite? She didn't know but she catalogued each one with a few photos for the scientists.

For the first time since the Exodus, Jules remembered what it was like to live and not just survive. This forest was life. Struck by the moment, she inhaled deeply and let it out to steady a sudden bout of sadness. Did humanity deserve such a second chance? After what they'd done to Earth?

Even before the planet was destroyed, she was a ravaged victim of industry and technology. They hadn't learned their lesson when the Mississippi became too polluted to fish or when the Appalachians had been strip-mined of all their natural resources. If Gaia was to be their home, they simply had to do better this time.

When Jules went quiet, Tom glanced back to check on her, dragging his forearm across his forehead. With Ozzy and Shiny busy with a contour map, he stole the moment to admire Jules's profile as she aimed her slate at another creature. He wished he knew what she was thinking, because he couldn't remember the last time he'd been so in awe of anything.

The leaves near him shuddered and a twig snapped, prompting Tom to use a hand signal for silence. Everyone froze, at least until the snout poked out of the underbrush and Shiny's naf, (she liked naming things). waddled from the shadows. "Looks like we've got a mascot," Tom smirked, recognizing the animal's colouring pattern from earlier.

Grinning, Jules squatted down in front of it.

"Hello," she said as the creature's back spines faded to the same greens around them. "I know those protein bars aren't that good. Are you our scout?"

The naf regarded her momentarily and snuffled at her outstretched hand before continuing past Tom. When he was a few paces ahead, he stopped and looked back at them. "Naf!"

"Carry on!" Tom nodded, motioning the creature to continue and his team to start moving.

"I guess it likes us," Jules smirked, watching the thing's chunky little backside wiggle ahead of them.

"It hasn't learnt better yet."

Looking up at him, Jules was surprised to see amusement on his strong features. Another layer to the man, then, when his cynicism was arrested by a fuzzy little creature.

"It's a he," Shiny pointed helpfully from behind them. "I guess he thinks he's responsible for us since we've been feeding his family."

"You mean, you've been feeding his family," Ozzy quipped over his shoulder.

"They got that second bar somewhere else," Shiny retorted, craning her head around Ozzy to find the naf. "Besides, I was being friendly. We trashed their home when our ship came crashing through their forest." She raised her chin defiantly, clearly repenting nothing.

Jules couldn't argue with that. In any case, the squints were delighted by the small family. More protein bars had been offered up while they ran all kinds of non-invasive scans to learn what they could about the creature's physiology.

"Well, when we get crops going, they can have my protein bars," she said, wiping perspiration from her forehead before reaching for the water bottle hooked on her belt to take a quick sip.

"Shiny, how far away are those anomalies on the map?" Tom asked, trying to get a gauge on the distance from what he could see through the trees. Usually, such marks meant caves of some sort.

"About three kilometres, Major." She looked up from the display of her tab. "According to our topographical scan of the area earlier, we're starting uphill."

Considering that, Tom walked back to her to study the map over her shoulder. "So, we could reach them in about thirty minutes, if we push it." That would give them time to get back to the shuttle. With the path hacked out, the group would move a little faster than the scout team.

"Naf!"

The bark got everyone's attention, especially since it seemed to hold a sense of urgency in it. Not so arrogant to discount the concerns of a native, Tom watched the creature cautiously, one hand resting casually on his sidearm. The naf remained still for a few seconds, making everyone strain to hear anything other than their own heartbeats. Just when he was starting to feel foolish for taking his cues from an alien wombat, a tremor vibrated the ground beneath their boots.

"Earthquake?"

Before he could answer, the ground shuddered again and this time, Tom felt the sensation. With the others scanning the forest, the ground trembled twice more. Three times. Four. No, this wasn't an earthquake. When the fifth tremor shook the trees around him, he recognized the pattern.

Footsteps.

"There!" Jules pointed to the suddenly rustling leaves several yards ahead.

Whatever it was, it was moving in a perpendicular direction and not towards them. Tom glanced at the naf, where it was sniffing Shiny's boot. "Stay here," he said quietly and headed towards the movement to investigate.

"Naf!"

"Step to, then," Tom told the animal as it hustled to follow him. "Don't suppose you can tell me what it is, eh?" The naf snorted at him as if grumbling at the stupidity of this strange, smelly creature.

"Don't worry, mate," Tom muttered in return, silently pushing through the shrubs towards the rustling trees. "I'll bugger off if things get ugly." Nevertheless, he still clutched his blast rifle firmly as he approached.

"Major," Jules hissed after him. "You get a one-minute head start and then we're coming after you."

"Yes, dear!" Tom called back, glancing at the naf. "Your bird that bossy?"

The naf chuffed in what Tom decided was sympathy.

* * *

About two minutes after leaving the scout team, Tom quietly stepped into a clearing roughly the size of a footy field. Around him, the dirt was worn down in what was clearly a migratory path, complete with tracks and scat in the fresh mud. Kneeling, he snapped a picture of a hoof print the size of a turkey platter. Lifting his gaze, he could see tall trees stripped of bark and leaves while broken branches gave evidence of recent passage.

The naf remained in the tree line, chittering at him urgently before circling nervously and pawing the dirt. He barked again, this time at something past Tom. Swearing and hoping there wasn't a three-headed, drooling dog standing over him, he turned silently and slowly.

There was no giant dog (thank God) but he was still awestruck with the animals gathered at the far end of the field. There was at least seven of them, languidly going about their business, oblivious to the human gaping at them in amazement. Giraffes, Tom thought at first, but even he knew these willowy beauties were nothing like the now extinct species. At least five times taller than any giraffe he'd ever seen, these were covered from knee to massive skull in articulated, leathery-looking scales.

"Wow," he said, glancing back at the naf with a smile. "This what you were worried about, you big girl's blouse?"

The entire herd turned towards Tom and the largest of them stepped forward, eyeing him conspicuously as its head bobbed down towards the ground.

Suddenly, Tom realized stepping out in the open like this might not have been wise. Especially considering even the smallest of the creatures could easily flatten him. *Like Godzilla.* He took a step back and the big male, (not that he was checking out alien giraffe junk, but it *was* kind of obvious), stepped towards him.

"Fuck me," he muttered, freezing in place, eyes not leaving the massive creature taking another step towards him.

Three more steps were all it took for the creature to be close enough to lower its massive head towards him.

"Gudday..." he offered quietly, when a large eyeball studied him silently. "Don't want to hurt you mate. Oh no... you don't..." He grimaced and tried not to gag as the giant lips gummed his uniform.

"At least buy me dinner," he told it, deciding that noise he was hearing was his heart pounding in his chest. Suddenly, the massive beast snorted against him and shook its head before rising majestically and returning to its herd with the same lazy, ground-shaking steps.

With its attention no longer on him, (bloody fucking hell, he felt violated), Tom tapped his radio link. "Hey, you lot, move in on my location, and be quiet about it."

In the few moments, it took for the team to join him, Tom retreated to the tree line with the naf. The little thing sniffed at him and sneezed.

"Oh wow!" Jules breathed in delight when she joined him, her slate already out to record. Like him, her gaze was on the graceful titans, who returned to stripping branches of leaves and chewing them lazily.

"Twigas," Shiny whispered, pronouncing the word in her graceful native accent.

"Twigas?" Jules could barely take her eyes off the animals to glance at the comtech.

"That's what we called giraffes." Shiny's dark eyes glistened briefly as she swallowed away the memory of her beautiful country of Botswana.

Giving her shoulder a quick squeeze, Ozzy shook his head. "Jesus, those things… Ugh, what's that smell?" he frowned, sniffing the air.

"Who smelled it, dealt it," Tom retorted, not willing to discuss the smell or his near molestation at this moment (or at all). "All right, enough sight-seeing, let's move out. We've got a bit of ground to cover."

* * *

Returning to the trail they were cutting, they resumed their search for a viable camp site. If the transponder plan didn't work, Tom wanted someplace that would offer both sturdy shelter and easy defence. After the loss of human lives to bloody sky crabs and those plant things, Tom did not want to risk the expedition sleeping in tents in the open. He wanted something solid and non-living at his back. The *Firefly's* current unstable position made it a non-option.

As they fought for every foot of trail, Jules continued to record the journey and the wildlife. Arachnids and the remains of a large web gave her the willies. All kinds of insects darted about and lizards with long, translucent tails paused to watch them pass.

A very distinct call caught Jules's attention, sounding above the surrounding symphony of bird trills and insect buzzing. Looking up into the canopy and trying not to trip, Jules finally spotted the source. Russet-coloured primates, about the size of capuchin monkeys congregated in the high branches. At first, Jules was relieved to see something sort of normal-looking, until one of the creatures jumped off its high branch and unfurled leathery wings to soar underneath the forest top.

"Flying monkeys," she told Shiny, who shook her head.

"Bat Mites."

"You are not allowed to name anything. At all. Ever," Ozzy started.

How did Tom stand it? "How much further are we going?" Jules called up to the Major, to distract herself from the banter. She swiped sweat off her face as Ozzy moved forward to take over cutting the trail. Despite being in good shape, Jules knew she would be feeling this hike for the next two days. Not that she'd say anything. For all she knew, the Sharks ran through the ship every day and were used to this.

"Shiny?" Tom motioned for her to come to him with the map.

Shiny glanced at her slate, studying the readings on the display for a few seconds before raising her chin to study the landscape and get her bearings. "We just crossed this creek, here," she said, tapping the screen. "There's a slope in front of us and the caves should be close by."

Taking a drag off his water bottle, Tom nodded and clipped it back to his belt. "Let's push on then," he said, motioning them forward. If the caves proved habitable, they'd have enough time to return to the *Firefly* and get everyone under shelter.

"Major," Ozzy said over his shoulder as he hacked away a vine. "What happens when we get back to the fleet? I mean, it's not like we got anywhere else to go and the rest of the planet might be as dangerous as this."

Tom glanced at Jules and shrugged, having no answer himself to the question. In truth, it didn't matter how dangerous the Babel site was, humanity was here to stay. The logistics of colonisation, however, were beyond him.

"I can't speak for the Council," Jules answered the young Shark. "I can tell you that if Babel isn't appropriate, then we'll have to find another landing site, somewhere temporary until we find a permanent location and prepare it for colonisation. Our resources have been stretched out as far as we can manage. We'll last maybe another month before we start running out of things."

Ozzy's face showed his horror at the thought. Hell, monitoring the ration handouts made the entire squad antsy. If rations were cut again, things were going to get ugly.

"I think Babel is fine," Shiny spoke up. "No place is going to be perfect. We're in an alien ecosystem and no matter how much we'd like to respect the terrain we're colonising, we're going to have to break some eggs to make the omelette."

"I'm more worried about the eggs dying," Ozzy muttered under his breath as he shook out the hand holding the machete. "Cramping up."

Tom motioned him back and slid easily to point. "Don't talk about eggs. I'd give up my first born for a bit of eggs on toast because that powdered stuff is shit," he grumbled, just as he realized the undergrowth ahead was thinning out. Thank Christ, he thought quietly. Despite sharing the duty, blazing a trail was hard work and his arms could do with a rest.

"Right there with you. I miss fresh juice," Jules sighed. Once again, fresh produce was simply impractical when space was at a premium. Like Tom's eggs, Jules's juice was of the powdered variety.

A breeze reached them through the spaced trees, making Jules sigh in the relief it brought. The trees had changed here, resembling delicate eucalyptus instead of redwoods. Through a gap ahead, she could make out tall grass swaying gently with the breeze.

When Tom pushed ahead, Jules hung back to grab her own water bottle. Shiny was right, she decided. The Babel site wasn't perfect but, then again, they didn't have a choice. She had a feeling most people wouldn't mind though, once they got off the ships and got busy with building the colony. With the ground underneath and the sky overhead, instead of everything grey, they'd feel better and more inclined to overcome the obstacles facing them, so they could stay. So, they could make a home.

"Jesus Christ."

Jules snapped out of her ruminations, frowning. She could just see Tom ahead, head canted so he was looking down. Glancing at the others, she pushed out of the brush to join him at the edge of a cliff. "What is it?" she asked, noting that Tom seemed frozen in place, his blast rifle hanging from one hand and the machete from the other. Between his feet, the naf had crouched down on its haunches, staring ahead.

He didn't answer so she followed his gaze across the valley yawning in front of them. Covered in more greenery, the land was cut through by an enormous river. Much larger than the one at the Babel site, this one hadn't seen the recent effects of a storm. Halfway through the valley, Jules could see the river dropping in subtle steps to another wide, flat expanse.

However, the view wasn't what had captured the Shark Major's attention. That honour went to the abandoned, stone city perched on a tabletop of land butted up against the hill on the opposite side of the valley.

"Holy shit," Jules exclaimed, staring openly at the stone ruins that reminded her of Aztec ziggurats. One of the structures was much taller than anything else in the small city and, from here, they could see three smaller ones arranged around the large one. Long overgrown, nearly every surface was covered with moss, lichens or creeping vines, except where stones had broken loose and tumbled to the ground. A high, thick wall ringed the entire city and was just as overgrown.

"I thought… I thought no one lived here," Ozzy stammered, running a gloved hand over his face. "I mean, there wasn't any sentient life here."

"We did all the scans we could," Jules answered, having conducted some of those herself. There was no evidence of civilisation, not anywhere on the planet. Not even in this location. "We picked up plenty of life but no cities and certainly no sign of any life form sentient enough to build that," she indicating the ruins with her chin.

"Well, someone built it," Shiny said, gaping like the others at the ancient spectacle.

Pulling his binoculars out of his pack, Tom switched them to the RR setting. Reflective radiance was pretty accurate when used on stone structures. Didn't work on metal worth a shit but stone and organic material were easy. Nothing would compare to an actual sweep of the land but, for now, this would do.

"No one's home but some bugs and those walking snake things."

"Slytherins," Shiny piped up.

"Better go with Slitherings," Ozzy retorted. "To avoid copyright infringement."

Jules ignored them, exchanging a look with Tom. He seemed to be thinking the same thing she was.

If no one was home, where had they gone?

XIV

Campsite

When Ren Richards opened her eyes, there was drab olive green above her head. She blinked as sound and other sensations returned to her awareness. When a breeze brushed over her face, she turned her head towards the thin sliver of light coming through the crack in the tent flap. Fresh air, hell yes, she thought, inhaling deeply. The crisp chill invigorated her, and she breathed deeply again before lifting her head to assess her surroundings.

A medical setup explained the fog over her senses. Only drugs could produce these kinds of holes in her awareness. Memories returned, flashing into place: the attack of the Audreys, the staccato rhythm of gunfire and, finally, the pain in her leg. Immediately, her eyes travelled down her body to examine herself. A blue Med Station blanket was tucked around her and she winced trying to tug it off.

"Steady there," Maya's tired voice made Ren look around quickly to see her best friend rising from a camp chair.

"Maya? What happened?" Ren's voice cracked, and she tried to lick her lips to get some moisture.

"Things went ass over tea kettle," Maya replied, snagging a water bottle and opening the spout. "Drink this."

Taking a sip of the water, Ren lifted a hand to grab the bottle from Maya. After a good thirty seconds, her friend put a hand on the bottle to stop her.

"How are you feeling? Any pain?"

Ren didn't answer as she took a quick inventory. No, her leg wasn't hurting. Not like she remembered it. She was tired, but the disorientated feeling was gone. She wiggled her toes and stretched her leg. Her thigh and calf felt like she'd done a good workout in the gym but that was it. "No. Just feels like I overdid it with my Thigh Master."

"Good," Maya gave her a tired, tight smile as she pulled the chair closer to Ren's cot. "I fixed you up and the squints synthesized some anti-venom to counteract whatever you were dosed with."

Ren nodded and gestured to the tent. "Have we made camp?" From what she could see past the opening, it looked like a standard Shark setup for an overnight stay, with a bunch of scientists thrown in.

"Sort of," Maya told her, pulling her tab out of a pocket. "The ship is currently not considered stable," she said, pulling up photos of the damaged shuttle. "Here," she said, handing over the slate.

Ren raised an eyebrow before taking the device. She stared at the first picture for a good two minutes, not believing that battered and ravaged ruin of metal was the slick hopper they'd boarded earlier today. She'd seen the shuttles hit by ground fire and even crashed but... damn. "What the hell happened to the ship!?"

Maya sighed and ran a hand over her hair, pulling out the elastic band to let her dark hair hang down. As she combed it back, neatening it up, she relayed the entire story of the sky crabs and the storm and how the ship ended up in its current demolished state. She finished with Dr. Hall's death.

When she was done, Ren was staring at her wide eyes. "You're shitting me?"

Laughing, absent of any mirth, Maya shook her head. "Crazy as fuck, yeah?"

That was one way to put it. She was about to comment on how she kind of wished she'd been awake for it when she finally noticed that her normally boisterous friend was quiet and sedate, her shoulders hunched slightly. Shit.

"Maya?" she put a hand on Maya's own. "Colin?"

Maya glanced up before her gaze dropped again. "It was too late."

"I'm so sorry," Ren squeezed her hand tightly.

"It's bloody stupid," Maya shook her head, her free hand dashing away the tears leaking from her eyes. "I mean we didn't know each other that long, just since we'd come on board the *Rutherford.* But with everything going on, it was nice to be with someone, you know?" she whispered, having finally reached her breaking point.

Ren nodded in sympathy. She did know. With so many loved ones lost, so little hope left to go around, just being in someone's arms for an hour or even a day was something to be cherished. "I know Maya, I know."

Maya wiped her eyes hastily. "We'd only spent a few nights together and stole an hour or two when we could, but it helped. It just feels so bloody unfair, not just for Colin but for Tonie and Dr. Hall. We made it here, we survived Earth being blown to bits. Six months of being stuffed into those ships. They should have had the same chance at a new start as the rest of us!"

Trying to hide her wince, Ren pushed herself up and patted the cot beside her. When Maya joined her on the mattress, she pulled her friend into a hug and held tightly. Maya didn't resist, didn't push away or try to put up a brave face like she was a tough as nails Shark. Instead, she just held on to her friend and cried her tears.

* * *

With Derick on a mission to retrieve the transponders and Tom away on a scouting mission, Luke was trying not to think about being separated from them. Especially now, with the nocturnal orchestra of insects and critters growing louder as the light faded from the sky.

The expedition members were listless, stricken with grief, and leaderless. Luke took it upon himself to step up because no one else did. He rallied the squints, assigning them duties and tasks like his father used to do.

Within minutes, they were all busy, checking data and equipment, calibrating meters. Whatever was reported damaged, he set the squint to repairing it if possible. Most of them came out of their fog under his direction, but he'd caught the occasional glimmer of tears here and there. He didn't blame them. Olivia meant so much to him too, and it hurt not being sure if he'd ever told her.

He was arms deep in the outer access panels to the communications array when he spotted his brother picking his way down the destroyed hill with Jag and French. Thank you, Jesus.

"Derick!" Luke called, waving his brother over, stifling the urge to run to him like he had when they were little.

"Hey," Derick greeted tiredly as he surveyed the campsite a short distance from the shuttle. Emergency shelters were erected. A row of chem-lights formed a three-meter shoulder from the cliff's edge, to keep anyone from inadvertently wandering off it. Jazz had done a good job, he decided, and motioned Jag and French closer.

"You got them," Luke stated, indicating the long, cylindrical devices tucked beneath the arms of each Shark. "Are they intact?"

"Mostly," Derick nodded, holding up the one he was carrying. "This one's busted though. Got yanked out of the ground and into a tree."

Taking it, Luke leaned over to hold it under his working lights. Dents and split casing marked the device up and he frowned, looking at the two held up by the other Sharks. "Those two look fine," he noted and tapped the 'broken' one with a knuckle.

"If I can't fix it, I may be able to salvage parts from it. The array is working but the signal modulator is damaged beyond repair. It won't be a strong signal, even if we do get the transponders to boost it."

Derick nodded thoughtfully as he gestured for his guys to set the transponders down on Luke's work table. "You two report to Jazz and then take thirty," he told them.

"We did get a fire going and some actual food cooking," Luke gestured to the corner of the camp, where one of the squints was stoking the fire. "Nothing fancy but it's hot."

"Anything that's not dried ration packs will be welcome," Jag said tiredly before he and French left the two brothers alone.

Derick cuffed Luke's hair affectionately. "Are you responsible for some of this?" he asked, gesturing to the camp behind him.

Sheepishly, Luke shrugged. "I figured I'd keep them busy, keep their minds off Dr. Hall. Getting them to help your guys set up camp was what they needed. Besides, who knew Dr. Andropolis could make a pretty decent stew with our supplies?"

Derick clapped his younger brother's shoulder and squeezed, letting his pride show as he grinned. "It was a good idea Brainiac. Thanks."

Like all the Rickman boys, Luke learned to be resilient and organised from their drill sergeant of a father. Still, he had to admit, hearing the pride in Derick's voice meant more than it ever had coming from his father. "Oh, Tom radioed back. They found something."

"Something?" Derick's eyes widened. "Like what?"

"He didn't say but they shouldn't be too much longer. He said it would knock our socks off, in a good way." Luke didn't know whether he liked the sound of that. They had enough surprises for one day already.

"If he wasn't dropping f-bombs or calling for back up, then probably," Derick grinned and glanced over a shoulder. Turning back to Luke, he indicated the fire. "Have you eaten anything?" Honestly, Derick knew the answer was most likely 'no'. "Come on," he said, grabbing Luke's arm.

As they returned to the campfire, Derick spotted Maya coming out a tent, where no doubt Ren was holding court. If she was conscious. Shit, he couldn't think on that. That's what he told himself even when he changed direction to intercept Maya.

"Hi Gunny, Luke." Maya nodded to both men as they fell into step with her.

"How's Richards?" Derick wondered if anyone aside from Tom knew what a monumental effort he was making to appear concerned yet nonchalant and not go running into that damn tent.

"Awake and kicking," Maya replied, holding up her chow kit. "I was going to bring her some soup."

"I'll take it to her," Derick offered, ignoring Luke's eyebrows jacking into his hairline. Instead, he focused on Maya, whose face bore the signs of her reaction to Edwards' death.

Maya paused, glancing at the tent before relenting. "Alright," she said, handing Ren's kit over. "But don't let her eat too much. I don't want it coming back up."

"I won't."

Within a few minutes, Luke was followed by his brother to the medical tent where the big Shark paused a few feet from the door. Deciding not to be a smart ass, at least for today, Luke nudged his free arm. "So that's the girl huh?"

Derick threw his brother a frown. "Just wanted to check up on her, like anyone of my squad."

"There's nothing wrong with liking her," Luke continued, forgetting his earlier promise already. "I mean, the human race is just ten thousand people now. We're going to have to start pairing up. Survival of the species and all. Hanae was saying to create a viable gene pool, women might need to have babies from more than one..."

"For fuck sake!" Derick growled, shouldering his brother out of the way. "I'm just going to see how she is. Stop with the Noah's Ark crap. It's freaking me out!"

Luke grinned and saluted him with a wink. He felt a little closer to normal now he'd got under Derick's skin. "Don't stay up too late. I expect the car back in the garage by the time the newspaper hits the pavement," he said, echoing their deceased father.

"Bite me," Derick hissed at him, motioning Luke away from him like he was an annoying fly.

Grinning, Luke took his leave and headed back to the campfire.

* * *

Derick ducked inside the tent, stopping just inside as Ren turned towards him. Her hair was back in a loose ponytail but there was no way it was 'tamed'. He didn't think those crazy curls ever could be and God knew, he didn't want them to be. She looked tired, in need of a good sleep, but he'd take it. Anything other than unconscious in his arms, covered in blood.

"Supper in bed, Gunny?" she teased. "Not how I imagined it was going to be."

Looking down at the chow kit in his hands, Derick fought a smirk before clearing his throat. "Yeah. Maya said you were awake and hungry," he winced inwardly. Had he just stood there, staring at her like some idiot? He stepped forward, setting his load down on the small table next to the cot and claimed the empty chair. "Dr. Andropolis made it. I can't guarantee it's edible," he smirked, getting comfortable.

Giving her a minute to dig in, Derick went to work on his own food. "Glad to see you're okay, Richards."

"Yeah," Ren agreed and leaned forward, running her hand across the blanket covering her leg. "Thank God for modern technology."

Blowing on her stew, she let the silence sit between them, at least until it turned awkward. Gunny was uncharacteristically not talking. She hadn't imagined the begging and what might have been a kiss on her temple. At least, she thought it was a kiss. She remembered only a few seconds of lucidity before the Audrey toxin dragged her into blackness. The worry she'd seen wasn't imagined then and even now it lingered.

"Mayday says we're stuck out here all night?" she asked, trying to break the silence. They'd always danced around flirtation, taking digs at each other and teasing. Anything more, i.e. Derick begging her to 'stay with me, baby', was uncharted territory. There were strict regulations for fraternisation in the ranks. Had he not been in her chain of command, a relationship would be technically all right.

Yet, she suspected the old rules were being rewritten even if it was not soon enough for either of their liking.

"Looks that way," Derick said, not mentioning Tom had news. Not yet. He glanced over his shoulder at the tent entrance, where he could see a sliver of the hopper. During the event, it had felt catastrophic. Looking at the craft now, it wasn't any better. "Luke's fixed the comms, but it took damage. Even with the transponders, it's going to be hard to get a signal through this atmosphere. When we get back, we'll probably have to recalibrate our communications equipment to compensate."

Ren nodded as she sipped the surprisingly tasty stew. "Thanks for getting me out of there. When that Audrey speared me, I thought I was done."

"Audrey?" Both eyebrows went up, making the connection immediately. "Like the musical?"

"Yeah, like the musical," Ren grinned, eyebrows shooting upwards. "Didn't figure you for a theatre fan, Gunny."

Derick laughed, and the tension bled out of the atmosphere, just like that. "Nah, mud wrestling chicks is more my speed. My mom loved musicals though. Dad hated them, so whenever he was shipped out, she'd drag Luke and I to them. High school productions, off Broadway, you name it."

Ren smirked, unable to keep the image of the big, bad-ass Gunny as a little boy, forced into his Sunday best, complete with bow tie and slicked hair. She could sympathize. Her own mother had practically bought out Harrod's and Macy's trying to 'tame' her obviously tomboyish little girl. Elizabeth Richards had desperately hoped the ribbons, frills, and Mary Janes polished to a high shine would bring out the female in her daughter. It did not.

Derick narrowed his eyes at her. "What's so funny?"

"Just trying to picture it."

"Uh huh," Derick rolled his eyes and shrugged a shoulder. "I couldn't let my best sniper get taken out by an Audrey," he told her pointedly, glad his voice didn't break. "We've lost enough people today. I wasn't going to let y... another Shark die."

There was more to it when it came to her, and Derick knew it. He remembered what he'd whispered to her on the way back. Right now, when they weren't safe, wasn't the time to act on it or even discuss it. Maybe later, when the regs changed — and he suspected they would — and the world was a bit safer, Derick might revisit his feelings about Ren Richards.

Who was he kidding? Of course, he would.

What was she expecting? Hadn't she just listed out why they couldn't move past whatever this was? Had she expected him to say more? Okay, the little princess locked away in the tower of her heart had. But the rest of her? The Ren that was sensible? She understood his reasons for maintaining the status quo and let it go with silent understanding.

A sharp barking interrupted her thoughts as the tent flap shuddered slightly. Looking around Derick, Ren spied the roly-poly creature trundling towards them.

"What the hell is that?" she asked, not sure if she should shoot it or name it. Behind the odd little thing, two smaller ones yipped in after her. Speaking of shooting, where was her rifle?

"Oh, that's right," Derick grinned at Ren. "Someone… Shiny and Ozzy… fed a family of them, so now we're friends. This is the momma and her babies." Digging out a ration bar, he opened it and offered up pieces to the family. The mother had just sniffed it when another, louder 'NAF!' echoed from a distance.

"NAF!!" The loud response made Derick wince, but he laughed as Momma hurried out, followed by her babies. He did note they had both managed to grab a bit of ration bar before hurrying after her. "Tom must be back. When the male disappeared, we figured he'd followed the Major's group."

"Okay. Where's Mack…" Ren began. Cute critters were great and all, but she loved that damn rifle.

"I have Mack Daddy," Derick grinned. The actual trip to retrieve the sniper rifle and the remains of Edwards and Macon hadn't been fun but, like most Sharks, pain was soothed by humour.

"Oh, thank God," Ren flopped back against her pillow. "It's bad enough I got taken out by a giant plant monster, but losing my gun too?"

"Death is no excuse. I would have written you up for certain," Derick offered dryly and jerked a thumb over his shoulder. "I'll clean it up for you when I get a chance. If shit will stop trying to kill us," he added.

That was typically Gunny but, again, the Little Princess declared he was doing it because it was hers. "Thanks, Gunny."

"Of course." Despite his joking and bad-assitude, he was rather modest when it came to some things. At his name being bellowed, Derick rose to his feet. "I'm being hailed. Rest up. I need you shooting shit," he grinned with a wink.

Caught in his gaze, Ren knew there were things she should say, despite the status quo. It wouldn't be much, just a promise to wait. Yet she opened her mouth, the only thing that came out was "Thanks, Gunny. I'm sorry I lost my head like some rookie."

Sparing her a slight smile, Derick brushed off the apology as he headed out. "Don't worry about it. Not every day you get attacked by an Audrey."

"No kidding." She sniffed. "A tongue that spears, that's gotta be someone's nightmare."

"I don't want to know!" Derick shot over his shoulder before leaving her.

* * *

"So? What is it? Jimmy Hoffa, the Yeti, what?" Derick near-demanded from Tom, wondering if the Captain would let him strangle his friend. Maybe. "A hundred virgins waiting for us?"

Jules rolled her eyes. These two were a walking public service announcement for sexual harassment.

Tom grinned but looked past his friend to the Sharks. "Shiny, Oz, go get some grub and rest up a bit."

"Thank you, Major!" Shiny sang out as the two Sharks headed off towards the campfire.

Derick eyed Tom sourly. "Permission to shoot him, Captain Curran?"

Chuckling, Jules pretended to consider it. The friendship between the two men was such she felt comfortable joining in the teasing. "Maybe the kneecaps. I'm getting used to him."

"Told you I'd wear her down with my charm," Tom winked.

"More like Stockholm Syndrome," Jules retorted, inclining her head towards Derick. "Tell the man before I change my mind."

Grinning like a little boy, Tom pulled the pictures up on his slate and turned it to face his friend. "A city, mate. Like fucking Machu Picchu, but it's a city."

Disbelieving, Derick took the device and dropped his eyes to it belatedly. After a moment, he let out a low whistle. "Fuck. Me."

"That's what he said," Jules grinned despite the implications represented by a city, even an abandoned one.

"You're a laugh a minute, Captain," Tom retorted, side-eyeing her before taking his slate back. "What's our status?"

"I got back about twenty minutes ago," Derick replied. "We were able to find three transponders. Jazz and Luke rallied the Sharks and the squints to get temporary shelter set up. Dr. Andropolis made some stew. With what, I don't know, but it tastes okay." Rolling his neck to stretch it, Derick continued. "We ran into a new lifeform that did NOT look friendly." It was his turn to show pictures. "They were heading for the river and didn't appear to notice us."

"Oh, God," Jules made a face over Tom's shoulder, staring at the slate in disgust.

"Looks like Jazz's tentacle porn collection," Tom smirked, swiping the screen to move to the next picture.

"Tentacle porn?" Jules made a face and shook her head, holding up a hand to still any response. Not that she would admit it, but she was sleeping with one eye open tonight. "They look like velociraptors."

"I guess," Tom said, studying them a bit longer before he paused and handed the slate back to Derick. "Right, we need this lot packed up and ready to travel ASAP."

"We going to march all these people through the woods, at night?" Derick could already imagine the complaints, but the risk was his primary concern. Not to mention the current injured list.

Tom shuddered a little. "Not exactly."

On the way back to the campsite, Tom and Jules discussed their options. While Tom's primary concern was the safety of the civilians under his charge, there was no denying the importance of their discovery, not just to them but also to the whole fleet. The presence of the city, as abandoned and ancient as it looked, changed everything.

If another civilisation existed on this world, they needed to make contact and reach some accord. Finding another planet would be impossible, not with their depleted resources and the population on the verge of all out riot. Still, the consequences of violent colonisation in the past three hundred years were not lost on modern humans. The memory of how badly things could go wrong if this was handled improperly was written in the DNA of everyone whose ethnic origins bore the worst of it.

Shifting his gaze to Jules from Derick, Tom shrugged his shoulders, indicating it was her place to explain. "Go head, Captain, it's your show."

She met Tom's gaze, sure of the plan they'd discussed on the way back to the camp. "We're going to fly. IF," Jules emphasized with a nod towards the ship. "IF the engines aren't damaged. We can't break atmo or even go that high in it but, if she lifts off, we can fly to the city."

XV

The Valley

After an hour of inspection and diagnostics with Luke Rickman, Jules and Tom finally decided the hopper was air-worthy. The *Firefly* would never break atmo again, not with her damage, but Jules and Luke determined it would survive at least a few trips to the valley and back. She'd keep it low and slow, skimming the tops of the massive trees they'd hiked through.

Ideally, they should have waited until morning, but their position was precarious at best and could turn downright deadly if the weather turned or worse, the sky crabs returned.

Especially if the sky crabs returned.

"You sure this is a good idea?"

A bemused smile crossed Jules's lips at the barely concealed anxiety in Tom's voice as he braced himself in the co-pilot's chair next to her. His presence at her side meant a lot to her but she didn't dare voice those feelings. Not right now anyway.

Initially, when Jules proposed this plan on the hike back, she'd planned on doing it alone. Firing up the ship after the damage it had sustained was insane. Period.

Naturally, Tom insisted ("Bloody hell you are…!") on joining her and here he was, despite Jules's best efforts to talk him out of it and what might be a case of the jitters.

"You're not scared, are you?" She glanced sideways at him, long enough to catch his scowl.

"Those are fightin' words, luv," Tom retorted, straightening and bristling even more when Jules chuckled. "I'm not bloody scared of anything, I'm just mentioning we might be a little hasty."

Smirking, Jules ran a thumb under the bank of switches that started the engines. With a solid click-click-click, she felt more than heard the whine of the powerful engine as it fired up. Tossing a wink at him, she said, "Don't panic, *Marine*. This is my thing."

Tom rolled his eyes. "Bloody wingnuts. I hope you're better at flying than making jokes," he teased back, giving his harness a final jerk to test it.

At what point this familiarity developed between them, Jules didn't know but she enjoyed it. After months of being the captain of the *Rutherford* where everyone saluted or tiptoed around her because of rank, it was nice to engage in the friendly relationships she enjoyed when she was just a pilot. She assumed the captaincy because it was necessary, but Jules was a pilot first and she missed the life. Remaining in charge of a big Bertha like the *Rutherford* was not what she wanted long-term.

Under normal circumstances, the conflict of their rank would never be an issue because they would be so far out of each other's orbit, it was a moot point. But the world was changing now, and she respected he'd never foisted unsolicited advice to her about running the ship or taking command or whatever. He never assumed she didn't know what she was doing, and he listened instead of telling her how to solve some problem. In the rare staff conference call, he often listened before speaking up and he'd never talked down to her, unlike that jackass in Engineering.

So, when the expedition called for a military escort, she had no problem letting Tom take the lead planet side, mostly because she knew he wasn't doing so because she was incompetent.

Jules also felt the friendship between them was evolving into... something. It was nice to know when they were back on the *Rutherford*, there was at least one person with whom Jules could be herself. Besides, she enjoyed their banter. It bordered on the flirtatious and that too, was something Jules missed. She was grateful to be seen as a woman by a man who appreciated it enough to not let it undermine his confidence in her as an officer.

Flashing her companion a smile she had no clue struck Tom Merrick deaf, dumb and stupid, she tapped her headset. "Gunny, is everyone at minimum safe distance?"

"Affirmative, Captain," Derick's crispy voice responded across the speakers. "How's the Major doing? He's not so good with the flying…"

"Screw you, Gunny," Tom retorted.

"Oh, didn't realize you were on the channel." Derick's smirk could actually be heard through the links.

"Oy! I know where you sleep at night!" Tom fired back, grumbling that maybe the big bloke's smart ass wasn't so funny anymore.

"He's a little twitchy but otherwise all right," Jules grinned, glancing at Tom. "I'm going to fire the thrusters. It's going to be messy but there's no other way around it. Once I gain altitude, I'll loop back and set down in the designated area."

"And make sure the squad is deployed around the squints," Tom threw in, knowing it would rankle Derick to be told something they'd already discussed. Suck on that, Gunny. "When this bird picks up, it's going to make a lot of noise. I don't want those MULKS you saw heading back to investigate."

"Mulks?" Jules raised an eyebrow.

"Motherfucking Ugly Lizard Kangaroos."

"Do you guys use acronyms for everything?" she retorted jokingly, turning back to the controls with a shake of her head.

* * *

The expedition had been moved as far back as possible, a good hundred feet from the hopper, near a gentle part of the hill abutting the flat plain before the cliff's edge. Reddish light from marking flares lit the space, bathing them all in a crimson glow highlighting their precarious situation and the worry on everyone's face. The Sharks, surrounding them at appropriate intervals, were surveying the jungle in all directions, keeping an eye out for any nocturnal visitors that might come to investigate the light and noise.

"Will the ship be okay?" Derick asked his brother quietly, standing towards the back of the group with him. He wouldn't admit it, but the butterflies in his stomach were threatening to turn into pterodactyls.

Luke shrugged, his gaze also locked on the bluish glow of the thrusters under the *Firefly*. "The engines and the reactor are fine, they're the most protected parts of the ship. It's the hull and the structure I'm worried about. The ribs took a beating from those what, sky crabs? Firing up the engines will put stress on them, I just hope it doesn't break apart."

Derick's face darkened. He'd been hoping for something a little more optimistic, but then again when had the Rickman boys been anything but blunt? Their father raised all his sons that way and their mother just apologised for them a whole lot.

A slight touch on his arm made Luke look over a shoulder, just enough to see Tammy behind him. His gaze softened, and he motioned her beside him.

"Hey," she greeted tightly, nodding towards the ship. "How much longer?"

Like the rest of the squints, Olivia's death had gutted the young woman. She'd looked up to Dr. Hall, nearly worshipping the woman, and Luke's shoulder bore the stains of her grief. Even those that hadn't known Olivia well, like the Sharks, were affected. Babel was meant to be the beginning of a new dawn, but those rosy coloured expectations were now smeared with a hard dose of reality.

"Not much," Derick nodded, glancing around Luke at her. "Just got the word from Captain Curran."

"You okay?" Luke nudged her affectionately with one shoulder.

Tammy's cheeks bloomed, a little embarrassed by her emotional display. Poor Luke had been her sole confidant since Earth's destruction. As nice as it was, she knew she needed to toughen up a bit, because the years ahead were going to be hard. Not for the first time, she realized how unfair she was being. After all, he'd lost family too.

"Yeah," she said, crossing her arms over her chest. "Shell-shocked, like everyone is, but better."

The thunderous roar of the *Firefly's* engines cut off any further conversation. Beneath them, the ground shook as the bluish glow of the ship's exhaust lit up the night. Around them, the jungle's flying denizens took to the skies in a flurry of panic and the closest trees and plants swayed at the outpouring of heated gases.

After a few seconds, the roar died down into a focused drone even though it still drowned out the nocturnal panic. When the ship moved, Derick swore he felt the suction of forty some odd breaths being held. The *Firefly's* engines fired again, tilting forward towards the edge of the chasm. Dirt and mud oozed into the now empty space under the hopper as a rock came loose and rolled over the edge into the chasm.

The vibrations loosened dirt on the hillside, sending it down and causing the gathered expedition to take a step back reflexively, despite being well out of the way. As they watched, the *Firefly* reached the edge of the cliff and dropped like a massive rock out of sight.

Near Derick, someone stifled a scream, but he ignored it. They didn't have the link feed he did, to know that Jules and Tom were okay. He was about to nudge his brother when he heard a familiar voice nearby.

"Two days of latrine duty says the Major's fainted."

Derick shot a glare behind him, nailing the culprit with it. "Harwood, no betting unless you want two full weeks of latrine duty."

"Just joking, Gunny," Cori replied contritely, waving off French's apparent acceptance of the bet.

Derick rolled his eyes just as another burst of sound washed over them and the *Firefly* appeared in the air over the chasm. Hovering in place for a few seconds, it lifted higher and shot across the chasm to circle around to the landing site they'd decided on earlier.

Once on the ground, it was only a few seconds before the hatch popped and the ramp lowered, revealing a grinning Tom Merrick. The ship looked like an aeronautical version of the man himself. Both had been to hell and back and fought like junkyard dogs the entire way. "All right, you lot! All aboard! We're going on a little trip!"

* * *

Despite the events of the last several hours, the expedition team hurried onto the ship in no time flat. Derick guessed the prospect of an ancient city dulled even the rawness of Dr. Hall's death.

Lift off, the short trip and the landing in the deep valley next to the city proved uneventful, which Derick welcomed. Not that he wasn't up for adventure but fuck a dead dog — he'd prefer it to be spread out.

As Jules set the *Firefly* down gently in a clearing between the tree line and the river cutting through the valley, she stared at the city silhouetted against the moons. "I wonder if this is how Hiram Bingham or Howard Carter felt when they made their discoveries," she said quietly, inhaling deeply and letting out a sigh.

"Shit scared they don't fuck anything up?" Tom remarked, studying the city. He wished he had time to sit here and enjoy the moment with Jules. To talk about history without being judged for the uniform he wore or his Ocker accent.

He glanced at Jules, watching her profile, and promised himself he would make that happen at some point. Right now, they all needed to rest and refuel.

* * *

An hour later, camp was fully set up, patrols were scheduled, and everyone was shouldering for a spot inside the hopper. No one had complained about being made to sleep inside the craft, despite the slightly cramped conditions. Derick suspected it was because pictures of the mulks had been circulated and no one wanted to wake up to that drooling on them.

He'd dropped his kit in a spot near the small medical bay, glad to find a space to stretch out all six feet and four inches of himself and got to work cleaning Ren's sniper rifle, Mack Daddy. The McAllister

4K Sniper Rifle, aka 'Mack Daddy', was truly a thing of beauty. Much like its owner, a little voice niggled at him.

Frowning, Derick ignored it and smoothed an oiled rag over the barrel, rubbing gently when his fingers hit a piece of dried on plant gunk. It was an expensive and valuable weapon Derick didn't want to be without. He definitely wasn't taking it apart and patiently cleaning every piece because it was Ren's.

Right. His brother hadn't bought that either.

Derick sighed, swiping his forehead with the back of a hand and grabbed the base stock. He blew into the latch, getting any last bit of dirt and snapped the barrel assembly into it. He thought putting the work into cleaning the damn thing would get his mind off everything, but it hadn't. Instead, he'd gone right back to the scene, arriving to find Ren out of it and a plant spear protruding from her leg.

Damn if his heart hadn't stopped and then sank into his boots while he watched Mayday work on her. Goddamn. Ever since day one, when she was a new private under his newly tagged sergeant, they had 'clicked'. Now, five or six years later, they finished each other's sentences, could exchange a look and just know what the other one wanted. They were friends, who entertained a kind of flirtation that suggested in a different life, a different situation, they might someday be more.

Until today, when time had frozen and he realized the love of his life was about to die.

Grabbing his portable work light, Derick moved it closer, so he could give Mack Daddy one last look over. Was it really love? He'd liked females that were in his command before. Denise Dawson had been a pretty, chatty blonde. She'd been in his unit before the Exodus. Chante Riggins had been another one. She'd been all dark skin and exotic. Neither of them had inspired the gut wrench of today.

In the last several months, he'd seen Ren suffer with the rest of them. Face down angry and frustrated civilians, injured in a brawl during the very first food distribution. She'd been covered in blood then, a lot of it her own because that whole thing had gone tits up in two minutes flat.

Never once before, not with Denise, not with Chante, had he felt like saying fuck all to the line of command that kept him from chasing after a woman. Not until today. Not until Ren. Not until he'd found himself carrying her bloodied body in his arms, whispering promises to her he never said to anyone and praying to a God he'd long ago forsaken.

Carefully, he snapped the laser scope back into place and smoothed a hand down the barrel. A voice carried out of the medical bay, making Derick look up. Mayday had taken her kit into the small room, grumbling about not wanting to listen to forty some odd people snoring. Derick suspected it was so she could be close to her friend and now patient.

Next, he clipped the strap back on the gun, giving each end a yank to test it. The webbing was still damp from where he washed it, but it would dry soon enough. Getting to his feet, Derick clicked off the work lamp and headed for the medical bay door.

Hesitating outside, Derick debated interrupting. The two women were thick as thieves and Mayday sounded like she needed a friend right now. Ren's rifle wasn't as important as the ear Mayday might need.

"'Ello, Gunnee."

Nearly jumping out of his skin, Derick reigned in the urge to murder the Frenchman for scaring the crap out of him.

"What?" he growled, realizing at that moment it might seem like he was lurking outside the medical bay, listening in. Which he wasn't. Jesus, he felt like he'd been caught spying on Chris.

"Luke said he needs to see you outside," French replied, oblivious to his near brush with death. He shrugged. "I do not know what for, just that he is with that petite squint."

Luke. How his brother managed to have such fucking timing, he didn't know. "All right. I'll be there shortly. Thanks," he said through clenched teeth and sent the Shark on his way.

"Gunny?"

Turning, Derick found Maya looking up at him. "Sanjay," he nodded, glancing past her to where Ren was sitting up on the medical bed. "I uh… uh…just brought Ren's rifle back," he said, pulling his gaze from the redhead to his medic.

Maya raised an eyebrow. "Uh huh. Well," she nodded and moved out of his way. "Come in. I'll leave you two…"

"You don't…"

"I have to check my other patients before I turn in," Maya explained, glancing back at Ren and giving her a slight smile. While Maya wasn't up to her old self, she couldn't help but be amused at the normally self-assured Gunny acting like a nervous school boy.

Before Derick could say anything else, Maya slipped past him and left him standing in the door. Right. Clearing his throat, he nodded at Ren, glad to see her awake.

"Hey, I brought you Mack, squeaky clean." He stepped forward to lay it on the bunk beside her leg. It wasn't flowers, but it might as well have been. They were Sharks after all.

Ren broke into a bright smile, eyes dancing in amusement and pleasure as she took the weapon, her fingers moving across the oiled surface as if she were inspecting something living for any signs of wear.

"Thank you, De…" Ren snapped her mouth shut, her eyes meeting his. Just like back in the tent, something connected them, something more than friendship. But they weren't alone, not really. She cleared her throat, going back to their standard operating procedure. "You going soft on me?"

Snark was good. Snark would keep her from wanting to call him Derick like she had when he'd swept her off her feet, literally.

Derick looked down, smirk tugging hard at the corner of his mouth. He worked his teeth over his lip, needing everything he had not to respond to her unintended innuendo. After a moment, Derick cleared his throat and indicated Maya's kit sitting on the small counter. "She going to be okay?" he asked quietly.

"I think so," Ren nodded sombrely. "They didn't know each other all that long, but after all we've been through he was someone to lean on, you know? I know she said it was a casual thing, but I think it might have been a little more."

"I wouldn't be surprised. Tom… the Major said she's pretty stiff-lipped about stuff like that." Which was at odds with the whole brash, loud personality, but Maya had her reasons. Tom had mentioned her parents but, considering how tight she and Ren were, Derick guessed the redhead might already know.

"GUNNY!! You coming or not?"

Luke's bellow made Derick jump and a twitch appeared in his jaw. "I am going to kill him," he told Ren and pointed at her. "Get some rest, you hear me?"

"Will do," she answered with a smile and then added, almost slyly. "Derick."

He didn't answer but when he left the medical bay, Derick was smiling and had decided NOT to kill his brother.

* * *

Since sleeping outside was out of the question, Jules chose to set up in the cockpit. Viewing the new world through safety glass was still better than the steel grey bulkheads on the *Rutherford* or the ones in the belly of the *Firefly*. Then there was the secret she was selfishly keeping to herself.

When the designers built these ships, someone had posited the idea that the pilot might need to sleep on board. Since there were no bunks, save for the Med Station, why not put in pilot seats that folded back into a more-comfortable-than-the-steel-deck reclining chair.

She couldn't remember who, but Jules was ready to put the ingenious forward thinker in her will. With the seat tilted back slightly so she could better see the night sky, Jules sipped at her water bottle. Chuck should be here. Chuck and Stefan both, she thought. Chuck would no doubt be snoring already while Stefan would be going on about all the plant varieties.

They wouldn't have paid any attention to the thousands and thousands of stars dotting the inky velvet night sky. Jules smiled to herself as she leaned back. She missed them and hoped Stefan was doing alright on the *Olympia*. She would check in once she got back on the *Ruthie*. Being Captain did have its perks.

A shooting star jetted across the sky and Jules closed her eyes, making a silent wish.

"You look comfortable," Tom stepped into the cockpit, carrying a rolled up sleeping bag with him. "Do you mind if I set up here. I promise, I don't snore and will keep my hands to myself. Me sharing billets with the squad is just going to make it awkward."

Tom thought for them it would be like having to share a room with your Nan but didn't need to put that picture in anyone's head.

Chuckling, Jules eyed him upside down before she sat up and indicated the other seat. "Be my guest. There's a button under the arm rest. I imagine having the Gunny in there will be terrifying enough." Running a hand over her hair, she pulled out the elastic band holding her ponytail back and combed everything back into a sloppy bun. "Did you see the sky?" she said, nodding towards the window.

Tom shifted his eyes to the glass and took in the sight of the glittering canvas beyond. It really was a spectacular view. "Now that's something to fall asleep too."

He didn't just mean the sky.

"You got that right," Jules replied, oblivious to any double meaning as she glanced at him, smiling. "No light pollution, no smog or haze." She went quiet and let out a sigh. "I don't want to screw this world up, you know?"

"I know what you mean," he said setting up the bedroll on the chair, "it's like we have a chance to set things up right. Not ten thousand years too late before we worked out the damage we were doing."

"Exactly." Settling her seat back again, Jules glanced at him. "So, what do you do when you're not saving the world from carnivorous plants or gigantic twigas," she asked, using Shiny's word for the massive beasts. There was obviously so much more to the man than he let on and whatever this thing was between them, she wanted to explore it once everything was safe.

Tom eased back into the chair and tossed her a beat-up copy *of A Town like Alice* by Neville Shute. The book was older than he was, the pages yellow and furled with creases in what was once a glossy cover.

"I read and try and get my hands on paper books like that one, aside from the drinking and picking up birds in bars, of course." He winked.

"Of course," Jules replied dryly, turning the book over so she could read the cover. She recognized the author from her high school days. "So, does everyone die in this one like they did in On the Beach?" Handing the book back, she sat up again and snagged her water bottle.

"Well it's about World War II and this bird who was a POW. The Nips were making civilian women on the other side do these death marches, but she meets an Aussie bloke and it works out all right." He resisted the urge to use the word romance because Derick had looked at him like he was reading Barbara Cartland.

"Hmm." Was 'it works out all right' Shark code for steamy romance? Jules gave Tom a look. Huh. Who knew? "I can't remember the last time I read an actual book," she continued, rolling over to face him and propping herself up on an arm. "What else?"

"What else?" He turned his head and cocked a brow at her. "Used to watch Rugby League matches, played the occasional bit of soccer but that's about it really. I'm not that complicated."

"And Godzilla movies. Can't forget the big guy." Her smile faded, and she inhaled deeply and let it out. "I'm sorry about your Sharks."

"It's the life," his expression sobered. "Ground pounders are always bullet catchers. I wasn't in charge of Macon or Edwards long enough to really know them. I hate that I didn't. Always swore when I got these officer's bars that was the one thing I would never do. I started out as a non-com and I hated officers that couldn't see the faces behind the uniforms. I should have done better by them."

"I forget you guys are just as cobbled together as the rest of the fleet." Jules squeezed his shoulder, the rock-solid muscle beneath his sleeve twitching minutely under her touch. "I don't know what you could have done better, Tom. Like you told me, you couldn't have known," she said quietly.

He caught her hand on his shoulder and held it in place, staring at those soft brown eyes.

"Thanks luv, I appreciate you saying it. You know," he added making no move to remove his hand, "considering you got thrown in the deep end, you've done a bloody great job as Captain. Holding the *Ruthie* together after the shit we went through leaving Sol, no one could have done better."

Jules felt her cheeks flare into a blush. She smiled slightly and nodded, not realizing just how much she'd needed to hear that. "I made a lot of decisions that I didn't want to make," she said quietly, flipping her hand to squeeze his.

"You were tops, luv, you were tops," he cracked a small smile, "and I'm not saying that because I think you have the prettiest smile I've ever seen. It's like a bullet to the brain, you know."

Her cheeks felt even hotter and Jules shook her head. "You're making me blush, you know." She was sure he did. Hell, the Sharks in the back could probably feel the heat. "Ruins my bad-ass Captain image."

"I won't tell anyone," he quipped and leaned across the space between their seats.

Since he'd met her this thing between them had been growing exponentially. Brushing his lips against her, his kiss wasn't rough and demanding like it was when he was partaking in the attentions of God only knew how many women in the past. It was as intimate as it was chaste. Everything about her was soft and luxuriant. Everything in him screamed she was too good for the likes of him.

When he pulled back, he waited with breath held tight in his chest, uncertain of what she would say.

Jules said nothing at first, how could she? When he started to pull away, she grabbed his shirt front to keep him from going too far.

"You should do that again," she said finally, licking her lips before she returned the kiss. Just as soft, just as sweet, because right now, this thing couldn't go any further.

"Now that I know you're not going to smack me, yeah." He smiled and leaned forward to do just that. Once again, it was an intimate, tender thing without demand. They stayed locked for a good minute, exploring and tasting, trying to savour this tiny moment in the eye of the storm.

It was Tom who pulled back first. He could still taste her on his lips and the scent of her was dizzying. There was much to say, and he was not a man who could express feelings easily, but this was not a woman with whom you could trifle with. Years of watching his father's brutality on his mother told him what kind of man he wanted to be if he ever found someone who meant something to him.

"I'm a mess, you know. An absolute pain in the arse. If you tell me to piss off, I'll understand but I want you to know, I think you're a ripper."

Settling back into the chair, Jules shrugged, lips still tingling from what they shared. "I think we're all some level of mess after everything that's happened." She patted his hand. "I'm not afraid."

Tom raised her hand to his lips and planted a small kiss on the back of one smooth knuckle. "You're braver than me, because I'm bloody terrified."

She let the back of a finger brush along his stubble and grinned. "Big, bad Shark."

"At least I'm housebroken," he winked at her as he faced front again, soaking up the stars as if they were looking back with interest.

He was more than that, Jules decided, but turned to face the window as well. She kind of liked Major Charming over Prince Charming anyway.

XVI

Deployment

Darkness still covered the camp like a shroud when reveille came for the Sharks the next morning. The nights were longer on Gaia, Tom realised, but it didn't matter. No rescue ship answered their call during the night, confirming his suspicions their signal was too weak to penetrate Gaia's heavily charged atmosphere. In the end, it didn't matter. Within a few hours past dawn, they would be overdue. The *Olympia* would send another ship to investigate and their first mission to Gaia would be over.

In the meantime, the city awaited, and they had a job to do.

"How's it going?" Tom asked by way of greeting as he and Derick approached the spot Luke and Shiny had chosen to set up the Mercator UAV. The unmanned aircraft would provide a bird's eye view of the ancient city as well as a glimpse of its interior. Tom wasn't sending anyone into the place until they had a little more information. While Sharks were trained to deal with almost anything, Tom saw no reason to be reckless when a little recon could yield a wealth of information.

"Almost ready." Shiny glanced up at the men from where she was squatting beside the drone. Hexagonal in shape, the UAV had four mini-turbines capable of keeping it aloft in anything short of a hurricane. In the centre, held in place by six support struts, was the orb-like sensor containing its scanner and communications relay, surrounded by a tough titanium casing. "We're lucky, the crash didn't do any damage to it or the guidance hub, just dented the case."

A few feet away from her and the drone, Luke stood in front of a small fold up table with a large, dark case perched on top. The open case revealed the drone's portable receiver and guidance system attached to a screen and the keyboard he was hunched over.

"Hey Bigfoot, hey Tom," Luke greeted, not looking up from the screen, brows furrowed with concentration as he synched the hub with Shiny's adjustments to the drone.

Raising an eyebrow, Derick nodded to his brother and Shiny and glanced toward the high city walls. The sun was rising behind the city, covering the encampment and the surrounding landscape in heavy, aged shadows. For the first time, in a long time, Derick felt the itch to record the moment, to try and capture the silent beauty. To study how the light awakened each room and how it glinted gold off certain red curls. Clearing his throat, Derick reminded himself that being hip deep in serious shit meant no skylarking.

"How much longer?" he asked, deciding that irritating Luke would keep his head in the game.

Bristling like a cat petted all wrong, Luke didn't stop typing. "Cut that out; this isn't like when you had to wait for me outside the bathroom at camp. I'll finish when I'm done."

"Ewww…" Shiny made a face at them both.

A Shark that went eww… Tom held back whatever comment that wanted to come. "But you're almost done, right?"

Luke didn't dignify the question with an answer.

"All right, Rickman," Shiny dusted off her hands and rose to her feet. "You're good to go, yeah?"

"Great," Luke flashed her a grin. Cute, he thought, baser instincts never too far away from his thoughts. "Let's make this bird fly."

Derick's glance cut to Shiny and back to his brother. He knew that grin and narrowed his eyes at Luke. N-O. NO.

Luke mouthed an innocent 'what?' and went back to work, tapping at the smooth keyboard and prompting the small turbines to begin their soundless whirring. As the four propellers disappeared into a circular blur of motion, the UAV lifted off the ground, rising steadily over their heads until only the glowing green light from its LEDs could be seen.

"How's it looking?" Shiny asked, wiping her hands on a rag as she stood beside Luke to watch the screen. She was happy for Luke's help, knowing full well the UAV could have been damaged beyond what her kit and expertise could fix.

Luke winked at her, incapable of not flirting with any unattached female in his proximity. Plus, it kept his mind off Olivia's death. "Signal's clean on all frequencies. I had to program some additional filters to compensate for the ionisation in the atmosphere, but we're getting telemetry. Right now, it's of Tom's bald head, but it works."

"Fuck you. It's a sign of virility."

"Yeah, that's exactly what it is," Luke snorted, smirking at Derick before returning his attention back to the screen.

Hiding a snort (and not successfully), Derick grinned to himself. What happened to the little kid he'd taken trick-or-treating? Or the baby he'd drawn a moustache on with his marker set? Mom had gone ballistic, so much so that now, two decades later, he still remembered. Had she realized then the trouble that he and Luke would be together? Luke's brains combined with his own general lack of fear for consequences had driven their mother nuts and was probably the cause of their father's grizzled grey hair.

In those first days of the Exodus, when he thought he was alone, Derick hadn't wanted to sleep. Closing his eyes only brought memories of his lost family. When news came about Luke, Derick had needed privacy. It took bribing a maintenance tech and a twenty-foot crawl down a bulkhead access to find it but when he did, he'd broken down and cried in relief.

As they grew up, Luke never ceased to amaze him and now, at the new dawn of humanity, his brother's genius intellect, his delight when something he made worked, and his ability to find humour still floored

Derick. He reached out and gripped Luke's shoulder softly in pride as he handed off the controls to Shiny.

Nodding her thanks, Shiny's brow creased as she went to work, her fingertip tracing the smooth surface of the slate control. The hovering craft immediately zipped forward, making a soundless beeline towards the *Firefly* where it started scanning the area in ever expanding circles. Tom and Derick stood behind Luke, watching his fingers fly over the smooth keyboard to enhance the bird's eye view of the camp being transmitted by the drone.

The image of the *Firefly* was displayed as a solid object on the screen, which was to be expected. Dented and damaged as the hull was, metal was a difficult substance to see through and the scanner had better luck when it headed out over the dense brush around the walls. Luke's fingers were a flurry of movement as the blurry images sharpened and provided them all with a reasonably clear view of the terrain from its vantage point above.

"Looks good," Tom complimented over his shoulder. "Can you operate the controls without Shiny? I'm going to need her in the sweep."

"Now that I got it all set up, no problem," Luke was happy to help. This was something he could do and, while not directly involved in what Derick was about to embark on, he was grateful at being able to help.

"Oi!" Shiny jabbed Luke's shoulder with a finger. "You didn't do it all yourself."

"Yeah." Just to be a dick, Derick jabbed Luke's other shoulder.

"Okay, okay," Luke gave an exaggerated sigh, "maybe she helped a little."

Tom gave Shiny an approving nod, just to show he was aware she had done a little more than just 'helped a little'.

"Right then, I want an initial scan of the area, especially a TRS survey of the structure so I know what we're walking into."

"No problem."

"Derick, get the squad ready to move out in fifteen minutes. We'll set up operational command here. Once we get the drone's intel, you'll go in and conduct a full sweep of the place. Sure, as shit the squints will be itching to get in there once they're up and about."

"Squints are already up," Shiny spoke up, glancing back at them from where she was watching the drone. "They fixed the hopper's coffee maker. Captain, can we keep them?" Hardly any of them was the coffee addict she was. Withdrawals those first few days after the Exodus began had been a bitch.

"No," Derick answered instead, motioning forward. "You heard the man. Equipment check in ten," he said, moving towards the camp. "SHARKS!!!" he bellowed, not caring that Shiny winced beside him. "On the line in ten mikes!! Starting now!!"

The camp had been stirring sleepily, like some entity coming out of a deep slumber. At the Gunny's order, it was as if a switch was flipped and the camp came alive with the sound of Sharks getting their hustle on.

* * *

Jules jerked awake at the Gunny's bellow. For a second, she stared at the metal plating over her in confusion until awareness hit. Falling back against the chair, Jules glanced beside her, a little disappointed but unsurprised to find Tom gone. Of course, he would be awake, and he better not say shit to her because if she wanted to get up at the ass crack of dawn, she would have joined the *Marines.*

Rubbing her eyes, she sighed back into the chair. Seriously, whoever designed it should be given something. Chocolate for life. Someone, Tom she guessed, activated the window's refractive shield so that she wasn't awakened by brightness stabbing her in the face. She inhaled and let it out, thinking back to their long conversation last night. They'd talked for hours, nothing deep and meaningful at first, just surface stuff to fill in the time.

Eventually, as it did for any refugee, darkness invaded. Jules read his file before the mission and was aware of the act of heroism that was the cause of it. She also suspected the action had come hand in hand with a mild case of PTSD kept at bay with alcohol.

The shadow in his eyes at the mention of the incident told Jules to avoid the subject for now. Still, if she felt confident enough to speak she would have told him the choice he was forced to make was an impossible one and while he had a right to his anguish, his guilt was undeserved. No one should ever feel guilty for being merciful. Just like he would probably tell her that choosing to dock her shuttle and save the people on board over helping her best friend dying on the deck beside her wasn't something to feel guilty over either.

Morning chatter reached her ears, along with the sounds of industry. And was that… coffee she smelled?? Even if it was the instamatic freeze-dried crap they'd been forced to subsist on since the destruction of Earth, she'd take it.

She was up a minute later, combing her fingers through her tangled hair so she could put it up.

* * *

"No."

"But Gunny…!"

"I said NO!"

Derick's reply was quiet but terse. After her years serving with him, Ren recognized when he was about to lose his temper but dammit, she didn't want to be left behind. Ren kept pace with him as he strode across the campsite proving irrevocably her injury of the day before was no longer an issue. Well, not much of one anyway. All she felt when she walked was a prickling across the skin where the wound had been. Her head was clear and with what Maya shot her up with, she felt fine if not a little euphoric.

"I'm fine!" she insisted, walking past Sharks who knew better than to get in between Ren and Gunny when they had one of their arguments. As much as the two worked like a well-oiled machine at times, Ren was infamous for her ability to challenge the Gunny the way no subordinate ought to be doing. Of course, when push came to shove, she was the first to have his back and he knew it. "Mayday cleared me for duty, you can ask her!"

Derick paused in his size thirteen combat boots and swung around, closing the distance between them with a menacing step. Not that he'd ever hurt her or any of his people, but he could be intimidating without realizing it. "I did talk to Mayday and she said you should be taking it easy but since you're determined to be a pain in my ass, she's cleared you for light duties. LIGHT!" He waggled a finger at her reproachfully.

"We're not going into a firefight! We're doing a sweep! I'll stick with Mayday and Jag. The minute I feel faint or get the vapours, I'll stand down! I swear!"

"Vapours...?" Derick stared in exasperation, uncertain whether to strangle her or dropkick her to the other side of the planet. In the end, it only cemented his admiration for her ballsy, no shit attitude, which was peachy if you wanted to date the woman but a complete pain in the ass when you wanted her to obey an order for her own damn good.

A gunny's word was law and her comrades would think her arguing with Derick like this to border on insubordination, but she didn't want to sit this one out. Not after spending months on the *Ruthie*, trapped in a sardine can, forced to maintain order against helpless civilians. Being out here, even after getting hurt, made her feel like she was a soldier again, not some jackbooted stormtrooper out of a dystopian novel.

"Please. I need to be out there."

This time, there was no guile or snark on her face, just simple entreaty and holy hell, how the fuck could he say no NOW? Especially when he understood where she was coming from without needing to hear the words. Still, responsibility as her senior NCO had to override his affection for her. Sentiment should never bleed into any decisions in that area and yet, he wasn't un-sympathetic.

It should have been a straightforward no. No, ifs ands or buts... but Derick dragged a hand over his face, rubbing the stubble he hadn't wasted water to shave. Despite the messy, decidedly non-regulation feelings he had for Ren, or maybe because of them, he understood her need to be with her team at a time like this.

Exploring a new world, making an ancient ruined city safe for civilians — that was a mission worth the risk. After what they'd been through the last six months, it would be cathartic. He knew, because if the tables were turned, he would be the one demanding to accompany his squad. Ren and he were more alike than either of them knew what to do with.

Glaring at her, Derick cursed inwardly and rolled his eyes. "Mayday!" he bellowed, turning sharply on a heel to continue.

Maya, in the process of checking her gear again, was half-aware of the argument as it progressed through the camp. She didn't have to be there to know why her best friend was dogging Gunny Rickman's heels like a bloodhound. Tightening the fastenings of her body armour, she stood up just in time to hear the man's exasperated call.

"Yes, Gunny!" Maya jogged over to them, falling in step and bracing herself to be the tiebreaker for whatever impasse the two had reached.

The medic's close friendship with Ren might be considered a conflict of interests but one of the things Derick learned about the Brit since she came to his command was her honesty. Personal feelings wouldn't get in the way of the mission and she was impartial when it came to the health of any Shark. Maya had joined the squad from the British Infantry and though they only served together on the *Ruthie*, her record proved that in a crunch, she could be as dedicated as any doctor who feared for their patient.

"Wonder Woman here insists she's well enough to join the recon. What do you think?"

Ren held her tongue, aware her request was going against the grain of his natural inclinations. Gunnery Sergeant Derick Rickman had the loyalty of his squad for good reason. He fought for them like a son of a bitch, but he wouldn't take their crap either. No matter what the situation, even when the brass was running around like beheaded chickens, Gunny held his shit together and got them out alive. Even if she didn't care for him the way she did, Ren would have still taken a bullet for the man.

"I'll keep an eye on her Gunny. If I think she even looks the least bit off-colour, I'll dose her and send her off the field. Which you will do, yeah?" Maya gave Ren a pointed stare to show she meant it.

Ren crossed her heart. "Scout's honour."

"You were never a scout," Derick grumbled, shaking his head and exhaling his lingering reservations into the ether. "Alright, go put on your party dress! We leave in ten!"

* * *

Ten minutes and a trip to the still functioning head (THANK GOD!) later, Jules had a cup of coffee in hand as she sought out Tom. The rising sun was painting the cloud-dappled green sky a kaleidoscope of colours, making Jules pause at the foot of the ramp. Should she? Screw it. Digging her slate out, she raised it up to take a few pictures. Call her a geek but Jules didn't care. This planet was going to be their new home and someday, she liked to look back at what it had been before colonisation.

Slipping the device back into the pocket of her flight suit, Jules spotted Tom hovering behind Luke, who sat perched on an equipment crate. He was hunched over the controls of what she recognised as the guidance hub of their Mercator drone. As she headed over, Jules scanned the sky to see if she could spot it. Ah. There it was, making concentric circles as it conducted a scan of the abandoned structure. She couldn't help feeling the thrill of excitement rushing through her and it showed when she greeted the men enthusiastically.

"Good morning, gentlemen."

Tom raised his eyes to her and though he didn't smile, she saw the twinkle of pleasure at her arrival. Luke's gaze was transfixed on the screen, focused on the telemetry provided by the drone. He glanced up briefly and offered a distracted greeting. 'Uh... good morning, Captain. You want a look at the telemetry we're getting from the Merc?"

"You bet." Jules quickly joined them, standing next to Tom as she leaned forward, staring at the flurry of images on the screen.

"We've just started," Tom added. "The first signals have just started coming in."

"I had to tweak the frequency to compensate for atmospheric ionisation earlier but other than that, the TRS is transmitting some great data," Luke leaned back further so the two of them could get an unobstructed view of the screen.

Jules's eyes widened in surprise at the radiographic representation of the forgotten city. As the UAV flew through the empty streets between the buildings, she could see plazas and courtyards as well as streets winding through the buildings. What looked like a road, led to the city's edge along a half-collapsed stone wall. At the entrance, an elongated piece of rock, that could have been a gatepost, lay sprawled against the ground like a lazy guard.

The valley was already reclaiming this abandoned civilisation, with tall grass fighting through cracks in the cobbled street like triumphant invaders, accompanied by their entourage of creepers. Bushes and shrubs flanked them, staking their own territory across the disused pathways where people might have once walked. Banners of vines and moss celebrated their victory, hanging down walls of the buildings as lichens bloomed across the rock, like bursts of artillery.

The buildings and towers were luminous images against a black backdrop, appearing ghostly as spectral outlines revealed rooms within rooms. There were chambers and stairwells ranging from wide and sweeping to corkscrew narrowness. Wide halls with high ceilings were surrounded by winding corridors, sometimes leading to small cellars below ground level. The floor plans resembled segments of completed puzzles, their mysteries laid bare for all to see.

A pulsing red dot at the corner of the screen caught her eye momentarily, telling Jules that the Merc was also recording its exploration. The TRS, capable of distinguishing the types of materials being scanned, exposed not only the internal framework of the terraced pyramid but also the objects contained within it. Furniture, trinkets and other objects made from stone and bone, were depicted in the same translucent shapes, with different colours denoting each new material. Detritus of civilisation, she thought.

"It's like they just up and left one day and never came back," Jules said.

Were they like the Romans and Greeks? Cultured, with philosophers and physicians and artisans? Or would they find the beginnings of civilization, with artefacts of culture and invention, signs of intelligence and promise? Even though humanity had charted most of Sol, the one thing they never found was intelligent life. They were alone, but it never hurt as much until Earth was going to be destroyed and they realised there was no one to call for help.

Had something catastrophic happened here and, like Earth, they had no one to call for aide?

"Tom," Jules said sombrely. "We've got to get in there. We need to know what happened to these people."

XVII

Reconnaissance

After a full equipment check, including helmet cams, bio-trackers and ammunition, the Sharks were on a careful approach to the entrance of the city. Monolithic stones fit together like the pyramids were covered in wrist-thick creeper vines and vegetation. Giant plants sprouted at the base, some of which had stalks as big as Derick's biceps. The Sharks ignored those unless absolutely needed and took machetes and serrated shovels to the rest to clear the path.

Reaching the outer wall of the city took a good forty-five minutes of chopping and trailblazing. The drone provided imagery of an entrance, blocked by the massive rock Derick was now standing in front of. A twin of a standing pylon at the left of the entrance, it had fallen haphazardly across the path. He ran a hand over the pitted surface, now cleared of any clinging vines and plants. They were going to need the hydraulic lift from the *Ruthie* to move the car-sized stone, but — for now — the crawl space underneath would let them through.

Kneeling, he felt the pads on his fatigues hit something too hard to be dirt and looked down. Clearing away the greenery, Derick saw flat stones fit together as tightly as the walls.

"Looks like it was paved," he announced, getting to his feet and dusting off his hands. "All right, Lorio, Anderson, clear this crawl space out and you're first through." He ignored the glances the two greenhorns shot each other. "Richards, you've got our six."

When his noobs didn't move forward, Derick nailed them both with a look. "You waiting' on a fuckin' escort, Shark?" he said, in a low voice that his people learned early on meant business.

"No, Gunny!!" they chimed as one and hurried past him as Derick shook his head. After a few minutes of grunting and cursing, both young men disappeared to the other side. Two seconds later, a strong and true 'Clear!!' was heard from the other side.

"All right, you heard 'em," he told the rest. "In you go!"

As the Sharks started to crawl through, Ren turned her back on the group, eyes peeled on the surrounding terrain. While the valley wasn't the nearly impenetrable jungle the Major trekked through, the river was bound to attract all kinds of wildlife. After being attacked by a giant plant monster, everything was suspect, and she was searching for anything that twitched.

Shiny had taken position near the redhead as she did a quick links check. Glancing into the sun, she shielded her eyes and turned to face the heavy walls. "Rickman," she hailed Luke, "You still read five by five?" she asked.

* * *

At base camp, Luke, enthralled by the camera footage, was surrounded by squints gathered around his worktable. After years of hearing his brothers describe their military action, this was the first time he was seeing it from their POV, thanks to the live feed.

"Hell yeah, it's better than All Access porn…"

THWACK!

"OW! Jeez Tom!" He glared at the glaring Major. "Yeah, you're five by five!" Luke grumbled, rubbing the back of his head. "Geez…"

* * *

Rolling her eyes, Shiny silently thanked whatever gods were listening that Major Merrick was up there. Sure, he could make the Foreign Legion blush, but he didn't take crap from his people.

"Radio check solid, Gunny!" she sang out as she approached the entrance. Slinging her rifle strap over her head, she dropped to her haunches to study the hole.

"Roger that," Derick nodded, listening to his link feed and the voices reaching him from the other side of the rock. He couldn't see over it, but he could hear them. Sounded like a lot of skylarking, but they'd let him know if there was trouble.

With Shiny, Maya and Jag now through, it was just him and Ren. "How's the leg?" he asked, resting an arm on his rifle.

"Peachy, Gunny," Ren quipped enthusiastically. "Feels like I'm back at Boot in Florida."

That was mostly the truth. Her skin felt odd, prickling with the sensation Maya warned was a result of tissue regeneration. For the most part, she tried to ignore it, save for the occasional tingle that felt like something crawling under her fatigues. A quick, surreptitious scratch usually solved it.

Even if there was more, Ren would never admit it. Not to Derick. He'd gone against his better judgement allowing her to come on this mission. By all rights, she should have remained behind with Beta, babysitting the squints. She wasn't going to make him regret the decision by complaining about the invisible ants she felt running across her thigh.

"Uh huh." Derick raised an eyebrow. He'd suffered through tissue regen before and knew what she was probably feeling. Hell, just thinking about it made him want to scratch. It was a creepy sensation and he hated it every damn time. Without thinking, Derick let his eyes drift down to the leg of Ren's in question and caught himself right around her belt.

Damn... Damn.

"Right." Derick cleared his throat. "Let me get through, give it a five count and then you come on, all right?" he ordered. Raised to let women go first, he caught himself before offering to make the offer to Ren. Out in the field, any chivalrous overture on his part would be met with a snort. If he was lucky. Not waiting for an answer, he dropped to his knees and crawled through the opening.

In just a short time, Derick was back on his feet, flicking an insect off his arm. Moving out of the way, he took in their surroundings. "Shiny?"

"Links are four out of five, Gunny," the young woman called out from where she stood closer to one of the massive stones making up the wall. She ran her fingers over a thick vein of black ore running through the rock. "Might be this, yeah? Static increases the closer I get."

"Noted. See if you can't get a sample for the squints," Derick ordered as Ren made her appearance, looking none the worse for wear.

Ren wiped the sweat off her brow, frowning because a tuft of red curls had managed to get into her face. Surveying the terrain once again, she welcomed all that green, even if it was a bitch to get through. Bugs zipped around them cautiously while mosquitoes the size of zephyrs eyed her fair skin with hungry desire.

"They're going to flip out over this place," she grinned. An honest-to-God alien civilization. Who *wouldn't* freak out? When she was eight, Ren and her parents toured Giza and she remembered soaking in the ancient monuments, built by people who had no concept of electricity. This place reminded her of those now destroyed treasures.

"Oh yeah." Luke would go nuts, Derick figured. "Shiny…?"

"Done!" She held up the small, plastic container with flecks of black in it as she stowed her knife.

"Good." The vegetation was less dense inside the walls, allowing Derick to spot what looked like paths disappearing into the overgrowth. "Just in case we're not alone here, heads up and eyes open," he began, eyeing the pyramids seen in the drone footage. "Ozzy, don't step in anything resembling shit this time."

There was a grumbled 'for the love of God, it was ONCE' behind him, making Derick smirk. Of the three pyramids, one was straight ahead and the other two canted off at an angle on either side of the main building. Derick waved nuisance insects away from his face.

"NAF!!"

"What the hell? Shiny?!" Derick frowned at her, dropping his gaze to the fur ball at her boots.

"I didn't bring him, Gunny! He must have followed us," the younger woman replied, trying to wave the creature off. "Shoo. Go back to camp, Henry."

"You named it?!?!"

Ozzy grabbed French by the battle harness when he went to scoop the animal up. He shot his friend a side glance warning '*if you value your life, come with me*'. Pulling him back to where Ren stood, he mouthed '*uh oh*' at the redhead (who was safe territory since she wasn't involved in pissing off Gunny). Plus, he didn't want to step in naf dung.

He'd simply never hear the end of it.

Ren winced in agreement. Shiny had done the unforgivable by not only feeding it but naming it. Those were Gunny 101 rules. Glancing at the creature, Ren found she couldn't blame the Motswana. The little fuzz ball was cute as hell. She narrowed her eyes and decided to use her power for good. This time.

"Hey Gunny, might not be a bad idea if the little guy tags along," she piped up, winking at Shiny. "For all we know, this could be Gaia's version of a dog or… a canary." Okay, sometimes she overshot.

"What?" Shiny stared at her in dismay as she gathered the creature in her arms.

Derick gave Ren a 'not you, too' look and rolled his eyes. He shoved his safety glasses back up his nose. She had a point, as usual. Frowning at the creature, he finally inclined his head.

"Fine. Bring Henry," he said dryly, his opinion on the matter clear in his tone. "Richards, take Mayday and Jagger to the left pyramid. Jackson, you've got Thing One and Thing Two, to the right. Ozzy, French and Shiny, you're with me, in the middle," he said, indicating the middle of the three pyramids. "Report every ten mikes, meet back here in one hour," he said, glancing at the chronometer strapped to his wrist. "Clear?"

"Crystal," Ren returned and gave him a little smile, nothing overt, just enough to thank him for letting her share in all this. She would have been gutted to be left behind. "See you later Henry."

NAF!

"Hey, it knows its name!" Ren smirked and headed out in search of Mayday and Jagger.

Derick would have winked at her if no one else was around but, instead, let a slight smile shadow across his face as he turned away.

"Fantastic. Do you all know your names because I don't fucking see anyone moving?!" he called out. The Sharks around him set to, quickly forming up and heading off in the directions he'd given.

Turning to his group, he yanked his machete free of its sheath on his back. "I've got point. Shiny, take our six."

"Roger that!" the comtech replied over a soft 'Naf!' "Shhhh."

Rolling his eyes one last time, Derick headed into the underbrush and sank the machete unnecessarily hard into the first plant he found. At least this would work off some of his pent-up energy.

* * *

Their pyramid, which Ren had started calling it not two steps into her team's trailblazing, was smaller than the others but no less impressive. Almost three-storeys high, the sides were meticulously terraced and doubled as steps. The tan brick used to construct the edifice was limestone. It made sense, Ren thought as Jag cut a swathe through the vegetation. Their scans of the mountains indicated an abundance of it and limestone was an extremely versatile construction material for a primitive culture.

The top of their pyramid was a flat platform, with a stone bench positioned in the middle. On the next tier, two small windows peered out at the world. Between them, a smoothed slide of rock reached all the way to the base of the structure. More Mesoamerican, Ren decided, instead of Mesopotamian. Wouldn't her mother be proud, using big words like that? Frowning, she pushed back a low-hanging branch and followed Maya.

"*Harah!*"

Maya glanced at Ren and turned back to Jag. After serving with him for the last six months, they recognised the word escaping Jag's lips as the Hebrew equivalent of 'shit'. While Ren felt sympathy for him, she also felt guilty, not being able to take some of the burden. Any suggestions otherwise and she'd get dirty looks from both of her friends (and a mouthful from Maya).

Pausing a moment to catch his breath, Jag wiped the sweat from his brow and squinted at the tall grass yet to be cleared. Driving the machete tip first into the ground, he took a sip out of his canteen, wincing as he shook his hand and wiggled his fingers to relieve some of the cramping.

"Let me see your hand," Maya ordered, holding hers out for it.

"I'm good," Jag obeyed. "We're almost there," he gestured at the path.

After Maya finished inspecting his hand, he gave her a crooked grin and tucked away his canteen. His eyes drifted to Ren and when she met his gaze, he smiled slightly. All the Sharks were close, but he felt more akin to these two than anyone else. Ren and Maya were family.

They filled the sizeable crater left in his heart after Earth's destruction took his beloved sisters and mother. Seeing Ren almost dead yesterday drove home their worth to him. He would do anything for these cackling hens, even when they were embarrassing him by asking the sexual orientation of every cute guy they encountered because they also knew a hot, single guy.

Or talking about shaving their nether regions.

Wiping sweat off her cheek, Maya held up her slate, snapping pictures like a tourist even as she kept an eye on their surroundings. Doing this kept her mind off the still fresh wound of Colin's loss. She frowned, actively reminding herself of how far she'd come, and loss was a Shark thing. Still, a tiny voice whispered. Bloody fucking unfair.

Six months ago, she lost a fiancé, something she hadn't worked up to tell Ren about yet. Not that she missed Vikram, she hadn't known him. Her parents arranged the marriage when she was twelve and he was fourteen. As adults, Maya was pleased to learn Vik hated the idea as much as she did. An arranged marriage for a Royal Marine medic?

Rubbish. Ancient, archaic, outdated rubbish. Nobody did that anymore!

She was pleased Vic didn't want it to happen anymore than she did. It was ignorant baggage from growing up Hindi. The caste system was abolished over a hundred years ago and with it, arranged marriages. Yet some families were too stubborn and steeped in tradition to abandon it. How many times had her mother droned on and on about how proud she should be of her Indian heritage?

And wasn't it just like *Amma* to be right?

Now, no matter how outdated those words were, Maya would have given just about anything to hear *Amma's* lecture on the importance of all of it one more time. Or sit by *Baba*, listening to him curse at the cricket scores. God, how she missed them!

Oblivious to her friend's thoughts and the caboose of their team, Ren kept her eyes peeled for anything Maya's bio-tracker detector did not pick up. She was grateful it was calibrated to filter out insects or the readings would have driven them all insane, since the world was teeming with bugs. Evidence of a healthy ecosystem, Ren's sixth-grade biology teacher would have said.

Waving away something buzzing at her ear, she wished the bio-tracker would have told them about the sky crabs. To be fair, the sky crabs rewrote their classification of recognisable organisms, (flying lobsters capable of creating hurricane force storms??), which explained why there hadn't been a peep from anyone's sensors. This time, they were caught with their proverbial pants down. Going forward, they needed to adapt better and faster.

Before more people died.

A grasshopper thunked against her body armour, making Ren smirk as it pinged off Maya's helmet. Crazy thing.

"*Good for planting, Miss Renee.*"

Ren looked down, digging at the dirt with the toe of her boot.

Mister Edgar, her family's gardener, would approve of the rich, loamy soil. Not for the first time, Ren wondered if their original landing site should be abandoned. This valley, with the river, good soil, and shelter, thanks to the surrounding mountains, might be a better place. Certainly, the architects of this city had settled here for good reason.

Stepping forward, Ren pulled back when she felt her boot push something hard into the dirt. To save time, they'd veered off the paved path to take a direct route to the pyramid. Looking down, something jutted out of the ground and Ren dropped a knee beside it.

"Hold up!" she called out, pulling a multi-tool from a vest pocket. Unfolding it to produce a flat blade knife, she dug in, brushing away the loosened dirt with the back of a hand.

"What is it?" Jag asked, flipping on his torch to give her some more light.

Ren grabbed the pale object and wiggled it, finally yanking it free.

"Oh wow…" she breathed, holding up a glazed figurine the length of her palm. If she had to guess, she would say it was carved from bone. Tapping her link, she hailed Derick. "Gunny, I found something."

"I'll say, look at the detail," Maya's eyes lit up as she grinned at Jag.

The artist in Ren agreed as she stepped into a shaft of sunlight and held up the figure. "Major, can you see this?"

* * *

Pausing, Derick slipped his slate from a pocket and tapped it as Ozzy moved around him to take up clearing their trail. "Luke, patch her feed to my slate," he ordered.

* * *

"Do I get my allowance if I do?" Luke's voice responded.

"Oi, patch him through!" Tom ordered, shooting the younger Rickman a look that said now was NOT the time.

* * *

Derick winced at the tone in his Major's voice and made a mental note to talk to (or shake him, shaking was good) Luke when he got back. Orders were orders and Luke ought to know better. A light blipped at him from the corner of the screen and he swiped a thumb across the smooth surface. A second later, he was looking at Ren's gloved hand holding up a small … thing.

"Okay. What am I looking at?"

* * *

"It's a carving of some kind," Ren explained, rubbing more dirt off with a thumb. "I think it's made from bone. There's a rudimentary glazing to keep it from breaking down. I've seen the technique in pottery made by the Mesopotamians in the 13th century BC but look at it, though. It's a biped," she said, running a finger over the two legs, the big round eyes and the prominent ridge above the bow-shaped mouth. The nose was wide and stubby and the body willowy but the hands… Ren turned it over in her palm and spoke again. "It's amphibian! Look, its hands are webbed." She pointed out the splayed-open long fingers and toes.

"Gunny, I think this is one of them."

* * *

Whoa.

Was that Ren? Derick stared at the slate. Sounded like her and yep, those were her hands. That was her voice (a rather posh Manhattan lilt the Marines hadn't been able to drill out of her) and the feed identified her as RICHARDS RENEE E. Still catching up from 'rudimentary glazing' and Mesopotamian, Derick blinked at her latest information. Damn. When did Orphan Annie turn into Indiana freakin' Jones? Even as he processed what he was seeing, a thought nagged the back of his mind. She was sooo out of his league, wasn't she?

"Should I bag it?" Ren was asking him. Right.

"Uh... Yes," Derick shook his head, dislodging something off his helmet. "Drop a locator next to anything else you find and leave it. I don't want to lose our daylight," he said, more business-like than usual.

* * *

Ren met Maya's gaze with a puzzled expression of 'what crawled up his ass and died?' "Gotcha, I'll bag this thing and flag any more souvenirs."

Maya dug a plastic Ziploc bag out of a pocket and handed it over. "Here. Off you go, Jagger," she grinned, making shooing motions with her hands. "Chop-chop."

Muttering in Hebrew, Jagger shot Maya the bird and yanked the machete out of the ground where he'd planted it. The Indian medic reminded him most of his sister Jacoba and the thought saddened him.

Sweet, bossy, big sisterly Jacoba. She should have been here.

XVIII

Worship

Hacking at the last of the vines curtained over the darkened entry, Derick yanked them free and tossed them aside. Stepping back, he snagged a rag from his belt to wipe down the blade before sheathing it. Dank, cool air breezed out of the passageway, brushing them all with the scents of greenery and decay. Frowning, he yanked more vines from the sides of the entry, revealing identical holes on each side. About six inches by six inches, they were mostly worn smooth, with gouges cutting up the edges.

"Looks like a locking mechanism of some kind," he said, bringing his rifle up. Thumbing on the torch snapped to the top, he shined it down the passageway. "French, you're with me. Shiny, Ozzy, you two stay out here."

"NAF! NAF NAF!!"

"You stay here too, Private," Derick glanced back, pointing at the critter. Not that he would admit in a million years, but the little fuzz butt was growing on him already. Nor would he admit to breaking his own rules and leaving a protein bar out for Mrs Henry. "Base, Shiny and Ozzy are covering the entrance. French and I are heading in. You got a good link on the visual?"

* * *

"Yeah, you're coming in five by five," Tom answered from where he now sat beside Luke and Jules, all of them glued on the feed. "Clear to proceed. You can see, Doc?" he asked, glancing to where Dr. Samara Nordin was standing behind them. While his Sharks were playing *Jumanji*, Jules ensured the appropriate personnel was present to offer their expertise. In particular, the cultural anthropologist attached to the expedition.

"I can, thank you, Major!" Dr. Nordin's face was lit up as she sat, practically dancing in her seat. "The artefact that Corporal Richards found is stunning and I think there is truth in what she said. The Mesopotamian people were one of the most artistic, next to the Egyptians. To think, they created full, anatomically correct figurines when your hunter-gather cul..."

"Oi, Gunny, say that again..."

Shooting Tom a hairy eye for his blatant attempt to turn the woman off, Jules winked at the doctor. All the squi... uh... scientists were demoralised by Dr. Hall's death and it didn't escape her notice this discovery was giving them all a little more colour.

* * *

Throwing a frown over his shoulder, in the general direction of the camp, Derick tapped his link again. "I said 'Roger that. Let's go, French'." Derick gave the Frenchman a pointed look, before receiving a sharp nod in return and fell into step beside the shorter man.

Moving forward as one, the two men advanced into the tunnel, flashlights cutting into the darkness. More cobwebs and interwoven flora blocked their way, but they made short work of it, finally breaking through after several minutes. Now free to concentrate on something else, Derick finally noticed the odd, crude carvings along the wall. In the beam of his light, he counted two bare, smooth tiles and one carved one. Two more blanks and a carved one. Following the pattern, he ignored Dr. Nordin's excited chatter in his ear piece.

Finally, the passageway emptied them out into a large chamber.

"Hold," Derick said quietly, noting the echo of his voice. He glanced up but only darkness greeted him. "Drop a light, French."

Behind him, Dupree pulled a chemstick from a cargo pocket, twisted it, and tossed it over a shoulder, keeping the light behind them. Within seconds, a soft greenish glow surrounded them.

The men moved forward, their torches lighting the ground in front and a trail of chemo light breadcrumbs illuminated their path from the door. Pulling the torch off his rifle, Derick held it over his head to try and get a better idea of the room they were standing in.

"This place is huge," he stated upon seeing that the beam of light didn't seem to reach any kind of wall or overhead. Only blackness.

Heading deeper in, Derick stopped short when an ornately carved column appeared in his path. He made to go around it when excited chatter filled his earpiece.

"There! Captain, I need to see that column!!!"

"You heard Dr. Nordin, Gunny."

Captain Curran sounded amused and a lot more patient than his best friend. Obliging, Derick took a step back, keeping his cam trained on the column to get as much footage as he could. Several hushed whispers chimed in at once before he was given an impatient 'keep going' from Tom.

As French into step with him again, Derick exchanged a smirk with his fellow Shark. They advanced into the room, leaving their bright trail behind them.

Only when the beam of his torch bounced off pale, white tiles did he stop. Another excited gasp hit his ear. Raising his light, it revealed the tiles leading to a dais or a raised platform of some sort. About twelve feet wide and ten feet high, the tiles continued up wide steps, flanked by pitted, rough statues.

"Oh, my word! That looks like some sort of altar," Dr. Nordin's exotic accent faded into another language for a moment.

Derick moved a little closer to the dais, where intricately carved images decorated nearly every inch of it. There were several figures, like the one from Ren's figurine with image upon image of plants and animals. There was even a formation that appeared to be a set of constellations.

"Yes, yes, yes, I'll need a closer look, but I would say this could be a historical record of their civilisation. Certainly, the room you are in held some importance in the lives of these people. Judging by the centre slab, this might very well be a temple. Are we able to see further into the room?"

"Yes ma'—"

"PUTAIN!! FAIS CHIER!!!"

The Frenchman's sudden, blistering curse caused Derick to bring his rifle up in a quick, practiced jerk. In the beam of light, French stared slack jawed above him.

"Gunny! Do you see thiz?" Dupree exclaimed, followed by several more words from the streets of Paris.

Standing beside him, Derick looked up. "Fuck a dead dog..." he breathed, light joining French's strobe to illuminate their find.

High above them, like some humongous blue whale display in a museum, a life size sky crab stood authoritatively over them, carved in stone. "Holy shit. Luke, you getting this?"

"Yep, Red Lobster made it out here. I'm trying to enhance the image."

Derick shined his light around him. "You think they worshipped them?"

* * *

"Well not surprising I suppose," Tom crossed his arms over his chest and stared at the 'monument', his memory still raw from the assault on the *Firefly*. "The beasties fly, generate storms and shoots electricity out of their arses. Primitive lot like these would think they're gods or something."

"Absolutely," Samara agreed. "The Mayans and Aztecs were sun worshippers while Native Americans identified their gods with the animals of their environment. The list goes on."

"Right then," Tom spoke up immediately, hoping to keep a full recitation of 'the list' at bay. "Resume your sweep so we can call it secured and let the squints get a proper crack at the place."

* * *

"There are some openings off the main room. We're gonna check those out." Derick glanced up once more and shook his head as he motioned French forward.

Like the main entrance, there were no doors, but the two men still approached cautiously. So far, too much crap had happened to them to assume they were safe just because the place was empty. Plus, Derick wouldn't admit it, but he'd probably watched Indiana Jones one too many times.

"On three," he told French as they took up position on either side of the first entry. "One, two... three...!" The Frenchman entered first, with Derick right behind him.

Their flashlights illuminated a small, not quite empty room. Like the rest of the place, cobwebs piled with dust, hung from every corner and nearly blocked a spiral staircase carved out of the same stone as the walls. Pulling his knife, Derick cut away some of the cobwebs, revealing carvings like those in the main chamber. In his ear, he could just barely hear Dr. Nordin's chatter and thought he caught a question from her. "Does she want me to clear the whole thing?"

* * *

"Negative," Tom replied after Dr. Nordin shook her head at him and went back to her assistant.

Glancing at Jules, he noted her pensive expression as she studied the screen.

Was she thinking what he was? Why no one had been here for millennia? If so, why? Even ancient ruins usually held kind of remains, right? More than one bit of figurine. Even with a mass evacuation or a plague, there was always something left behind.

Pompeii had its skeletons frozen in time. The lost Roanoke Colony left behind food and tools, material too important to discard if its people left on their own volition. Hell, his first mission with the SAS was to a planet where the entire terraforming survey crew was killed by a spore contaminating the water supply. When his squad was sent in to investigate, all they found were the dead.

So, where the fuck were the bodies here? The tools and weapons? The skeletons?

Frowning, Tom hit the link again. "Gunny, keep an eye out for anything that might explain why this place is so empty?"

If Derick didn't find anything (which Tom suspected would be the case), then whatever had taken these people out, did it by complete surprise.

A chill raced down Tom's spine and he swore he heard his old crazy cat lady neighbour droning about someone walking over his grave.

* * *

There was nothing here but cobwebs and enough dust to send a germaphobe into cardiac arrest. Derick acknowledged the order anyway and glanced at French. "You heard the man."

"Oui." French's reply was solemn and quiet.

Yeah, right, there with ya, bud, Derick thought to himself as they returned to the main chamber and headed for the second door.

* * *

How the fuck did I get here?

This was a question Private Jeremy Anderson, aka Thing One, asked himself nearly every day for the last six months. Of course, he knew the answer. He was a petulant, blue-blooded little bitch (his father's words) who turned down Harvard and in doing so, had apparently thrown his life away.

Jeremy (he preferred Remy) could still feel the burn of his father's words in his conversation with the head of admissions. Of course, the old man hadn't listened. Hadn't bothered to find out his son got accepted to the Massachusetts Institute of Technology, where he really, really wanted to go.

No, instead the elitist fuck told Admissions his 'ungrateful pissant of a son' had made a mistake and was 'listening to his dick' and 'of course, he would attend Haaavaahd' (the monied pronunciation). How could he not? It was his 'legacy'. Seven generations had graduated from the Ivy League school, everyone except Grams, who had apparently gone to Duke. Major *Escandelo* in the Anderson and Wentworth families.

Remy sighed. If he missed anyone from home, it was Grams. She would have brought him back down to Earth and talked to her son about her grandson. She would have punched gentle holes in his glorious, naive idea of travelling the systems, writing gritty tales about the life and adventures of a space Marine.

Yeah, if he missed anyone, it was her. She would have told him the truth. Reality sucked ass and boot camp was fucking HARD. Despite a background in team sports like crew sailing and football, he'd struggled. But boot camp did exactly what it was designed to do. After Remy Anderson, Captain of his school's crew team enlisted, he'd been deconstructed and rebuilt as Private Jeremy Anderson, US Marine (now SHARC).

His last phone call home, to tell his family where he was assigned, had been full of his father still being pissed at him. The fuck hung up on him before he'd had the chance to tell them.

He hadn't been on the Eisenhower two weeks before everything had been destroyed. His assignment saved his life, and, in the end, it had been Private Anderson still standing when Edward Reginald Anderson and his Haavahd blue-blood burned with the rest of Earth.

Standing in the shadows of several trees, taking up the six as Sarge chopped and hacked his way into an alien jungle, Remy realized something.

He had plenty of material for that book.

CLANG! "FUCK!"

Startled out of his memories, Remy winced. Someone's mamma bore the brunt of Sarge's temper as the darker skinned man shook his hand out. The machete dangled from the wrist strap of his other hand as the ancestors of someone's mamma were now cursed.

"Sarge?" Remy asked from his position, craning his head to see around the stockier Private Frank 'Frankie' Lorio.

"I hit something," Sergeant Jackson growled, yanking at the high grass in front of him and shoving it all apart to find a hip-high, bullet shaped piece of stone sticking out of the ground. It had been smoothed and polished white and was covered in odd symbols, etched right into the rock.

"Huh…" Sarge grunted as he hacked at some of the thick grass to clear around the stone.

Meanwhile, Remy surveyed the immediate area. Spotting another one of those bullet shaped rocks through a group of saplings, he headed over to it. "There's one here, too."

A moment later, Frankie also chimed in with his own discovery. Within ten minutes, the three men uncovered at least a dozen stones. While shaped the same, each stone was carved with a unique set of glyphs.

Running a thumb over the markings, Remy frowned before turning to study the others. Wait a second… a flash of inspiration, followed by dismay struck him.

"Shit!" he yanked his hand back as if bitten. "Sarge, it's a graveyard!"

"Yeah, I just realized that myself. Don't disturb any of them."

"Aw man!" Frankie crossed himself quickly and muttered something about forgiveness as he danced from one foot to the other, trying to find a safe place to stand.

"Dude, it's not like lightening is going to strike you dead," Remy rolled his eyes. This wasn't the first time he'd seen his friend's very Roman Catholic, Italian sensibilities challenged. "Just stand still."

"Lorio! Chill the fuck out!" Sarge snapped. "They ain't gonna mind where you stand."

"But Sarge…" Frankie didn't look up, too busy trying to find a place to put his boots.

"Am I fucking talking to myself? STAY PUT!"

Frankie froze and hell, even Remy froze. Sarge was turning into Gunny.

"Gunny, we've found what I think is a cemetery. We found several…"

"Twenty," Remy spoke up.

"Approximately twenty gravestones."

* * *

They had cleared the two other rooms and were now debating the spiral staircase. Derick didn't relish crawling through all that dust (and probably fucking spiders) and he could tell French wasn't too fond of the idea either. When Jackson first called him, static crackled through the line. Derick thumbed his link. "A what? Say again?"

The sergeant's second time was heard clearly.

A cemetery? Crap.

"Luke, take a scan and find him a way around," Derick ordered, just as he heard the rasp of a lighter. Where French had found a Zippo, he didn't know but he motioned for the man to put it away for the moment. "Sergeant, you know the drill."

Wars had been fought over holy land and even though the people of this world were long gone, they still had protocols to follow when encountering consecrated land.

* * *

Luke was beginning the survey when he'd heard Sergeant Jackson's announcement. On his screen, the headstones glowed pale and nearly luminous next to the grey silhouettes of the Sharks. Tapping the spectral coloured screen, he zoomed out to study the surrounding area.

"Okay, Sarge, take ten steps to your left and then proceed compass north for 35 meters. That should get you past it and up to the walkway around the structure."

* * *

"Copy that." Sarge made the careful half turn to his left as Luke relayed directions to Lorio and Anderson.

"Copy."

Remy could hear the relief in his friend's voice. It didn't matter if the body in the grave beneath him wasn't human, it was still a grave, and Catholic doctrine dictated a healthy respect for any gravesite.

"First, we find their city, then we find their graves? Those eggheads really dropped the ball huh? I thought we was gonna be the only ones here?"

"Well," Remy kept his eyes down to count his steps as he moved across the ground cautiously. "It's not like we had much of a selection, or time to be sure of anything."

"True dat. It's just… its turf, you know? Where I'm from, turf is a big deal. You don't mess with another people's turf. You do, and bad shit happens, man. Real bad shit. They may not be so happy to see us moving in."

"Both of you, stop jawing and pick it up!!"

Sarge's rebuke startled them both and spurred them into moving faster than before. Remy had just stepped onto something hard when he heard Frankie's shout behind him.

"Fuck!"

"Frankie!?" Remy shouted, turning just in time to see Frankie disappear into the brush. "Frankie!! SARGE! Lorio's in trouble!" he called out, already moving to the last spot he'd seen his friend. He could hear something crashing through the underbrush.

"What's going on?" Sarge appeared next to Remy so fast, he did a double take. Before Remy could respond, he'd touched his link.

"Not sure yet! Standby!"

Remy shoved past a sapling, not caring when he heard green wood cracking under the pressure.

"Frankie?!" he called out, skirting around a thorny bush with the Sarge close behind him. He was about to hop over a downed tree when he was yanked backwards by his harness.

"Stop!" Sarge ordered and pointed over the tree to where Frankie was standing at the bottom of a crater, getting to his feet.

"Frankie, you okay?" Remy called down to him, noting the trampled greenery and discarded Shark equipment marking his friend's path.

"Yes, dammit..."

Remy tossed the Sarge a smirk. "He's okay if he's cussing." When the Sarge only frowned at him, Remy cleared his throat. Right. "I'll uh... I'll toss him a rope," he said as Sarge turned away to talk to Gunny.

"Everything's okay, Gunny. Lorio fell into a hole."

Glancing back at his sergeant, Remy shrugged out of his pack and dropped it the ground. Kneeling beside it, he pulled out the high-tension steel lined cable the Sharks called 'rope'. He listened with one ear while he secured the line around the nearest thick tree.

"Looks like a crater of some kind. Tough to see because it's all over-grown but you wouldn't see it until you were right on top of it. Yeah, hold on."

Tossing the cable down to his friend, Remy waited as Frankie searched out his lost equipment.

"You alright, Thing Two?"

"Yeah, Sarge. I'm fine," Frankie grumbled as he claimed his gear. "Just feel kind of stupid - like Timmy in the well you know?"

"Well no one's digging your ass out so on your feet soldier, unless you broke something."

When the sergeant had turned back around to finish his conversation, Remy shot his friend a sympathetic look. "Ready when you are," he called down, wrapping a length of line around his gloved hands.

After a few minutes, a disgruntled Frankie was dusting himself off and trying to inventory his gear.

Helping him get sorted, Remy looked over to where the Sarge was aiming a laser ruler across the opening. "What do you think? Meteor?" he asked Frankie, who shrugged.

"Don't know. Didn't get many meteors in Little Italy, man. The only craters we saw was the dimples in our grandma's thighs."

Remy rolled his eyes. "Classy," he retorted, shaking his head as he collected the line.

"Come on, Thing One, Thing Two. We've still got a lot of ground to cover."

Too conditioned to jumping when a senior soldier ordered them about, Remy and Frankie hurried to fall in behind their sergeant.

XIX

Ancient City

They named the city Babel.

'They' being the eggheads who argued for an hour before reaching their decision. Jules who was volun-told as the mediator for the discussion, had sat through staff meetings less boring. The suggestions ranged from the poetic, like Babel, to the overly romance-novelish Serengettica. Seriously? More like Bullshittica, Jules thought contemptuously. In the end, it was Luke who ended the argument with the best choice.

Babel. It was what Dr. Hall chose.

Jules agreed. Olivia and Dr. Nakamura chose the name Babel for their landing site even before the expedition set foot on the planet. It was biblically poetic. Babel was the first great city of man to be struck down by God and this city, with its overgrown grass and chambers filled with dust and cobwebs, had apparently suffered a similar calamity. Further to that, everyone agreed (or chose not to argue), the valley should be named after Olivia Hall.

It was fitting because Olivia Valley was a much more appropriate location for establishing a colony than their original landing site.

The mountain protecting the valley on either side kept out the worst of the elements and the storms generated by the sky crabs. Even with the wide river running through it, a good portion of the valley was above the floodplain, making it perfect for setting up housing. Not unlike the Nile Delta where the early Egyptians began building their civilisation.

The soil was also given a high passing grade by the team's pedologist. Declaring it extremely fertile for growing crops, he believed the odd rows of trees here and there were perfectly situated to prevent soil erosion by the wind. More and more, it was becoming clear this was a better alternative than their original landing site. It was certainly more conducive to the large-scale agriculture they would have to put into effect almost immediately. With no signs of catastrophic flooding, there was very little chance of crops being wiped out.

From her vantage point at the main gate, Jules saw none of these things. Instead, she saw Angkor Wat, Mohenjo-Daro, or Teotihuacan. After college, and before joining the Space Corps, she'd spent a year backpacking and visiting those landmarks, cognisant she'd never have the time afterwards. How right she had been. They were all gone now, each and every one of the seven wonders, from the Great Pyramids to the Leaning Tower of Pisa.

Profound loss stabbed her heart and for a moment, Jules's eyes misted over.

* * *

With a little Luke Rickman ingenuity and a whole lot of creative cussing, the broken monolith blocking the main entrance was heaved out of the way by the Sharks. Putting their backs into it, they tipped the limestone block into the brush off to one side, promptly crushing the verdant overgrowth beneath it. More sweat, cursing, and encouragement from the nafs followed and before long, the greenery under their boots was cleared, revealing an ancient cobblestone path.

For now, there was no longer any need to crawl under the massive rock or through waist-high weeds, but more drastic measures would be needed later, Tom thought. Maybe a controlled burn once the expedition completed its analysis. Or maybe next time someone ventures down to a planet full of grass, they could bring along a bloody lawn mower and a whipper snipper.

A group of squints swept past him and Jules, chattering on about bloody theorems and WhoGivesAFuck's Law of Disorder. He couldn't fault their eagerness. This discovery was bloody Christmas morning for this lot. Stepping back out of their way, he took advantage of the moment to get a good look at the pyramids.

"Got to say," he admired the craftsmanship and the sheer balls that went into building something like that with primitive tools. "It looks even more impressive now we're up close."

When she didn't answer immediately, he glanced over to see the deep introspection on her lovely features. "Oi, you alright?"

"I'm fine," Jules straightened up, schooling her face. This wasn't the time or the place to get melancholy. Despite exchanging spit last night, she wasn't ready to let her guard down just yet. She gestured to the overgrown jungle and the ruins beyond.

"It's impressive, you know? I half expect spider monkeys or snakes to come out of the undergrowth."

"Well, I can shoot those," Tom patted the sidearm at his hip affectionately. "It's the big buggers that fly and zap you I'm more worried about."

"You can't shoot spider monkeys!" Jules snorted, eyeing the weapon at his hip. "Besides, that won't do a damn thing against sky crabs," she said, hitching her pack a little higher. "I know what they did to the shuttle but they're animals all the same. They were just defending their territory. If we must shoot them…" Jules didn't finish her thought. She didn't like the idea of shooting an innocent animal at all.

"We're not going to repeat Earth," Tom offered quietly, glancing at her.

Humanity had systematically buggered every environment they landed on by having little or no regard for its natives. The sky crabs scared the shit out of him but in their way, they were also magnificent. It was like finding out you'd landed on a planet of dinosaurs. Killing them wasn't something he'd like to entertain.

"I'm keeping my fingers crossed this lot can figure out a way to scare them without resorting to that. Maybe some kind of repellent."

Surely, there had to be an answer in that giant smear of sunblock that just walked past them.

"Maybe." Jules went to her toes for a second, absently dropping a hand on Tom's bicep to keep her balance as she scanned the groups for Luke. "My money is on Luke," she said, going back to the flats of her boots. "So how long have you known the Rickmans?"

From the way they acted together, she'd guess longer than just the six months spent on the *Ruthie* together.

"Oh, since the big bloke was a bloody hippy hanging about Miramar on Earth and Luke was shoo...uh... gawking at every bird that walked past. I ran into Derick at a local bar and started talking in between drinks. He wasn't a Marine yet."

"A... Gunny was a hippie?" Was he pulling her leg? After a moment of side-eye, Jules decided he wasn't and glanced at the tall Shark who looked like he'd been born with that roguish high and tight. She couldn't picture him in flip flops and board shorts. "How long ago was that?"

Tom stared for a moment. How long had it been?

"About ten years I think," he calculated out loud and blinked at just how much time had passed.

Ten years? A whole fucking decade? Had it really been that long? Suddenly, the passage of years from that kid at Miramar, suffering the loss of a brother who meant everything to him to the best 21C Tom ever served with, made Tom feel inordinately old but also proud.

"He was in a difficult place at the time. You know the one where you have no idea what the fuck comes next until some drunken bastard at the bar gives you a kick up the arse?"

"And the drunken bastard, was you?" Jules grinned at the expression on his face, the one that suddenly realized he was closer to forty than he liked. Had she ever been in a 'difficult place'? When her dad died, yes. She'd felt so empty because a man like her father was supposed to live forever. "What were you doing in Miramar then? I was stationed there for a couple of years."

"Prisoner exchange," Tom joked as they resumed walking down the paved street bringing them to the foot of the largest pyramid in Babel. Sharks were hacking away at the vegetation around it, trying to clear space for the squints who would need room to work. For a moment, they looked like worshippers bowing repeatedly in front of their god. "I was in town to take part in a joint live fire training exercises with your Marines. Spent two weeks in San Diego, went to Sea World, and charmed the ladies with the accent."

"The ladies at Sea World?" Jules smirked, deliberately misunderstanding. "You must have made quite an impression on the sea lions and the seals. Probably broke some hearts, huh?"

"Well I had something special with a manatee, but it was the lasses at the local bars that liked the accent," he winked. "And no, I didn't leave a lot of broken hearts behind, just celibacy vows."

"Oh, for God sake!" Luke's exasperated voice exploded in their ear pieces. "Turn off your headset already!"

"What's the matter, Rickman? Not into sea creatures?" Jules retorted, eyes twinkling at Tom. Was she embarrassed at being overheard possibly flirting with Tom? Maybe. Maybe not really.

"Tell them about the octopus, Luke." Derick's dry remark left Jules giggling in an undignified manner.

"All I can say is you can't always tell whether they're female or male." Luke's voice sounded pained and there was a very female 'eewwgh'.

"If the hole fits," Tom threw in, prepared for the response that comment was about to get. It was all a bit of fun, wasn't it?

Jules eyed Tom in amusement. "Anything else I should know about you?"

"Nothing I'm willing to say on an open channel," Tom grinned and then laughed when he heard Luke's voice in the nearby distance.

"*Thank Christ!*"

* * *

When they arrived at the entrance to the main pyramid, the Gunny and his team were already present and waiting. Nearby, the squints were unpacking their gear, eager to study this new playground and talking a mile a minute.

Of the nearest group, Tom recognized Hanae and her assistant Mahmud trying to collect insect specimens for study. Mahmud was a tall, skinny kid and he moved like he wasn't quite sure what to do with his long legs and arms. When he finally finished fiddling with his net, Hanae shooed him off and turned her attention back to the insects already occupying several specimen jars.

Behind Hanae, Dr. Andropolis had commandeered French to help him move what Tom assumed was a weather sensing device to the top of their pyramid.

Dr. Hall should have been here. Not for the first time, Tom felt a pang of sorrow at her absence. Sucking in his breath, Tom resolved he and Jules would do right by her and her team. They would try and keep them as safe as possible. She deserved that much, and Tom was determined her final expedition would also be her greatest.

Nodding once to himself, Tom moved closer to the Sharks. "Right then," he regarded his troops, "Reports!"

Predictably, Derick spoke first.

"So far, no one's showed up to claim the place," Derick crossed his arms over his chest, resting them on the butt of his rifle. "Altars are in this one. The graves are that way," he jerked a thumb over his shoulder, indicating a freshly cleared path of chopped up undergrowth. "Lorio and Anderson are working on clearing a path to Lorio's Crater…"

"Why's it got my name?" the younger man's voice was thick across the links.

Grinning at Tom, Derick wiggled his eyebrows. "You fell in it, it's now your hole." There was a collective groan from the Sharks.

"At least it was a hole he fell in," Ozzy grumbled under his breath to Jazz, who snorted.

"Hey, we can name any steaming pile of unidentifiable stuff, an Ozzy," Ren quipped, ducking behind Maya, who smirked.

"Fucking comedians. You and Gunny shouldn't be allowed to name anything!" Ozzy grumped, rolling his eyes.

"Score one for Orphan Annie," Derick laughed, winking at her without realizing it. "Richards's statue was found in that pyramid." One hand waved in the general direction of the third building. "We secured it according to Dr. Nordin's instructions."

"Thank you, Gunny Rickman," Dr. Nordin stepped forward. Despite being in her fifties, she had a head full of dark hair coiled into an elegant bun.

There was an air of authority about her that reminded Tom of Mrs Butterworth, his fourth year English teacher. The woman could make him piss himself with a single glare through her bejewelled glasses. To this day, he still had nightmares about conjugating verbs and now, his nightmares would include Mrs Butterworth in fatigues.

"Under normal circumstances, I would cite the preservation of the site's integrity to avoid contamination, but these are not normal circumstances," She explained. "Might I suggest the first thing we do is scan the cemetery and the bodies there. These people left a perfectly good city in a predominantly fertile and well-irrigated valley for no obvious reason. We need to know why. We must investigate all possibilities, especially disease."

Judging from the Sharks' reaction, no one liked the sound of that. Tom didn't blame them. There had been diseases on Earth. Smallpox remained viable even decades after the fact. A raging sickness was the last thing humanity needed right now.

"Let's make that a priority," he said sharing her concern. "Also, I'd like to know what made that crater. You lot got anything in your bag of tricks to figure out what caused it?" He scanned the scientists present.

A slender, Asian man raised his hand and spoke up. "I am Jae-Sun Park, the team geologist," he introduced himself. "I can conduct a survey to determine what might have created it. It does not appear to be the result of natural erosion or a meteor crater. I may not be able to give you any definitive answers, but I can rule a few things out."

"Thanks Doc," Tom nodded, appreciating the honesty.

"We'll also conduct a C14 scan of the remains," Nordin added. "That will tell us just how long the bodies in the grave have been interred."

"Good." Tom swept his gaze across the entire group, Sharks and squints alike. "No one goes anywhere alone. We've done a sweep, but this is a large place and as we all know by now, the ionisation levels on this planet plays silly buggers with our sensor equipment. You want to go for a walk to scan something pretty, you take a Shark. That is not negotiable."

"You heard the man. Jackson, put two on the wall there to keep a look out," Derick stated, just as he spotted what looked like a staircase carved into the outer wall. At the top, where it ended it looked flat. "Belay that," he snapped his fingers, changing tracks. "Richards, on the wall," he ordered, hoping to keep her out of trouble with the medical staff. "Jag, you're with her."

"Gunny…"

Ren opened her mouth to protest but the look he shot her brooked no argument. She didn't like being sidelined for sentry duty, but she owed him. She nodded obediently, before heading for the wall. "Aye Gunny. Jag?"

"Right behind you, *ahot.*"

"A what?" Ren stopped short, causing Jag to bump into her from behind.

"It means sister. It slipped."

Their voices died off as Derick continued, half-listening to their conversation. With no protest from Ren (finally!), he'd almost pulled her back until she reacted to Jag and shot him an evil look. Yeah, she was fine. "Mayday, you're on the ground with us. Sharks, I want any movement radioed in, especially if it takes you off a cleared path. Understood?"

"Hold up, Gunny," Tom spoke up, not ready to dismiss his people yet. "What about the structures themselves?" he asked Dr. Nordin, looking the main entrance and the wall above up and down. "Are they sound? I'd like to use the main chamber as a base," he said, ignoring the baleful eye the woman turned on him.

"Scans put it in the affirmative," Luke answered confidently, no traces of snark or juvenile behaviour in his voice this time. "They built these things strong, probably to withstand the storms."

"Alright then! You lot know your jobs, no larking about, smoke breaks or humping trees! Dismissed!" Tom's bark prompted everyone to disperse like he was the pebble thrown into a pond.

"That leaves you and me to set up base camp," Jules said, grabbing her pack off the ground. "Let's go see what we've got."

"Yes ma'am," Tom threw her a snappy salute and waved her ahead of him like a gentlemen. Who was he kidding? He just liked the view.

* * *

The Slurry rippled.

A thing it had not done in years. In the crucible of its confinement, deep in the dark places where no living thing save themselves dwelt, they felt the presence of the others far above them. The disturbance hummed through the rock, nudging them gently awake from their long, black sleep.

As the sleepers awakened, each new quiver in the Slurry brought the promise of prey and a deep, aching hunger. In the rotting putrefaction of their previous victims, limbs uncurled, and bodies jerked as the sleepers shook off the effects of their long hibernation.

A vibration echoed from the Giver, a song of need and demand, to bring her sustenance flowed through. Like drone bees, the creatures slithered through the Slurry to silently breach the surface.

Freed from the surface, feelers tested the slurry-free air and detected the sweet scent of prey. Lots of prey. Enough to sustain them through another long sleep. One by one, the dark shapes scurried into the dark undergrowth and prepared to feed.

XX

Mulks

Needing more supplies from the *Firefly*, Luke and his Shark escort trudged back to the ship. Approaching the shuttle, he was once again struck by the damaged it sustained during the sky crab assault. Thanking his lucky stars, Derick's lucky stars and whatever the hell it was Tom counted on, they'd survived not only the attack but also the flight to the valley. Her demolished state reminded him of some wrecks he'd inspected during his first year out of college.

The analytical part of him, removed from the ache of Liv's death, was surprised she'd been the ONLY casualty.

"Don't get too far ahead, yeah?" Shiny's elegantly clipped voice reminded.

Slender, with exotic dark skin and almost his height, Shiny looked like she belonged on a catwalk somewhere instead of standing hip deep in thick grass, toting an automatic rifle. At her feet, Private Henry, the furry critter who'd adopted them, trundled along with the occasional 'naf!'

"You know," Luke paused long enough to let her catch up. "You didn't have to come back with me."

Like Derick would have let him come out here alone. That had been a *fun* discussion.

With still no contact or acknowledgement of the signal they'd sent to the *Olympia* that morning, Luke assumed the worst. The signal was probably too weak to penetrate the ionised atmosphere. Taking this as a personal challenge, Luke decided the next thing to do would be to prepare a locator beacon.

According to Captain Curran, they would be considered overdue by nightfall. Since they moved locations and couldn't count on the update getting to the fleet, they needed the beacon for the ships to find them.

Shiny snorted, a dark eyebrow lifting. "You heard Gunny, no one goes no place without a Shark, okay?" How in the world did the Gunny keep his patience with his brother? She rested a hand on the butt of her rifle, where it was clipped to her vest and motioned him forward. "Come on, while it's still light."

"Okay, okay, but it's hard to take 'Gunny'," he raised his fingers to emphasize his brother's rank; "Seriously, when he used to sit on my head and fart."

Derick had been ten and he'd been five, but Luke had been vindicated when Chris ran Derick down and did the same thing. Nevertheless, her point was taken, and he hastened his pace, aware that she was just looking out for him.

"That's it!" Shaini closed the distance between them and yanked him around to face her. "You don't get it, do you?" She glared before rolling her eyes. "Of course not, or else you would not be showing such disrespect. I don't care if the two of you peed on each other like my little cousins or picked boogers out of each other's noses! Out here, he's Gunny! No quotation marks, no sarcastic remarks! If anyone of us spoke to him like you do, we'd be finding pieces of our ass between here and those mountains! You talk to him like shit and you don't respect him. It makes every one of us want to shoot you when you open your mouth!"

She paused and caught her breath, aware she'd crossed a line, but it was too late now. She would say her piece.

"That man has had the shit for the last six months. People in his face, spitting on him, calling him all sorts of names, threatening him, all because he's wearing a uniform. All because he's doing his duty and he never once lost his shit and gave those fuckers what for." She stepped closer to Luke.

"He took the brunt of it, you know. He wouldn't let the survivors take their anger out on us. He stood between us and them. Before word came about you, he did this despite mourning his entire family. You will not disrespect him in my company, brother or not, you hear?" she finished, nostrils flaring in anger and her eyes black.

Woah. Luke actually took a step back. Shiny looked that damn scary. As her words sank in, he regrouped, meeting her glare eye for eye. This wasn't the first time he'd got yelled at by a soldier, not when you grew up in the household of Daniel Rickman. Hell, after the death of his favourite son, yelling was the only way to get through to Derick.

After a long pause, Luke bowed his head slightly. "I'm sorry, Corporal. Have you been a soldier long?"

"Six years," Shiny retorted, hands going to her slender hips. "What of it?"

"I've been in the military all my life," Luke replied, wondering if she'd understand. "When your father and brothers are soldiers, you don't get a choice. You go where they go, you live with all the other soldiers on base. Its life, until they get shipped."

He didn't know why he was explaining himself, but her anger made him feel it was necessary. There was no denying the respect and awe in her voice as she fought for his brother. He respected that.

"No one other than soldiers' families understand the weight of that hangs over us, the dread of seeing the chaplain or another officer walking up the driveway with bad fucking news. I've been through that. I watched it change my brother from the hippie surfer boy to…Gunny," he said, thrusting an arm in the direction of the city. "He and our dad nearly tore each other apart from grief."

Stepping closer, Luke tried not to appear confrontational, but he needed her to know that in no way did he disrespect his brother.

"Trust me, I know the sacrifices he's made, I know that he could die any day. Jesus, if anyone knows that, it's me. What you call disrespect keeps me from begging him to leave the Corps… I mean the Sharks, because I don't want to lose him too." His voice threatened to bottom out and Luke cleared his throat. "Trust me. I respect him, just like I respect you and all the Sharks."

Even Henry had gone quiet, perched back on his haunches, one paw on her boot. "You have a funny way of showing it," Shiny retorted finally. "You could show it occasionally, too, you know? Right now, it's nothing but disrespect."

"Do you have brothers?" Luke bit back, using restraint because her critique was coming from a place of affection for his brother.

"I'm the oldest… "Shiny's hesitation was almost unnoticeable. "Of five girls. Why?"

Five girls. Well that explained *that*.

"Well the disrespect you see, is how brothers always behave towards each other. When I was little, Chris and Derick, *your* gunny, use to put bugs in my bed. The number of times I had to eat something that was meant to be fudge but ended up being motor oil… I've lost count. We give each other shit, that's how it is."

"Motor oil?" Shiny stared at him in disgust. "I suppose that's as bad as convincing your little sister that fish slime is good for her hair…"

"Or being forced to go on a play date with Betty 'the Spitter' Scolari because she has a hot older sister your brother wants to date."

It was *so* not worth the five bucks Derick had paid him.

"NAF!!" Shiny glanced down at Henry before looking up at Luke, ignoring the creature pawing at her pants leg. "I had to go on a double date with my little sister once. Mother would only let her go if I went. The boy brought his older brother, who was still two years younger than me."

"NAF!NAF!NAF!!!"

Scooping him up, Shiny rubbed behind an ear. "What's all the noise for?"

Henry paused long enough to sniff her hand before wiggling to prop his forepaws on her shoulder. "NAAAAF!!"

"Oy…" Shiny pulled him back into her arms. "Luke, look!" she called out, holding Henry up for him to see. Along the creature's back, the furry spines had turned blood red, as if the little guy came complete with its own version of Condition Red. Henry wiggled and barked again, his cries getting more urgent. "Ouch!! Alright, calm down…"

"Maybe he smells something off!" Luke replied as he headed around the ship towards the rear cargo hatch of the *Firefly*. He was only a few steps from the corner when something emerged from behind the ship.

UGG-LEE was Luke's first take on the nearly seven-foot-high creature that stopped him in his tracks.

Holyfuckingshit…was the second. Standing upright on powerful hind legs, it had a muscular serpentine neck that didn't seem to have a head. No eyes, no snout, even nostrils. Just a star shaped mouth that opened to reveal rows upon rows of glistening, sharp teeth.

"Uh… Shiny…" Luke hissed as he retreated. The thing reared up. "You know what I said about not wanting to be a soldier? I TAKE IT BACK!" He yelled, jumping back just in time to avoid the swipe of a long, three clawed hand.

Jesus, Mary and Joseph's Dead Uncles!! Tossing Henry to the ground, Shiny snatched her rifle into position. "DOWN!!!" she bellowed just before the report of her blast rifle sizzled through the air. The bolt impacted the creature's head, lifting it off its feet and sending it backwards to the ground in a spray of fluids and wet meat.

On his belly to where he'd dropped after she'd shouted, he was scrambling away from the thing when it was ripped to shreds. Not far enough, he realized, recognizing the fluid sprayed over him and the wet thuds he could hear smack down around him.

"Luke!" Shiny rushed to his side, yanking him hard by his field harness. "Are you all right?!" she demanded, shaking him.

"Yeah… no… the fuck was that thing?" he grimaced, flinging gunk off his hand before wiping it on the grass. Swiping at his cheek, Luke made a face when he realized the liquid was blood.

"Fucking mulk!" Shiny retorted, hauling him to his feet and shoving him towards the shuttle. Behind her, Henry naffed frantically and loudly. "Get the transponder and come on!" she ordered as Henry ran off a few feet and turned to bark at them again. His back spines were still an electric red. "Christ on a pogo stick, Henry knew they were there!" She jabbed the button on her link. "Gunny, we made contact! Mulks!"

"What?" The Gunny's voice was broken up over static.

"Mulks!" Shiny yelled into the link just as Henry tugged at her pants leg with his teeth. "Henry, all right, we're coming, I… shit…." Her eyes went wide at the sight of two more mulks breaking out of the tree line. "Gunny, one Mulk dead and two… shit… three… more!"

It's odd how a little bit of death and possible rending could bring two people together, Luke thought as he raced up the ramp. His foot slid on something gory, but he didn't stop to inspect it, intent on getting what he came for and getting the hell outta Dodge. The broken transponder he hadn't managed to jury rig into the ship's communications was lying comfortably against the floor. Snatching it up, Luke hurried back, skirting the dead mulk before leaping over its carcass.

Skidding to a halt beside his escort, Luke followed her glare. "Fuck me…" he muttered, spying the group at the tree line. Two more emerged from the woods and one of them let out a sharp, trumpeting bellow.

When it was answered, Luke stared at Shiny as a second call echoed in answer.

"Oh shit…"

"RUN!!" Shiny ordered, shoving his shoulder. She plucked a hand grenade off her belt and thumbed the timer for it.

"Shiny!! Come on!" Luke demanded. Like hell he was going to leave without her. Derick would kill him.

"Ten more seconds," Shiny told him, never taking her eyes off the approaching monsters. Finally, she yanked the pin free and hurled it with an arm worthy of a World champion bowler. Not waiting to see if she landed it, she gave Luke a shove and scooped up Henry. "Run!!"

As she and Luke ran flat out for the ruins, a still bright red Henry clung to Shiny's back. The air sucked back a second before a muffled WHOOMP exploded in their ears. Behind them, more of those brassy, trumpeting calls sounded. Tapping her link as they ran, Shiny hailed the camp. "Gunny, we're coming in hot! Mulks on our tail! Whole fucking herd!!"

As the link opened to all channels, Shiny heard the Gunny call for Richards to cover them. She glanced at Luke, but her gaze went past him. "Shit! Gunny, on our left!!"

Just as she said that, the head of one of the mulks closing flank on them exploded in a haze of bluish mush. Richards! Shiny thanked whatever God had given that woman her sniper's eye as another braying call sounded. Risking a glance over a shoulder, she cursed. Too damn close!

"Luke, keep going!!" Skidding to a halt, she turned to face the oncoming threat, ignoring Henry's frantic barking. Seven more mulks, the closest about twenty feet away, were advancing quickly. Suddenly, the leader's chest exploded out of its back. Yes!!

Planting her feet, Shiny opened fire just as a plasma bolt zipped overhead to blow another chunk out of a mulk. The thing roared in pain, its odd tubular head thrashing as it went down.

"SHINY! Fall back!!" Other shots echoed the first, giving her the cover, she desperately needed to get back to the city.

Luke paused when he saw Tom firing over the stone fence and risked looking over his shoulder at Shiny. For the first time, he wished he had a gun in his hand, so he could help, even though the idea of firing a weapon was something he had trouble with. Another reason why soldiering wasn't for him. Something nipped at his boots and he looked down to see Henry. Suddenly, over the creature's insistent barks and yaps and the sound of weapons fire, he heard a loud, clear voice.

"LUKE, GET YOUR ARSE MOVING BEFORE I SHOOT YOU!"

Dan Rickman had NOTHING on Tom Merrick when the Major was properly pissed. Luke's feet were moving before his brain could even engage. Henry 'naffed' in encouragement, ducking out of the way of the two Sharks coming towards him.

"Keep going!" Ozzy yelled at Luke as he and Dupree ran past to assist Shiny.

"They're turning back!" Shiny's voice was breathless over the links as she turned on a heel and ran for Luke and her fellow Sharks.

Ozzy hurried past Shiny, to cover her back. Tapping his link, he kept moving, backing up towards the city and keeping an eye on the retreating beasts. "Gunny, that's confirmed! They're running off."

"Fall back!" Tom ordered over the link and instructed Richards and the others to keep an eye out as he met Shiny, Ozzy and Luke at the entrance.

"Major! Did you see…?" Shiny began, peeling Henry from where he'd dug into her pack.

"I saw," Tom frowned, still watching the retreating animals. Derick's description hadn't done them justice and that was saying something, considering the big bloke was quite articulate. They were something out of a bloody nightmare. Evil looking, they could run like hell and from what he'd seen just now, they worked as a pack on the hunt. Shiny had no idea how lucky she was, she could have easily been lost to those bastards.

Tom didn't move for a long while.

As he watched them retreat, he did so with the suspicions something was wrong. There was no doubt in his mind, the bloody things would have kept coming until every one of the pack was dead. No, they'd stopped because their pack leader had uttered a weird, trumpet call during the gunfire, like a signal to break off the attack. Not one of them had come any closer than twenty feet of the city.

Why? Tom turned around to study the ancient construct of looming walls and pyramids in a new light. Was it this place? Come to think of it, during the work clearing out the ruins, they'd seen nothing larger than bugs and lizards. No scat, no skins, no bones. By rights, it should have been overrun by wildlife.

Not liking where this was heading, Tom broke into a jog to catch up with Shiny. "You all right, Corporal?"

"All body parts accounted for, Major," Shiny answered without looking at him. "Did you hear that last noise they made? Like a braying noise?" she asked, glancing up at him. "It was different than the others." Not that she was an expert but something about that sound had sent a chill down her spine.

"NAF!" Henry propped his paws on her shoulder, watching behind them.

"You did good, Private Henry," Shiny grinned, running a soft hand over his back spines. "They aren't red anymore."

Tom glanced down at the little beast and noted it had indeed returned to its normal russet colour. "Situation normal, eh, fuzz ball?" Tom gave the naf an appreciative smile before replying to Shiny's question. "Probably some kind of rudimentary communication system. They're pack hunters, like wolves howling at each other. When you get a chance, get some of the vid together from your approach."

"Yes, Major." Pack hunters? Shiny shivered, thinking of the hyena in her native Botswana. Letting out a breath, she scratched behind Henry's ears. "Oh, Major? I think Henry knew the mulk was at the shuttle. He kept barking at us and pawing at me. He knew."

"I guess Orphan Annie was right," Tom didn't look at Henry as he spoke. "They are this planet's version of dogs. Might pay to keep more of them around. We can start a naf unit," he joked until he realised it was not a bad idea. Any sort of warning system for mulks was going to save lives. "Did Luke get the transponder?"

"Yes, he did," Shiny replied, still coddling Henry as they walked.

"Good. Nice work, Corporal. Now go grab the vid," Tom ordered, catching sight of Derick clapping Luke on the shoulder. Jesus, if they'd lost the younger Rickman, Derick would have gone ape shit.

"Yes, sir," she nodded and hurried off, Henry in her arms.

* * *

Twenty minutes later, at the base camp set up inside the main pyramid, Tom was standing with Derick, Jules and Luke, watching video footage of the encounter and not liking it at all.

"There." Shiny replayed the section where the mulks had turned back. The footage was shaky, but it was from her body cam. She tapped a small box at the left hand of the screen and its image appeared. "This is Corporal Richard's footage."

Watching it again from the new angle, Tom's jaw ticked. Both he and Shiny were right. That last call was different from the others before.

"Am I seeing what I think I'm seeing?" Jules asked quietly, eyes fixed on the screen.

"Jesus." Not for the first time since Luke returned, Derick squeezed his little brother's shoulder. The gesture served as a reminder Luke was still alive.

"They turned back when they got to the columns," Tom confirmed.

The question why opened a whole new can of worms. Why had the buggers run off? What could scare something that visceral and atavistic into turning tail?

"Gunny, I want both squads up. Put Alpha on patrol, buddy system. Check in every fifteen minutes. I'll take Dr. Nordin personally," he said, glancing at Jules, whose expression mirrored his thoughts.

He wondered if the alarms going off in her head were as loud as his?

XXI

Instinct

Upon the eerie revelation the mulks had turning back from the city, Tom decided a scouting mission was in order.

Two hours and a hike through dense woods later, Tom dropped his kit in an out of the way corner inside the main pyramid chamber and squatted down to dig out his water bottle. Dropping back onto the paved tiles, he took a long drink and then another before digging out a protein bar. Chewing steadily (really the only way to eat the damn things), he surveyed the large room and the industrious changes made while he'd been out scouting.

Worktables and work lights had been set up, the latter connected to cables running out to solar gennies parked outside. Squints milled around, some of them coming, some of them going and all of them giving him a wide berth.

Tom really hoped it was because of his reputation and not his smell.

A low chuckle caught his attention and Tom's gaze easily found the source of it. Jules was sitting with Luke, bent over a drone produced map of the compound. She didn't seem to notice him, so Tom took the moment to observe one Juliana Curran.

Not for the first time, Tom found himself thinking she was far, far out of his league. She was a classical beauty, with thick dark hair and tawny skin, courtesy of her Hispanic mother. Him? He was a colony mug, straight from the loins of Aussie miners. She'd gone to the Academy, become a pilot, whereas he'd earned his bars through a field promotion.

She belonged in the beautiful sky and he belonged on the plain old dirty ground.

Snorting, Tom shook his head. Fuck me. One kiss (and what a fucking kiss…) and he was waxing poetic like one of those wig-wearing poofters in a Shakespearean play.

Wolfing down the last of his protein bar (which tasted nothing like snags and mash, despite the label's declaration), he stowed the wrapper in his kit and got to his feet, confident no one would disturb it if he left it behind. He'd found something odd in the ground behind the pyramids and wanted to run it by Jules. It was the least he could do for the trust she'd shown in him.

She hadn't questioned him earlier when he took them to DEFCON 1 even though she was perfectly within her rights to do so. He was acting on instinct and wondered if Jules's own instincts trusted he knew what he was doing. Someone had once told him that flying any aircraft was 10% skill, 25% guts, 60% instinct, and 5% luck. Tom could see that. You couldn't pilot those Zephyrs for long if you didn't have some sort of superior intuition.

Over the years, he'd flown with blokes who could pull a ship out of the atmosphere when everyone else thought they were going to fry, without breaking a sweat. Jules was the same.

"*Relax, Marine. This is my thing.*"

Fucking hell, it was. She took the damaged *Firefly* off the cliff and let the bloody thing plunge into the ravine, pulling up only when they had mere meters between them and the water. Throughout the dive, she stayed cool as a cucumber, which only made him grit his teeth harder and suck it up. It was sheer will power that kept him from fainting when his stomach ploughed into his throat.

And he thought he had balls. All the skirmishes and full out firefights. The extractions to get negotiators out of mining riots and facing down mutinous colonists… yeah, he had brass ones all right, but Jules? Hers were made of fucking diamonds!

The joy on her face when she flew made him sad she wasn't still zipping about in a Zephyr. She was right, flying really was her thing. Being the Captain of the *Ruthie* was a waste of her talent. Then again, he hadn't expected to like being an officer, let alone in charge of the *Ruthie's* contingent. He'd never intended to wear officer's bars, just like she'd probably never intended captaining an entire ship.

Whole new world, Tommy, he told himself. Everyone's adapting.

"Hullo," he said, by way of announcing himself as he approached the table. When she glanced up, he couldn't help but smile.

"You weren't eaten, awesome," Jules grinned, scooting over to make room for him at the table. "We were just reviewing the drone map," she said, with more warmth than she'd addressed anyone else.

"Yeah? Good, because I have something to add it," Tom began, tugging his slate from a pocket to show her the pictures he'd taken.

Before he could get even one open, an excited 'Captain!!' rang out, drawing his attention to Dr. Nordin who'd just emerged from one of the side rooms. "Oh, Major! There you are! Come! You both need to see this!" she said breathlessly, motioning excitedly.

Glancing at her, Tom turned back to Jules. Her warmth was gone, with the facade of Captain Curran in its place. "After you."

* * *

By the time they joined her, Nordin was standing under the massive spiral stair while a trio of squints hovered nearby.

"What have you got, Samara?" Jules prompted, crossing her arms over her chest.

"I believe we have made an amazing discovery, about the crater," the woman began, stepping back to show off one of the many friezes in the building. From top to bottom, pictographs and symbols filled the stone. "As we suspected, this is a historical record of sorts. Corporal Richards was correct in her assumption the artefact she found was depicting an image of the dominant life form. Their language is a mixture of symbols and pictograms, bearing similarities to Sumerian cuneiform and Egyptian hieroglyphics. It's given us a snapshot of their culture and history."

He needed to see this? A bunch of scribbles? Unless there was a way to detour the sky crabs or a record that The Purple People Eater had devoured the previous population, he didn't see why he had to be here. His annoyance must have telegraphed because the next thing he knew, Jules's elbow 'accidentally' thumped his bicep. Tom cleared his throat, shooting her a raised eyebrow as the doctor turned her back to them to point out some important squiggle.

Biting her lip to keep from laughing, Jules cleared her throat. "I'm sorry, but you mentioned the crater?" she asked simply.

Soldiers, Nordin sighed inwardly. "Yes, of course," she nodded and then gestured for them to bend over a little, so they could see the symbols for themselves. "They charted significant events in their history. The first planting, the construction of the city and this temple, and so on, but down here…" she pointed to a specific set of images and symbols, fingers just brushing against the stone.

Tom bent over and reminded himself to thank Jules later for cutting off the woman before she went into the history of the first circumcision or whatever. Not that he wasn't interested in the history of these people. He was. But now was not the time for superfluous information. That gnawing in his gut was growing and Tom was bracing himself for the worst when it finally manifested itself.

Staring at the pictogram she was pointing at, Tom saw it revealed the faded depiction of Babel's first people, paying homage to what appeared to be some type of stellar body, a meteor or possibly a comet, in the night sky. Doubled over in reverence as the elliptical object with the flowing tail flew above their heads, their heads were bowed in worship. Even if he wasn't a student of history, the scene was clear, something had come down from space and most likely created Lorio's crater.

But that was not the worst of it.

It was the last pictogram on the column. There were no further depictions of what came after the object's arrival in Babel. Unlike the column on the other side of the altar, filled with writing and symbols from floor to ceiling, there was nothing recorded after, as if its scribes had nothing left to say. History seemed to have come to an abrupt halt.

"That's it?" Tom looked up at both women in question.

"Correct," Nordin nodded, staring at both officers solemnly.

Jules frowned at the blank space and then the round object, dropping down to one knee to inspect the drawing.

Tom might not be an astronomer, but he knew impact craters. "Lorio's crater isn't big enough to wipe anybody out. It probably caused a little bit of a mess but not enough to wipe them out."

"Agreed," Nordin said, motioning one of the squints behind her to join them. "This is Vadim, my glyph specialist, and he has a theory on the pictographs," she said, motioning the young man forward.

With permission given, the slight young man picked up the conversation.

"Our carbon dating puts this last set of pictograms at 300 years. I believe that these," he said, indicating all but the last set, "were meticulously done by someone with time, superior skill and proper carving tools. These... Excuse me, Captain," he said, indicating the ones in front of Jules. "I believe these were done in haste. Look at the letters and you will see they are different than the others. They were not rounded out or sanded. The glyphs themselves are not carved as deeply as the others. That indicates that either they did not have the proper tools or..."

"...or they ran out of time." Nordin concluded and raised a hand to the temple around her. "I believe sentient life began here but abruptly halted, never allowed to spread across the rest of the planet."

Keeping an ear on the conversation, Jules studied the images. There were two, one with the meteor coming down and one with it on the ground. Around it, people were bowed before it, hands in the air offering what looked like welcome gifts.

From the young Shark's description, Lorio hadn't really fallen into the crater as much as he'd tumbled down an incline. Jules turned her attention back to the meteor, pressing her fingers against the outline. Earlier, this same thing had earned her a decent lecture from Dr. Nordin about skin oils, ancient rock, and something. Something, something…

To be honest, Jules had zoned out.

She tilted her head this way and that, automatically processing the trajectories, the speeds and the impact, compared to what Lorio described. Her fingers crept over the image until she'd found a straight line. Man, what she wouldn't give for a piece of paper and a pencil. Carefully, Jules dragged her finger around the line and froze.

"It wasn't a meteor," she looked over her shoulder at Tom, motioning him forward.

Tom shot her a look immediately. There it was. Four little words that made everything fall into place. It *wasn't* a meteor.

"Here. Feel…" Grabbing Tom's hand, ignoring that he was practically standing on top of her, Jules pressed his fingers against the image. "Look, there's ridges, there's an opening," she said, the implication crushing her voice to a whisper.

Without hesitation, Tom traced his fingers along the same path she'd taken. Yes, he did feel the striations and grooves giving the shape more detail. And it made perfect sense. No meteor landed in the middle of a city, without damaging anything. Only God was that precise in his aim and he had better things to do than lob asteroids at developing civilisations. The answer was obvious, and it had taken a pilot to see it.

Jaw tightening, Tom tapped his link as he squeezed Jules's shoulder. "Gunny, come in."

"Gunny here. Go ahead."

"I want motion trackers and scanners on," Tom glanced at Jules, his eyes dark with worry, "We may have sentient company."

* * *

Derick blinked, a chill starting up his spine. "Roger that."

Moving off the secure channel, he raised Richards first. "Ren, go to FLIR and Bio-Scan." Her sniper rifle was connected to her slate, with software to give her a good look over the area she was surveying. "Jazz, Shiny, bio-trackers, confirm."

All three replied in the affirmative.

* * *

"Should we leave?" Nordin asked the two officers. As much as she wanted to stay, she wasn't a rabid academic with no sense of real world urgency. They'd already lost Olivia, she didn't want to lose anyone else.

"No," Tom answered promptly. "There are mulks out there in the woods and if the sky crabs come back, this is probably the best place to be. If there's anything about, we're in a better position to handle it than this lot probably were. Blast rifles are bloody good equalizers. We've only got to hold out until the rescue ship arrives later today."

"The *Firefly* won't survive another attack," Jules agreed. "And she is no longer capable of breaking atmo. This is shelter; if we need to, we can barricade ourselves inside, right?" she directed to Tom.

"Definitely. If we need to, we can strip the hull plating off the Firefly and use it to replace the doors. We're not there yet, but we will be able to reinforce any barricades if we have to," he turned towards the doorway. "Right now, I want a closer look at the crater."

* * *

With sentient life now discovered on this world, Dr. Steven Kim, bio-chemist and confessed nerd, felt alive for the first time since the Exodus started. Even though the mysterious race might have died out, the fact they existed at all was a tantalising thought to the humans who thought they were alone in the universe only a few short months ago.

When they had first geared up for this expedition, he'd worried about the inclusion of the Marines or Sharks, whatever they were called now. Too many times, he'd been on so-called scientific expeditions only to have the military stomp in and take over. Before they'd left, Dr. Hall had assured him that wouldn't happen. Now that she was gone (may she rest in peace), he hoped that Dr. Nordin and Luke

Rickman wouldn't put the expedition at the mercy of Major Merrick and Captain Curran.

His task had brought him to the cemetery, along with the requisite Shark guard. The man looked like he belonged on a recruitment poster somewhere. "So where are you from?" he asked the Shark as he calibrated his slate.

"St. Petersburg, Russia," Nikolei Lukashenko replied, glancing over at the doctor. His accent was heavy on the hard sounds, despite having spoken English since he was a teenager. "What about you?" Shiny was always telling him he needed to be more sociable.

"Singapore," Steven answered, glancing up at his companion. "Unfortunately, there is no town, just a city that's the whole country." He thought of a joke he'd heard once about it size. *It's so small, we can lay wall to wall carpeting from one end of the country to the other!* God, he missed it. "Would you like to see what I am doing?" he offered.

Would he? Nikolei stepped eagerly to the scientist's side. "Of course," he replied enthusiastically.

Once upon a time, Nikolei had been a little boy wanting to grow up and dig for mummies and ancient civilizations. Those dreams died when his father did, when he was just seventeen. As the oldest child, he joined the Russian National Army, to help support his mother and siblings. During the Exodus, he'd only managed to find two of his younger siblings.

They were worlds apart in everything, from physicality to upbringing, but Steven recognized the yearning in the younger man's voice. "Do I see a scientist in you?" he prompted with a knowing grin.

Nikolei returned the grin, the pink of his cheeks incongruous to his hulking form. "Once, before my father died," he admitted. "I was the oldest."

"Ah. Your family...?"

"My brother, Andrei and my sister, Irina, are dead"

What could he say to that? Steven had considered himself one of the lucky ones. Both he and his wife Miranda never had time for children and were together on Ganymede when everything went to hell. Fully prepared to meet their fate together, they'd booked passage on the first ship available, the *Outpost* and were on their way to Earth when Sol chose to go nova early.

Their captain, something of an operator by the name of Seth Yukovski, was smart enough to join the ragtag fleet amassing to make the crossing through the Ribbon and even though his ship lacked an Em Drive, one of the capital ships had allowed them to latch on. The small ship was almost ripped to pieces in the journey but reached the other side with few casualties.

Nikolei pulled his water bottle off his belt. "I have been to Singapore," he said, effectively changing the subject. "Very nice place. Have you been to Petrograd?"

Smiling, Steven nodded, a slight smile on his face. "I have, actually; my wife and I honeymooned there, and we took a trip down the Neva River and saw the Winter Palace. It's a beautiful city."

"Yes," Nikolei replied solemnly, sending up a prayer to his long-gone family. He missed the beautiful city and his boisterous family and thinking on it would lead to no good. "So, are you finding anything?" he prompted, shifting to his other foot.

With Sharks, it was so easy to forget under their armour and guns, they were young men and women with families. Add to that the stress of being a thin blue line between the civilisation and anarchy these last six months and instantly Steven had a new appreciation for these soldiers. He considered apologizing, but the young man was the image of typical Russian stoicism and probably would not appreciate anything seen as pity.

Instead, Steven focused on the GPR scan results chirping at him. He'd been careful to stand a few feet away from the pellet shaped tombstone, not wanting to disrespect the person interred here. Yet the screen showed nothing beneath them. Not one damn thing.

"That... is the question," he replied, brow furrowed as he pushed through the thick vegetation to the next marker. Aiming his slate at it, Steven repeated the scan and frowned again. Nothing. Nada. A few traces of metal but nothing of bio-organic, carbon-based remains. Quickly, Steven went to the next one. "Hmm. These graves are… empty."

Nikolei frowned at that. "What do you mean, empty?" These weren't the great monoliths of the centuries-old cemeteries of his home, but there should have been something.

"No bodies, no bones," Kim's concern deepened, and he went to the next grave. When nothing was found, he shook his head and looked up to his escort. "That's the fourth one. This is not normal. I mean, there is evidence of some materials, like metals, but there's nothing else," Kim replied, shaking his head. "Something was there but it's now gone."

"Can you scan the rest?" Nik asked, frowning. That was strange.

"Yes, of course," Steven replied and got to work.

Fifteen minutes later, 'strange' had fully evolved into 'creepy'. Not that Nik believed in things like ghosts and monsters, but when you had an old babushka who told little boys stories of the *strigoi*, empty graves took on new meaning. "This is the kind of strange thing the Major needs to know about. Excuse me," Nik activated his link, taking a step away from Kim. "Major Merrick, this is the Ruskie," he said, using the officer's unoriginal nickname for him. "Dr. Kim has made an interesting observation."

"Standby, we're on our way."

"You didn't reach out to your Sergeant or your Gunny first?" Wasn't that a breach in protocol? Steven didn't want the Shark getting in trouble for his excitement.

"Gunny authorized us to contact the Major directly if we found something weird." Gunny's exact words had been 'fucked up'. Nik gestured to the stones. "This qualifies."

* * *

Tom led the way towards the cemetery, noting pleasantly Jules matched his stride without him adjusting it at all. The thigh muscles… Oi. His conscience slapped him on the back of the head and he forced away all thoughts of tawny skin. Mostly.

As they entered the clearing, he was glad to see neither carnivorous plant nor mulks. When he heard a sigh of relief, Tom glanced at Jules to see she too had apparently been thinking the same thing.

"What do you have, Doc?" he asked by way of greeting and acknowledged Nik with a tilt of his chin.

Steven glanced at Captain Curran, who nodded encouragingly. Showing them the screen of his slate, he tapped one of the rectangles there. "The graves appear to be empty. There is evidence of biological and carbon-based material, but it is trace amounts."

"Gone?" Tom exclaimed, glancing at Jules. "As in decayed?" Surely, they wouldn't have called him here for bits and dust.

"No," Kim shook his head. "I saw no evidence of it. They're just gone or… looted." Sounded better than body-snatched.

"So, are you saying there's no remains in them?" Jules shot Tom a look that spoke volumes. No bodies?

Just as Steven opened his mouth to reply, a blood-curdling scream rent the air, startling even Tom. Before he could even raise Derick, his link came alive with the chaos of a situation going to hell.

XXII

Underground

Herded into the main pyramid for safety, Hanae Akiyama listened like the others to the shouts and calls. She was relieved to hear when one of the Sharks standing guard reported that everyone was back safe. Glancing at Mahmud, Hanae could see she wasn't the only one relieved.

Within minutes, they were released, and she and Mahmud joined the squints filing out of the pyramid once more to continue their work.

"…probably killed all of them. Fucking jarheads. I'm sure they'll burn the carcasses or something. Won't even listen to us scientists."

"We could ask, Dr. Thomas," said a quiet voice. Both voices were behind Hanae and she recognized them instantly.

"I didn't ask you, did I? Besides, neither of us are built like Captain Long Legs, so he's not gonna listen to us," the voice said with snide arrogance.

Hanae glanced at Mahmud, who was shaking his head, lips pressed tightly in anger. She didn't blame him. Dr. Rachel Thomas was not a friend of many in Olivia's team. Especially Sanjit, her assistant. In fact, Hanae was certain Olivia had kept the bitch on solely because she was one of the best entomologists. Even before the Exodus, Rachel Thomas was considered an expert in her field.

And the bitch never let anyone forget it. As if they could, with the woman shoving her opinion into everyone's research and work. With the world gone to hell, Hanae couldn't believe anyone could retain such a petty and bitter personality.

"Dr. Thomas." Hanae announced each word sharply as she spun on a heel, ponytail snaking around on her shoulders. Smiling tightly, she took a step forward. "When you're done insulting and passing rumours on of what's left of humanity, I believe you have work to do." Giving her a sharp nod, Hanae turned on her heel once more and shoved her way through the crowd.

* * *

When Mahmud joined her a few minutes later at their workstation, Hanae's face was still stormy. Not for the first time, he refrained from telling her how camera-friendly her pretty, Asian features were. Earlier, she would have rolled her eyes at him. Now? She'd probably shank him with a pipette.

"So," he began, taking his place across the worktable from her. "I hope we build a BIG wall when we finally set up a colony. One of the Sharks had pics on their slate."

He'd been a film student back when there had been an entertainment industry. Now, he'd found purpose in falling back on his biology minor. While he mourned not being the new Spielberg, Tarantino or Capello, he made a pretty good assistant and he liked working for Hanae.

"I never want to meet those things face to face."

"You survived Dr. Thomas face to face, I'm sure you'd survive them," Hanae grumbled, frowning at the small specimen jar in her hand. "This thing was purple when we got called in, right?" she asked, thrusting it at him.

Squinting at the now orange contents, Mahmud nodded, just as perplexed as she was. "I didn't add anything to it. Did you?"

"No." Hanae shook her head and set the jar down as she glanced up. "Where's our Shark? Abrams?"

"Anderson. I don't know, I'll go look for him. Maybe they forgot about us in the chaos."

"Okay. But hurry. I don't want to get him in trouble." Turning back to the portable spectrometer behind her, Hanae went to work on analysing the water froth in the jar. After a second, she was humming to herself.

Yep, that was his sign. Mahmud only smiled at her back and went to find the Shark.

* * *

Parking herself on a small camp chair to study the results of the orange froth, Hanae set her slate on her lap and pulled the hair elastic from her pony tail. Looking at the information scrolling by, she absently pulled her hair back into a ponytail and secured it. The calcite content of the water was off the charts and so was the selenium content. Interesting. There was another substance, something that wasn't on the known periodic table.

Holy monkies! Hanae blinked. Three hundred some odd known elements on the periodic table and she'd just discovered a new one. A. New. Element. Hanaekomium? Ew…God no….

Something shook the vegetation in front of her and she looked up in reflex. Nothing. In the distance, she could hear Mahmud's voice, so this wasn't him. Was it a naf? The large plant in front of her shook once more. Spooked now, Hanae stepped back when something huge shot out of the ground in a rain of dirt and greenery.

When her brain registered the creature, Hanae screamed.

* * *

"So where are you from?"

Mahmud glanced back at Remy, his answer interrupted by a horrified scream he recognized immediately. "Hanae!!!" he yelled, breaking into a run towards their worksite with Remy hot on his heels.

* * *

Was it wimpy of him to go find Tammy after everything that happened? Like a kid seeking out his blanket, Luke headed for Tammy's workstation beside one of the smaller pyramids. Still a little shaken from his encounter with the mulk, Luke had difficulty concentrating. He needed to see Tammy because she knew how to help him focus, like she'd done in the months before he learned of Derick's survival.

He'd call her Baby Sister and she'd call him Dumb-ass and all would be right again.

As an exobiologist, she was probably gathering everything from soil specimens to plant mould. Or as Luke put it, elbows deep in plant and insect goop. Maybe even have it smeared across her nose. Heading down the cleared path, Luke spotted her and her Shark escort.

"Hey!" he called out, grinning.

"Luke!" Tammy beamed, arms going up for a hug. Luke had to laugh when mud landed on the Shark's cheek and he paused before wiping it off. "Glad to see you're in one piece. I was worried!"

"I'm too tough to kill," he grinned looking down at her.

"Riiiight." Tammy rolled her eyes before turning to the soldier. "Luke, this is Private Evan Chu."

"Hey man," Luke jutted his chin out in greeting. Chu nodded in return before heading off to stand a few feet away. Grinning at Tammy, Luke wiped mud off her cheek. "I just wanted to catch up. We haven't seen much of each other since we got here." He would never admit, even to Tammy, she was kind of like his stuffed Glo-Worm from his toddler days.

Grinning, Tammy hurried back around her table, eager to show him what she'd been working on. "You have been busy," she began, beaming at him in pride. Did he know how proud she was of him? Taking charge of the scientists like he was born to it? "Evan has been keeping an eye on me."

"My pleasure, Dr. Adelaide."

Doctor Adelaide? Luke turned to face Tammy, only to find her smiling doe-eyed at the Shark. "Uh huh," he replied after a moment, narrowing his gaze at the Private. He suddenly felt protective of his friend...who was still staring at Chu. "So, you were saying...?" Luke waved a hand in front of her and pointed to the table. He'd grill Derick about Chu later. Maybe ask his brother to assign someone else if this Shark turned out to be a trouser snake. Yeah.

"Hey what?" Tammy blinked at him owlishly and then looked at his hands. "Hey, if you have nothing to do, grab that specimen case. I've got bugs to collect."

"More like bug poop," Luke fired back, grabbing the case she indicated. No, this wasn't his idea of fun, but he was taking a break from work. "You have me for twenty minutes and then I have a date with a transponder."

"That sounds like a personal thing!" Tammy smirked over her shoulder at him.

Suddenly, something large erupted out of the brush in front of Tammy and when the dust cleared, Luke found himself staring at the most terrifying thing he'd ever seen. Held up by four spindly but powerful legs, its tubular body was covered in dark, leathery flesh. There seemed to be no distinction between its body and head, resembling a worm on legs. Where a head should have been, were a mass of tentacles surrounding a maw of glistening, razor-sharp teeth.

"Luke, what…"

"GET DOWN!!" Chu shouted from behind them, a plasma bolt zipping over Luke's head so close he felt the heat.

The thing undulated to the left, dodging the bolt and let out a high-pitched hiss that made Luke clap his hands over his ears. The beast lunged forward, snapping its upper limbs around Tammy's slender body and yanking her off her feet. "Tammy!!!!" Luke yelled.

"HEY!" Chu shouted over Tammy's screams, pushing past Luke with his machete out. Swinging at one of the limbs, the private didn't stop when one was flung off in a spray of liquid.

With a squeal, the monster shoved at Chu with a powerful leg, sending him flying back against a tree. As Luke watched in horror, flesh curled back from its mouth as its neck rolled back. Suddenly, its head shot forward, expelling a gelatinous ball of something that slapped over Chu's entire face with a wet squelch.

"TAMMY!" Luke shouted as Chu started to scream and claw at the gunk on his face. Shit!! Snatching up the man's discarded machete, Luke ran forward, slashing at the limb reaching desperately for him. "Take my hand!!" Their fingers had just touched when something slammed into Luke so hard he fell backwards.

The pain was immediate and crippling, sending Luke into screams of his own as a clawed tentacle gashed him open again. Clamping a hand over his bleeding leg, he looked up just in time to see the creature... and Tammy... disappear into the dirt before her screams stopped echoing against the pyramid walls.

"TAAMMYY!!!!"

* * *

Lance Corporal Cori Harwood was on her way to relieve Private Chu for a break when distraught screams of panic cut through the air. Realizing they were coming from the direction she was going, Cori broke into a run. A minute later, she skidded into the clearing just in time to hear Rickman's agonized wail for Dr. Adelaide. Both Chu and Luke were down and there was so much fucking blood all over the younger Rickman.

Cursing, Cori ran forward to Luke, tapping her link. "This is Harwood! Grid 8, Bravo Two! Luke and Chu are down, I need Mayday!!!" she called, not bothering to check on Chu. Not that she was a medical expert, but she knew the release of death in the air. It was too late for the private.

Grimly, Cori dropped to the ground beside Luke. Slapping a hand over the gushing leg wound, she dug out the mini first aid kit secured in a cargo pocket. It wasn't much, gauze, some tape and an alcohol swab but it would do. Snatching the gauze, she piled it on top if the wound.

"Luke, where's the squint?" she asked, patting Luke's jaw with a bloody hand to get his attention. When he didn't answer, she cursed. He was going into shock. With the link still open, she hailed the others. "Gunny! The squint's missing!"

Luke's eyes seemed to roll back in his head and Cori caught his chin. "Hey…"

"She's gone…" Luke said hoarsely, eyes locking on the last spot he'd seen his friend. She'd been so scared, so aware of what was about to happen. "She's… It took her. That… thing… I let it take her!!" he said, trying to shove the Shark off him.

"We'll find her!" Cori stopped short of promising because it just wasn't something she could do. She grabbed his flailing hand and pressed it against his chest. "Which way?" she asked as she heard people approaching.

"Down there. Down…" Luke's voice broke. "It took her into the ground. I think that's where it came from. I couldn't stop it, I couldn't stop it from taking her…!"

* * *

Luke… Derick's gut churned into his throat as he turned automatically for that section. "M…" His voice broke like he was twelve. "Mayday…Tom…"

"On my way, Gunny!!" Maya's reply was strained and punctuated with grunts as she ran for Harwood's location.

"Go!" Tom's acknowledgement over the link shot Derick forward into a run, racing for his brother's location.

* * *

Arriving on the heels of Maya, Derick stopped short as she dropped to her knees at Luke's side. Joining her on Luke's other side, he grabbed one of his flailing arms. "Luke!"

"Gunny, I need him still!" Maya barked, shoving at the large gunnery sergeant with one hand. "You're in my light!"

With Luke being seen to, Cori turned her attention to her friend, Evan's body. Squatting beside him, she meant to close his eyes when she realized it was too goddamn late for even that.

"Oh fuck…" she whispered. Chu's face was gone. Just… gone. Down to bloody, bloody bone. No eyebrows, no eyelids and barely any flesh on the bridge of his nose. Just a macabre grimace and his eyes...Jesus.

What she'd thought were his dark eyes were gaping, bloody holes full of gelatinous goo.

"Jesus, Evan..." she whispered and shouldered off her kit to start taking care of the body.

* * *

At his brother's voice, Luke finally looked away from the spot where Tammy had disappeared. "Derick!" he said wildly, half-pleading with none of his usually cocky demeanour. "You have to find her! It took her into the ground! I couldn't stop it from taking her! You have to go after her!" he begged, ignoring Mayday's orders to be still.

There was only freshly turned earth where Luke was pointing. No hole or opening of any sort. What did he mean? Took her into the ground? Was that even possible? Maybe it ran off and Luke was delirious. "Harwood, see if you can find a trail," Derick ordered over a shoulder as he ran a hand through Luke's hair. "We'll find her, I promise. Mayday?"

"He's going shocky," Maya answered, checking the bandage secured around his leg. "I need to get him back to base camp and I need the shock packs from the Med Station."

"There won't be a path, Der!" Luke grabbed his brother's harness as Derick lifted Luke to his feet. Mayday slipped under his other arm, but Luke wasn't paying attention. "It took her into the ground like some of kind of trapdoor spider!"

"Okay, we'll look. I prom..." Derick was cut short when Tom's voice came through the link in his ear.

"Derick! Something just snatched Hanae Akiyama! I want everyone back at the camp immediately for a roll call."

Derick exchanged a look with Maya, who looked as concerned as he felt. "Dr. Adelaide was taken as well. Luke's injured, we're bringing him back. Mayday needs a shock pack from the Firefly. Jazz, get someone on that ASAP," he ordered, hearing the various Sharks acknowledging the return to base call. "Harwood?"

"Yeah, Gunny?" Cori had just shouldered Evan's rifle and tucked his sidearm away into her kit.

"Belay my last and cover our six."

XXIII

It

In the hour since he'd called the emergency muster, Tom was again impressed with what his Sharks were capable of. Not one argument, one complaint (or it was kept quiet). Not so on the Squint side. That lot, he was ready to shoot. However, anyone bitching was quickly shut up by a look from Jules that could have peeled paint. Jesus, he didn't want to be on the receiving end of that glare. Ever.

Deciding to let her handle the expedition team, he went back to his plans and sent out three teams of Sharks. One with Harwood to retrieve Private Chu's body, a second with Jackson to recon the site where Dr. Akiyama was taken and lastly, he'd sent Derick with a team to the *Firefly*, to start stripping off what hull plating they could salvage. Orphan Annie was still on the roof, ready to cut anything and everything down.

In the meantime, Mayday made use of one of the rooms off the main temple chamber, setting up a makeshift infirmary. The room wasn't very big, but it afforded the injured some peace and quiet. Right now, it was just Luke and the room (and Mayday's guard dog ownership of it) that kept pitying eyes off him and gave him the privacy to deal with his grief. Derick had told him what the young doctor meant to Luke and it twisted Tom's gut knowing he'd lost the girl he'd adopted as his baby sister.

His chest tightened and for a moment, Tom was back in a burning passageway staring at Lisa as plasma ignited the very air around her. Blinking back the burning in his eyes, Tom shook his head. Lisa hadn't been a sister to him, she'd been a lover. *Fuck, this was not the time mate,* Pod's voice chided him.

He had more important things to deal with.

"What's the verdict, Mayday?" he asked, glancing over where Luke lay on a cot facing the wall. The vibe coming off the younger Rickman screamed 'leave me the fuck alone!'

Looking up, Maya glanced at Luke and then gestured at the hallways beyond the room. Tom got the message and headed there first. Behind him, he heard the audible snap of the case she was repacking, before she joined him a second later.

"He is as well as can be expected, Major." She sighed and ran a hand over her thickly braided hair. "Nothing vital was hit, although the leg wound was pretty deep. I'm more worried about his state of mind. He won't speak or respond and he's refusing painkillers."

Bugger, Tom knew all about that state, didn't he? Hell, he had a waterfront plot there, overlooking Grog Creek and Wasted Dam. "Can I have a word with him?" he glanced at Luke through the open doorway.

"I'll give you some privacy, sir," Maya nodded, pointing towards the main temple room. "You know where to find me."

* * *

Everything around him was on mute, drowned in Tammy's screams burning up his memories. Hell, he couldn't close his eyes without seeing her with that expression on her face. The horrified realization she was about to die because Luke couldn't rescue her.

Why the fuck couldn't the damn thing have taken him??

If he'd hurried a little more. If he hadn't stopped to… hell, if he hadn't gone to get the transponder, he could have been there. Tears leaked from his closed eyes into the blanket under him. Boys don't cry. How many times had their father drilled it into their heads? So many times, he and Chris and Derick had been forced to hold grief inside of them until it channelled down every nerve ending and burned them up.

"Luke."

Tom. Luke didn't acknowledge him, sure of what was coming. A pep talk. Suck it up, son. We need you to be strong. You were spared for a reason. Blah, buh-blah, fucking blah. He didn't want to fucking hear it.

There was a sigh behind him and a hand squeezed his shoulder.

"I have no right to ask this right now, but we're gonna need you Luke. Something's coming and I need to know what it is. We're gonna need you, mate. When this is over, you and me will find some god-awful grog, a quiet place and toast those we've lost. And then I'll tell you about Lisa and a secret not even your brother knows."

That got his attention. Luke turned and looked over his shoulder to find not the Tom he knew, but one suddenly aged by fifteen years and steeped in grief and pain. Tom always seemed older than his years, but this was a raw and angry version that screamed loss. After a minute, Luke found his voice. "You couldn't save her?"

Clearing his throat, Tom shook his head and looked at his hands, clenching them so Luke wouldn't see the tremor. "No. I couldn't. I had to kill her."

Before Luke could reply, Tom's link went active with the Captain requesting him. Clearing his throat again, Tom pushed himself to his feet and ran a hand over his face. He glanced out the door for a moment before turning back. When he did, the Tom Luke knew was back. "For now, get yourself together. I need to know what attacked you and I need you to help me figure out a way to kill it."

* * *

When Tom re-joined Jules in the main chamber, he found a hot and sweaty Jackson and his team back from searching for Dr. Akiyama. They smelled like the damp earth outside and it looked like they'd tracked it in on their clothes.

"Sergeant," he said, motioning the man over to join him and Jules closer to the wall, for a bit of privacy. "What did you find?"

Jackson took a swig of his water bottle and dug into a pocket.

"We didn't find any kind of trail, Major," he said, shaking his head. "Just the ground, all churned up. No broken branches, no prints, nothing. Just this," he said, holding up a dirty silver chain with a locket on the end of it. "It's Dr. Akiyama's. I remember telling her to tuck it in her shirt when she was leaning over the water. Shiny found it when she dug up the ground at the…place." He held it out to Tom. "She found it two feet down."

A chill raced up Tom's spine at the news and he gently took the locket from his soldier. Had Luke been right? Had the thing taken Hanae and Tammy Adelaide *into* the earth? He glanced at Jules, to find the disquieted expression on her face matched his own thoughts. How was that possible? Finally, he nodded, winding the chain around his hand.

"Thanks, Jackson," he said, dismissing the sergeant as he stared at the locket.

He thought of Hanae in the river the day before, wading through the water with bare feet and her pants rolled up to just below her knees. For a few spare minutes, she had looked less like a scientist and more like a kid catching frogs. Tom hadn't been able to bring himself to remind her of the dangers possibly lurking under the water. Did she have any family on the ships or was she like most of humanity, the sole survivor of her blood line?

"I liked her," he said, aware of Jules standing beside him, her hand on his arm.

"So did I."

Glancing at Jules, Tom smiled, but it was weary and sad as he tucked the necklace into a pocket. "I won't lose any more of them, Jules," he said firmly. "This planet's made it clear she won't let us stay unless we earn it. We've got to make it safe."

"Agreed…"

"Major!"

Tom looked up at Mayday's call, finding Harwood and Anderson toting a stretcher between them. The lance corporal looked pale and

Anderson looked like he'd tossed his cookies already. Motioning to Jules, he followed behind the pair as his medic directed them into the room with the spiral staircase. Thoughtfully, Maya had decided to keep Chu's body separate from Luke. Tom made a mental note to make sure her record got updated with something that said, 'above and beyond the call of duty'.

"What'd you find, Lance Jack?" he prompted, glancing at the tarp-wrapped body.

Letting out a sigh, Cori pulled her helmet off and shoved sweat-soaked hair off her face. "No trace, sir. No kind of trail or path or anything. Private Chu..." She swallowed thickly and glanced at the tarp. "You were a dredge, right sir? An ice miner?" Cori's eyes flicked to Captain Curran before she corrected herself.

"That's right." Tom nodded, recalling Harwood's upbringing had been on a mining colony much like his.

Rubbing her face with one hand, Cori continued and gestured towards Chu's body. "You've seen the lye blowback victims, right? When the lye wash for the permafrost blows out? There's no flesh left," she said quietly, having lost a step-brother to one such accident. "It's like he was hit with lye or acid..."

"I'm pretty sure it's an acid-based composition."

Luke. Tom took the younger man's appearance as a bittersweet victory, but a victory nonetheless. He looked pale and there were dark circles under his eyes, but he was on his feet, holding up his slate.

"What've you got?" he said, joining Luke at the door instead of making him come closer to Chu's body.

"I made a preliminary sketch of the..." Luke's tongue flicked over his lips. "It." He showed the sketch to Tom, not looking up when the women joined them. "Based on what I saw."

"Bloody hell..." Tom grimaced as he took the slate to study the drawing. Like a worm with limbs, the creature was a thing of nightmares. Noting the measurements Luke had scribbled in a corner, he swore inwardly. Seven fucking feet? He showed it to Jules who swore.

"The acid is fast working, from what I saw." Luke's jaw worked as he fought back his disgust. "Chu's small calibre bullets dented it, so I think the plasma rifles will do the trick."

"Good," Tom nodded, handing the slate back to Luke. "Anything else?"

"It did go into the ground." Luke cleared his throat when his voice cracked, and he ran a hand through his hair. "I haven't figured out how yet, but I will. I…"

"Luke." Tom squeezed his shoulder. When his friend's eyes raised to his, he nodded, a silent thank you. "This is a bloody good start. Get to Shiny and make sure this gets to everyone's slate. Next step, we're gonna need a door. Your brother and his team are stripping the outer hull plating off the Firefly. It can withstand re-entry, it should be able to stand up to that acid, right?"

"For a while, yeah," Luke nodded, brow furrowed as he did the mental calculations. "Good thing with hull plating it's made to withstand everything from plasma to solar flares, corrosive acid will strip off the ceramic coat, but it's not going to eat through titanium."

Inspiration struck Tom then as he saw Luke working it out, devoting his considerable mental abilities to the question. The lad might be somewhat shell-shocked after what happened to his bird, but he was a fighter. After meeting their father, Tom was convinced it was in the Rickman DNA. Spawned from a bastard, they could be nothing else but scrappers.

"Can you build me a barricade to keep those fuckers out?"

"Yeah," Luke met Tom's gaze. He could do that. He could build something to ensure none of those things got in here to take anyone else. The way it had taken… *stop, just stop*, he told himself. He needed his head back in the game, he needed to be useful, or he was going to go crazy with despair.

"Yeah, I can do that." Then with resolve, he repeated. "I will."

"Good," Tom clamped his shoulder and squeezed. "As soon as Derick gets back, get to it."

XXIV

Subs

She could see forever.

Ren snorted to herself as she lowered an eye to the scope of her sniper rifle to check on Derick… Gunny's status. At this angle, she had an uninterrupted view of the man as he worked to pull sheets of hull plating off the shuttle. Never one to just give orders, Gunny was masked up, wielding a laser cutter on the shuttle's roof. Rising to his feet, he lifted the mask and hollered at one of the Betas on the ground.

"What do you suppose he's saying?"

"Jeez…!! Jag!" Swatting his arm, she scowled. How in hell had she forgotten that her spotter and his slate would have the same view as her scope?

Laughing, Jag elbowed her and waved a hand at the expansive valley and the horizon that stretched on and on, beyond it. "The Gunny is very good-looking, but you should be looking at all of this," he teased, indicating the scenery. "You've been gawping at him for the last six months."

"Like you haven't been! And I don't gawp," Ren retorted, eyes narrowing as she spotted something on Jag's vaunted horizon. She twisted slightly, bringing the rifle with her to look through the scope. "Oh, check that out…"

Against the backdrop of the pale green sky, a flock of birds rode wind thermals and soared across the sky, dipping and rising like ballet dancers on a stage. Ren zoomed in on them. "Whoa."

"They look like pterodactyls," Jag replied with a wrinkled nose as his slate blipped an incoming message. "Kind of ug…" He descended into Hebrew curses and tapped Ren's shoulder, putting the slate forward so she wouldn't have to shift much. "Look at this. That's what got the squints and killed Evan."

"Well, there goes any sleep tonight," Ren grumbled as she studied the screen. Across the bottom of the screen, in neat handwriting were the words Subterranean Ugly Bastard aka SUB. "The major's been naming things again. It spits acid? Fantastic," she growled and went back to the scope.

Instead of focusing on the Gunny, Ren widened the range so she could view the area around the shuttle. Eventually, she'd get together her fellow Sharks and share a moment over the loss of yet another Shark. She made a mental note to talk about how Evan had been a dynamite poker player with more stories about horrible dining experiences than any man alive. The guy loved food and would travel halfway across the system to sample a meal.

Hell, he'd even showed her and a few others how to make rations taste a little more palatable with some things he'd snuck aboard in his duffel. Yeah. When this was over, the Sharks would make their goodbyes to Chu, Edwards and Macon.

"We'll show them not to mess with Earthers."

"Gaians," Ren replied without looking up from the scope. "We're Gaians now."

"Gaians." With Jag's accent, it sounded a little more exotic. "Oh, the hopper team is headed back now."

Ren felt more than saw Jag shift to his belly next to her. "I see them." Suddenly, she cocked her head and glanced at Jag. "Do you hear that?"

"Hear what?" Jag didn't look up from his slate.

"I don't know. Like… a *tiktiktik* noise?"

Quirking an eyebrow at her, Jag pushed up so he could look around. "I don't hear... Oh. Yeah, I hear it now. *Tiktiktik tiktik...*"

The noise got louder as Ren and Jag exchanged bewildered glances until another noise caught her attention. A rock or something. A loose stone tumbling and bouncing against stone. Hefting up her rifle, Ren put a finger over her lips and quietly flipped the tripod shut. Using hand signals, she indicated the edge of the pyramid's flat-topped apex.

Jag nodded, all business now as he quietly got to his feet.

Ren bent into a crouch and silently crossed the stone to the opposite edge to peer over it cautiously. A heartbeat passed before she slapped her link open, thumbed the rifle to automatic and opened fire.

"INCOMING! Subs on the back wall!!"

* * *

When had it got so fucking hot? Tom groused as he hefted a piece of hull plating up the steps to the pyramid. Or had being stuck on a ship with recycled air for six months taken away his tolerance for humidity? Piss on that, he grumbled as the cooler air inside the temple enveloped him. Humans just weren't made for being canned up like sardines.

Wiping his brow, Tom sidestepped the squints who volunteered to help with retrieving the plating. He'd originally ordered all of them inside, screw their research for now. A reminder of the Subs kept the bitching in check but he'd been pleasantly surprised and impressed when many of them stepped forward with offers to help. With the extra hands, they were quickly organized into two groups, one to strip the plating and the other to carry the pieces back as they came off.

Now, watching them work, he might just yet take back everything he'd ever said about them. Not that he would tell anyone. Well, maybe Jules.

Speaking of... he sought her out automatically. She was leaning over Luke's work table with the younger Rickman. Both looked involved in the transponder laid out on the surface. Luke looked beat to hell and honestly, Tom felt guilty about that. He just hoped the kid would forgive him.

"*INCOMING! Subs on the back wall!!*"

For a split second, everyone in the room tensed and Tom met Jules's eyes across the room. He nodded and ran for the door, palming his link open. "Gunny!! Time to come home! Jackson, get a squad on the back wall to cover Orphan Annie!"

"*Jesus, they're coming outta the ground!!*"

As he emerged on the steps, Tom found himself in the middle of surreal calm compared to the fight in his headset. That only meant one thing. They weren't bothering with a frontal attack. Yet. "I want everyone who's not running their ass off to form up on the gate. Shiny, I want cover fire to get the Gunny's people in!" he called, heading towards the main entrance to the temples.

* * *

Normally, Ren would have the Gunny's back by laying down suppression fire to get her teammates back to base safely, but this situation was anything but normal. Not with six… five (nice shot, Jag!) of the ugly fuckers making their way up the wall. They jumped from foothold to foothold and how they weren't tumbling back…

"Ren, your right!!"

At Jag's yell, Ren turned to her right automatically just as something tightened around her leg and yanked her off her feet. Hitting the ground hard, her rifle clattered to the smooth stone beside her.

"Shit…!" Scrambling for it, she was tugged out of range and swore. Eyes darting at her feet, Ren's eyes widened at the sight of a thick, ropey tentacle extending from a Sub's mouth and wrapped securely around her calf.

"Oh, HELL no…" Jerking her machete free of its sheath on her back, Ren swung at the appendage. The blade sliced cleanly through as the beast screamed. Not wasting time, Ren kicked free of the remnants and lunged for her rifle. Rolling over the weapon and bringing it up with her, she opened fire on the creature and the one that appeared behind it.

"These things are fucking ugly!" Jag yelled behind her.

"I'm not arguing!" Ren retorted as both creatures tumbled backwards over the edge of the wall. Scrambling to her feet, she hurried towards Jag just as another beast appeared, it's long, muscled neck rearing back. Without thinking, Ren tackled Jag just as something wet splattered against the back of her body armour. Shoving Ren off him, Jag shot the Sub with a torrent of filthy Hebrew.

"Jag!! My armour!" Ren scrabbled at the quick release under her arm, feeling pricks of pain pierce her fingertips as they brushed against the acidic spit. The back of her neck prickled with tiny spears of heat and Jesus, it stunk!

"Here!"

Ren felt a slight thump against her ribs and then the armour loosened. Shimmying out of it, she let it drop and backed away from the already disintegrating carbon fibrete. "Jesus!" she swallowed as the hardened material literally disappeared before her eyes.

"Got two more!" Jag called, making her look up. Sure enough, two more were attempting to clear the edge of the roof. "Where's the Sarge?"

"I don't know but we're not waiting! We're getting off the roof!" Ren tossed the strap of her rifle over her head and half-dragged Jag towards the open corner of the plateau. She paused at the edge, swearing at the long, smooth expanse of rock. "How do you feel about slides?"

* * *

"MOVE!" Derick bellowed over gunfire as he slid down the ladder of the shuttle. Before they'd come out here, the squints had been instructed to make for the temple in the event of an attack. Don't stop. Don't look back. Run. They had taken the order to heart and were now running pell-mell for the opening in the wall as Sharks poured out, laying down cover fire.

As his squad formed up, Subs emerged from the ground, throwing dirt and debris everywhere. Shouts of surprise and pain added to the chaotic scene. A shriek caught his attention and Derick saw someone on her hands and knees in the high grass.

"MOVE! On your feet!" he bellowed, taking aim but just like that, she was gone with the Sub, her scream cutting off like a tap.

"Fuck!" Movement in the corner of his eye made him look up in time to see more Subs burst from the ground. Shit, the number of Subs was catching up to the number of people! He needed to do something about that. Jumping onto a nearby large rock, Derick thumbed his rifle to full automatic and fired bursts into the oncoming creatures.

"Gunny! Get your arse to the bloody temple!!"

Hopping off the rock into a dead run, Derick sprinted for it, knowing the order wouldn't be given until Tom had everyone inside. He cleared the gate opening in no time flat and made for the steps, where Tom and a couple of other Sharks were keeping the way clear for him.

Just as Derick was closing in on the steps, a Sub burst from the ground directly in front of him, spraying him with dirt and debris. Lunging to avoid the beast, Derick cursed when the ground gave beneath his feet, signalling the arrival of yet another Sub.

* * *

"Major, Gunny's down!!!"

The edge in Ren's voice made Tom's stomach hollow as he spun around, searching out his best friend automatically in the mess the courtyard had become. There were two or three of the beasts focusing on something about thirty feet away. A quick glance at his sniper told him that's where the big bloke was. Still was. Shit.

"Keep him covered, Richards!!" Charging down the steps, Tom jumped the last two and hit the ground at a dead run.

As he approached them, the head of one exploded in a spray of gunk before the body collapsed. A second one reared back just before its head was also shredded, no doubt from Richards's sharp shooting. The third screamed in defiance, yanking at Derick's leg, and trying to dislodge its prize from the tree the Gunny was holding onto for dear life.

Yanking his machete free, Tom swung for the back of its legs, the blade cutting into the meat and spraying cold, oily blood. He swung again at its back, then a third time in the same cut before going for the tentacle wrapped around Derick's leg. When it snapped loose, Derick hit the ground with a thud.

"No time for lying about, Gunny! Get off your ass!!" he joked, extending a hand for his friend.

"Fuck you!" Derick growled as he grasped Tom's hand and got to his feet.

"*Fuck you both, get inside NOW!!*"

Tom shot a glare over his shoulder to see Jules standing on the steps, a rifle in her hands. To his left, two more Subs shot out of the ground and he slapped Derick's shoulder. "Run!"

The Subs seemed to understand their prey was going to escape because as Tom and Derick ran for the temple, the beasts seemed to surge from the ground. Between the sprays of dirt and the rifle fire, it was chaotic as they charged up the steps and ran for the now smaller opening.

"SEAL IT!" Tom shouted as soon as they were through.

"Harwood, blow alpha point!" Derick called over the noise as the last of the plating was dragged quickly into place. Several Sharks descended on it with torque drills from the shuttle just as something thudded against the heavy metal sheet. A second later, there was a loud whoomph that puffed dirt and dust around the edges of the plating and made the Sharks holding the sheet stagger.

"Get your backs on it!" Derick ordered, rushing back to the door to put his weight against it.

Tom quickly joined his friend and the other Sharks, until someone yelled that the entrance was secured. Glancing at Derick, he saw his friend still leaning into the metal as if not quite trusting, not at least until he saw for himself.

Two by three, they backed off the makeshift door as something thunked against it. There was a second and third hit and then a rapid-fire set of something heavy pounding against the metal.

A few minutes passed by with no one moving before Tom realized the noise had stopped. Glancing at first Derick and then Jules, he stepped forward and pressed his ear to the metal. "I think they're gone," he said after a minute, moving back. "Probably looking for another way in. I want another sweep of this place! If there is a patch of soft dirt anywhere, I want to know where it is and I want it covered! Check every bloody corner you can. Luke, come here!"

"Beta squad, fan out!" Derick ordered. Alpha's orders were clear. Hold the door. Around them, the members of Beta fanned out and disappeared into the various open doorways.

As Luke and then Derick joined him in the corner Tom indicated, he set a hand on Luke's shoulder. The younger man looked tired, probably like they all did, and it was salt in the wound stinging Tom right now. "We need that transponder beacon, mate. What's your timeframe on it?"

"Um…" Luke blinked, glancing at his brother before replying. "Maybe an hour…"

Harwood's voice broke in on the link. "*Gunny, there's windows on the third level. More like slots, about three inches across and two feet high. Four on each wall.*"

"Post a guard on them," Tom ordered, turning to Luke. "We need it as soon as possible, yeah?"

"Yeah but I…"

"No buts, Luke," Tom shook his head, hating what he was about to say. "Make it work or we die."

Luke jerked, shooting Tom a frown before he nodded and moved off. Tom glanced at Derick, who was watching his brother with a concerned look. "You too, go be with him for a minute."

Derick nodded and headed after his brother. Tom watched the big guy go and finally let out the huge sigh of relief he'd been holding in. After losing Lisa, Tom wasn't sure he'd survive the loss of his best friend too. He dragged a hand across his head, feeling the stubble of a day's worth of not shaving. Rolling his shoulders, Tom surveyed the group in front of him.

Like before, his eyes went to Jules automatically, where she was helping Mayday tend to an injured squint. They were all stepping up to comfort each other, even that battle axe that liked to bitch. There was no laughter, no chatter like before… not that he expected there to be. Instead, there was terror and tears, the sounds of lost innocence and crushed naiveté.

Finally, his gaze moved to Luke, who had the transponder in his hands. Tom let out a breath, his teeth grinding. He didn't like being an ass to the younger man but as Tom surveyed the room, he knew he made the right choice.

The thought was cold comfort, knowing first hand that sometimes, to save everyone, you had to be an asshole.

XXV

Barricade

Luke was on autopilot.

Forced into a gear he didn't know he possessed, the reality of Tammy being gone from his life warred with the orders given to him by Tom. Anguish and grief were waiting in the shadows to take him down, like it had right after the Exodus, when he faced a world without his family.

Derick spent a few moments with him, at least until someone yelled for the Gunny. His big brother, in every sense of the word, bumped their foreheads together like they used to and left without even hesitating. Luke let him go and turned back to his work table. Nothing had been upturned but a good five minutes went by before he realized he was just staring at the transponder. Rubbing his face, Luke glanced up to check on his brother. Right. Back to work.

Fifteen minutes later, Luke was frowning at the electronic guts spread across his table when a shadow fell over his work. He looked up, surprised to see Tom studying him thoughtfully.

"How you going?"

"I'll live." Maybe. Luke sniffed and picked up the damaged motherboard. He needed to keep working.

"I know you will," Tom nodded, wishing like hell they were in a position where he could offer the kid a shoulder. Instead, he indicated the transponder. "What's our status?" He felt like a shit for pushing but they were literally on borrowed time.

This, Luke knew. Shut it down. Push it away. Courtesy of one Dan Rickman. Tammy's death became a dull ache as he pointed to the dissected equipment and showed Tom his findings. "The beacon's motherboard needs resoldering. Someone was trying to locate my soldering iron but I have other options."

A loud noise, something clattering to the stone floor made Luke jump and just like that, panic and grief swept in. He gripped the table tightly, eyes smashed shut as he tried to get himself under control.

The noise startled Tom but nothing like the panic he was seeing in the younger Rickman.

"Luke..." he began, stomach clenching in sympathy. He knew that look, knew that grip and bloody hell, he hated to see the boy like this. Luke was a smart mouth bugger, arrogant and brash. Tom liked that about him, liked he didn't give a shit about airs and graces even though he was usually the smartest person in the room.

"Hey... hey...." He took Luke by the arm and glanced behind him. Derick was with the Sharks and Jules was talking to Dr. Nordin. Mayday was attending to some of the other injuries incurred during their mad dash into the pyramid. Basically, everyone was busy and they wouldn't have interruptions. "Come here."

Not giving him a choice, Tom pulled an unresisting Luke towards a corner.

"Look, can I tell you something? Something not even your brother knows?" he asked in a quiet voice.

That got Luke's attention. He'd nearly forgotten what Tom had told him earlier. He nodded, brow knotting.

Tom dragged a hand over his face and let out a deep breath before he began. "Derick probably told you I've been drinking." When Luke tried to protest, Tom shook his head. "No, mate, I have. Can't seem to sleep properly without a nip from the bottle." How he wasn't blind from cheap grog, he didn't know. "The *Ruthie* was hit with solar flares just before the sun went nova. Since we were in port, we were down about a quarter of the personnel and I was on duty. When the cargo deck took a hit, I helped the wounded get to medical."

The next part was bloody hard and it required Tom pausing, taking a breath deeply and exhaling before he could start up again. "A plasma fire broke out in one of the shuttle repair bays. The emergency systems fired up, sealing the hatch into the repair bay, trapping six people with the plasma fire." He paused again before continuing, as if fighting to get the words out.

"One of them was a sheila I knew. We'd taken a tumble a couple of times. Bloody beautiful blond hair and a smile that would break your heart. Blue eyes that could make you forget what you were thinking. Her name was Lisa."

They hadn't been a couple, just a few quiet moments during voyages, sharing a bottle and intimate company. "She must have been closest to the door when it shut. She was screaming for me to open it. I couldn't hear her, not through the fucking door but I know that's what she was saying. When she realised..." Tom trailed off, jaw clenching as he looked away. "All that lovely hair went up. She looked like she was glowing from the inside, like she had a halo." Rubbing his face, Tom met Luke in the eye. "They were all alive but it was Lisa who saw me. I was looking right at her when I decompressed the bay and blew them into space to put the fire out. She knew I couldn't..."

"...save her." Luke finished, staring at his friend. He had known Tom for several years but never once had seen him look so... broken.

Tom nodded. The kid understood. "I don't regret it. If I'd opened that door, I would have compromised the rest of the ship and chances are, they wouldn't have thanked me for saving them anyway. Not in the shape they were in by that point. They were in agony. The rational part of me knows I ended to their suffering and saved the ship. But none of it fucking matters when I close my eyes and hear her screaming in my sleep. I keep thinking I should have been able to save her, I should have been able to do something."

"I should have been able to save Tammy…" Luke interrupted him, staring at his friend with hard, shining eyes before he looked away. "If I hadn't stopped to…"

"You did the best you could," Tom looked up then, grabbing Luke's vest to get his attention. "Nearly being gutted counts as doing everything you could. You had no choice, mate. No options. Just like I didn't. You hear me?"

Luke didn't want to believe that Tom was right. Despite his intellect, despite multiple degrees in physics and engineering, there was no way he could have known what was coming, no way he could have saved her. At best, he was hurt and she was gone. Worst case scenario would have been both of their deaths. He nodded once. "I'll try to keep that in mind."

"Good." Tom let him go and stood up straight. "I think Lance Corporal Harwood has your solder kit. She's the mouth-"

"I know who she is," Luke nodded, familiar with the brunette under his brother's command. He started to move away but stopped and glanced back at Tom. "Thanks."

Tom shrugged one shoulder. "Even before this mess, you and Derick were family, mate. Now go on before I start picking out bloody curtains."

Chuckling despite the situation, Luke headed off in search of Harwood.

* * *

With Luke on the move, Tom sought out Jules. He found her, sitting next to a young woman who looked barely old enough to be out of high school, let alone a full-fledged scientist. Jules leaned in close, telling the woman something in soft and no doubt reassuring tones.

Moving into her line of sight, Tom waited until he caught Jules's eye and canted his head towards the passageway.

Jules nodded and gave Dr. Chin Yi Liu a quick squeeze around her thin shoulders. "We'll get out of this. Look what we've survived so far."

After Yi nodded and offered a quiet 'yes ma'am', Jules quickly joined Tom in the passageway.

"I saw you talking to Luke. How is he doing?" she asked once she was close enough for them to speak quietly.

"Better," Tom explained, crossing his arms over his chest. "Got him focused on the transponder. It's going to sting for a bit but he'll be okay. He's a tough bloke." Tom knew he was vastly underplaying what passed between them but he wasn't ready to tell Jules about Lisa yet. "How about you?"

"I'm good." She had to be. For everyone here, for the *Ruthie* and even, she suspected, for the man in front of her. Later, once the rescue ship was here, maybe they could find some time to forget about everything else but each other for a while. "So, I was thinking," Jules said, looking out across the room. "How about we get some of the scientists to set up shop in the other rooms. They can get started on their analysis and get distracted," she added, glancing up at him.

"Great, it will get their minds off things and maybe get us some more intel on those creatures. There's got to be some kind of beastie expert among them, right?"

Jules winced remembering who their xenobiologist had been. "I'll check, but I think that was Dr. Adelaide. There has to be more than one, though. It might also be a good idea to have people start drawing what they remember of them. Do you have any artists among the Sharks?"

Tom thought about it and was there something about Richards? He'd read her file when he was putting together his squad. "Yeah, Orphan Annie went to some school … sounded like one of those liberal places… Art Student League or something in New York."

"Then I say we get her on a slate with a stylus." From their vantage point at the entry to the passageway, she could see the redhead in question sitting with Maya, the Gunny and the one they called Ozzy. The four of them were going through packs she assumed belonged to the dead. Watching the Gunny grimly pull several ration bars from one of the rucksacks, Jules frowned. "We might need to start rationing water," she said, barely above a whisper. "And maybe food."

Tom stiffened because fuck, she was right. He'd been more worried about ammunition and the rifle plasma packs that would need recharging at some point. Rations hadn't even been a thought because of the promise of a rescue ship. Now, though? When they weren't even sure the signal had broken the atmosphere?

"Yeah," he nodded. "We might see if one of the squints managed to do an analysis of the water in the river. If worse comes to worse, we can make a supply run." The idea of going out there didn't please him much but, if the rescue ship was late or — worse yet — didn't show, they were going to have to consider it.

"Let's hope it doesn't get to that. I wish like hell I knew if the signal got out or not." Jules let out a sigh and rubbed her face.

"Hope for the best, prepare for the worst." Pod's words. Paraphrased. "I'm also going to find the best place to make a hole if we need bug out and the door's not an option."

"I'll speak to Corporal Richards," Jules said, glancing back to the woman in question and her friend. "Do those two always look like they're plotting world domination?"

Tom cracked a fond smile. "I think it's worse than that; its world domination where all the blokes are enslaved as beasts of burden." And there was no question on who Ren would pick first, he smirked.

That made her laugh. "Maybe I'll throw my hat in with them," Jules retorted and headed off to speak to the redhead in the pair.

* * *

Even though she'd known Luke for a couple of years, Cori swore he aged another ten today. His normally bright blue eyes were dark grey with grief and shadows mapped his face in new paths. Having lost people, she cared about (and not just in the Exodus), she wanted to say something. Wanted to tell him he wasn't alone. But she didn't. One of those lost used to say Cori had a heart of gold, a head of rocks, and a mouth that was too smart for her own good.

Translation - she meant well but would probably just succeed in upsetting or pissing Luke off.

She remained quiet while he inspected the backpack with RICK-MAN, L written across the webbing with a black magic marker. In the fall-back rush, she'd spotted the pack lying on the steps and had snagged it in a last-minute decision. Eyeing him, she glanced at the contents. "Did I break anything?"

Luke didn't look up. He knew Harwood, had spent a few holidays with her when Derick dragged home any of his people that couldn't make it to a home-cooked meal of their own. This exposure embarrassed him.

"Uhm no…" he said quietly, not meeting her eyes.

"Good." Cori gave him a grin that faltered when she remembered the situation. Right. Next topic, moving on. She indicated his work. "How can I help? I was raised in a mining colony and apprenticed as a drill repair tech before I signed up."

For a moment, resentment flared in Luke, despite knowing it wasn't fair. He didn't want hers or anyone else's help. He wanted to work alone, he wanted the whole damn world to go away for a while. One hand closed tightly around the pack strap and he smoothed it out three times before answering. She meant well and he knew better than to send her away.

"We need to," Luke grit his teeth when his voice broke. He swallowed against the dryness in his throat. "We need to rig the transponder to generate a signal capable of being detected through the ionisation. So, the rescue ship knows where we are."

"All right. Is it anything like the beacons on an A90 Speitz Ice Drill?" Some of the parts laid out on the table looked familiar, just like the look on Luke's face. She got it. He didn't want her here but that was too damn bad. Gunny said to help but she didn't feel the need to rub that in his face.

"Close," Luke nodded, waving off the water bottle with a muted 'thanks' and indicated the table. "The A90 is a straight up beacon. This one is more like a relay. We've got to turn it into something capable of generating a signal strong enough to pierce the atmospheric ionisation." This was good. Concentrating on a problem he could solve distracted him from the battles already lost.

Cori bit her lower lip for a minute, fingers drumming on the small table he was using as a workspace. "You know, the geologist squints have those core sample tubes. Some of those have a GPS kit on them. It's a real basic design but the code for them is written in HT29." The computer language was one of the most basic but it was also one of the most adaptable. She didn't look at him, instead choosing to search the room for the squints in question.

Luke hid the mild irritation at the suggestion. It was a smart one; he should have thought of it since he'd been responsible for caring for most of that equipment to begin with.

"That's actually... a good idea," he offered, nodding.

"Better write that down. I don't get good ideas that often," Cori grinned at him. "Bad ones, sometimes. Questionable, all the time."

Harwood's laugh was kind of infectious and Luke found himself fighting to hide a smirk. Devastation still ruled him, but at this moment, she made the broken pieces inside of him, grind a little less.

* * *

It felt odd sketching for the first time in years.

When Captain Curran approached her earlier, Ren expected a request to perform some Shark-related duty. Instead, the woman handed her a pad and a pencil (an honest to God, graphite pencil) scrounged from one of the squints and asked if she could sketch an image of the subs. It would be useful for them to study. The request took Ren so completely by surprise, all she could do in response was to nod like some dumbstruck kid.

Not that she couldn't draw the nasty fuckers - her earlier, up-close encounter with them made sure of that. No, her astonishment came from the fact that — of all the Sharks — Captain Curran singled her out for this duty.

As the pencil rhythmically scratched and rasped against the paper, she was reminded of the art school scholarship she'd won. A full ride because she was *that* good. Being invited to join the prestigious Arts Student League was the first time in her life Ren ever achieved anything on her own, without needing her parents' money as a buy in.

Thinking of her parents prompted a wave of sadness through her and even though they were estranged when Earth was destroyed, she missed them.

Of course, missing them was a far cry from forgiving them, which was something Ren would never do. Perhaps if they'd bothered to show up to the funeral, Ren might have tried to rebuild their fractured relationship. But no, they were dead set against Emma's birth to begin with. Why the hell would they care when the baby died?

She hadn't drawn a thing since the day she found Emma and now, something as simple as sketching had cracked everything open again.

It had taken a moment to get started. She used to sketch a subject for hours, without any sense of time. She'd been known to stop everything she was doing and start drawing due to some trick of the light, or the shadows loving the lines on a person's face. Other times, it was the scene, a need to capture the feeling of the moment. Back then, it felt like hunger, where her mind was starving and her fingers needed release.

Ren didn't want such flames rekindled. Not only was this new world too dangerous for such distractions, but also, she didn't want the reminders of her old life.

She knew her mother. Adele Richards would have ended her last day on Earth with a high society luncheon with her country club set, toasting the end of the world with the last of the good wine. Her father, Ren thought with a pang of sadness, would probably aim for a last round of golf with his buddies.

They would have made no attempt to save themselves, not when the future awaiting them would be undoubtedly meaner than the high society life they'd known since birth.

And what about David? Had David tried to find a way off Earth with his new family? Last time they spoken, he'd welcomed a second child and she was touched by how hesitant he'd been to tell her about baby Anson. Ren didn't blame him for moving on, and often reminded him he'd lost too. Of the two of them, David was the one who really moved on.

Ren didn't blame him for the things that happened. They'd been two stupid kids thinking they could make it work on their own with school, jobs and a baby. For a time, it had worked. And then the bitch that was Fate steamrolled through their lives and ruined everything in a single night. Fate was the one Ren was truly angry at, stealing away her beautiful little Emma, not even allowing Ren the badge all mothers earned when they fought to save their child.

She and David had stayed together for just a few short months afterwards, but it was too much. Seeing him every day only reminded her of the beautiful, happy, red-headed baby. David had felt the same and they split. David had returned home to his family estate. Ren joined the Sharks.

Now she found herself in a quiet corner of the temple, sketching the subs from memory. While she would have preferred a different subject for her first piece of artwork in years, Captain Curran convinced her it was important. That, and you just don't tell a ship's captain 'no'. Maybe she'd be lucky and the subject matter would keep those stirrings at bay.

She was about to put the finishing touches to this so-called masterpiece when a loud crash reverberated and echoed through the entire building. Dust showered over them, sending people ducking and grabbing up equipment to keep the dirt out.

"WHAT THE FUCK WAS THAT?" The hysterical pitch to the demand made Ren think it wasn't a Shark.

"SHARKS! Form up on the door!!" Gunny's bellow was loud enough to be heard over everyone as Ren set the drawing aside, snatched her rifle and hurried to join the others as everyone (so it seemed) started moving and talking over the top of each other.

With an order from Sarge, the Sharks tiered up in three rows, facing the door as the temple room went quiet. They waited, some patiently, others fidgeted on the line as every eye in the room was on the makeshift barrier.

BOOM!!!!

Dust rained down again when a different noise caught Ren's attention. Glancing over her shoulder, she was just in time to see the rear wall shudder with another crash.

"Gunny!" she called out, turning towards the wall as mortar cascaded to the floor. "It's not the door, it's the back wall!!"

XXVI

Expendable

Tom had just left Jules with some of the squints on the second level and was descending the narrow-rough-hewn stairwell to the main floor when the first hit impacted the building and showered grit and dirt around him. The second hit made the stairwell drop a few inches, slamming stone against stone pillars with a deafening crack. Not wasting time, Tom all but jumped the last few steps as the building shuddered and groaned around him again, over top of the voices shouting from the other room. Too well-seasoned to let the shock stay for long, Tom hurried into the temple room he tried to raise Jules on her link. Another boom shook the building again and this time, he felt it in his bones.

"*We're heading down now!*" Jules finally responded.

"Watch the stairs, they've come loose!" Tom replied, his gaze going first to the Sharks, expecting to see them formed up on the newly erected door to fend off the subs. The *titanium plated* door: his logical mind argued the impossibility of anything breaching four inches of stuff that could withstand atmospheric re-entry. Then again, this bloody planet kept reinventing 'possible' every chance it got.

Except the squads weren't facing the door. Their attention was fixed solidly on the back wall of the temple, rifles raised.

"What the fu…"

BOOM!

This time, he saw the wall in question shudder as mortar cracked and tumbled pieces of the ancient frieze to the floor below, sending up clouds of dust. Fuck, he hated being right sometimes. The ugly bastards did have a plan and, worse yet, they weren't wasting time putting it into action.

The former occupants of Babel probably had no idea what hit them.

Jazz was not-quite-shouting at the squints to halt their rising panic, his voice calm but loud enough to be heard over their noise. Amid the packing up to move upstairs, most of the science teams returned to that task, albeit hastier than before. Others were anxiously looking to the Sharks for direction, uncertain of what to do next. Another deafening thud against the wall startled everyone, making them jump like ants about to scatter.

"That wall is two feet thick!" Ren shouted over her gunsight. "How many of them are there?"

Tom wasn't sure he wanted the answer to her question. While the bombardment masked the sound of fracturing rock, he could see the damage with his own eyes. Fuck them sideways, that wall wasn't going to hold. A sick sensation churned in the pit of his stomach at the thought as he scrambled to get his helmet on. Flipping his eyepiece into place, he scanned the wall, hoping to catch a glimpse of how many of the fuckers. Nothing, just blobs. Not surprising, considering the outer wall had interfered with their signals earlier.

"Harwood!" Tom called over the next thunderous hit. "Get upstairs to the windows and get me a sitrep! Watch those stairs!"

"On it!" Cori broke from the formation and headed for the stairs at a run. As she rounded the corner through the door, she sidestepped Captain Curran and two other squints, one of whom limped along between the captain and the other man. "Mayday, you're needed on the stairs!" Cori said quickly into her link as she headed up the way they'd come.

At her nickname, Maya glanced at Gunny, who nodded quickly in the direction of the stairs just as the Captain appeared.

"Sprained ankle," Jules told the medic as she passed the wounded doctor over.

"I got him," Maya replied but Jules was already joining Tom and Derick. "What the hell is going on?"

Tom pointed several cracks in the wall. "I think they're trying to breach the wa…"

"*Fuck me running…*"

"Report…" Tom ordered, not liking the sound of the normally un-phased Lance Corporal Harwood's voice.

"*Sending you the feed, you gotta see it…*"

Tom glanced at Jules as he pulled out his slate and slid it on. A second or two later, a live, jilting feed appeared on the screen from where Cori had stuck her slate through one of the slotted windows. When he realized what was on the screen, he decided *fuck me running* was an understatement.

It took a lot to shock the buggery out of him, but Harwood's feed certainly qualified. The spectral outline of the thing assaulting the outer wall like a battering ram wasn't any man-sized sub. Not even close. What was determined to smash its way inside the pyramid was BIG, like Godzilla fucking big The wall coming down wouldn't be an if but a 'when'. He could almost hear a computerized countdown to critical mass, as if this was one of those awful science fiction movies.

"*They're all joined together like fucking blocks!!*" Cori called out, giving up on proper radio etiquette altogether. "*Maybe… Ten feet or mo… Ohshit!*"

"They what like what?" Jules glanced at Tom and did a double take because the experienced combat veteran, had gone pale. Worse, there were no answers in his face.

"*It's using its spit to destroy the wall!*" Cori's voice resounded through their headsets.

As if brute force wasn't enough, Tom thought.

WHUMP!

This time, the impact rattled everything, walls, equipment, and personnel. Someone screamed in the gathering of scientists. "Harwood, get back down here!" Tom ordered, doing a mental inventory of their ordinance. "Ozzy, how many Thumpers are left?"

"Three!" Ozzy replied, swearing under his breath as he glanced at the Frog, who was crossing himself and probably praying to every French saint available. Shit. If they lived through this, Ozzy would learn every one of them as well.

Three Thumpers and the C4. The power pack and fire pod from each rifle, any of which might be running low.

The mission to Gaia had been a scientific expedition with most of the *Firefly's* cargo space taken up by the squints' equipment. They'd come to Babel to conduct a survey mission, not to engage in jungle warfare. There didn't seem any need to stock up on ammunition when it was just as easy to leave if things got rough.

Of course, no one counted on the ship getting demolished by whale-sized cockies from Hell.

Scanning the room, frightened faces stared back at Tom Merrick. For a brief second, Olivia Hall flashed in his memory. He remembered seeing her for the first time when they stood on the deck of the *Olympia*, ready to discover the new world. The squints soldiered on even after she died, displaying as much mettle and dedication as any Shark who'd lost a fallen comrade. And they hadn't lost just Olivia, they'd also lost Hanae and Tamara Adelaide.

Their fear was the lens he needed to see clearly and come up with the only plan that mattered at this point. Getting the civilians to safety. What it all boiled down to was the scientists in this room needed to survive. Humanity needed their expertise. His soldiers were like all soldiers, expendable.

While he had no intention of re-enacting every Kamikaze remake, he had to be realistic. Getting the squints out was going to get bloody, and everyone who'd signed up knew it.

Tom turned to Jules, oddly calm, he noticed, even if a slight twitch of her fingers gave away her own anxiety. Brilliant, brave, bloody beautiful — and whether she knew it or not, she'd saved him. Up until a few days ago, when he'd met her face to face, he was prepared to wallow in his self-imposed misery and die at the bottom of a bottle. She restored his wounded heart and gave him something he never thought he'd feel again: hope.

Whatever happened today, he was grateful for that. Looking at her now, he could feel that hope starting to burn.

"Luv, I need you to take the squints out of here and make a run for the ship. The *Firefly* may not be able to get you back to the fleet but it can take you far away from here. We Sharks will be right behind you but it's going to be a shit fight all the way there, you know that."

What he wasn't saying was the Sharks might need to hold the line for the civilians to get away, but she'd figure that out herself.

Realization hit Jules hard. Her eyes widened, and she shook her head. "No. No, Tom." This time, she grabbed him, one hand snatching his combat harness. "There has to be another way. I'm not leaving anyone else behind!"

"Jules, we're not going to be left behind, but that wall is going to come down," Tom gestured to the fractures were now spreading like fine webs across the limestone. The massive two by two-foot bricks were rippling like they were fluid, weakening with each impact. "We're going to blow the door so you lot can get out. We'll be right behind you. I'm not letting my people die any more than the squints, but this is the only chance we've got of getting them out of here alive."

Pilots had done this. Pulled a last-minute Hail Mary so others could get to safety and Jules had yet to meet any pilot who'd survived such last-ditch heroism. She glanced around the room, at the walls and the truth sank like a rock in her stomach. He was right. They had no time for anything else. No time, no other option. Like him, she understood. Get the civilians to safety.

"Fine," Jules yanked Tom to her, pulling him down to plant a hard, fast kiss on him, absolutely not caring who saw. "You come back to me," she hissed, pressing her forehead to his. "You get the fuck out of this place in one fucking piece and you come back to me. That is a fucking order, Major!"

Helllloo. Tom blinked and grabbed her face, returning the kiss with just as much intensity. Jesus, Mary and Joseph, she tasted sweet and invigorating! This bird could change your life if you gave her a chance. Tom accepted he might never know for sure but as long as she lived, he was okay with that.

"Yes ma'am," he said, planting one last hard kiss on her lips before letting her go. "If I make it back, can I get my own office? I mean now that I'm a kept man and everything."

"When, not if," Jules retorted and glanced towards the door. "Where's Godzilla when you really need him, huh?"

"Probably mucking around in a volcano somewhere. Lazy fucker," he winked, stepping back, ending the moment whether it was over or not. "Gunny!"

"Right here!"

Jules turned away from them. "Luke! Dr. Nordin!" she called out, picking out the two people she was certain could help her the most without breaking down.

"The exit we spoke about earlier," Tom said when Derick reached him. "We need it now. Captain Curran is going to take the squints and make a run for the ship. I need three bodies to escort them there. The rest of us will hold this position until they're clear, then we get the fuck out, but not before we blow this bastard back out its arse." Blowing things up should make the big guy happy. "Get this place rigged with enough C4 to bring it down, preferably with some kind of remote switch. Jackson! Get over here."

Jazz, who gratefully turned over charge of the squints to the Captain, jogged up to his superiors.

"Sarge, we're blowing the door so you and Captain Curran can get the squints out. You're going to make for the *Firefly*. Take Lorio and Anderson with you for backup."

The sour look on the younger man's face spoke volumes as to what he thought of this plan for him to leave them behind. "Sir…" he started to say before he remembered himself and bit back on what he was going to say. He wasn't happy and it was clear.

"Jazz," Tom grabbed his sergeant by the arm and glanced around, making sure Jules was nowhere in earshot when he spoke. "If it becomes problematic for the *Firefly* to come back and get us, you tell her my last orders were to take off. This mission is still under Shark command. I want her to leave and get everyone to safety. Understood?"

"But sir…" Jazz shot the Gunny an entreating look, hoping the guy would say something. They didn't leave people behind and the idea of just turning tail and running…?

If Derick knew anything about Tom, it was that he couldn't be persuaded from some things. Like now. He stared right back at Jazz, face unreadable. "You heard him, Sergeant," Derick said, knowing the formality would make Jazz toe the line.

Not for the first time, Tom thanked the high heavens that Derick was his Gunny and his friend. "Use the Thumpers on the door but do not detonate until I give the word. The minute those buggers break through the wall, they're going to swamp us. That's your window, while we're dealing with them, you take the squints and run your arse off."

Still hating the idea, Jazz nodded. He had his orders, didn't he? "We'll get them home safe, Major. I give you my word."

"Good bloke," Tom patted his shoulder and looked over the temple, saddened by what they needed to do to the place. "Derick, let's get to work setting those charges."

* * *

By the time the first ray of sunlight cut through the dust-choked air, they were ready.

Standing next to Derick, Tom cast a brief glance over his shoulder at Jules, their eyes making contact. She stared back at him with those soulful blue eyes, full of promise and sadness. Full of everything they could have been to each other. She gave a quick nod and turned back to the scientists she would be leading out of the room in a few seconds. Tom refocused on the task at hand, making Jules a promise that he'd do everything possible to get back to her.

Rock buckled around the ragged hole, a large piece breaking free a second before a section caved in. Tom barely had enough time to blink in the bright sun before it was blocked by The Big Motherfucker. "Short, controlled bursts. Make every shot count!"

Suddenly, the wall exploded inward, sending large chunks bouncing and skittering everywhere along with an enveloping cloud of dust that rushed across the floor. The Sharks that weren't masked up had hidden their faces behind bandannas. To Tom's right, one of the now shadowed soldiers yelled as he went down.

"Get him up!" Derick bellowed from Tom's right and the shape regained its feet.

"Are you hurt?" Tom asked and received a negative in reply. "Steady on, hold your fire!"

Backlit by the sun, The Big Motherfucker finally revealed itself to those who hadn't been privy to Harwood's feed from earlier. Even though Tom had seen it, he still wasn't prepared for what was filling up that hole. More than ten feet tall, closer to fifteen, Tom estimated. The subs had formed into a tinker toy monstrosity, connected by tentacles and clenching limbs. The head wasn't something he'd likely ever forget, a cluster of tentacles whirling like hair. There were no eyes, just... jaws. Multiple jaws, snapping away.

For a moment, there was dead silence, both entities sizing up the other.

"FIRE!"

In a bone-shaking roar, every rifle and firearm opened up on the beast. Beta went high, targeting the chest carapace while Alpha went for the lower body. Ren was perched on the dais to get a bead on the beast's head with her sniper's aim.

Long, thick tentacles lashed out across the room, retaliating against the plasma fire. There was a yell as someone was yanked off their feet. The big Maori, who kept his head and was swinging at the tentacle with his machete as Tom fired at the appendage. When he hit the floor, he rolled back to his feet and let out a war cry.

Another tentacle raced along the floor, heading for Derick. Ren reacted immediately, her trained sniper's eye pulling the trigger on her rifle even before it got anywhere near him. The short, abrupt burst of plasma severed it mid limb, sending meat and dark fluid spurting everywhere.

Suddenly, the creature roared, rearing back as Tom realized what was happening. "TAKE COVER!!"

The Sharks scattered. A huge gob of fluid shot from the beast and splattered against the big stone altar, sending Harwood, Richards and the Maori diving behind the big rock.

This was their window, Tom thought. It was time for the squints to go. "Jazz, now!"

A split-second later, the titanium barricade exploded violently, the shock wave making everyone stumble and covering them all in eons worth of dust. Tom blinked through it in time to see Jules ushering the squints through the opened doorway.

Beside her, Luke hesitated, staring at his brother. Sarge and the Captain were shouting at him and the rest of the civilians to move, but Luke couldn't make his feet work. If he left, he'd lose Derick and after Tammy, he couldn't lose Derick. Not now. Not...

"Luke, go!!"

Someone pushed at him and Luke found himself staring at an insistent Captain Curran. He almost refused until Derick's bellowed order drew his attention to where his brother was steadily firing on the monster. He'd never seen him in action, not like this and with sudden clarity realized why his brother fought so hard. For him. For him to get free. He had to go because it was what Derick would want — no, needed — him to do. With a curse of anguish, Luke let himself be ushered out of the room, praying he'd see his brother again.

* * *

"Beta! Cover the squints!"

With his back pressed against one of the large columns flanking the altar, Tom barked his order over the discharge of blast rifles. Only when they were mostly gone did he turn back, laying out his own hell. Two shots struck a knee, destroying the sub and disrupting the creature's movement. About to issue an order to aim for the joints, Tom blistered the air with curses when an individual sub crawled up to replace the ruined joint.

"Switch to grenades! FIRE IN THE HOLE!!" Tom called over the noise, yanking a grenade off his own belt, arming it and hurling it at the monster.

Ren followed suit just as Harwood grabbed her arm, pointing to where three subs had just oozed their way into the temple, past the mother beast. Jesus Christ. They were like rats, Ren thought, boneless and dangerous at the same time, slithering over one another. She lobbed the grenade expertly, a pitch any major leaguer would be proud of, and snatched back her rifle as the device flared brilliantly and disintegrated the three creatures.

An outraged scream filled the air as the beast focused on Ren, stomping towards her as it reared back. She was yanked downward just as another glob of acid spit splattered against the stone altar, eating into the already weakened bricks.

"I think you pissed it off!" Cori shouted over the noise.

"I'm good at that! Fall back, I'll cover you!"

Rising to her feet, Cori opened fire on the beast as she and Pookie backed away to re-join the others. "REN! Heads up!!" she yelled as a massive tentacle slammed into the column beside it.

The abused stone finally crumbled and gave, sending rock, dirt and stone tiles washing over Ren. She had just enough time to pull her limbs close and shield her head before it all came down on her.

"Richards!!" Derick moved towards her on instinct, barking at Harwood to cover him.

"Gunny!" Cori swore under her breath and aimed her shots higher, to get the beast's attention.

Sliding through the rubble, Derick easily tossed a large tile off Ren and breathed a sigh of relief to find her not fully covered. He grabbed her by the harness and hauled her over a shoulder before scrambling back to the others.

"On your left!!" Tom yelled, opening fire on the sub making straight for his Gunny and his unconscious corporal. Behind that creature, more were pushing their way into the temple, around the big one. "Beta squad," he ordered. "Take out all the stragglers. It can't do a Lego on us if there are no extra pieces. Alpha squad! Concentrate all firepower on the big bastard!"

A barrage of shots exploded before he even finished giving the order, cutting down the subs flanking the behemoth and driving them back through the ragged opening. The big one was still outraged, forcing itself ahead and determined to reach its prey.

With its size, Tom figured it wouldn't take long for the beast to reach them. Unless... he popped up from the fallen boulder he'd taken cover behind to assess the expanse of stone in front of him. He could do it. It would be a Hail Mary pass, but it wouldn't be the first time he'd pulled a miracle out of his ass. Snatching one of his last grenades, Tom darted towards the altar and jumped onto what was left of it. Using his momentum, he launched himself off the altar and hurled the incendiary into the centre of all those tentacles.

Sure in his aim, Tom didn't watch to see the grenade land, too busy with not breaking his own neck as he hit on the stone. Rolling out of the drop, he threw himself behind another huge rock just as the grenade went off, evaporating at least four of the subs making up the head and bathing the upper half of the body in fire. For a few seconds, Momma Beast stood in place, her tentacles whipping around like Medusa's snakes before subs started shedding off and breaking apart.

"Take them out!" Derick encouraged as the beasts seemed to lose their organization. "Keep 'em from regrouping!"

Separated from his squad, Tom was a man alone against the wall as two subs advanced on him. Blasting away at the nearest one, he was relieved to find the second one was shredded into meat. Looking up, Tom nodded to Ozzy and French before rushing back to safety. Near him, someone cursed as they ejected a fire pod from their rifle and kicked the smoking capsule away from them. Others were doing the same, changing out the plasma containers and, when he looked, more subs seemed to be spilling through the opening.

It was time to bug out.

Tom tapped his link. "Jules, what's your status?"

"We're at the *Firefly*!" came the broken, static filled reply. "We're coming back for you!"

"We'll meet you in the compound!" He replied, relieved to hear her and turned his attention to the squads.

"Beta squad, start to withdraw through the main doors! Alpha, lay down suppressing fire to cover them. WE ARE LEAVING!" While dying was something they were all prepared to do, unnecessary martyrdom was not on the agenda today if he could help it.

As the units separated to their tasks, Tom heard Ozzy shouting. He spotted the guy shortly, one hand firing his sidearm and the other holding onto French's harness for dear life. The former Legionnaire was caught in an absurd tug of war, between Ozzy and two subs, tentacles snaked around his legs. Just as Tom raised his gun to fire, a thick tentacle lashed out of nowhere, slamming into Ozzy, making him release French as he was sent tumbling backwards. He scrabbled unsuccessfully along the stone as Shiny appeared beside him, using her weight to keep him from going after the Frenchman.

"ALAIN!" His yell was eclipsed by French's scream as he was sucked into the whirling, slithering mass of carapaced bodies.

XXVII

The Slurry

"You hear me, baby? Hold together."

Tom would appreciate that line, Jules decided when Dr. Nordin said nothing from the co-pilot's seat beside her. Jules pulled back on the throttle a second time and heaved a sigh of relief when the tell-tale vibration of the engine igniting, rumbled through her boots. She waited a hot minute to make sure the shuttle wouldn't stall out again before glancing back to the main compartment. "Everyone buckle up, NOW!" she bellowed over a shoulder.

The Bobbsey twins, she forgot their names, quickly relayed the order in a tone that promised future command positions if... no... *when* they made it through all this. "You too, Doc!" Something groaned as the shuttle levitated upwards. When something thudded against the deck plating under her boots and a yellow light started to flash on the console, Jules repeated the famous order under her breath.

"What's that?!" Dr. Nordin asked, staring at the warning light.

"Nothing, she's just bitching. We're fine!" Jules replied, quickly acknowledging the hopper's attempt to inform her of the O2 leak in the rear coolant access hatch. Yes, she knew about that. Or expected it. The sky crabs' attack and subsequent salvage of anything that could reinforce the temple left the shuttle in a perilous condition. In fact, the short flight Tom envisioned for their continued survival might be the *Firefly's* last.

Second to last, dammit. They still had to fly somewhere else.

As she brought the hopper around to head towards the temple, the yoke stuttered in her hands, shaking for a brief second before it steadied out. When Jules pushed the throttle, the craft lurched forward. They picked up speed, creating a whole new group of noises as wind whistled through various openings. Something tore loose, making a lot of noise before stopping altogether. One of the Sharks yelled an order to ignore the equipment. He was right. Equipment could survive falling out. A person couldn't.

Cresting over the outer wall of the city, Jules could hardly believe the damage. Fresh new craters, courtesy of weapons fire, grenades and even the subs left the verdant greenery pockmarked and trashed.

"Tom, we're here!" Jules announced over the link as Subs spread across the main pyramid like a swarm of fire ants returning home to their hill. Spying an opening in the underbrush nearest the temple, she turned the shuttle in that direction and keyed in the landing sequence. Not that the computer would help much in its present condition. She was going to have to do this manually. Otherwise known as 'by the seat of her pants'.

Hoo-ya.

Three new lights flashed red on the console but Jules ignored them as she muscled the hopper into touch down.

"Brace for landing!!" she yelled, not breaking her gaze from the contours on the fritzed digital screen.

When the shuttle set down with a jarring thump, Jules swore it breathed a sigh of relief.

* * *

Time screeched to a halt when Dupree was taken by the Subs.

Ozzy's scream was an aria of anguish and the seconds it took to reach crescendo moved like molasses. Everything was drowned out in that horrified cry; the bass *thumpthumpthump* of blast rifle fire, Derick's booming voice and the Subs' chilling war cry. Even Tom, who was only Dupree's commander for a matter of months, felt his granite constitution fracture.

Shiny was wrestling with Ozzy, using her full body weight to keep him from diving into the writhing mass after Dupree. There wasn't anything to get back, Tom thought, the kid would be ripped apart by those fuckers. You didn't have to be a twenty-year lifer to know that.

"Ozzy! HE'S GONE!" Shiny's voice was sharp and shrill and just like that, everything snapped back into motion. With Dupree taken, Tom knew they didn't have much time left. Hurrying over to his distraught corporal, Tom yanked his harness to get his attention. "LOOK AT ME CORPORAL!! Pull your fucking head out!" When Ozzy's mouth opened, as if to protest, Tom yanked at him again. "LOOK AT ME!" he ordered.

When the younger man's head snapped around, focus solely on him now, Tom was glad to see Ozzy wasn't too far gone to ignore his conditioning. "He's gone! And if you don't move it, we'll be gone, too!!! Now lay down suppressing fire and RETREAT!"

Ozzy blinked, his body starting as his fugue released him. Tom saw the pain and sorrow, watched as the kid forced it into the lock box all Sharks kept inside of them.

"Yessir," Ozzy swallowed thickly and nodded.

Tom patted him on the shoulder. He knew those eyes. The kid would survive. His heart might not, but the kid would make it. Now it was up to Tom to make sure the rest of them did. Turning to the rest of the Sharks, Tom bellowed. "Anyone with grenades, we're not saving them for Christmas! USE THEM and get the fuck out!!!"

On cue, several dark shapes hurtled by overhead as the Sharks vacated through the tunnel. Staying behind until he was sure the last one was out, Tom primed his last two grenades and dropped them where he stood before heading for the passageway and the outside.

He had just cleared the tunnel on the other end, breaking into the sunshine when heat washed over him. The concussion wave tossed him down the stone stairs to the ground, hitting it hard and rolling over and over until he came to a crunching, pained stop against a tree.

Before he could register what was broken or even get to his feet, someone grabbed his harness and hauled him up.

"Stop trying to impress the ladies!" Derick yelled, just as a second explosion erupted from behind them and sent them both scrambling for cover. Dirt, stone and unidentifiable objects showered down all around them. "Claymores! You okay?" he shouted, pulling Tom back to his feet.

"What?" Tom shook his head again, shaking Derick off once he was certain he wasn't going to kiss the ground again.

"Jesus, Tom…" Derick began, cutting off when he glanced behind his friend. "Shit!! RUN!!!" he bellowed, giving Tom a shove.

Looking over his shoulder, Tom swore as he took off for the hopper. The subs were coming up through the ground again.

"DIE YOU MOTHERFUCKERS!" Ozzy's voice carried above the dull roar in Tom's ears as weapons fire raced over head. Tom spotted him standing on a rock with Ren's sniper rifle with Shiny next to him firing on anything that wasn't a Shark.

"GO! GO! GO!"

Derick's order urged him into a run for the shuttle behind the other Sharks.

* * *

"I see them!" Jules flinched at the ear-stabbing burst of artillery through her headset as gunfire erupted at the rear of the hopper. She fervently hoped that was cover fire and not because the subs had gotten wise.

The ship's console whined ominously but the sound of boots stampeding into the back drowned it out. She patted the console once more. "You can do it, baby," she murmured. Someone in the back called out that Beta Squad was on board. She leaned over the link, not even sure if Tom's was still working. "Come on, old man!!"

A very Australian curse was sent back in reply. Jules grinned, not even caring what he said because if he was talking, Tom Merrick was still alive.

* * *

Shiny ran onto the shuttle, quickly turning to keep covering the Major and Gunny, who were running flat out. They ignored burning piles of plasma and detritus, leaping over them and only breaking their stride when a sub shot out of the ground. "Don't let anything live!" Shiny yelled to her team as they fanned out to each side of the ramp and opened fire.

* * *

To her untrained ear, the gunfire seemed to change pitch and Jules desperately hoped it wasn't because they were running out of ammunition. Just then, she noticed a single, blinking blue light to her right. She did a double take before slapping it hard, filling the cockpit with a most welcome voice.

"...peat... Capt... lles, Shutt... fly... this is Lieu..." Static scoured the air and the voice came back on. "Please... Rutthh... Er... land... Zone..."

"This is Captain Curran!!" Jules's voice cracked. "We are under attack! Close on my coordinates!" Rattling off the numbers, she heard something crash into the hull of the shuttle. "What was that?!" she yelled behind her.

"Subs!" was the frantic answer over the top of someone screaming and what sounded like a fire extinguisher being set off.

"Captain Curran, this is... Rae... ETA six..."

More static and Jules cursed. They didn't have six minutes. "TOM! We need to move!"

He didn't answer.

* * *

Where she came from, they called her the Devourer.

In a time far removed from the present of this day, she'd consumed whole cities and left haunting emptiness in her wake. Like a scourge out of the depths of the Great Darkness, she was a destroyer to all she encountered. On the world that first birthed her, she'd emptied a continent, held back only by the hated ocean.

Then, the feeding had been good and the soil soft and pliant. Her children moved in the land beneath the sunless earth, basking in the black sea of the Slurry. With the rich meat of brain matter nourishing the Slurry, the thought stream connecting them all was like living lines of currents. Taken from their primary prey, the sunbacks who built and tilled above ground, their soup was the sweet ingredient needed to give life to the Slurry. No other prey would do.

Until the day, they swept over the hated ocean, in numbers greater than she had ever seen. Fierce and vengeful, they found the Slurry and destroyed it, murdering all her children with their unholy weapons, incinerating them. She still could picture inferno in her mind's eye, howling with the screams of her dying children. Instead of killing her, they scooped her up, like a great hand and placed her in a cell she could not escape.

And without a second thought, flung her into the endless void of space.

Whether it was by cosmic design or mere luck, she came to a world where the prey was just as sweet and weak as they had been when she first feasted well. Within hours of reaching this new realm, she awoke, ravenous. To the prey, she was a goddess sent from the heavens. She allowed them their belief. After all, a god needed sacrifices.

Once more, she ate well, mining their brain matter to create a new Slurry; but, like before, she'd been careless. Bloating herself without thought, she'd exhausted the supply and there were no more sunbacks who tilled and built. The lower animals sensed the Slurry and stayed away, forcing her children to scavenge the dead husks already rotting in the dirt. But it wasn't enough, and the Slurry began to wither. Fear of its complete stagnancy drove her into hibernation.

Now there was a new prey but these were of the kind responsible for her exile in the void. Oh, their brain matter was sweet indeed. The few brought to the Slurry were quickly consumed but the others, the others were filled with hatred. They fought back and now she could hear her children screaming again, their agony reaching her in the Slurry. She felt their deaths, each strand of their lives cut one by one with such speed, it was dizzying.

It enraged her and gave birth the black need for vengeance. Her children were dying and, like any good mother, she had to protect them.

* * *

"FUCK!" Derick yelled, nearly falling backward when a sub appeared out of the ground in front of them. A shot over his shoulder exploded the creatures head just as the ground shook beneath his feet. "What was that?" he asked Tom.

Suddenly, dirt and torn greenery washed over them like a dam had broken, knocking both men off their feet and sending them tumbling in the mess.

"What the fuck…" Derrick spit dirt out, trying to clear his eyes. This time, Tom hauled his friend to his feet.

"Not stick…" He began, glancing behind them and froze. "Bloody fucking hell!!!"

Towering over them was forty feet of monster, rising and shedding flora like water. Its shadow eclipsed them as its mouth opened. The resulting roar was deafening and shook the ground at their feet. Almost on reflex, Tom emptied what was left of his ammo into the trunk of the thing.

It did not make one slight bit of difference.

The creature screamed indignantly like an angry god. Tentacles writhed, Medusa-like, around the mass of its head. When its mandible shuddered, Tom cursed loudly, knowing what was coming.

"The fence!!" he shouted at Derick, glancing back one more time… and it was too late.

"RUN!" He yelled, his steps stuttering as he heard the nightmare's sickly heave. Diving for the nearest rock that wasn't nearly big enough, Tom skidded face first into the dirt seconds before something massive and wet splattered against the rock and the ground around him. He had just started to his feet before he realized exactly what had happened or even register the sticky, gel-like clumps clinging to his armour.

The smell registered before the pain did, seizing Tom in what felt like a shower of burning coals. A fire that burned sickly sweet as it ate into bits of his flesh. "Shit!!" he hissed, too distracted by his slagging armour to see the second danger until Derick roared his name.

He looked up, just in time to register the tree-thick tentacle coming at him like a speeding train. Later, he wouldn't remember the actual hit but the monster swept Tom off his feet like he was nothing, hurling him through the air a good thirty feet. He slammed full-body into a thick, high rock fence and bounced into the wild overgrowth below.

* * *

"Fuck me…" Jules breathed as she gaped at the creature emerging from the ground.

Whatever that Lego thing had been earlier, it was a puppy compared to this thing. Four slithery limbs framed a massive eyeless head the size of a hopper. Two curved tusks, easily six feet long flanked a mouth full of rows and rows of teeth. The body was twice as thick as one of those sky crabs and it seemed to ooze more than step forward.

"LUKE!!! I need all power diverted to the engine!!" she yelled.

* * *

"TOM!! I need cover!!" Derick yelled into his link as he crashed into the bushes in search of his friend. "The Major's down!!" Hauling a sapling out of the ground and out of his way, he spotted a flash of bald head. "Tom!"

"Get this fucking thing off me!" Tom barked, pain hitching his voice as the nerve endings in his fingers lit on fire. "Get it the fuck off!"

Just then, a shadow zipped over them, front cannons already blazing as a Zephyr lit up the beast. Derick snatched his knife from his boot and quickly worked it under the side that wasn't melting. With a yank, he cut the remaining straps, barely getting his knife out of the way before Tom stripped off the now useless body armour.

Tom could hardly think straight for the pain as he fumbled for Derick's battle harness. "Der… Derick?" he gritted out as he was hauled to his feet.

"Just a second," Christ, blood was fucking everywhere! Derick hurriedly cut at Tom's shirt to try and get the soaked pieces off him.

"OY! Derick!"

"What!?"

Tom blinked, not used to Derick pulling Gunny Mode on *him.* "Okay. You're in charge now."

Then Tom Merrick, the Commander of Tiger Platoon, fainted.

* * *

Despite the Sharks' beyond heroic efforts, Jules couldn't help but notice the line of sub bodies was getting closer and closer. Something zoomed by in the corner of her eye and she looked up. "YES!!" she cried exultantly when she spotted the Zephyr and two more descending from the sky.

As the fighter came around, tracer fire danced up the monster's torso before larger detonations imploded against its shell. The creature roared in defiance, refusing to accept its coming death as it fell backwards in slow motion, limbs flailing, toppling like a building going down in demolition.

"*Mayday, meet me at the ramp!!*"

That was the Gunny. Jules's stomach leapt into her throat.

* * *

"…did not fucking faint…I don't…fucking…faint!!" Tom protested when he regained a moment of lucidity and realised he wasn't where he'd landed. In fact, the *Firefly* loomed over him, which meant he lost time. Derick was raving, not unlike the occasion when some bright spark of a recruit had substituted his shampoo for hair dye.

"MAKE A HOLE!!" Mayday's voice carried to them before she appeared through the throng of bodies. She took one look at Tom and motioned to the Med Bay. "Back here, Gunny!"

"Where the fuck she get those bloody lungs?" Tom mumbled as he was moved to the med station. A blanket had been laid out of the floor, mostly because the bed had been stripped down. The process to get him on the deck hurt more than he could have imagined. In the last moments of his consciousness, he wondered if this is what Lisa felt that night. If it was even a fraction of her pain, then spacing her was a kindness he'd never again regret. Absolution loosened months of self-pity and anguish out of his body and let him slide peacefully into unconsciousness.

* * *

With the all clear to take off, Jules pulled the throttle back to lift off. The shuttle shuddered and… Nothing. "Come on!!" She yelled, kicking the console. Several lights blinked and fluttered as a shadow passed overhead.

"Captain Curran, this is Lieutenant McRae. Target destroyed, ma'am."

"Excellent job, L.T.!" Jules barely held back the sob of relief that wanted out just as another idea crossed her mind. "Lieutenant, are you carrying a bunker buster?" When the affirmative response came through, she nodded. "Drop everything you have on that hole the creature came out of."

"Roger that, ma'am."

Jules touched the throttle again and the little hopper that could, roared to life once more and lifted off the ground in a lurch. "That's it, baby!" she grinned, heading away from the hot zone to rendezvous with the shuttle that just appeared on the horizon.

* * *

As per orders, Lt. Sloane McRae circled the large rip in the earth where the creature had first emerged, sighting the pool of dark sludge that pooled at the bottom of it. Her nose twisted in disgust beneath her oxy mask as she adjusted her trajectory to place it in the crosshairs of her targeting computer.

"TARGET ACQUIRED."

The computer announced dutifully and McRae wasted no time dropping the plasma payload into the orifice that stared at her like a blight on the pristine world's surface. She felt some measure of disappointment regarding the structures she was about to destroy and looked forward to the landing team's report about the civilisation birthed in this valley. McRae had no doubt they'd have a hell of a story to tell.

The missile struck the target and the explosion that followed was eclipsed by a wall of sand and dirt filling the air, almost reaching the Zephyr's hull. McRae adjusted her altitude and rose easily above the blast, watching the shock wave ripple destruction outward from the kill zone. Sand, rock, architecture and history disappeared as the ground liquefied. What had been in the epicentre of the blast was no more. It had been vaporised.

The Slurry and all its kind were gone for good.

XXVIII

Reflections

Ren Richards spent the two days after their rescue in the *Ruthie's* Medical Centre. She suspected she was being kept an extra day to make up for the time she should have spent recovering after the Audrey made her a shish-ka-bob. Honestly, Ren didn't mind the rest (and it would take a whole mess of Audreys to get her to admit that) because she *hurt*. Her body was bruised almost everywhere and, thanks to a concussion, the inside of her skull pounded with a raging headache. A good soldier knew when to surrender to superior forces and for Ren, this was it.

Besides, convalescence provided her with time to think.

Dr. Whelan told her she was lucky to be alive, but Ren didn't need the *Ruthie's* CMO to state the obvious. She knew it. How many had died on Gaia? Olivia Hall, Tammy Adelaide, Hanae Akiyama, Colin Macon, Tonie Edwards, Evan Chu, Dee Sheridan and Alain Dupree. Her name could have been easily added to the list of the dead and each one drove home how damn lucky she was to be still breathing.

Maya became a frequent visitor during these two days. During one such visit, the medic reluctantly gave Ren a final roster of those who'd perished on Gaia, until she got to Colin's name. Only then, in the privacy of the hospital room and with her closest friend, Maya let him go. They both did, holding onto each other, Maya shedding tears for Colin and Ren, weeping for her fallen comrades.

Despite Colin and Maya's protests to the contrary, Ren knew their relationship was more than just casual. It might have begun as a fling between two strangers seeking comfort after a catastrophic loss, but it had become something more. It was plain to anyone who saw them together they were, or were very close to, falling for each other fast.

Ren thought about the other Sharks who fell on Gaia. For the members of Alpha Squad and most of the armed services, Sol's destruction meant the loss of everyone they'd ever loved. The only connections not obliterated by civilisation's end were those formed in the ranks. During the six months in space, these relationships sustained morale and deepened so much that none of them were strangers to each other. When someone died, they weren't some faceless soldier you knew in passing, it was a person you talked to and saw every day.

Like Tonie, whom Ren would miss every day because of her irrepressible energy and optimism, like some demented cheerleader. Ren initially found Tonie's obstinate refusal to let the grey walls and bitterness dampen their spirits somewhat irritating. But the truth was, they had needed to hear Tonie's constant reminders of a better life. The cynics among them never appreciated Tonie. Now it was too late, and Ren wished in hindsight she'd been kinder.

Before Maya left, Ren sent her on a last errand, to go through Evan Chu's locker before someone placed his gear in storage or, worse yet, divvied it up among themselves. Months ago, during a late-night drinking session, Evan showed her the seed packets he'd managed to save from his parents' house before Sol became a memory.

Unlike Ren, Evan never intended being a lifer. Instead, he was using his military service to travel the system like some culinary Jack Kerouac. When that plan died with Sol, he adapted it on the fly. He would plant these seeds and open a restaurant. It would be called The Dragon's Wok, after his parents' place in Los Angeles.

The death of that dream left a bitter taste in her mouth and Ren vowed to see those seeds planted, even if she had to dig the dirt herself.

And then there was Dupree.

Ren was already out cold by the time Dupree died. During Shiny's visit, Ren asked how Ozzy was handling his friend's death and the comtech revealed sombrely how she'd had to restrain Ozzy from going after Dupree when the subs took him. While her heart bled for her friend, she wasn't surprised. Even more so than Colin and Maya, Ozzy and French kept their relationship discreet. She'd only found out because she had come across them discussing plans once they reached Gaia. They'd asked for her secrecy and she'd willingly kept that oath to protect the two men.

Like Maya and Colin, their relationship had burned brightly and knowing Ozzy, he was probably mourning in silence, too afraid to tell anyone what Dupree really meant to him.

In the months after Earth's destruction, the Major had overlooked things like fraternization, but the stigma remained. It was easy to compromise a situation with personal feelings, and in a firefight, it could be deadly. She made a vow to find Ozzy when she was released, since he wouldn't come to her, and let him know she was there for him.

Because grief was something she knew about too.

During their bout of shared tears, Ren showed Maya the folded picture of her beautiful daughter Emma, stashed in her foot locker. Though Ren kept the photo close to her, she almost never looked at it. Maya sat and held Ren while she relayed how the little one had died of pneumonia in the second month of her life.

As Maya brushed a gentle finger over the photos, Ren found herself realizing she'd missed her so much! In her friend's delight at Emma's hair and her eyes and even her toes, Ren remembered those moments of sheer perfection. The feel of Emma's newborn skin the first time Ren held her. How her little smile would take Ren's breath away and the strength of a tiny fist around her finger made her promise Emma the world, every time.

Gaia had taken even more from a desperate population, but as Ren talked about Emma for the first time in years and studied the picture she'd stowed away until now, she realized they had also gained.

Everyone would see grace and beauty again. They'd experience the wonder of discovering a whole new planet where twigas drifted by in boneless grace and little balls of fluffy personality brought smiles to people in dire need of hope.

Ren had rekindled her passion for life amidst the horror and realised there was someone who cared for her as much as she did for him. Derick, just Derick, kept a vigil at her bedside the first day. He was there every time she'd opened her eyes. They hadn't talked much but they didn't need to. His eyes had been the first thing to capture her attention years ago. Hazel and expressive, he could rock the flinty-eyed poker face but when Derick Rickman wanted to, those amazing eyes could say everything he felt and reveal a world of emotion.

Loving Derick made the years behind her a little more bearable and the years ahead hopeful.

* * *

"Don't work too hard, yeah?"

Luke made a face at his brother's grainy visage on the screen. "Look who's talking." He wouldn't go into it with Derick now, not over the link.

Working was the only way Luke Rickman knew how to get past what happened in the ancient city the squints were now calling Roanoke. Where it once stood, only a huge crater existed now. The flight wing dispatched to 'sterilize' the area had been remarkably efficient. There was no trace of the city or the creatures responsible for destroying the nascent civilisation. The expedition team hastily collected every bit of data before the final destruction and it was hoped they could use it to provide a memorial for the dead race.

While Roanoke's fate was being carried out, the bigwigs argued *ad nauseum* over the location of the new settlement, named Babel. When the dust settled, and the feathers were swept away, it was determined Babel would be built in Olivia Valley, ten miles from Roanoke Crater, along the banks of the Hanae River. Luke had been extraordinarily pleased they'd accepted his naming suggestions for both locations.

Honouring Olivia was a no-brainer, but he'd liked Hanae's sense of adventure. Naming the river after the first person who was brave enough to wade in barefoot was fitting.

Somewhere in all that, he had been put in charge of some of the engineering projects on the ground. While the military was highly efficient in establishing a firebase, setting up permanent operations was needed and fast.

So now here he was, snagging a quick break and a cup of coffee while reaching out to Derick. For once, their schedules meshed, and he didn't have to leave a message.

"Hey, I'm just nodding my head and keeping fights from breaking out. You're doing all the real work."

When Derick grinned, Luke nodded tiredly. Truth was, mapping out the new proposed settlement was hard work. Trying to manage a ship's worth of surveyors, civil engineers, and environmental scientists was like trying to herd cats. More than once, he was glad for the presence of the Shark contingent. The *Olympia*, the *Ruthie,* and the *Beamer* had sent squads down and the place actually felt secure.

Besides, anyone complaining about the number of Sharks down here changed their tune very quickly after seeing a mulk, an Audrey or the trashed *Firefly*.

As Luke made his goodbyes and disconnected the call, he downed the rest of his coffee and got to his feet. Heading to the trash, he spotted a tired-looking Cori Harwood lower herself onto a bench with a meal packet and bottle of water.

He hadn't intended on speaking to her. Not yet, anyway. But it wasn't lost on him how much of a wreck he'd been after Tammy's death. He would have been no good to anyone if he'd been allowed to let the grief swallow him up. While Tom's talk had served to bring him back to the here and now, it was Harwood who kept feeding that fire.

She'd nudged his intellect, pushing him to keep working to get them out of Roanoke. Her ideas fuelled his own and together, they'd done what was necessary to get a message back to the fleet. There was a lot of back slapping when they'd gotten back to the *Ruthie*, but Luke wasn't sure Harwood had received her due.

Changing course, he headed over to her table and offered a friendly smile when she looked up. "Hey, can I sit?"

"Sure." Cori smiled back at Luke, glad to see him. She'd been too busy to personally check on him, but she'd bugged the Gunny a couple of times for Luke's sitrep. Going strong had been the answer and now, Cori could see that for herself. Good. "Did you eat yet? You don't mind if I eat in front of you, do you? I mean, my grams would kill me if she was alive ... Oh." Cori's eyes widened. "Shit. I'm sorry."

"Nothing to apologise for," he dismissed the perceived slight with a wave of his hand and took the seat in front of her. "I wouldn't want you to snub years of tradition."

Smiling, Cori didn't waste a minute tearing into her meal. "I'm starving," she said, making a face at the first bite. "This is so not chicken alfredo. How have you been? I heard you were put in charge of the surveying?"

She hadn't been surprised at the news. Gunny had told her once Luke's IQ was higher than most. The work would do him good, keep him busy and keep his thoughts off his dead girlfriend. Someone had told her they weren't sleeping together. Yeah right, a guy like Luke Rickman? Nope. She wasn't buying it.

"If you mean being in charge is me telling them we got bigger things to worry about than what we name that rock, yeah that's me." He offered her a ghost smile, hiding how much satisfaction he drew from being the go-to person capable of herding squints.

Sitting across from her, Luke noticed for the first time that, beneath all that jungle-bunny kit she was wearing, she was pretty. Hot, Luke. The word is hot. Baser instincts fought the current of his wounded emotions to kick start the charm needed when in proximity of attractive women, except Luke didn't want that right now. Reducing her to 'potential tail' was cheapening what she did for him and he didn't want that.

"Look," he spoke, refocusing his thoughts. "I wanted to thank you for your help in Roanoke. I wouldn't have been able to get through it without you."

"Oh!" Cori shot him a warm smile and shrugged. "Just helping out. You would have made it. You're tough. I just hate not doing something, you know?" Her words bore the worn bitterness of experience. Her pretty features hardened for a split second before she beamed her trademark grin at him. "So, are people seriously naming rocks?"

"Rocks, the squishy thing that just crawled by, you name it." He noted the gratitude made her uncomfortable, but he had to get what he wanted to say off his chest. "Anyway, I just wanted you to know I'm grateful for what you did; and I hear you, I'm down here because I need to do something too. Besides," he raised his eyes to the world outside the tent, "we get to be here."

"Amen to that, right?" Cori grinned at him. "I can't get over how green everything is! I was raised by ice miners. Our landscape had two basic colours: white and a hundred shades of grey. If there was colour, it was because we planted it," she chuckled, digging her fork into the meal packet. She made a face and scooped out a bite, wolfing it down despite her apparent distaste.

"Chin up, Shark," Luke teased and indicated the packet. "When I can manage it, I'll cook you something much better than that."

Yes, he, Luke Rickman, could cook. With a sizeable gap of time between his arrival and that of his younger sister Lily, their mother wanted to pass on family traditions not involving the best way to police an area or store your weapon, (yes that was a thing in the Rickman household). Luke became the recipient of all her culinary expertise, which helped when he was on his own, living on a budget. It was also a great way to end a one night stand the next morning.

An eyebrow went up dubiously as Cori put another bite in her mouth. "You cook?" she asked when she'd finished chewing. "Like cook, cook? Something that doesn't involve lichen or squishy, crawling things?"

Luke made a face. "I won't ask, but yeah I cook. My mom wanted one of us to know her recipe for Thanksgiving stuffing and my sister Lily was a few years away."

There was also the fact that while Chris and Derick were very much Dan Rickman's boys, Luke was his mother's son. He spent the most time with her at home and his success with women had a lot to do with Janice Rickman's teachings about how they should be respected and treated.

"Oh my God, it's like you're a Rickman, but not really. Cornbread stuffing?" Cori asked, eyeing him because really, honest-to-god home-made cornbread stuffing and gravy?

"Oh, I'm all Rickman, baby," he puffed his chest, feigning great ape posturing, "I just stayed out of the family business, and that meant staying at home longer. I came home every day from college to save on dorm fees, so I spent a lot of time with mom."

At the time, he'd thought it was limiting, having to come home, but it meant the world to his mother and now, he wouldn't have traded those extra years for anything.

"Oh yeah? That is so cool!" Cori didn't show it, but she sighed inwardly. He was so far out of her league. The kind of guy that usually went for her didn't cook with his mother, unless it was a narcotic. "I make a mean roast beef sandwich, but that's about it," she grinned. "My sister wouldn't let me near the kitchen after an unfortunate incident while making divinity. Before it sets, that stuff is like napalm...." An alarm from the vicinity of her link made Cori look down at her wrist as she tapped the earpiece everyone carried. "Oh shit," she exclaimed, rising to her feet just as several other sharks in the galley did the same. "Have to go, survey team's coming in hot..."

Without saying goodbye or even a hesitation, Cori hurried off to join the other Sharks as they hustled out of the galley tent.

Even growing up around them, Luke was always impressed at how fast Sharks could get it together. Getting to his feet, he grabbed Cori's trash and deposited it in the recycle bin before heading out himself.

Warm, mid-afternoon heat sheathed him as soon as he stepped out into the open and the sun's glare made him squint. His brain identified the faint odour of animal spoor, pollen, and dust in his lungs when he took a breath. In a second or two, the Sharks would be rallying them up, no doubt to avoid the next scary thing with too many teeth, discovering human was now a tasty part of the menu.

For now though, Luke took in the sight of the new world and knew as long as Tammy and Olivia were buried here, he was anchored to Gaia and Babel.

They were home.

Sleep

Meeting after meeting... after meeeeeeting. How the hell did Tom do it without shooting something? Derick yawned as this last one adjourned, which drew a raised eyebrow from the big Russian general. When the man, who dwarfed him, approached afterwards, Derick expected a reprimand. Instead, he received an order to get some sleep and a fatherly smile.

With that order in mind, Derick made a strategic retreat and went in search of a shower and his rack. If he could sleep. The last four days saw him living off jet fuel disguised as coffee and a few protein bars. His earlier conversation with Luke got him through the last meeting, but Derick was running on fumes. He knew this...but damn, it was good to see Luke with some life in his eyes! With everything Derick had to do, he worried about his little brother, but it relieved and humbled him when both Harwood and Shiny stepped up. Cori kept Luke from wallowing in his grief while Shiny mothered him, forcing him to eat, etc.

Making his way through the tight confines of the makeshift bunk room at the Cave, Derick had one destination in mind. Well, two, counting his own bunk. Right now, he was there to find Ren and make sure that she was following doctor's orders. She probably wasn't, knowing her. Turning down the aisle to her bunk, Derick froze.

The light in her bunk was on, illuminating Ren, and in a single heartbeat, Derick realized there would never be anyone else for him. She was glowing, from her bare legs to the gold tones sparking off her hair like fairy lights as she bent over a sketch pad. For once, her hair wasn't muscled into its tight braid but instead, hung slack over one shoulder. A long, lithe leg hung off the side of her bunk, with toes tapping the deck to some unheard tune. Warm skin disappeared under her shorts leading to a body he'd only dared to map in his dreams.

When he first met her, a few years ago, Derick had been entranced. The red hair, the curls, the grin, the swagger, the way she was so damned determined to carry her own weight. All of it in was wrapped in a gloriously hot package of femininity and smell-pretty. In short, Renee Richards was the kind of beauty a guy automatically pegged as *waaaay* out of his league. Like she was the frigging Milky Way and he was an Earth-bound primitive, captured by beauty he'd never understand, much less have. Their ranks, him being her senior non-com, didn't even register.

About two years ago, at some function or other, his mother met Ren and spent the evening with an enigmatic smile. Derick hadn't understood then but damn, he sure as hell did now.

These past six days had seen the noise in his head coalescing into a single song. He stared at her now, struck dumb with a clarity that explained the peculiar way his gut twisted when he'd carried her out of the temple. And his mother, God love her, *knew*. Susannah's gaze had reached across the horizon and saw the coming dawn.

In the years they'd served together, Ren became so much more than ethereal hope. Peace, when his mind needed calming. Light, when the darkness of combat and loss threatened to swallow him whole. He knew what his mother saw that day and he wouldn't deny it now. He was in love with Renee Richards.

Just then, she looked up at him and grinned. Derick's breath actually caught. All his tension, all the fretting over Tom, his brother, those god-awful meetings… it all melted right away.

"Hey," he said, though he didn't move forward. "You're listening to the doc for a change."

Yeah, he might be in love with her but that didn't mean she was getting a reprieve from his teasing.

Normally, Ren was so attuned to the Gunny's presence, she would have noticed the moment he entered her orbit. Not today. She'd been so immersed in her own world, he slipped right into her presence without her being the wiser. How long had he been standing there watching her? The thought made her stomach flip.

"Hey Gunny," she beamed at him automatically before her eyes narrowed upon getting a closer look at him. "I thought I was in strung out shape." She gathered up the loose sketches around her bunk to make room for him to sit, "but you look like crap."

Tit for tat.

"Thanks, I was hoping for shit but I'll take crap," he retorted dryly, moving towards her. Her bunk was tempting in oh, so many ways... but he didn't take it. Instead, he lowered himself slowly onto the empty bed opposite hers and stretched his long legs across the narrow aisle. "How's your head?"

Neatly tucking the pulled sketches back into the pad, Ren set it aside. "Better," she admitted, cautiously shifting to face him. "I mean, I'm not ready to do cartwheels, but I'm well enough to work on these." She tapped a pencil on the cover of the sketch pad before flipping it open. Gently thumbing through the sketches, she removed one and held it out to him. "Here, for Luke."

While she'd been at Medical, Maya dutifully fulfilled all of Ren's requests, including hitting Supply for a sketchpad and pencils. According to Maya, many tears were shed for a child with terminal lycanthropy who just wanted to make drawings for his mummy when she came to get him. Only, his mum was dead and wasn't coming...

Hell only knew if Maya was telling her that preposterous story to make her laugh or did she actually try to pass that by the techs in Services. But hey, she'd come away with a sketch pad. With the desire to indulge again in her long-buried passion and a self-prescribed mission, Ren got to work.

Capable of sketching from memory, Ren breathed life into the empty canvas with images of the temples, the wildlife and, most importantly, the people lost on Gaia.

The portraits, when they were completed, would go to the friends and family of those lost. She knew it was a small thing, but for years the folded photo of Emma was such a comfort because Ren could hold it in her hand. That tactile bit of contact was worth more than a thousand tera quads of digital data. Giving the mourners something, they could touch or trace with their fingers was Ren's way of easing the anguish of their loss.

Carefully flipping the page over, Derick paused at the extremely life-like sketch of Tammy Adelaide smiling back at him.

"Wow..." he whispered, staring at the picture. The portrait captured the little wrinkles in Dr. Adelaide's eyes when she smiled as well as the young woman's quiet, understated grace. Even if he'd known her for only a day, Derick was able to see it.

"This is amazing," Derick's voice was reverent with sincere gratitude as he smiled at Ren. "Seriously. Thank you. Luke will definitely want this."

Even though she'd received praise for her artistic talents for most of her life, his genuine appreciation caused a swell of pleasure to flow through her.

"I don't know how long he knew her, but he must have cared a lot about her. I thought he ought to have something to remember her at least." Everyone saw Luke's devastation over Dr. Adelaide's loss, and if this helped then Ren considered it mission accomplished. As her favourite teacher once claimed, art capable of touching the soul, was also capable of healing it.

"He met her right after he was assigned to Dr. Hall's team. They took care of each other after the Exodus." Derick's words felt bittersweet as he studied the face of someone he'd never be able to give his gratitude.

Just then, Ren realized the shadows on Derick's face weren't from the lighting. There were dark circles under his bloodshot eyes and a hint of stubble, all indicators of a man on the edge of exhaustion. She wanted to take care of him, just like he took care of her on Gaia. Screw their ranks. Nudging his leg with a toe, Ren dropped her gaze enough to distract him from the drawing.

"How are *you* doing, Gunny?"

Even though she used his title, her tone implied he was so much more than her senior NCO.

Derick didn't reply at first. Instead, he handed the paper back to Ren. Normally, he wouldn't admit to just how fucking dead on his feet he was, but this was Ren. Only to her did it not feel like an admission of weakness.

"Hold on to that for now, it will be safe." He indicated the drawing as he dragged tired hands over his face. Whatever fumes he'd been on were gone. He was completely tapped out. "I am so tired, Ren. I need to sleep and..." He paused, caught up in her pretty green eyes. "Would...you know...I slept better when I knew where you were in the room. Would you... The only thing I can think about is sleeping near you because I can't sleep anywhere else."

Such a simple request, even so stuttered was more romantic than any love letter. Scooting to the edge of her bunk, she smiled and crooked a finger for him to come closer.

Dear God, that smile was lethal. Derick eased off the bunk to his knees and leaned in, one hand on either side of her hips. He leaned in close, knocking on the edge of her personal space. "Yeah?" he smiled.

Ren met him there, kissing him just enough to taste him before she pulled back and caressed his cheek.

"Sleep. You know I always have your back, Derick."

Derick watched Ren for a minute before his eyes dropped to her lips. When she raised her hand, he grabbed it, instead of seeing out her intent. If he kissed her back, he wouldn't stop. He put a soft kiss on the back her hand and let it go. "I know."

He pushed back to the empty bunk and rolled into it. Dropping an arm over his eyes, he was asleep almost instantly.

Ren watched him for a few minutes until he surrendered to deep sleep and his breathing became a light snore. With a little smile, she flipped open her sketch pad and started to draw.

This portrait would be for her alone.

* * *

"Captain…?"

Jules entered the infirmary at a brisk walk and didn't stop, forcing the nurse to side-step and follow her. "You haven't seen me," she stated quietly, heading for the small room Tom had been given for recovery.

In the last two days, Jules had become a constant fixture in the medical centre. That is, when she wasn't on constant teleconferences with the bigwigs as they debated *ad nauseum* on what needed to be done, who would live where and… Yadda yadda yadda. She wouldn't admit it but she'd zoned out until Anisimov had quietly nudged her foot with his boot.

"Ma'am?"

"For the next two hours, you haven't seen me," Jules repeated as she stopped in front of Tom's door. "Unless it's an emergency, all right?"

The nurse, Lieutenant Winchester, finally understood and she shook her head with a shrug. "Captain who?"

Jules winked and slipped into Tom's room. The door slid shut, leaving her in dim lighting. She could still make out a clear path to the bed and Tom's sleeping form stretched out on it. His peaceful sleep belied the seriousness of his injuries. The acidic phlegm (the term alone made her gag), had eaten through the Shark Captain's body armour and into his skin, burning through the subdermal layer to reach his lungs. It was saying something that the least of his injuries were the broken bones he sustained tangling with Mama Sub.

By the time, the CMO got to him, he was already in shock and Whelan had stated it was only his armour that saved Tom Merrick's life.

Don't go there, Jules, she told herself. Kicking off her boots, she tugged her slate free of its pocket and slid it onto the table beside the bed. Carefully, she climbed in, into the spot she'd slept in for the last day, whenever she'd been able to.

Propping her chin on a fist, Jules softly pressed the back of her free hand against Tom's cheek before leaning in to gently kiss his chin. Two days' worth of beard scratched her lips but Jules didn't mind. She was just happy he was breathing on his own, save for an oxygen cannula stretched across his face. Bandages covered his broad chest, where the subdermal skin had been repaired and then covered with a regen product.

Settling back cautiously, Jules slid her hand into his uninjured one and closed her eyes. Two deep breaths later, she was sound asleep.

* * *

When Tom Merrick woke up an hour later, he almost thought he just surfaced from an all-night bender which somehow culminated with a shag he couldn't remember. For starters, he felt like shit. Everything ached. There was pain. His mouth was dry and his memory foggy. Then there was the unfamiliarity of the place. How many times had he awoken and wondered where the fuck he was? Finally, though this bit was pleasant, was the warm body pressed against him.

Until he tilted his head to see who she or he was, (don't ask, don't tell), and realised it was Jules.

Suddenly, he remembered everything with blinding clarity. Babel, sky crabs, mulks and subs, the violence and the losses, the gorgeous lavender sky and green tinged clouds and the woman he kissed with the moonlight bathing their faces.

The woman who was still here, despite his shit for brains.

Looking down at her, she was resplendent in her beauty as she slept next to him. He studied the lines on her face, the curl of her lashes, the soft rise and fall of her body as she snoozed. She fit so perfectly next to him he had to wonder how he ever managed without her until this point. Perhaps it explained why he felt invigorated, even lying in what he knew now to be Medical, with tubes sticking out of him and fresh wounds marking his body.

Before Babel, he'd been broken and while he wasn't magically fixed, Tom recognised he was on the mend. Because of Jules. Because he felt lightning struck when she smiled at him. At *him*. A junk-yard dog of a kid with a drunk for an old man. She knew his record and *still* crawled into the bed with him. Strewth, would he ever measure up and be the man she thought he was? He didn't feel like it right now, not when Lisa's screams still haunted his sleep, but he'd get there. It was like the universe was giving him one last shot, putting Jules in his path.

Tom studied her sleeping form, memorizing every bit. *Earn this*, the universe was saying. He intended to. There would be nightmares and shrinks. Normally a career soldier like himself would balk at the suggestion, but he'd do it. If only so the universe didn't take her away.

He settled back on the bed but realized he couldn't sleep without getting a sitrep. He glanced at Jules. Like hell, he would wake her. Something blipped quietly and he focused on it, realizing someone's slate, maybe hers, was on the bedside table. His mind might have been mostly alert, his body was still sore and his movements were slow. He managed to pull the table until the slate was within arm's reach. Once in his hands, he logged into his own profile.

Rhys had dutifully sent him every report regarding the expedition, even though the man probably didn't expect him to read it until he was discharged from Medical. Tom skimmed them, getting the gist. The mission was a success, even if it was a pyrrhic one. They'd lost people and, with a heavy heart, Tom noted Dee Sheridan from Beta Squad was on the list. Like Dupree, she'd been killed during the retreat from the temple.

Despite the deaths, Tom believed they weren't in vain. They'd spent twenty-four hours on the surface and look what they found? The sky crabs, the nafs and the twigas. More importantly, the expedition gathered enough intel about the valley to conclude it might be the place to settle. Once it was clear that Wormandra and her offspring were well and truly gone.

Olivia Valley (that soothed an ache in his heart he hadn't realized was there) was large enough to establish the colony a good distance away from the ruined city. As Tom and Jules first reasoned, the mountains on either side sheltered the valley from the worst of the storms generated by the sky crabs and Hanae River, (bloody hell, what was in his IV to make him this weepy?), was large enough to support their numbers.

Naturally, fortifications would be needed, if only to deter the mulks from deciding the humans were a new delicacy. Despite all of that, despite the dangers, Tom still recognized that it was paradise to ten thousand people desperately in need of blue (greenish in this case) sky, fresh air and most of all, hope.

Logging off, Tom slid the Slate onto the table and settled back against the bed. Jules shifted slightly, her hand searching his, so he caught it and twined their fingers together. They'd talk later, exchange war stories; but right now, they both needed to rest.

They had paid for it in blood but now he and Jules, and the remains of humanity, had a lifetime to enjoy.

Dear reader,

We hope you enjoyed reading *Savage World*. Please take a moment to leave a review, even if it's a short one. Your opinion is important to us.

Discover more books by Jennifer Slusher at
https://www.nextchapter.pub/authors/jennifer-slusher

Discover more books by Linda Thackeray at
https://www.nextchapter.pub/authors/linda-thackeray-science-fiction-fantasy-author-australia

Want to know when one of our books is free or discounted? Join the newsletter at http://eepurl.com/bqqB3H

Best regards,
Jennifer Slusher, Linda Thackeray and the Next Chapter Team

Savage World
ISBN: 978-4-86751-501-3

Published by
Next Chapter
1-60-20 Minami-Otsuka
170-0005 Toshima-Ku, Tokyo
+818035793528
2nd July 2021